THE
RAVEN
THIEF

ASHLEY OLIVIER

Cover Design by Bianca Bordianu Design
Editing by Nick Beard
Proofreading by Carolyn McSharry
Map and Illustrations by Melissa Wright
Interior Formatting by Qamber Designs and Media

THE SAINTS

Saints are unique to the fae religion following the faerie goddess Eethra, who is said to have created the world as we know it. While common beliefs in Skeyya and Brasova, there are differing religions across the Great Sea in the East. Some even believe the goddess to be an old wives' tale. Nonetheless, there are saints from each country based off stories and legends from centuries long since passed.

SKEYYA

Saint Abbana – The Saint of the Seas

Saint Gabrian – The Saint of the Sick

Saint Baldredon – The Saint of the Dead

Saint Finthan – The Saint of the Sun

Saint Brigidda – The Saint of Healing

Saint Colline – The Saint of Storms

Saint Olivett – The Saint of Peace

BRASOVA

Saint Iberius – The Saint of Knowledge

Saint Dumitru – The Saint of Sacrifice

Saint Simu – The Saint of Suffering

Saint Dina – The Saint of Spirits

Saint Stefan – The Saint of Wisdom

Saint Theo – The Saint of the Forest

Saint Sophia – The Saint of Freedom

CARDEK

Saint Pellin – The Saint of Martyrs

Saint Jeyan – The Saint of War

Saint Canan – The Saint of Fire

Saint Nida – The Saint of Wealth

Saint Irena – The Saint of Marriage

Saint Esra – The Saint of Rivers

TOBUHAN

Saint Nyima – The Saint of Health

Saint Rinchen – The Saint of Beauty

Saint Zopa – The Saint of Patience

Saint Palden – The Saint of Power

Saint Dawa – The Saint of the Moon

Saint Gelek – The Saint of Honesty

Saint Sonam – The Saint of Success

THE FAE COURTS

Beyond the human world lies an unseen realm of the fae ruled by four courts. This includes the Winter Court, Spring Court, Summer Court, and Autumn Court. Each possesses both unique and shared abilities, and each is stationed in different hidden places on the map.

WINTER COURT RULERS

King Cezar

Queen Sabina

SPRING COURT RULERS

King Kunchen

Queen Lhamo

SUMMER COURT RULERS

King Mehmed

Queen Vahide

AUTUMN COURT RULERS

King Darren

Queen Aisling

To those who believed in me, and to those who didn't.

PROLOGUE

Enya – The Beginning

THEY SAY that overcoming your past can be one of the hardest things to do. Memories can steal your passion, your happiness, even your soul, until you're nothing more than an empty shell.

Maybe that's why I tried so hard to forget.

One moment, you're screaming, agonizing over the pain pulsing in your chest, clawing its way out. The next, you wake up one day, and it's as if nothing happened. You don't remember, and it's bliss. The saints in all their mercy have allowed you to forget, if only for a moment, and you have peace.

But you know there's something missing; you just can't remember what. Sometimes, though, it's better to remember. That way, you can forgive yourself and others for what happened. Damn, I'm so childish for even bothering to write these letters.

Maybe one day I'll forgive myself.

PART ONE
ROYALS AND THIEVES

Arden, Skeyya

WINTER'S ICE-COLD winds swept through the industrial capital of Arden as its citizens woke to brave the day.

Already, some poor, homeless souls were dropping from frostbite on the docks at the edge of the river cutting through the city. Their corpses sat feasted upon by dark and curious creatures that lurked within the shadows.

Inside a nearby rebel warehouse, Enya trudged up and down several rows of barrels and boxes, counting wares and tallying shipments.

She hummed along to the screeching song of a drunk-en sailor outside. His slurred words seeped in through the worn-out wooden exterior of the building, earning occasional chuckles from the other rebels inside, accompanied by a few of her gang members, a ragtag group of people better known as the Grims.

Brutal cold also crept through the cracks in the walls, sending a shiver down her spine and a faint breeze through her long black waves that spilled like ink over her shoulders.

She pulled her jacket tighter against her small frame, wishing that her leather boots fought off more of the chill.

Enya peered over a cracked-open crate full of ammunition, soon hearing shoes scraping against the wooden floor behind her. She saw Carson's shadow towering over her. His husky breath brushed against her collarbone, and she froze. Whatever it was that caused butterflies to take wing in her stomach, she hated it. It made her feel weak and delicate, like a rose without thorns. But thorns were the best weapon of all. Unexpected and pointed, just like her wit.

Enya straightened and set down her clipboard on a nearby crate, one among many others. She turned, giving him a side-long glance. He grinned back.

"Is there a reason," she began, "you're invading my personal bubble? I'm pretty sure we've had this discussion already. Do you need another intervention?"

She'd meant to sound strict, but the words came out too kind. Too gentle. A playful air enveloped them, one that only revealed itself when he was by her side. Enya didn't know why, but his mere presence made her soften.

She hated that too.

Carson chuckled, stretching his long, tan Cardekian arms up towards the ceiling while he stepped back.

He hailed from a land across the Great Sea, one full of

sand and spice. But the tattoos peeking out from under his dark coat sleeves were an indication he no longer followed his childhood religion.

He dropped his hands, jammed his fingers in between the loops of his trousers, and leaned against a wooden beam. "I think we're done. Or does the Raven have a trick up her sleeve to make more weapons and rations magically appear?"

Enya reveled in the nickname she'd been given, and she owned it as best she could. The Raven. The name of the infamous gang leader that controlled the streets of the capital with a glimmer of shadows and sharp eyes. Of palace secrets gleaned from her time as a child in the king's service, not that she remembered much after the fact.

But memories were worthless if they didn't give her leverage over her enemies. In any case, that was neither here nor there, and she had no time to sit and dwell on the past. Not if she wanted to survive the myriad of threats levied from the royal guard and rival gangs like the Wraiths and Blood Spiders.

But when Carson said it, he was only teasing. He'd known her long before her rise to power, and he liked to remind her of that fact. Also, he liked to remind her of the fact that he was older than her despite her being in charge; her being seventeen, him being nineteen.

"Give me a second," she told him.

Enya glanced around the space, taking in the endless shipments they'd either stolen or acquired through the narrow supply of funds granted by Mihaela, the official leader of the rebellion growing in Skeyya.

A few rebels and Grims stacked barrels of black powder, guns and ammo, and heavy sacks of smuggled grains and vegetables, not that there were much of those to go around. After all, the king had to take his hefty cut from the nation's farmers in order to keep his troops on the Brasovian frontlines fed. They were currently embroiled in yet another pointless war to try and expand Skeyya's already extensive borders. That and hefty taxation for the war efforts were enough to cripple what was once a mighty country.

But greedy kings did what was to be expected of them: steal from those they were meant to lead.

There were other warehouses and strongholds stationed around the city, but this one had been running low. They all had to keep up stock so their fight could carry on; lives depended on it.

When Enya saw that all was well and there was nothing left to jot down on her paperwork, she nodded.

"Let's go. I'm sure the other Grims are waiting for us back at the Bowman's Pub," she said, tossing the clipboard down on a nearby crate. Striding towards the entrance, she shoved open the heavy doors, with Carson following close behind.

Winter air bit into her cheeks, stinging them and no doubt turning them a crimson hue. She stepped outside and pushed the wooden doors shut behind them.

Before them was an empty scene of ice sheets and cargo containers that had been dropped off by foreign ships. In the distance, she could hear the grinding gears and machines of a few factories, ones that wafted smog up into the sky. Based on the gray clouds above, Enya guessed either snow or icy rain would be pelting them soon. Crates and stacked wood decorated the gravelly road that led to the main streets of the capital.

"I'm surprised you were able to get that thing open by

yourself." Carson chuckled with a wry grin.

Enya rolled her eyes. "I'm surprised you can even fit through the doorway with those big muscles of yours." She flushed beet red once she realized the implications of what she'd said.

"So, you think my muscles are big." His voice was teasingly smug, and he leaned closer. She shoved him back, her embarrassment quickly shifting into anger. He stumbled into the warehouse door with a thud.

"Shut up," Enya snapped, her breath frosting in the air with her biting retort just as hot.

Carson's expression darkened. "Sometimes you can be so infuriating."

A noise around the corner caught their attention. The crunching of leaves under unsteady feet. Enya's breath caught, and her hand instinctively reached for her pistol. Carson did the same, and they nodded to each other in silent understanding. Anyone lurking too close to rebel properties could mean trouble.

It was better to be safe than sorry.

Slowly, they inched along the rickety warehouse wall. Once they'd rounded the corner to the main thoroughfare full of passing carriages, they let out identical sighs of relief.

The drunken sailor who'd kept them entertained earlier now danced awkwardly with a broomstick, humming more sea songs while he sloshed his stout all over the frozen ground. His dark clothes were soaked with alcohol.

Enya wrinkled her nose at the stench, lowering her gun.

"He's harmless." She snickered, holstering the weapon back in her belt. Carson's lips turned back up into a smile.

"Come on." She signaled for them to start moving with a wave of her hand, amusement shadowing her features.

"I'm sure Podge has something good cooking," Carson said, rubbing his hands together and blowing on them. He frowned once he caught wind of her raised brow. "What? I can practically smell the food from here."

She doubted that; they were still several blocks away from the pub. Sighing, she quickened her pace.

Besides, Podge, the Bowman's middle-aged owner, was usually never around for much else besides delivering shipments and showing off the joint to his flavor of the week. Whoever the woman was usually stood draped in jewels, clad in dainty fabric, and laughed way too much at his jokes. She was also just as likely to only be interested in his money.

He was hopeless in romance. But Enya couldn't deny that his culinary creations were some of the best. The thought of roasted fish, salted and buttered, made her mouth water.

There wasn't much meat to be found on the menu besides what Podge personally butchered himself from his black-market hogs kept in his backyard; soldiers needed the meat more. Commercial livestock had been bought out by the king for over two years now. Farmers were pleased. Everyday people were not, if their growling stomachs and hollowed cheeks had anything to say.

Momentarily distracted by her thoughts, Enya nearly missed it: the silence. Something was wrong. Her eyes searched the street for any signs of trouble brewing, and an uneasy feeling knotted in her stomach.

"What is it?" Carson whispered, keeping pace with her as she walked, his own eyes scanning the area.

"I don't know yet."

It was suspiciously quiet, with only a few families meandering along the cobblestone road that slipped around tall shops and homes, some with horse-drawn carriages and some without. Passing gulls squawked overhead, and the wind carried with it the powerful hissing of nearby ships along the docks several blocks down.

The carriages. There were too many of them left unattended. Families would never—

Enya flung Carson back with a sudden hand to his chest once she caught the glint of a rifle atop a nearby building. Her mouth moved to form a warning, but by then, it was far too late.

Bullets rang out from behind the parked carriages and towering rooftops lining the narrow street. One tore through Carson's jacket, grazing his shoulder. He cursed, grabbing the searing wound.

A flash of anger rippled through Enya. Her pistol was up within mere seconds. The flash of barrel almost seemed to go off in slow motion, illuminating her face and sending a bullet flying. A male scream rang out. But she didn't have time to smile at her successful shot before someone was shoving her down with firm, calloused hands. She fell with Carson behind a merchant's cart full of newspapers. Just in time, it seemed. Above them, a hailstorm of hot lead shredded paper and wood.

"Who are these guys?" Enya shouted, quickly firing back from over the cart. She yanked her hand back when a few stray bullets nicked the chapped skin atop her knuckles.

She snarled several obscenities, biting her lip so hard she tasted blood, which only added to the pain.

Enya could barely hear herself over the sounds of the

blazing weapons. Bystanders screamed and shouted, scrambling to get behind cover. A few weren't so lucky, succumbing to the blasts in a heap of spewed red and tattered clothing.

Her breath caught in her throat, and her blood ran cold. Whoever this was didn't care about casualties.

"How the hell did they find us?" she hissed. Carson attempted to fire back when another volley of shots zoomed past them, forcing them back down. She swore again, her grip on her weapon tightening so hard it hurt.

"Someone must have ratted!" Carson yelled. He took a blind shot, keeping himself below their quickly dissipating cover.

Whoever was responsible would be shown no mercy by her Grims or the rebels. Broken fingers and pulled teeth were only a fierce whisper of what her gang was capable of.

More gunfire erupted, this time from their warehouse, the heated exchange earning screams of pain from their assailants. With a shuffle of heavy boots, Enya guessed their attackers were now ducking for cover.

She took a deep breath, trying to calm her racing heart.

"Are you guys okay?" a male voice called out from the iron catwalks hanging along the second floor of the warehouse behind them. Enya turned her head up finding Brendan, who had been stocking black powder. By his side were a few other rebels and Grims. They aimed from the rafters, keeping a steady exchange of blasts.

Firing and reloading one after the other, they operated like well-oiled, deadly machines.

"We're alive enough. Who the hell is attacking us?" Enya hollered back, crouching further down behind the cart.

Her pulse quickened in her ears, and her palms began to

sweat. Judging by the number of bullets ricocheting off the brick walls around her and shattering nearby windows, they were heavily outnumbered. Carson peered over a few stacked newspapers, his mouth a fine line.

Brendan called down, "It's the police!" He paused, his voice growing unsure. "A lot of them."

Just our luck, she thought to herself, scowling in contempt. They must have been sent by the king.

King Eamon, the unfortunate ruler of Skeyya, had been looking to put the Raven's head on a stake for months.

"We took out the ones on the roof!" a girl's voice, Emer, could be heard from above.

Enya took advantage of the lull. She stood, quickly firing out two shots. Each hit their mark; one man fell out of a two-story window, and a second dropped from where he was crouched behind a carriage. She ducked back just as a torrent of return fire ripped into their cart.

The rebels above covered for her, only adding to the roar of bullets and black powder through the street.

"What are our options?" Carson yelled during a brief reload.

"We have a load of pipe bombs and dynamite."

Enya stared at her hands for a moment, wondering what sort of damage an attack of that magnitude would have on the surrounding area. What other lives might be lost. Guilt coursed through her like a tidal wave, but she immediately turned her resolve into cool steel, unwavering and sure.

It was either they die now, or they fight their way out of this. There was no other choice.

"Do it!" she hollered back up to her rebels before holstering her weapon. She and Carson ducked down further, terrified for what was to come.

Enya closed her eyes and waited, covering her ears with her hands.

Shouts echoed through the street when she guessed the bombs were tossed, likely from the officers and others attempting to flee. She squeezed her lids tighter, trying to calm her tumultuous nerves.

"Enya—" Carson began, his mouth close to her ear, but his voice disappeared in the shockwave of several explosions.

Black powder and fire spiraled through the street, causing a cascade of rubble and dust to settle along all those unfortunate enough to bear witness to the sight. More glass shattered around them, and for a moment, Enya couldn't hear anything, the ringing in her ears almost painful.

She coughed at the stench of ash and bone wafting through the air, waving her gloved hands in an attempt to ward off the cloud of dust filling the area.

Sound returned in the form of piercing screams.

When she glanced up from behind their cover, flames and tendrils of darkness could be seen licking at rooftops surrounding the street.

An oppressive cloud of smoke blocked her view of the enemy line. She helped Carson to his feet, and they staggered across the soot-covered stone. "You alright?" she asked him, rubbing her brown eyes furiously to rid them of floating debris.

She stifled another round of wheezing, her throat burning from the haze that had managed to wedge itself inside her lungs and nose. Explosives were something she dreaded using even at the best of times, but unfortunately for everyone, they were necessary today.

"Better than those guys," Carson retorted with a humorless smile, gesturing over his shoulder with his thumb.

She followed his callous gesture.

Dozens lay dead. The bodies that weren't blown to bits were stiff from the impact. Blood decorated their uniforms like cruel splashes of paint.

Their war-torn section of the city was unrecognizable, disguised with fire and soot. A few undoubtedly innocent people laid among the corpses, ones who had been unable to avoid the blasts coming from both sides. Enya was sick to her stomach to witness what had unfolded before her, but desperation brewed desperation.

She had to distance herself mentally from such things if she wanted to stay sane. Not that she had time to dwell.

A surge of police barged onto the scene from a nearby alleyway, already barking orders and making threats.

Enya inhaled a long breath, catching a hold of Carson's sleeve. They tore off down the street and into a different borough of Arden, silently begging the saints to get them out of this mess. Wind whipped through her hair, impossibly cold and unforgiving. She willed herself to be the same while they darted around horse-drawn carriages and pedestrians clad in expensive suits and frilly dresses, each scrambling as a result of the explosion.

Furtive whispers followed them, telling the tale of what must have been a terrible accident in the warehouse district.

News hadn't spread yet, but it would.

The bustling crowds of the city filled their view when they reached the canal, one full of massive steam vessels and travelers busy finishing the day's work, not at all bothered by the freezing temperatures and instead fretting about the lack of paper bills filling their pockets. Citizens traded in Cardekian liras and Tobuhanian yuans, shouting over each other to try and snag the best deal of the day.

Beyond the wooden docks, steel ships flew by like birds in the murky blue water, creating waves of ice and slush.

The bustling waterfront reeked of fish and coal, and Enya wrinkled her nose. The sky overhead was full of gray clouds with barely a hint of sunlight in sight.

While men unloaded cargo, Enya and Carson blew out cool breaths, and shivers climbed up their spines.

But when she turned the corner around a stack of old boats, a firm hand snaked out to capture her wrist. Her hands ached, but she was ready to fight her way out of this mess by any means necessary. She turned her eyes up and met the foreboding eyes of an officer, one who towered easily above her.

The older man sneered, "This is the little rat we're chasing?"

Enya's brows pushed angrily together. *Little rat*, she repeated in her head, scoffing. *Even rodents can bite.*

In an instant, the officer's other arm wielding a gun was ripped into the air by Carson's right hand. He fired out a shot, earning startled shouts from shoppers around them. Enya grabbed the baton hanging at the man's waist. With a swift move, she clocked the policeman right between his legs, making him drop the weapon and groan out in pain, flailing back. Another blow to his temple laid him flat on the ground, unconscious.

Enya and Carson breathed heavily, but there was no time to lose. Reinforcements would arrive soon.

"No point in waiting around unless we want to take dirt

naps with the wraiths," Enya snapped.

Carson shoved two onlookers out of the way and pulled her into a run. They continued their escape through crowded docks, their booted steps pressing harder against the ground the faster they ran. Their goal was the Bowman's Pub, but at this point, anywhere but here was looking better and better. They needed to escape prying eyes and loaded guns. Needed to find cover.

A few people grunted and yelled when the duo shoved them aside, one startled merchant falling face first into a barrel of trout and salmon, sputtering at the stench. The shadows of docked ships danced along their path, as if leading the way to safety.

Merchants cursed soundly when a few of their ragged stalls toppled to the wood below their feet when the sea of hagglers jostled into their merchandise. Delicate goods such as glass and pottery shattered. Food tumbled across the ground and was snatched up by stray dogs roaming the marketplace. "Saint Nida! Who's going to fix this?" one man shouted. More obscenities chased the young rebels through the docks with a vengeance.

But Enya couldn't think about that now. She could only keep her mind focused on getting the hell out of this mess.

More authorities stumbled across the road off in the distance, shouting for the rebels to turn themselves in. A few were captured, thrown against the ground, and cuffed. Others outright gave themselves up, shouting for the Raven to keep moving.

Enya redoubled her efforts, panting hard.

She shook her head, an exasperated noise slipping from her throat. "We'll have to make for the rooftops." She pointed over to the stacked crates that would lead them on top of a butcher shop at the end of the canal's market district. "Come on!"

The fight to climb the building with Carson was more crowded than she preferred. Other rebels, ranging from tall to short, from posh lady to brute pub-crawler, frantically stomped up the crates to access the rooftops.

Guards below pulled more rebels down, halting their bid for freedom before they'd even started. Their screams tore at her heart, but she couldn't stop, not yet.

When she reached the top with Carson, they fled.

Wooden planks drawn across buildings led the way while smoke wafted up from chimneys, drawing a thick darkness into their lungs, despite them holding their breaths.

Her eyes scanned the scene, searching for an escape.

Throughout the capital, hideouts were scattered like pin-pricks of light through a canvas of shadows.

Enya's gaze landed on a large open window to her right, far ahead on the never-ending expanse of rooftops. It was the closest hideout near the warehouse, resting in what appeared on the outside to be a florist's shop. Well, they certainly sold enough buttercups and lilies to stink up any rich man's home, but their secret room in the back was the perfect spot to avoid police detection.

They could wait for all this to blow over while the shop-keeper brewed them nettle tea to battle the winter chill.

Without a moment of hesitation, she quickly grabbed Carson and pushed him towards the grimy, frosted window, earning a grunt of surprise. They slid through with ease, followed by several others, landing in a heap on the dusty wooden floor with a loud thud.

Enya winced from the pain searing through her still bleeding hand from the bullet graze earlier. She pushed herself to her feet and dusted herself off. Her knees were sore from the impact, but she'd survive to fight another day.

Carson stood up beside her, already ready to jump into action if needed. "Well, that was fun," he said, still gasping for breath.

She nodded, still catching her own while she gazed around the room.

Wide-eyed rebels stared back, a mixture of human and faerie alike. Some with pointed ears, some without. It was like a melting pot of magick, all wrapped up in a bow of forbidden, treasonous goals. If they were caught, they'd be killed on the spot. And there was nothing evil kings hated more than treasonous fools.

"Think we're safe here?" one of the rebels asked, one named Breena. A girl no more than sixteen, if Enya recalled correctly. Her round, hazel eyes stared anxiously into Enya's.

Enya nodded. "We should be—" She stopped short, her brows furrowing in thought.

Carson caught the look and whispered, "What is it?"

"I can't help but wonder how they found us at the warehouse to begin with. That sort of thing seemed too planned out. That kind of ambush would be weeks in the making, at least."

Carson sighed. "Like I said, someone must have ratted."

"Who, though?" It wasn't like they didn't know everyone that worked there. She knew all the rebels by name. Knew most of their faces better than her own. They were all united by the same hatred burning in their souls for the king.

Carson cleared his throat, distracting her. "We should

bandage your hand, Enya. You're still bleeding."

She waved a dismissive hand. "I'm fine. We'll worry about that later. Right now, we need to figure out how we'll get back to the Bowman's Pub."

"Enya, come on. Stop being so stubborn."

She glanced warily at him, taking in his glower. Finally, she let loose an exasperated sigh, fumbled to remove her glove, and held out her hand.

He took that as his cue to pull out a medical kit from one of the cabinets full of dust sitting nearby. Cracking open the box, he pulled out a roll of gauze. "Come here."

She did as she was told, annoyed that he was telling her what to do. But her hand did look pretty bad. Sticky red oozed out from her knuckles, and searing pain pounded beneath her wound with a heartbeat all its own. He slowly wrapped her hand, looping the gauze around her palm and back again before securing it with a knot.

He must have seen her troubled expression because he next asked, "You okay?"

She shrugged, pulling her black glove tediously back over her injured hand. "If King Eamon knew about the warehouse, what else does he know about? I mean—"

Her thoughts were cut short when the back doors swung open, revealing a new horde of trigger-happy policemen. Their boots stomped along the ground when they pushed in, shouting words so angry and jumbled, she could barely understand what they were saying. Those in front of the squadron began grabbing at the rebels with rough, gloved hands while others pointed rifles, ready to shoot those now screaming in horror inside. Moments later, they did just that. Screams erupted, and bodies dropped like swatted flies to the floor, drenched in blood.

She and Carson glanced at each other, a hundred thoughts passing between them in mere seconds. His eyes darted to the door that led to the shop, and she grimaced.

They had no choice if they wanted to survive.

Enya bolted, shoving through the crowd while Carson followed. More bullets rang out, bouncing off crates and walls and nearly hitting the duo as they struggled to reach the door to the main shop. Their noses were immediately met with the cloying perfume of countless flowers, and she stifled a cough, stumbling towards the front door. Patrons gasped, falling back into display stands to get out of their way while she and Carson disappeared through the entrance and back into the frigid street.

A faint flurry of snow had begun to fall, casting a bluish tint upon the city. She took a deep breath. Cool, white specks threaded themselves into her hair.

Set up outside the shop was a blockade of police wagons. Gun barrels lined hitches and open shutters. Enya internally groaned, her lips curling back. Uncertainty crept up her spine, but she did her best to ignore it. Now wasn't the time to dwell on possibilities.

Enya immediately pulled out her pistol, but Carson deftly caught her hand, giving her a warning look. "Don't be stupid, Enya."

She angrily shrugged him off, raising the gun higher. They'd killed countless rebels and were now likely going to kill them too. No, they had to pay, and she wasn't going to go down without a fight.

Usually, the inner circle of her Grims would be there to

back them up, but she'd let them stay behind at the pub while she and Carson ran this errand. They were supposed to meet back up before supper. She could see now that was a mistake.

Several armed men hopped out the wagon, pointing rifles at the two. Enya swallowed. That was a lot of ammunition just to capture two teenagers.

"Drop your weapons!" someone shouted, his booming voice full of loathing. They weren't fooling around. Enya and Carson looked at each other, hands now in the air. He appeared to be the Chief of Police, a man named Kelman, with all his medals and the same famous mustache that graced countless newspaper articles. "Or we'll shoot you where you stand!"

With a frustrated sigh, she threw hers forward. Carson released his and kicked it over. Their weapons skidded across the pavement towards the man who spoke, narrowly missing his brown leather boots.

There goes our insurance policy, Enya thought bitterly, glowering at the men who had them tightly surrounded.

The chief was tall and muscular, with a network of scars covering his neck. It was a scary sight to see, even for Enya. Rumor was that a wolf had bit him as a child and that he'd fought him off with nothing more than his bare hands.

It was the kind of legend you'd expect to hear about some saint or woodland faerie king, not so much a regular man.

She couldn't help the tightness that bloomed in her chest as she stared down the men with an unflinching glare.

Uniformed and organized, they stood poised to fire whenever the order was called. There was not an ounce of pity or remorse in their eyes. They didn't care about anything but tallying deaths and following orders like dogs.

"Now, now. Let's not get too hasty, gentlemen." Enya gave an innocent smile, casually playing the part of the everyday teen who didn't just knock out a policeman and kill dozens of Kelman's men. "What is it that you think we've done?"

"We were just on our way to lunch after morning classes." Carson nodded, seeming to try and stand in such a way as to hide the ash on his jacket while he flashed a look as guileless as a choirboy. It was ironic since he looked way too much like a brute with his broad shoulders, thick black hair and beard, and art-covered arms.

Enya nearly smiled in amusement, but she bit the inside of her cheek instead, trying to keep her face emotionless.

Kelman spat, "If it was up to me, I would have the two of you hanged, but that's not my call. Someone special wants you alive."

She narrowed her eyes in suspicion, her eyes flitting from him to his squadron and back. "Someone special like who?"

He glared back, holding up a wrinkled stack of papers emblazoned with blue royal seals and black ink.

"King Eamon sent out a warrant for the Raven months ago. I guess today was our lucky day. I sure didn't expect a tiny woman, though. Complete waste of military resources if you ask me."

He waved his officers forward, and Enya bristled at his sexist remarks. She and Carson didn't struggle when the officers hoisted them into the back of the police wagon and chained their hands. Enya exchanged a sneer with a passing guard, who rolled his eyes at her insolence. Chief Kelman just looked annoyed that he even had to be there, babysitting.

To him, they probably appeared like a bunch of runaway thugs not worth his time, though he so craved their untimely demise.

But she refused to present herself as anything less than stoic and unreadable.

Fear made people weak. It made them easy targets as they squirmed, trying to find a way out of the black webs woven by the Raven and her hidden eyes strategically located around the capital. Fears revealed truths people never wanted to tell. Revealed their true nature. That's why Enya concealed her fear at every turn. She wouldn't be made into such a weakling in front of others.

Besides, if she were just some lowly scoundrel to them, why send an army to arrest her?

That only fueled her confidence further. It wasn't every day the king wanted an audience with a prisoner. That meant she was important.

Enya smiled viciously at her captors.

She would prove to them they weren't untouchable. That even the king should fear her. Captive or not, she would show them.

She would show them what it meant to be afraid. What it meant to live in the hell they had created. She would prove to them that the Raven and her Grims were not to be underestimated.

A bump in the road made her chains rattle. Enya scowled, turning her face to her bound hands in disgust.

But she would have to live first.

Renmare, Skeyya

SCENTS OF coal and smoke became that of fresh-cut grass and endless flowers while they moved along the dirt road. Snowfall had turned dirt into wet mush and the fields of Skeyya's countryside into a brilliant white.

The wheels of the wagon broke up the marshy mess as it tore across the road, batting away the cold blasting outside.

Inside, Enya tried to focus on anything but the reeking smell of sweat and soiled britches. She stifled a gag, rubbing her eyes and glancing back out her blessed peephole.

While they had passed a flower field once or twice, this area housed wealthy manors more than actual farmland, but Enya doubted the rich would like to have the stench of pigs

27

and sugar beets near their fancy residences, anyway. Gleaming columns and newly refurbished rooftops sprung up from the trees. Homes intricately crafted for undoubtedly the wealthiest among the country's citizens, like the king's cabinet members.

Other parts of the country held cattle, horses, sheep, and chickens. Produce, too, but more than half of it was for the troops in the North. Such things were also too fine for these noblemen to view from their windows, naturally.

But the country of Skeyya used to be a mystical place. Ancient creatures described in terrifying tales told over flaming hearths once roamed the lands and lured innocent people to their deaths.

They still did, but it was a lot harder ever since iron bullets were invented. Now, you'd only see a few of the lowlier creatures, like the faerie folk who had been subjugated by the royals. It made Enya's stomach turn. She despised having to be herded back to the palace after witnessing their cruelty both inside their opulent halls and on the streets. The former during her servitude as a child in the palace stables.

"Are we almost there?" Enya asked with an annoyed sigh as she gave up on taking stock of her surroundings outside and leaned against the wooden boards behind her that made up the frame of the wagon.

It felt like they'd been riding for hours. Hours that had been wasted doing nothing useful. She hated such inactivity. Well, she hated everything about this situation, really. Being powerless and controlled. Especially by spineless fools eager to run this country into the ground and dance upon the ruins. Ones blinded by their own heavy pockets and pride.

The chief whacked above the hole with his baton, flashing her a dark expression that would knock the socks off just about any peasant. But she wasn't just anyone. "Keep quiet. We get there when we get there."

Enya glared back. Fine. She'd be silent, but there would be hell to pay when they got out of this mess. One glimpse over at Carson's set jaw said he agreed wholeheartedly.

It looked different out here. *Felt* different.

There didn't seem to be that almost impossible-to-avoid feeling of despair and exhaustion. The typical feeling of the city with its factories and giant ships to maintain. There was a sense of calm among the brush and buzzing bees. There was no desperation for justice, only contentment. Whoever lived out here hadn't felt any of the unrest, not when their homes reeked of money.

Enya soon heard giant iron bars slam shut behind them, and the police wagon finally screeched to a halt, making everyone inside sway left and right uneasily.

She and Carson were roughly shoved out onto the dirt and mulch, cold air stinging their faces while they staggered to regain their balance. She hadn't even realized how much warmer the inside of their ride had been. Now the clutches of winter were upon her once again, chilling her bones and making her breath frost. She shivered, her body instantly dissolving into shudders and clattering teeth.

The police behind her snickered at the sight of their struggle, and she scowled, rolling her eyes.

"Need a hand?" one asked, holding back his chortles with a hand against his lips. "I see yours are a little tied up there. Not that we could, uh, help with that."

The officer next to him groaned. "Really, Lucas?"

Kelman struck them both in the shoulders, and they stood straighter, masking their faces again to be stoic and unreadable, as they should have been all along.

Enya inwardly scoffed, *How professional.* These were the men sent after her? She couldn't help the dark amusement that flooded through her.

His stony gaze was ruthless, and his eyes narrowed dangerously. "Both of you, keep your mouths shut. Let's move." The chief turned to Enya and Carson next, barking his next words, "Keep walking."

Kelman thrust them forward toward the pavement, and they stumbled, casting the chief dirty looks. A mountain of stone steps led them up a well-kept grass hill and to the palace entrance. The white stone of the grand building still glistened from a recent rain shower, one made evident by gray and black clouds hanging low in the air, while snow swirled down, leaving ice crystals in Enya's hair.

Nostalgia hit Enya like a sack of bricks. This place looked too familiar, sounded too familiar, and smelled too familiar, like violets and fresh mint.

It also reminded her of being on the receiving end of senseless beatings from the king as a child for even daring to befriend his precious sons, ones who were now long since dead. Maybe that was one of the reasons she hated him so much, aside from his never-ending ego and totalitarian reign.

She had already begun mentally plotting their escape when they were pushed inside and towards the throne room. The long, decorated halls were plastered with gold trim and painting after painting of whichever royal felt egotistical enough to sit for a portrait that year.

Her eyes raked over the luxurious display, hatred growing with each fateful step she took atop the colorful tile floor.

The wooden doors to the throne room were broad and heavy, earning grunts from the armored guards who pushed them open.

The room was massive, with large, twinkling chandeliers hanging in neat rows leading up to the throne and a few pews behind half walls on either side of the aisle. It was there that the king's advisors, otherwise known as his cabinet, sat. And there were plenty of them. Their eyes followed her like hawks waiting to pounce on their prey. Enya shuddered. So many harsh eyes on her made her legs feel wobbly and her pulse quicken. It took courage to keep moving.

There the king sat in all his self-absorbed glory on the famous golden throne atop polished, white marble floors that had never seen a speck of dirt.

King Eamon's long red hair and beard hung down the front of his black robe, eyes thoughtful. His mouth was set in a tight line and his brows furrowed just enough to show he meant business.

Beside him was Queen Ciara, a good enough replacement for the former queen, but much more narcissistic from what Enya had heard. Just like her husband, this woman had no empathy and cared way too much about her little tea cakes and moss puddings. Flowing brown hair fell past her shoulders, and a dark-red gown enveloped her tightly as she sat beside the king.

Her lips twisted into something less than pleasant, as if her guests were nothing more than the dog crap the housekeepers had failed to clean off the floor.

Chief Kelman bowed deeply, earning a smirk from the king. "We retrieved the Raven, as you asked, Your Majesty. We were fortunate she had one of her friends tag along, too." Kelman grabbed a hold of their chains. "They're all yours, Your Majesty." He thrust Enya and Carson onto their knees before the king, metal rattling in his hands. She landed hard, grimacing in the pain from the impact.

"Thank you, Chief." Eamon waved him away, his gaze now fixed on Enya. "The infamous Raven under my roof. You're not at all what I expected," he scoffed with a mocking smile. "And here I thought you were some grand threat to my kingdom."

"That plan was already in the works," Enya offered with a sarcastic grin, earning a wary look from Carson.

This was breaking all sorts of etiquette rules, and there would be steep consequences if she wasn't careful. Not to mention she was threatening the king's life. But right then, she didn't care. This man deserved to have his head on a stake for not only what he'd done to her, but also his own citizens. People who trusted him to lead. He was failing miserably.

She added, "Lucky for you, we got caught."

"Yes, lucky me that a puny girl did not raid my bed chambers in the dead of night." Snark seeped into his words while his piercing gaze roamed over her small frame. He was taunting her. Egging her on to say something else that would give him more of a reason to utterly destroy her.

And it was working. Enya's expression darkened further, her shackled hands clenching into fists, pressing even harder against her bonds. "Yeah, well, street life tends to turn you hard. Not that you'd know anything about that. I bet you've never even missed a meal," she snapped, earning a shove from Kelman. She snarled back, baring her teeth. "Watch it, pig."

"The prisoner will be silent," Queen Ciara commanded with a disapproving look. Her sultry voice echoed off the throne room walls and forced a breath of silence to settle over those inside. The hairs on the back of Enya's neck stood up. "You will have respect for your rulers, girl."

The king yawned, appearing bored. "Can someone bring me over a list of crimes committed by the accused?"

Eamon motioned in the air, almost dismissing Enya's failure to manage a respectable demeanor. A servant rushed up. She bowed deeply and dropped a stack of papers in his hands, looking to be holding back her disgust at his arrogance with a sucked-in cheek.

"Ah, here we are. 'Numerous crimes against the crown including but not limited to smuggling, vandalism, forgery, impersonating a police officer, impersonating a nun, theft, perjury, illegal possession of arms not limited to guns, explosives, and swords.'"

Hushed silence fell over the room as the impact of her crimes was realized by both guards and advisors alike.

Enya would have crossed her arms had she not been bound. Instead, she rolled her eyes. It wasn't *that* bad. Others had done far worse in the ruthless capital streets. Besides, she would even go as far as to argue that she was justified due to the cruelty of the police and politicians, but that point was mute here. No one would have cared.

"You forgot 'fleeing from police and assaulting an officer,' Your Majesty," Kelman chimed in happily. "That's from today."

"Oh, silly me. Thank you, Kelman." Eamon sat back and

stroked his beard, looking between the two kneeling before him while he tapped the now rolled-up papers against his thigh. "And what about this one?" He gestured to Carson, uninterested.

"He's an accomplice to her crimes," Ciara offered. "I'd say he deserves to share equally in her punishment. Don't you, husband?" Ciara flashed a devilish grin, seeming to come to the decision with as much ease as she would if it were her choice for brunch.

"I like how you think, my love. Very well. Death for both of them," Eamon declared, his voice booming off the walls of the throne room.

Carson's wide eyes met Enya's, and a million thoughts passed between them. For once, she was scared. Death was usually a nebulous concept, something off in the distance in the form of guns and smoke, but never so close and definite. Never punched onto someone's calendar. Now, it was tangible. Right within her grasp—or rather, the grasp of a noose around her neck.

Her nerves ran wild. "You can't do that!" Enya blurted out, unable to bite back her words. "We're barely of age to be tried!"

This made the king and queen laugh outright.

"You may pretend to be an innocent child," King Eamon said. "But we both know that you are a murderous thief— Enya, the Raven. Death would suit you like the darkness that lurks behind that title of yours." Eamon's words dripped with contempt evident on every syllable. "Besides, how do I know you wouldn't rise up in the ranks and do some *real* damage to my men?" He sneered, turning up his nose. "No," he reflected. "Death is almost certainly the right call." Enya and Carson gasped as they were lifted off the floor. "Take them to the dungeons. It'll be by hanging just before noon tomorrow."

Enya finally managed to pick her jaw up off the floor. Rage swelled within her chest, and she had to remind herself they were outnumbered by the royal guard. "You won't see the last of my men, Eamon. The rebels won't forget what you've done. No one will," she spat, still seething.

It was only a matter of time before he was taken down.

Rough hands yanked her and Carson up and led them out the throne room, chains clanking with every step. Servants stared curiously but kept their mouths shut. Guards kept their faces unreadable, but everyone knew their fate. No prisoners were kept in the palace dungeons except those with a death sentence.

Those with hands against their backs now shoved them behind iron doors. There was no mercy upon their jailer's aged face as he turned the key and walked away. Darkness crept in as their lamps moved further and further away.

Her eyes adjusted quickly enough to the faint light from the halls, but unfortunately, her nose took longer.

The holding cell was filthy and reeked of rotten eggs, but Enya couldn't figure out the source of the stench. The room contained only a lone metal bench placed on the stone floor while walls blackened by water damage boxed her and Carson inside. That, and there was a house goblin in the corner, munching away on what she hoped was a pile of chicken bones.

Every few minutes or so, a guard patrolled outside the iron bars on their door. Carson sat with his head resting on his legs on the floor while Enya laid on the bench, staring at the ceiling. *We'll figure a way out of this,* Enya thought to herself, *Just like we always do.*

"Any idea on how we're going to get out of the palace before noon tomorrow?" Carson muttered, playing with some dust on the ground and watching the tiny monster scratch its balding green head. "Or did you not think about that while you mouthed off to the king?"

Enya sat up, now glowering at him. "He's a tyrant who deserves whatever the saints give him. I don't regret anything."

"Oh, great. You can tell them that when you're hanging from the noose." He sighed, running a hand through his hair. "Enya, you know I'd follow you anywhere and do anything for you, but—I don't know. I just didn't think we'd end up in this mess."

Her heart fluttered with something she couldn't name. She hated how his words made her feel, along with his stupid face. Enya swallowed. She'd never felt anything like this, and she didn't like it at all. It made her feel good and strange all at once, and she hated such confusing things.

"I'll get us out of this. I won't let you or the gang down."

"I believe you. I just don't have any idea how you could possibly do that," he replied flatly, prompting the nearby creature to look up at them curiously, picking flesh out of its sharp teeth. The creature met their gazes with a man-eating smile, one which showed its yellowing, razor-sharp teeth.

"Just have faith, Carson. You'll see." She tugged off her black gloves, staring down at her hands, whose crescent scars were pulsing with slight pain. It always happened when she was in action, and sometimes it happened randomly, but she never knew why. It had been that way since she was a child, but Enya couldn't recall experiencing any injuries. But pain was a reminder that she was still breathing, still alive, so she welcomed it.

It meant she could fight another day.

Give it just a bit longer, and I'll have that slimy king right where I want him, Enya told herself, clasping her hands atop her knees.

Evil kings were simply broken people. The only way to take them down was to find their weak spot and strike. They'd fall, soon enough. She was counting on that fact if their rebellion was ever going to make any progress for the people of Skeyya.

A sudden clang caused both their eyes to spring over to the guard unlocking their cell. She quickly slipped back on the gloves and stood, Carson doing the same.

The house goblin shrank farther into the corner. A few more prisoners were loaded into their cell, making it quite cramped once the door slammed behind them.

"What brings you to our humble abode?" Enya attempted to make light of the situation, but really gloom was looming over everyone's heads. They were sentenced to death, just like she and Carson had been. Otherwise, they wouldn't have been brought to this crap-hole of a place.

"We stole some food from the ration line," a woman said, shoving her tangled honey hair out of her emerald-green eyes. "Apparently, that's a hanging offense." The two beside her nodded.

Enya thought her sentencing was harsh … Eamon must have been getting desperate. His concern about the growing rebellion had his finger twitchy on the trigger.

Another prisoner stood tall, and despite his lanky figure, he reeked of danger. Enya liked that. It made her think of a few ruthless rebels she'd admired while growing up on Arden's bustling streets. The last of the three was a dark-skinned old man covered in battle scars, likely earned from the last war.

With a welcoming wave from Enya, they took a seat on the worn-out stone floor.

The older man frowned, eyeing her and Carson up and down. "What about you two? You look a little young for death sentences."

Enya shrugged, foregoing any pretense a proper lady would have. Proper, she was not. "I'm the Raven, and I run the gang in Arden called the Grims. We got caught after bombing some cops." That earned gasps from the others. Beside her, Carson bit his lip with a grin. She'd expected such a response, of course. Not only was she young, having only just become an adult, but her name was growing in infamy across the country.

"But ... but you're so young!" the woman said, her eyes going wide. That was true, but Enya had accomplished quite a bit in her short life despite her scant years in this world.

"Why would a gang follow such a young girl?" the old man asked, his face plastered with disbelief.

Enya wasn't entirely sure of that herself, but she had a pretty good guess. "I knew enough inside information of the palace to gain some credit on the streets," she began, a thoughtful look now on her face as she pondered over the last decade living in the capital. "Instead of using that to gain wealth, I used it to gain trust and help others. I don't like selfish people, and I suppose I wasn't the only one who felt that way in the capital."

"She also rescued me from a linen mill operating on child-labor." Carson shrugged nonchalantly, like such things were an everyday occurrence. "That was kind of a big deal."

The others looked at her in awe, as if amazed a young girl

could be capable of such a deed. She supposed it *was* a big deal when one put it that way. That was another thing she tried to do: save others. In fact, most of her gang was simply made up of rescues from the streets that'd unfortunately, just like her, been dealt a poor deck of cards in life.

After ending up on the streets, she'd quickly begun using the king's secrets she'd learned from working in the palace against him, thus making friends with even the most dangerous of street rats and thieves. Intercepting cargo, supplies, stealing child slaves to free them.

You know, the usual.

That's how she became known as the Raven. She symbolized bad luck to all that dared cross her and the rebel cause.

The lanky man replied cautiously, "If what you say is true and you really are The Raven, how do you plan on getting us out of here?"

She hadn't quite figured that out yet. Maybe she'd dream of a way while she slept, or maybe she'd dream of her childhood in the palace.

Or maybe, if Enya was really lucky, she'd dream of nothing but a life not obsessed with making daring escapes and avoiding death at every turn. His question remained unanswered while her mind drifted off in thought. Eventually, the others made conversation without her, and she was back to pressing her fingers against her lips with a furrowed brow.

Her hands pulled out a crumpled sheet of paper and a pen that she kept hidden inside her coat pocket.

"Is she mental?"

"She's thinking. Give her a moment." Carson, ever her protector, murmured. Most of the other inmates slowly lost faith in her, they found some odd corner of the cell to try and sleep. All of them made it a point to avoid the goblin's bone covered corner. She paced around the small space, pen and paper in hand. When she didn't know what to do or what to think, she would write letters to herself. Her mother had suggested doing that as a kid—something about dealing with feelings or whatever, and it worked, so the habit stuck.

When she was certain that everyone was drifting off to sleep, the words began to flow.

Renmare, Skeyya

ENYA WOKE groggily from her sleep that next afternoon to be met by the sound of iron bars clanging against stone walls.

"Time's up. Follow us," a guard declared, throwing open their cell door. Enya was surprised she'd managed to sleep for so long on such an uncomfortable stone floor, now noticing a hunger pang in her stomach. Another man joined him in forcing Enya and Carson out, leading them up the stairs and back to the main floor of the royal palace. But with each step, her mind flooded with dread. They were being marched right to their deaths.

Enya couldn't help the scowl on her face when she and Carson were marched through the decorated rooms. Then again, being sentenced to death would ruin anyone's day, even a notorious gang leader. She held her head high, though her stomach was flipping in all sorts of ways.

We're about to die. We're about to die. Her mind willed her to repeat it, but she tried her best to focus on what they could do to get out of this mess. She hated fear. She hated feeling weak.

Enya knew they had to be smart. It's not like they were some everyday fools. They were rebels. They'd gotten out of worse situations before.

The soldiers guided the two down the hall towards the gallows outside while sunshine dappled the walls. It was no longer snowing outside, but the ground was still treacherous with ice and frost from what she could see. When Enya was sure there was no one else in the corridor, she stopped short, causing the guy behind to bump into her. Carson shot her an incredulous look.

"Keep walking," the man growled. She kept her feet planted, waiting for him to make his move.

Come on. Come on, Enya thought furiously.

He grabbed her shoulder, likely to push her forward. Enya immediately gripped his hand and snapped him to the side into the other guard. They both grunted out in pain, scrambling to turn back and restrain her.

Carson grabbed the other guard around the neck without hesitating. He fumbled with his chains, pressing them hard against the man's windpipe. The soldier gasped for air, legs going rubbery as he desperately yanked at Carson's arms. Now was her chance. Enya grabbed the one closest to her by the hair and snuck a leg around his. She slammed him to the floor as hard as she could, cringing at the crack his skull made against the tile before his face went slack.

It made her sick, but she let herself turn cold.

"Grab their guns," Enya huffed to Carson when he had effectively knocked out his captor. "Kill him. We don't leave loose ends." With that, she bristled with unease at her own words. Now she was starting to sound like the king, and she wasn't sure if she liked that. But it was reasonable to not leave loose ends, wasn't it? Never mind the fact these soldiers likely had families waiting for them at home … but she couldn't think about that when their own skins were on the line. *It's us against them,* echoed through her head.

Carson shrugged before crushing the man's throat with his boot. Guilt tugged at her heart strings, but she'd save that for another day when she had time to sulk in the mirror. He grabbed his pistol and threw the other firearm to Enya who stuck it in her belt. Once he'd retrieved the keys from inside the guard's pockets, he then released the uncomfortable chains encircling their wrists. That was that, and it was time to run before they got caught again.

Reality didn't wait for feelings to catch up. You just had to keep moving and hope for the best.

"Follow me. I know a way out," Enya panted after they'd wandered a bit through the hallways, always careful to rush behind housekeeping carts or within service closets when someone passed by. She was certain they'd look out of place with their dark street getup, even if they tried passing for servants.

Well, she'd *thought* she knew a way out.

It had been so many years since she'd roamed through these halls as a child. Enya had tried for so long to forget that now it was becoming hard to remember much at all.

Their footsteps rapped hurriedly down the west stairwell, one crafted from smooth stone, careful to be as quiet as possible.

"You sure you know where you're going?" Carson quietly asked while they hid behind the left wall at the bottom of the steps from a palace guard around the corner.

"I spent half my life here as a kid. I know the ins and outs of this place like the back of my dartboard at The Bowman."

Carson winced, not seeming to like the sound of that.

Enya hissed back, "Would you just trust me?"

"I always do, but sometimes you make some really questionable decisions." Carson glowered, averting his gaze. She hated seeing him disappointed in her; she was supposed to be the crew's leader. "You offended the king. I'm sure that didn't help with our sentencing."

"I like pissing him off." Enya shrugged, giving him a dismissive wave of her hand while she stuck out her head to get a good look. "Let's talk about this when we aren't trying to escape?"

Carson nodded with a roll of his eyes.

Enya slid down the hall. The guard never heard her coming, and she was on his back in a split second, her hands encircling his head. With a sharp turn of her hands, he was on the ground with a broken neck. Carson caught the lamp in his hands before it fell from the man's grasp, carefully setting it down to avoid too much noise. With his arms under the guard's shoulders, he roughly shoved the man into a nearby linen closet.

One wrong move and they would be caught. Their lives would be over.

It was a truth she repeated over and over in her head, willing herself to remember which way to go, where to hide, and who to kill. The doors that led to the outdoors were just mere steps away.

One look through barred windows said the courtyard full of sweet-smelling flowers was mostly empty, all except a few souls gathered by the fountain in its center. This area must have gone mostly unused during the day. It was also the only way out of this part of the palace.

Adrenaline pushed her forward, but quiet feet kept her from being noticed by the group before them while they slipped behind a short stone wall. The sound of water bubbling in the fountain was unnerving, as was the overwhelming scent of pink berry flowers and roses. It almost made it hard to focus, but she managed to take a deep breath and remember why they were there.

"On three, okay?" Enya said quietly, gripping the pistol tighter in her gloved hands, earning a sharp twinge of pain. She gritted her teeth, and Carson nodded. With a deep breath, she whispered her next words. "One … two … three!"

They sprang into action, lifting their guns to fire as they stood. But those in front of them were certainly not members of the palace guard.

"Jackson? Finn? Miriana?" Enya's heart nearly stopped in shock, the gun trembling slightly in her hands. "What are you guys doing here? Are you trying to get killed?"

"We're here to rescue you, of course!" Miriana said in her typical singsong voice, as if the matter were obvious. She ran a soothing hand over her bead-covered arm. "Rumor has it someone snitched to the chief." Enya and Carson nodded, faces grim.

Carson holstered his gun and crossed his arms over his

chest in exasperation. "We could have shot you."

"Ah, but you didn't!"

Miriana wore a dark violet skirt and pale green bustier above short black boots. A thick brown coat kept her warm from the wind whipping around them. She was a petite thing with brown skin and cropped hair. Her parents immigrated to Skeyya from Brasova due to the war before they were killed in enemy bombings a year ago. Being only sixteen at the time, it was lucky the Raven found her on a job up in Thomond smuggling arms and ammo.

Miriana was a Banya, or as most would say, a witch, and considering her nationality, hated by many. The war certainly couldn't be blamed on Brasova, but that didn't stop the more bitter and hungry souls from taking out their frustrations on innocent Brasovian targets—and especially on the "lowly" fae.

According to her, she was an Unseelie faerie from the Winter Court, which covered all of Brasova, though the world was unseen. Only through hidden entrances were any allowed in such places, and human rulers had to sign treaties with the high fae rulers, agreeing not to interfere with worlds unless required.

Not that Eamon was very ... diplomatic in such matters. Especially given his barbaric treatment of the creatures of the woods and their ilk.

The Autumn Court of Skeyya couldn't have been pleased.

Those from the North were usually cold and reserved, the exact opposite from the bouncing Banya standing before the Raven today. She'd taken her tragedy and transformed it into a bubbling love for every creature who drew breath, even her home country's enemies.

Even those who killed her parents. Or so she said.

Enya had no doubt Miriana could take on trouble, but anyone should know better than to sneak into the palace.

Jackson, a gangly teen with just the barest hint of stubble, blue eyes, and a head full of tousled blond hair, grinned mischievously. He gestured to the rifles concealed within their arms, his own being covered with a black jacket lined with fox fur. "We may have had a bit of fun in the palace's armory on our way here." This pleased Enya, who was grateful for the additional weapons in their arsenal.

"Well, at least there's that." She let out a breath of relief before her eyes went wide. Two guards were chatting and about to head right for the courtyard from what she could see through a decorated window.

"Get down!" Enya ordered.

With a start, their newfound companions darted behind the stone wall beside them, eyes now peering over the ledge to watch the palace goons pacing the stone pathways while their rifles clacked on the paved ground. They were so close to escaping. But were they? What about those still locked up in their cell?

The idea of escaping without them put a sour taste in her mouth and spoke of guilty dreams. In any case, it was already hard enough to catch any sleep in Podge's cramped attic what with the rowdy patrons drinking and carousing below.

"Think we should take them out?" Finn, a pale-skinned teen with pointed ears, brown hair, and a wry smile, asked.

He wore only a dark button-down shirt rolled up at the sleeves and a pair of gray slacks. Finn was a Seelie fae, one whose own magick was slim in comparison to a Banya's but powerful all the same. He claimed to come from the Summer Court, which resided in the unseen world of Cardek, far from humans.

"I wouldn't mind the challenge," he continued, his brown eyes now gazing over to where Miriana crouched. She stuck a tongue out in return, sparkling power now visible at her fingertips.

Enya shook her head. That would be way too dangerous and attract way too many watchful eyes. The gang needed to be smart about this. "No, we need to be careful about leaving too long a trail of bodies and drawing attention. Can't you put some sort of invisibility spell on us?" she asked.

Both Finn and Miriana nodded, speaking words that Enya could only guess were exclusive to those who wielded their kind of power. Enya felt nothing different, but reassuring waves from the two said they were good—for now.

"We need to do something about those three locked in the holding cell over in the east tower," Carson finally said after several moments of looking thoughtful, clearly having been planning their next move just as much as she was.

"I've got it," Miriana whispered, pink eyes now going black. She sat there quietly while the others waited. "I found them," she said, eyes now back to normal while glancing at the rest of the crew. Her heart-shaped face grew determined, her mouth turning up into a confident grin. "I can grab them while you guys escape."

"No. It's dangerous to split up," Enya retorted quickly, trying to keep her voice level and calm. It was hard to keep her temper in check when they frustrated her like this sometimes. They needed to lay low. Why was that so hard to understand?

Carson seemed to weigh this before responding.

"She has powers, and we're invisible right now. I'd say if Miriana could make it in safe, she could make it out just fine, considering her talents," he said, giving Enya's arm a reassuring pat, one that made her skin cover in goosebumps and stomach turn with all kinds of tricks, something only he could manage to do. "Let's let her go help them."

"I can go with her!" Jackson offered without hesitating, his abrupt reply startling Enya.

"Keep it down!" she hissed. They'd be toast if they were spotted—and not the kind slathered in butter and washed down with whiskey at the Bowman's Pub.

He turned his head down sheepishly, as if this realization had only just struck him. He was too eager for his own good about everything and nothing all at once, like a kid in a candy store. Raids and missions kept Jackson on his toes, always joyfully ready to jump in at any moment. His hopeful reply regarding Miriana, however, left Enya guessing she wasn't the only one harboring not-so-business-like feelings for one of the Grims. In any case, the witch blushed at his offer, her expression growing shy and reserved.

Enya considered this all for a moment, gaze never leaving the guards as their backs disappeared within another door to the palace. If she let the Banya take care of this, and she knew Miriana *could* take care of this, that meant three less deaths on their way out. Ones that were preventable.

"Fine—but be quick. I don't want my best Banya to get butchered by the king's men. Or my best weapons dealer." Enya sighed, waving them on. She paused, remembering someone else that had been in there hiding in the dark. Her features turned sympathetic. "Don't forget the goblin in there. I'm sure he didn't deserve his fate either. They never do."

With that, Miriana and Jackson disappeared silently back the way she and Carson had come from, leaving them to their own devices. Enya knew that they could handle it. They'd have to handle it, after all. But there was no time to dwell on possibilities.

It was time to get moving.

She motioned for Carson and Finn to follow her while she crept across the courtyard, ignoring its inviting roses and vines crawling up the stone walls of the estate's exterior. Her memories flickered, begging her to notice them, but she did her best to remain stoic and emotionless. She needed to forget.

Enya had to if she wanted to make it out of the palace alive.

The inside of the palace was bustling with visitors and servants, some obviously having recently immigrated from the nearby countries such as Tobuhan and Cardek from across the Great Sea or Brasova from beyond the Galtymore Mountains of Thomond, where war brewed day and night.

Enya couldn't help but think only the craziest would ever dream of setting sail across the Great Sea on such a journey to Cardek, or its neighboring country, Tobuhan, which was full to the brim with mountains and mystery. And monasteries, if you were the religious type, all in reverence to the high fae rulers of the Spring Court. Enya was not particularly devout, and neither place had ever seemed worth the dangerous excursion.

But that didn't stop traders and diplomats from braving the impossible to predict threats lurking beneath the waters. Gaining allies and resources was considered well worth losing a few men and ships, but with King Eamon's greed, both were quickly growing scarce.

She frowned at the visitors, her eyes raking over them like the potential targets they would likely become if Mihaela, the rebellion leader, had her way.

Anyone who had dealings with Eamon was a target to her. Enya, however, wasn't so cruel. Monsters could be tamed. Deals could be made. If they had the guts to brace the Great Sea, she could only imagine the ferocity they'd bring to her ranks.

They dressed up in top-hats and suits, but they were fighters at heart. Otherwise, they wouldn't have survived the journey here. She smiled to herself.

Enya, Carson, and Finn, however, were already out of breath from constantly ducking behind pillars and statues back inside the palace. It was becoming harder and harder to avoid detection, what with the housekeepers fluttering by with their cleaning carts and diplomats easing along, chatting about national issues while they brushed icy raindrops off their fancy ensembles.

A few halls down, they saw the king himself taking a stroll with his wife and son, an heir who shared in his mother's hair coloring and his father's striking features, something that sent chills down Enya's spine and hatred flaring through her heart. They were so similar that she wondered if he'd be the next evil king.

King Eamon and his monstrous reign would meet an end soon enough. All tyrants and their legacies did. When the boy came of age, she'd weigh whether he was worth her bullets. Perhaps he'd have a change of heart.

With a breath of relief, they finally reached one of the back exits of Whitstone Palace.

Waiting outside were practicing troops working out in the field nearby, their shouts reverberating through the winter air. Enya had to admit they sure were a sight to see with their shirts off, but Carson didn't look too happy at her expression. She simply shrugged, unsure what there was for him to be upset about.

She was allowed to enjoy such simple pleasures, and why shouldn't she? Who was there to stop her?

They kept moving until they were out in the woods, safely away from watching eyes and dangerous guards.

Branches and leaves crunched under their boots, and the scent of pine and moss filled their noses, bringing a sense of ease they hadn't felt for the past day or so.

As they walked farther, though, they realized they weren't alone. Three young men were being escorted by a few guards through the brush, ones who had all the gait of royals. Their clothes looked deceivingly plain from behind, but no peasant would gesture so dismissively to an armed man in the way the leader of the three did.

They'd make easy targets, Enya thought, smiling viciously.

The Raven had to get a closer look.

Kidnapping these boys could mean a hefty sum from the royal family or whichever noble family they came from and a victorious upper hand for the rebellion. It was almost impossible to ignore the calling to move towards them, the impossible pull their mere presence had on her. In her mind flashed images of money—and loads of it. This was what they'd been waiting so long for.

An upper hand.

But when the one in front turned his head suspiciously

at her boot cracking a twig much too close for comfort, Enya realized she knew him. When the others spun to see what he was looking at, she realized she knew them all.

These were the three dead princes, and it seemed that the Grims' invisibility had worn off.

4

Renmare, Skeyya

IT WAS almost impossible for Enya to ignore the recognition that made her hands twitch and her chest tighten. The guilt that captured her breath and almost stole it away like leaves in the wind.

Had the anticipation of death caught up with her and made her mad enough to see royal ghosts? Surely, this couldn't be real.

In cases like these, she'd usually just focus on something—anything that would distract her mind from the horrible memories of her past.

She was innocent … or was she? *Murderer. Traitor. Deceiver.*

All these thoughts swarmed her mind, almost keeping her

from reaching for her pistol. Almost. She drew, fast enough to kill any skilled shooter. But before she could squeeze the trigger, the princes' escort aimed with their rifles. It was only a strangled noise from an older gentleman, one she'd also recognized, that halted fire.

"Enya?" the man breathed, whose name she remembered to be Farrell. Shock painted his features.

He didn't look to be much older than he had been when she was a child, but he had definitely grown into his sharp jaw. His blond hair was still tousled and a mess He also sported a neatly trimmed beard. Medals decorated his uniform, indicating he had risen through the ranks from lowly cadet to captain.

Farrell slowly lowered his gun. "I thought you were dead."

The other three with him gasped when they also realized her identity. Still, only Farrell had lowered his weapon out of his squadron. Both his men and hers aimed high, waiting for whoever would fire the first shot. Even the eldest prince, Rowan, was poised to shoot.

Finn and Carson didn't seem at all pleased for them to have been caught up in this discussion. They were supposed to sneak out undetected, not get spotted by members of the royal family. This was dangerous. If things turned bad, they were outnumbered, and Enya could only guess how much the king's trigger-happy dogs would enjoy peppering them with lead.

She took a deep breath, keeping her eyes trained on the guards, steadying her grip on the weapon in her hands.

The Raven wouldn't go down without a fight.

"Well, sorry to disappoint. As you can see, I'm still very much alive," Enya retorted. *And I'm going to keep it that way.*

"And I'm sorry too. Sorry you decided to show back up,"

Rowan snapped. She'd never forgotten his stern brown eyes or dark-red hair. He had been the heir to the throne before rumors began that they were dead. But now they were here, standing before her, appearing alive as any sorry soul. Enya wondered if this was some sort of faerie trick. That perhaps woodland ghouls sought to lure them to their deaths. It wouldn't have been the first time something like that happened.

"For god's sake, Rowan, lower the gun. It's Enya," Niall pleaded with his older brother. A few of the guards looked to their commander, unsure of what to do.

Niall was the youngest of the three princes, from what Enya could recall. He looked just as meek as he had as a child. He was much more slender than his siblings, and his hazel eyes spoke a sad tale, one Enya couldn't quite decipher. Like both of his brothers, he had the signature red hair of the king.

"Niall, let us handle this," Captain Farrell ordered with a disapproving look. Sunlight glistened against his men's muskets, and he wouldn't let them back down so easily. "Why are you here?"

"I could ask you all the same thing. Rowan ... Niall ... and ..." Enya struggled to find the words.

They'd all been so friendly as children, but that was so many years ago. She could recall playdates behind the king's back in the stables she had served in. Laughter with royal brothers she'd considered her own kin. But those days were long gone. So was her sympathy for foolish kings and queens, never mind their children.

They were all rotten to the core.

"Prince Beacon." The last one gave a half-hearted wave of his hand, his golden-brown eyes almost apologetic, as if he were sorry that they had to see each other again. She was too. "We were never close, I guess."

Carson let loose a disgusted scoff, cocking his weapon. "Royals. They make for good leverage over the king, don't they?" He turned his head to both Finn and Enya. The creature of the woods nodded, but Enya stayed still. She was unsure.

Farrell brought his gun back up and aimed as well. "Don't get any ideas. Why are you really back at the palace, Enya? And don't lie. You know I can tell when you do."

Enya gave a weak shrug, trying to appear as nonchalant as possible. It was becoming hard when their faces made so much fear flash before her eyes, fear of her past.

So many feelings consumed her, but the fake, cocky grin on her rosy lips did well to hide them all. "We may or may not have been arrested. And sentenced to death. We're kind of in the middle of our daring escape if you couldn't tell."

The Raven couldn't let her new identity, that of a ruthless leader on the streets, falter.

She wished it were something more than that, though. Something higher up in the rebellion called to her, and she was *trying* to answer. Either way, she needed to be smart about her next move here. She needed to make them afraid, just like how their mere existence made her feel at this moment.

Was it fear doing somersaults in her gut? She felt exposed here, trapped by their gazes. Like a raven in an iron cage, and someone had thrown away the key. They reminded her of feelings she had refused to allow herself to feel for so long. Of memories she'd locked away deep inside her. But right now, they were screaming for her to notice them. To acknowledge them.

"We're leaving this polished prison. Give us one reason

not to kill all of you," Carson demanded.

Enya hoped it wouldn't go that far today. She felt that she'd hurt them enough in the past, especially by leaving them. They'd been best friends, after all. Killing their father, the ruthless tyrant that he was, would be easy. He was a monster. But these princes? If she remembered correctly, they had hearts.

"Carson," Enya gave a nervous chuckle. "Settle down. I'm sure we can work out some sort of agreement."

Farrell's eyes narrowed. "Agreement? Like what?"

Enya noticed the trunks and packs the three brothers were carrying. It was obvious they'd be going on a trip and seeing as though she was sure no one else knew they were alive, now would be the perfect time to use that to her advantage. They needed a way back to the city without Eamon and his goons being notified, and the insurance of having these three under her wing made her heart and mind steady.

Emotions were gone, and now it was time for the notorious gang leader and thieving schemer to return.

"We'll escort you through the city. Think of us as your personal bodyguards." Enya offered a man-eating smile, gauging their skeptical reactions. "You wouldn't want anyone else to know the king's sons were stumbling around the streets unguarded, would you? Without us, you'd be discovered much too easily."

Carson eyed her hesitantly before he spoke. "You either let us tag along or you'll get killed out there," he snapped with a wave of his gun at the three brothers. "You need us to survive against the rebels, anyway, seeing as though they trust us to run the capital city. If you try to leave us behind, we'll just kill you and your men—and we don't hesitate, unlike your captain here."

"By the looks of it, they're too weak to face anything but the queen's powdering room." Finn laughed, nudging Carson with his elbow. Always the joking fool. Enya shook her head. Now wasn't the time to say such things. They used fighting words, but they were still outnumbered. These were empty threats, but maybe the captain would buy into their charade.

"Now listen here, you little—" Rowan's face filled with rage before Farrell cut him off with a lifted hand. The prince was just as arrogant as she remembered, and then some.

"You will protect them in Arden, Enya? I have your word?" Farrell demanded.

"Of course. When have I ever done you wrong?" Enya batted her eyelashes in an attempt to look like a sweet young girl. Meanwhile, she was hoping their crew could ditch them as soon as they got back to the capital. Or kill them. Or kidnap them for ransom. Whatever suited her and the Grims best at the time.

"Fine. You may escort them, but only because I know you, and we can't risk word getting out about them."

After the guard captain had lowered his own gun, she followed suit, having her own men lower their weapons. She was silently thanking the saints for helping her pull off that bluff. Nonetheless, they weren't out of danger yet, and they still had to make it back to the capital.

They were all herded by Farrell to a waiting carriage at the end of the trees. It was quiet in the forest, aside from sounds of fluttering bats and the burbling of a nearby stream.

There were no ice flurries today, merely sunshine warming their backs and the never-ending hills leading off into the deep forest. In the distance, she saw sheep prancing around a field. They seemed more free than she'd ever be. Eaten eventually, sure. But at least they didn't have the worries of the world stretched out before them. Besides, who was to say Enya wouldn't be eaten by some faerie creature one day? It would make an entertaining tale for the descendants to come after their time, should she be of any worth to the rebel cause or the world enough to be remembered.

Enya almost felt bad for the old man driving the carriage who had to shiver in the cold on their journey while they were safely tucked atop the warm velvet of their seats. The carriage door shut behind them, and they sat cramped inside much too close for comfort.

Jackson and Miriana would no doubt catch up with them back in Arden. At least, Enya hoped they would.

"So … how's life been since you left the palace?" Beacon asked, breaking the tension in the carriage. Enya didn't blame them for being on guard, of course. She was a wanted criminal, after all. "I see you've been … busy." He cracked a nervous smile, scratching his head and tousling his rust-shaded locks. Even after all these years, he almost looked to be the same age as Rowan, along with matching brown eyes like the other two brothers.

She thought for a moment before offering a mocking smile. "I had to live in the filth of the streets as a child and build up my reputation on a mound of death and debts. How about you?"

Carson stifled a laugh with a convincing cough.

"Why did you leave? If I remember correctly, we had all been good friends. As good as a servant and royal could be, that is," Rowan said, raising a cocky brow and shifting in his seat. His chin was turned up, but she could sense doubt in his features.

Her stomach turned with guilt once again along with the bumps in the road.

"I was forced to. That's all you need to know," Enya said, as if it were all that simple. It wasn't, but they didn't need to know her sob story. Not now, not ever. The past was the past. If you got too caught up, you were killed.

"Well, excuse us, pretty princess," Rowan mocked, mask once again firmly in place. "Not like we haven't seen you in over ten years."

Before she could answer, Carson interjected, "Why are the king's dead sons going out to brave Skeyya armed with nothing more than tiny pistols and trunks full of clothes? Must be important." He locked eyes with Finn, who narrowed his own in agreement. Enya had thought the same.

Why would three supposedly dead princes be out on the town after all this time? It was highly suspicious and hinted towards the possibility of some serious coin if their crew got in on the job. With that, she was eager to hear. The other Grims looked to have the same idea, both exchanging a glance and turning to face the princes.

Rowan glanced over to his brothers. Niall just fidgeted with his cravat, obviously trying to avoid scrutiny. With his silence, Enya had almost forgotten he was there.

Beacon cleared his throat, straightening up his jacket that had clearly been borrowed from a servant. "We were told to find the Sword of Bas for Queen Ciara. We haven't been out of Renmare in a very long time, so we could really use your help."

"What's so important about it?" Enya asked, cocking her

61

head. Some silly faerie trinket, no doubt. Maybe the queen was growing bored of all the treasures brought back by diplomats and soldiers from faraway lands and needed new interesting things to add to her collection. Her nose scrunched in disgust. Why did royals have to care so much about material possessions?

"It can call upon armies of dark creatures and pierce souls, so the legend says—" Beacon began before a quick strike from Rowan to his shoulder. "Okay, fine. It's important," he grumbled.

That sounded really expensive. And dangerous.

Enya would have to be careful with this. In the wrong hands, it could kill a lot of people, and now that these guys were searching for it to give to the queen ... "We'll help you find it," she declared after stringing her thoughts together and reviewing their options, prompting a shocked look from Carson and Finn. "But we want payment."

If Enya found the sword, she could use it against Eamon and his army of mindless dogs to finally make something of the Grims—and gain an upper hand in the rebellion. Or, at the very least, she could keep it out of his hands so he couldn't hurt any more of her fellow rebels, much less his people. Either way, these boys had no clue what dangerous game they'd just signed up for.

"How much?" Rowan studied her with a set jaw, chestnut hair barely resting over his furrowed brows.

"One hundred thousand pounds," Enya said simply. The three men in front of her gasped. Carson just gave a disbelieving shake of his head. Finn seemed pleased at the idea of a new job, one that would pay more than a mere pittance.

Such was the day to day in Arden. You broke your back to stay broke. There weren't many other options.

"That's—that's way too much!" Beacon exclaimed, loosening his collar with a nervous laugh. "Fifty thousand pounds is more than enough."

Enya sat back into her seat, sizing them all up.

"You're royal, so you can afford it. Eighty thousand pounds or we ditch you in the slums."

Rowan glared, eyes shooting daggers. She met his furious gaze with her own, and he backed down. "Fine. It's a deal," he snapped with an angry huff. Niall gave them all a nervous look.

"So, you will help us?" the quiet prince finally piped up. "Our lives depend on it."

"What do you mean?" Enya asked, brows pushed together in confusion. They were royals. What could they possibly have to be afraid of?

Niall went pale, loosening his shirt collar. "The queen will kill us if we don't find what she's asking for."

Her mouth fell open in shock. Had she heard them correctly? "She's … going to kill you?"

Well, that certainly would raise the stakes. Sure, the queen was a real piece of work, but death? Their lives were already in danger, anyway, if anyone found out who they really were. But Enya couldn't wrap her head around why the queen would want these three dead. Wouldn't the king be against this?

The poor boy looked like a scared mutt fetching the daily paper out in the rain with his wide eyes and limp curls. She pitied him; he reminded her too much of her younger self when she had to brave the streets alone. It had been brutal, full of hungry nights, bruises, and bartering for a measly place to rest her head.

But she'd pushed through, and she was certain that he could gain some courage too.

"Yes, we'll help you. No need to be all worried and whatnot." Enya gave him a reassuring pat on the shoulder.

She'd get this done, take the money, and the crew could finally stop living like common thugs in the attic at the Bowman's Pub. Maybe they could make a living for themselves and do something *real* for the rebellion. Maybe she could become its leader, too. Maybe, just maybe, they could find a new king to replace this current monster on the golden throne. She'd much prefer no king at all. Most if not all royals were evil, anyway. Or so she thought.

Enya smiled. This was going to be a fun ride.

Arden, Skeyya

THE ROAD back to the capital city was uneven and smelled putrid compared to the fresh notes of lavender and moss Enya had grown used to in Renmare.

They rolled along the road, passing dilapidated wooden homes and stores, muddy streets and grime-coated stone. Citizens toiled about, carrying firewood to heat their homes or ushering their children back inside from the cold. A few faeries stared at their passing carriage, giving them curious looks.

She hoped no one would notice the princes. That would make this situation all the more dangerous.

When the sun turned into an orange sunset across the lands, and mossy hills turned into Arden's city suburbs, she almost regretted leaving her old home from her time before the Grims.

She was still piecing together how she'd ended up on the streets and out of the palace, but that part of her memories was always fuzzy.

Enya didn't know if she even wanted to remember.

"What are you looking at?" Carson asked, a curious flush now spreading over his cheeks. Enya hadn't even realized that she'd been staring right at him.

"Just thinking. That's all." She gave a dismissive shrug and shifted in her seat so that her body faced the frosty window of the carriage instead of Carson. She had no idea how he always managed to catch her staring. Truthfully, she wasn't even sure why she did.

Beacon gave a huge grin when he realized the streets had become wider and full of other vehicles and people while buildings had grown taller than trees.

Old houses became sprawling two to four story buildings, with homes and shops intertwined in a dance for dominance over the tangled streets. Merchants haggled from corners and courtesans beckoned from doorways. Others were off to work, be it on the docks or in the factories. But some, like those she'd stumbled over a day before while they were trying to put some distance between them and the police, were not so active and instead lay unmoving and pale blue, like the winter haze breathing life into the sky.

The streets were teeming with life and death, and Enya almost scoffed at the prince's reaction. What was so special about this place? She'd much rather be surrounded by the tranquility of the countryside.

"Can you believe we're actually outside the palace?" he asked his brothers, his eyes going wide in awe.

Enya couldn't help but frown at the reminder of their makeshift prison sentence for the past twelve years. It sounded like a new kind of sick for Eamon to have locked his children inside a tower and cut them off from the rest of the world.

Well, he was a monster, after all. Monsters did horrible things. It seemed to be just a matter of time before his cruelty extended to his children. Yet she couldn't help but wonder what part Prince Aiden, Ciara's son and the "current" heir played in all this.

Was he truly the heir, or was Rowan? Why had everyone been told they were dead by King Eamon? Enya pursed her lips, staring back out the window.

The Raven would keep quiet. She was sure that the princes would tell them at the right time.

"It's not that great, brother. I mean, just *look* at these people." Rowan cringed. "How do they live like this? *Dress* like this? Do they not know of class and decorum?"

Enya shot Carson a knowing look.

Hopefully, the prince wouldn't be like this the entire trip, or else she might sock him in the head long before they got paid. If she didn't, Carson would. The thought made the corners of her lips turn up, and she subtly covered her smile with the back of her hand.

Rowan glared at her. "Something funny?"

Enya shook her head. "Nope. Nothing." He didn't seem convinced in the slightest, but he averted his gaze.

Beacon leaned out the window and waved. A few women

draped in fur coats and linen gowns giggled at him, their rosy lips turned up into serene smiles and their bosoms decorated with the finest jewels someone outside the palace could care to own.

He whistled, only encouraging their laughter. Enya paled. Someone might recognize him. She was about to say something before Rowan groaned.

"Please tell me you wouldn't settle for peasants. These are not royal women," Rowan pleaded, rolling his eyes.

Beacon sat back and nudged Niall, who appeared sick from the ride. "I'm just having fun. Maybe you guys could learn a thing or two from me." Enya grimaced, looking over at the young prince who still appeared green with nausea.

He'd better not throw up all over the Bowman's Pub, she thought. The owner, Podge, was already unsure about their crew watching over the place and sleeping in his attic. He likely wouldn't be too happy about one of their 'friends' spewing bile all over his custom-made carpets.

There was also that tiny detail about them being outcast princes. That'd have to stay a closely guarded secret, or else Enya would face getting their crew kicked out of the rebel cause. Their reputation would be ruined.

The driver finally stopped outside their destination, yanking the reins on his horses and earning several annoyed noises from the beasts, who shook their manes with indignation.

They seemed nearly as displeased as she was, being cast in this situation with these supposedly dead princes. Enya sighed.

An unwavering group of bystanders greeted their group when they stepped out of the carriage, and one silent hand held in the air by Enya told them exactly who'd arrived. All went quiet, and the scramble to get out of the way was almost immediate, earning a prompt nod from Carson and an exasperated sigh from Enya while Rowan, Beacon, and Niall followed behind with Finn.

This crowd full of rebels, what with their arm bands engraved with the rebel insignia revealed only around safe houses, knew she was the leader of the Grims. Her gang was a force to be reckoned with, according to anyone you asked in Arden.

These boys better not embarrass us, Enya thought with a skeptical glance at the three, ones who were looking just as concerned at the large crowd. They needed to hurry this along.

A tall, middle-aged man covered from head to toe with taut muscle and a myriad of tattoos tipped his bowler hat to Enya as he stood guard by the front door. "Good to see you, boss."

She nodded, shoving the door open and leading the group inside.

Inside was all one would expect of a pub; a wooden bar sat along the far wall adorned with intricate glass art. Worn out stools held men and women grubbing down on their morning breakfast of beans, toast, and bacon while others talked way too loud for Enya's liking at the tables haphazardly strewn around as they slurped down their morning beers and tea.

Enya's stomach grumbled at the sight.

"Where the hell have you guys been?" Maxon, a dark-skinned teen whose arms were covered in scars, asked from across the room. He dealt out cards to a group of patrons before biting his lip and surveying the board. "Sorry, Declan. Looks like you lose." The master of cards said it almost regrettably, but Enya knew this was his job: to win every game. That meant more money for their tiny apartment upstairs, and more money for the cause.

Being nice didn't keep debts paid nor stomachs full. The Raven's kindness could only extend to so many.

The man across from Maxon threw his hand in anger. He rested his head in his hands while others seated at the table comforted him with whispers, no doubt attempting to stroke his fragile ego.

Enya had to hide her smile at Maxon's guiltless shrug while he stepped around to greet them within the sea of early-morning patrons. He sauntered over, crossing his arms and leaning up against a wooden post near their group. He was a sight to see, with lean muscle and a tailored outfit ironed to perfection, one that most in this pub could only dream of affording. She guessed he'd paid for the services rendered with some of his winnings along with a thick paycheck from the Grims, something she couldn't blame him for.

What was that saying, again? The poor fought for bread, but roses too. And they enjoyed roses, indeed. Ones of cool steel, gunpowder, and silk cravats. Well, much of that was stolen, of course, but the point was still the same.

"The other Grims didn't tell you?" she called back, now approaching to give his hand a good shake, wincing at her own hand's tenderness. "We were arrested."

"Interesting. Nope, I don't remember hearing that particular bit of news."

"I thought we did," Finn said before sauntering up to the bar and ordering a drink. He appeared at her side moments later with a beer mug dripping with froth, silently mouthing the number of game chips in front of Maxon's perch at the table. His eyes went wide, and his mouth fell open at the cut the dealer would no doubt take from these winnings after paying up to Podge and Enya.

Finn looked to be holding back a joke, but thinking better of it, he kept his mouth shut and took a sip of his stout.

Maxon shook his head, brown eyes now set on the three princes seated at the bar across the room with Carson. Enya hadn't even realized he had left her side, but she suddenly felt cold—like her warmth had just packed up and walked away. It was an empty feeling. "Who are those three talking up hot stuff? New bloods?"

"We're temporarily babysitting," Enya muttered, blushing at the comment on Carson's good looks. She knew he looked good, so why was she reacting this way? She needed to get it together. "It's a boring escort job, but the payment's good."

Maxon nodded in return, understanding the obvious. They would need the money now more than ever considering the growing threat from Sean's gang, the Wraiths, and the increasing pressure from police. That earlier explosion probably didn't help much in the way of lowering their profile.

Finn suggested with a raised brow, "I think a meeting is in order, don't you? I'm always happy to touch base with my band of thieves. My dynamic posse of death-bringers."

Enya sighed, tired of being around people for the day. Would she manage a break before this misadventure? "Fine," she snapped. "But after that, I'm sleeping, and no one can stop me. Don't forget that I'm the one calling shots around here."

Soon, Enya would also be calling the shots for the entire rebellion, not just the Grims, if she had her way. She definitely valued their loyalty and wanted to make sure she delivered the best leadership in return—and getting them out of this dusty old bar was part of that.

"You got it, boss. I'll gather the troops for the meeting," Maxon replied before stopping short to look over her shoulder. "By the way, Miriana and Jackson just popped in."

The two waltzed right through the double doors, hand in hand, until they realized everyone had noticed. With red cheeks and a scramble to distance themselves, Miriana and Jackson approached Enya. They were obviously head over heels for each other. But did they realize it?

"Welcome back. We were just about to start a meeting upstairs," Enya announced before noticing the three fugitives missing. She narrowed her eyes. "Where are the ones you rescued?"

"They went home and took that goblin with them. We figured they deserved to rest after everything they'd been through." Jackson shrugged, brushing a lock of hair out his eyes. He and Miriana didn't seem nearly as concerned as Enya now was.

"Home? They're wanted by the palace guard," she exclaimed. She couldn't understand how anyone could be so careless. With a deep breath, she spoke her next words over the sound of the growing crowd of the Bowman's Pub. "We need them to be at one of our bases at *least*."

Their faces paled, and they exchanged a worried glance. It wasn't often that she raised her voice at her crew, but when she did, she could be a terrifying force. They all knew what she was capable of.

As if on cue from her distress, Carson was already at her side. "What's going on?" he asked, startling her. His eyes seemed so earnest, and she hated how much she liked it. Enya froze for a moment at how close he stood, trying to regain her composure. But he had calmed her anger, at least. She hated that too. Hated the way he made her feel like he was one of the only things keeping her sane at times.

With a hard swallow, she was able to speak again. "Send one of our messenger birds over to Amir in the southern warehouse. Quickly. Tell him to go pick up our stowaways before the police beats us to the punch."

Sometimes, rebels would use literal ravens to communicate across the country, which was another inspiration for her nickname.

Their messenger birds would have red bands around one of their legs, and on command would go wherever their crew needed them most at the time. It was a hell of a lot faster than running around like mad on foot or on horseback, and it was great for urgent matters like this one.

Hah. Ravens just like me, Enya thought, smirking to herself in amusement at her nickname.

She gazed over to the princes at the bar, ones who were now throwing olives into each other's mouths in some sort of game. Seriously? They needed to move, not horse around.

"Carson, get them situated upstairs. I'll be right up," she finally said, now walking over to the bar. The others, following Carson's lead, now trudged up the creaking stairs near the bar, earning curious glances from patrons seated around the worn-out steps.

No one ever went up there during the day unless something important was happening.

The three princes stopped their game as soon as she reached them, green olives dropping out of their hands to the dirty floor. Enya eyed them up and down, considering how ill-prepared they were for this kind of journey. They'd never been outside of the palace before, had little to no combat training, and they were a bunch of dimwits when it came to anything resembling street smarts.

Her gaze hardened while she stared them down; they'd better not make this job more trouble than it was worth.

"We're having a meeting upstairs. We'll be talking about this job and a few other things," she began, watching their expressions. If they were plotting anything nefarious, it didn't show. "I'd like you to join us." She added a tone of finality. This wasn't a suggestion.

Rowan looked to the others seated beside him. He appeared to be the decision-maker of the bunch, which made sense with him being the heir—or, having been the heir.

"Is it really necessary that we come up there with you thieves?" he demanded, his eyes growing bored, as if he were talking to the lowest of peasants in the street. Rowan tossed another olive into his mouth.

This had Enya taken aback. They were *helping them*, after all. He had some real nerve. Rage thrummed under her skin, but she bit her cheek, fighting for control.

Rowan, judging her flash of anger, waved her off. "Alright, we may come up in a bit."

Beacon and Niall looked just as shocked as she felt. Beacon looked like he would say something, but Enya snapped before he had the chance. She grabbed Rowan by his collar and yanked him off his stool. It must have been an entertaining scene for those enjoying their morning meal, as the royal prince yelped and nearly lost his footing.

Chuckles and gasps echoed through the boisterous crowd, which was now watching intently for what would happen next.

Rowan stumbled forward when she pushed him towards the stairs, catching himself on the tarnished wood. She cracked her knuckles, nodding to the stairs.

"Move," she barked.

With a few mumbled curses, the heir was on his way upstairs, followed by his brothers, who each held apologetic looks. With an exasperated sigh, Enya joined them, stomping not far behind.

They were going to have to cut their holier-than-thou attitudes if they expected to get very far with her. She may just wind up robbing them and leaving them behind altogether.

After passing a few dusty barrels of beer and boxes of restaurant supplies, they reached an old, wooden door. Across the hall was their tiny apartment space.

Everyone was already seated when they entered, and Enya made her way to the head of the table, her eyes scanning the scene. She found the gang snacking on crab sandwiches, one of the owner's specialties. Her stomach rumbled with a hunger she'd forgotten most of the day when she took a spot beside him and took a bite. It tasted fresh, having no doubt been caught this morning by Podge.

Jackson then placed a tray of mint tea in front of the three brothers. "Bottoms up. Right from the shrubs Podge grows in his own backyard." They nodded a thank you in unison. Enya couldn't help but notice they didn't seem too eager to drink any, though.

That's strange. It's just tea, she thought, wondering if she'd been too harsh on them earlier.

"Did you take care of the message?" she asked quietly of Carson, who nodded with a small smile.

"Have I ever not done as I was told?" he retorted, exuding confidence and maybe something a little more than that. Something more than friendly. "You know you can trust me."

She grinned back—faintly, but all the same.

"So, this is your home?" Beacon asked over a few mouthfuls of his own grub, seeming to ignore the drinks. He swallowed and gazed around. "Everyone here seems so free from expectations … the usual social hierarchy thing, if you know what I mean."

"They have reason to be. I'm here. My gang keeps them safe from Eamon's platoons of stupidity on the streets. All we ask is for payments when they're due." Enya shrugged and glanced over at Carson. "This is a place where everyone can be themselves and be free to do what they want. Only rule is no fights unless there's a fee to watch."

"Where will we be sleeping?" Niall asked quietly, clearing his throat. "While we stay with you, I mean." He hesitantly picked up the glass to sniff it. Enya paused; that was a good question. They only had enough beds for the crew, and she was pretty sure they wouldn't like the floor. Rowan would probably try to punch her if she suggested such a thing. The thought made her smile slightly, though she tried to conceal it in front of all the eyes at the table.

"Well, we're set up with rooms at Tucker's Inn by Queen Ciara. There are keys waiting for us," Beacon chimed in.

"You really think it's a good idea to trust the queen after she threatened to kill you guys?" Enya made a face, leaning back in her chair to clasp her hands behind her head. "That just sounds stupid."

"I'd have to second that." Carson briefly placed a protective hand on her shoulder, earning a slight jump from her and making her straighten and lower her arms. He cleared his throat and quickly stuffed his hands in his pockets, as if embarrassed. "If she's trying to get rid of you—and I'm not saying that she is, but *if* she is, the queen probably tipped someone off about your location."

"If not her, then someone else did if they saw you. Our best bet is to keep you under our noses." Enya eyed each of the brothers. "Besides, we have a journey ahead of us."

"Wait, the *queen* sent you here? You're spies?" Maxon accused, reaching for a pistol inside his dusky jacket. Carson deftly caught his arm, holding him back from sending a sea of bullets straight into Rowan.

"We're getting to that. Settle down," Enya commanded, giving him a dangerous look. They needed to stick together on this. There was no need for uprisings from their own gang members. The Grims needed to be a team now more than ever before.

Her words seemed to settle him for a moment. Maxon bristled, shoving Carson's hand off and sitting back in his chair, grinding his jaw in an attempt to stay calm.

She didn't blame him in the slightest for being upset. After all, the royal family had sentenced his own relatives to work in the mines after finding out they supported a newspaper speaking out against the king's atrocities. Maxon had never seen them again.

"Why haven't you had any of your tea?" Jackson asked the three brothers quietly, confusion turning his mouth into a hard line.

"Our mother, the former queen, was poisoned with strychnine in her tea. None of us drink that anymore," Niall murmured, looking down. Enya's face darkened. Her mother was also dead as a result of pneumonia, based on what little she could remember of her past, and her father was never in the picture to help in the aftermath. The reminder tugged at her heart, but she willed her face to be a stoic mask.

The past was the past. If you couldn't change it, keep moving.

"Wait, so you're the three dead princes?" Miriana gasped. She pursed her lips. "Why are you not dead?" she blurted out. She had a serious lack of tact ... but you had to admire her bluntness. Enya had been wondering the same thing, and she could tell she wasn't the only one. The others at the table waited, and anticipation hung heavily in the air.

This was a well-known tale—that of their deaths. The country mourned for years, and so had the king.

Or so they thought, anyway.

Everyone knew the rumored fate of the three dead princes. Drowned in a bog or eaten by sluaghs in the woods, spirits who could turn into birds and peck one's soul dry.

"When our mother was killed, it was revealed that some rebels were planning to kill us too," Beacon explained, looking down at the floor, his expression growing troubled. "So, our father hid us inside the west tower."

Rowan cut in, "He's had us locked up all these years to prepare us for our rightful ascension to the throne. That way, no one could kill us and steal our birthright. My birthright, more specifically,"

Enya's jaw dropped, and she struggled to close it.

For all these years, she'd thought that they had died with their mother. Her palms grew damp, and her chest felt heavy, like she was underwater. Enya toyed anxiously with her gloves.

No one noticed her silent drowning.

"So, what's this all about, then?" Miriana asked, motioning around the table. She propped her head up with her hands and her elbows on the table. Her round eyes turned to Enya. "And why are we not ransoming these three should-be-dead princes to the king?"

Rowan cleared his throat, his face saying he wasn't so happy to be here with Enya or her crew. "We're looking for the Sword of Bas and need help finding it. We've already promised payment."

Miriana gave him a harsh look. "'The Sword of Death.' How do you know about that? Its location is a closely held secret among the faerie courts and has been for generations."

Enya and Carson turned curiously to the three brothers whose eyes went wide.

Beacon stammered, obviously being surprised by the sudden spotlight poised on him by the gang, "We were sent to retrieve it by the present queen. Otherwise, she'd kill us for taking the throne from her son and not proving our worth as possible rulers. She only, uh, just found out about our whole not-being-dead thing. We aren't sure who told her."

"And how does she know about the sword?" Miriana demanded. "Considering the crown spits on our kind, I can't imagine why they'd suddenly be interested in our myths and legends."

"I ... I'm not sure," Beacon admitted after a long moment of thought. "We had to play a card game with her. If we lost, we had to find the sword. In her eyes, if one of us died, that made the others next in line." He loosened his collar with a nervous smile. "She couldn't have any of that. Not with Aiden."

"She beat each of us," Rowan said with a huff. "Not sure how, either. That woman doesn't look like the gambling type."

Miriana had frozen in place. The witch's tiny white goat—well, phooka might have been a better word—entered the room from behind some beaded curtain, disrupting the silence that had fallen over the room.

"What they said." Niall nodded. Enya was surprised he even spoke at all. He seemed scared as a fish out of water.

The Banya stood to look at them over the table, shooting them all a wry look with its black eyes. "You ... played a game with her?" Mirana gasped, nearly falling out of her chair when she flew back, wood screeching along wood. "It's a demon—the wicked one. She made a deal with the devil."

She attempted to collect herself, her hand pressing against her throat while she inhaled ragged breaths. Enya's eyes darted around the room and her hand immediately grasped her pistol, as if something were waiting to pounce. They seemed safe enough in the Bowman, but what sort of unseen forces lurked beneath the shadows, their lanky claws threatening to reach out and snatch a fleshy meal or soul?

Miriana had mentioned a demon, which wasn't an unknown creature anywhere. Each language had their word for it, but the result was the same, from what Enya understood. Unholy, vile, and unspeakably wicked creatures. Ones who embodied evil in every sense of the word. It made unease coil in Enya's stomach.

Finally, Miriana spoke again, her voice teeming with immense apprehension of something Enya and presumably the others had never encountered.

"The Crimson Witch."

Arden, Skeyya

THE TENSION in the room was so thick one could cut it with a blade, but Enya was much fonder of guns. She also wasn't a big fan of awkward silences.

"Who's that and why is she important? Spit it out," she ordered, growing restless.

Miriana gazed between the lot of them for a moment, almost lost in thought while petting the phooka—Lina, beside her. It seemed to bring her calm, albeit the thing smelled like a dead fish.

She did have to admit that it was kind of cute.

Enya had always been a sucker for animals after working with horses for so many years. The feel of soft fur, of happy hooves. These things always raised her spirits. Phookas were friendly enough but could be evil in some cases, being wicked shapeshifters. This one looked about as clueless as any farm animal while it attempted to nab the sandwich from its master's plate, but Enya knew better.

"Are you going to tell us what we want to know or what?" Rowan glowered, looking about ready to get in her face from his seat on the far side of the table. Enya shot him a fierce glare and he scowled. She wasn't going to put up with his blatant disrespect. Not in this meeting room, at the very least, and not in front of her team.

Miriana began, meeting Finn's eyes, "She's a demon. Used to be a big trouble for us all, back in the day. Well, back in my great-great-grandmother's day. There was a big war over a hundred years ago between her army and all the faerie courts. She lost and was cursed to dwell in one of the ancient ruins beneath the Black Lake."

He nodded solemnly, and his expression turned sour. Finn was a jokester, one who laughed and smiled more than anyone, but Enya read through that façade in an instant. Those who laughed the most often had the most to hide.

Miriana's words alone sent a chill through the room, and the shadows decorating the walls almost appeared to grow more sinister as everyone listened intently for more. Enya felt like someone was watching them, but when she gazed around their makeshift office space, there was no one else but them.

Enya pulled her jacket tighter against her small frame, as if that would defend her from forces unknown. The grip on her pistol tightened, and she ignored the pain searing through her hand.

"She has to roam the lands on foot now," Finn explained. "And her army's pretty limited. Not much magick left in her anymore except the ability to change her face and those of her men." He gestured to his own with a grimace. "She and her men can appear to be anyone."

That would make her harder to kill, but Enya was definitely up to the challenge. The three princes, however, didn't seem comforted by that in the slightest.

"What about the cards?" Beacon questioned, his brows furrowing. The playful prince had grown serious, his mouth pressed into a firm line. "I thought we had just been playing Switch for kicks." Recognition dawned upon the others sitting around the table. Switch was a common game—one played by sailors at the docks and brewers at the pub.

Miriana replied with a frown, "She uses many ways to trick people into making deals with her. The Crimson Witch gives out magical items that are supposed to help them, but really they're cursed."

"So, what does that mean for the queen?" Beacon pressed, his voice wavering. Enya was just wondering the same thing. It could mean a swift change for the nation if she fell. With the throne teetering from the fierce rebellion, it would have been a turning point if she were to die. In any case, while Enya *did* want them both held accountable by the firm grips of justice, she wasn't sure an evil demon was the right way to go about it. "What'll happen to her?"

"She'll turn evil, just like the Crimson Witch. Her very soul will be splattered with darkness," Miriana said simply, as if it were so obvious that even a child should understand it.

This was really bad. Not death, but still pretty bad. An evil queen with an influence on the rest of the royal family *and* the government just spelled out much more trouble on the horizon for the people of Skeyya. Enya inhaled deeply, trying to calm her quickening heart.

"What about the Sword of Bas?" Enya demanded. "How does that have anything to do with this demon?"

"It's the key to unlocking her army and her powers." Miriana shivered, clutching the goat closer. "But it's also the key to defeating her for good. It was lost in the faerie war."

"Where do we find it?" Carson asked. "If this demon has a hold of the royal family now, imagine what she's capable of even without the sword. She'll have a hold on the entire country."

Enya nodded in agreement, and the corners of Carson's mouth twitched, holding back a smile. It seemed he was happy they agreed on something for once. The matter was a rare sight, indeed; Enya knew she was too stubborn for her own good.

"That's true," she allowed, running an anxious hand through a long black strand of hair. "We have no choice but to stop her. I'd say that demands more payment." She gave Rowan a wry smile, who then paled at the idea. Enya snorted. "Just kidding! Relax, prince-y."

These royals are so cheap for people rolling in money, she thought.

"We can start with the Pentacle of Glac. It's hidden somewhere within the caves in Belsale. We'll need that before we can find anything else," Finn finally said, earning a nod from the Banya sitting not far from him. "That was the last rumored location for it, anyway."

Enya nodded, taking this in.

"Okay. I'd say this is a two-person job, but I have no doubt that these three royals will want to tag along, seeing as the queen has it out for them and whatnot."

"Well, you have something right for once." Rowan rolled his eyes, arms crossed. "We're not going anywhere until this is finished."

"In nicer terms," Beacon added quickly, leaning closer across the table. "We'd love to come with you, if you'd have us." He smiled earnestly, something that made Enya's chest tighten. She hated seeing them trust her. Would she let them down like she did as a child?

Niall offered a weak shrug, still unsure.

Enya swallowed hard, meeting their eyes and then that of the Grims. With a sigh, she said her next words. "You three will come with me and Carson, and we'll get this taken care of. It's bad enough having an abusive prick running the country, but a possessed queen at his side, too?" It was too much evil all in the same place. Someone had to balance the scales, so why not an outlaw who actually cared for her country?

This was all a recipe for disaster.

Enya hoped they'd be able to put a stop to the queen's plans. But it seemed that evil lurked beyond the palace walls— and not just that of human nature. Everything had the chance to be corrupted. You only needed a spark; a match to set off the blaze of madness.

She was now dead set on extinguishing that fire.

The rest of the gang nodded.

"We can watch our territory while you're gone," Miriana promised, giving Enya an earnest smile. "You can trust us. Just make sure to stay safe on your journey."

She flashed a silver, metallic wing. This was the symbol of their gang; a promise to stay moving, no matter the cost. She had been inspired by birds when she came up with the idea—and her own nickname, of course. *The Raven.* They, like all birds, never stopped flying towards their mark: freedom.

Now it was their turn to be free.

They always carried these wings as a reminder of their motto whenever they had to split up.

With a shuffle of hands, each member of the Grims revealed their own wings, holding them up in the light of the sun gleaming through the dusty windows.

"To stay moving, no matter the cost," Miriana said aloud, almost like a prayer; a toast to the future.

"To stay moving, no matter the cost," everyone else echoed, earning strange looks from the princes. Enya smiled to herself. This was her family, and she wouldn't let them down. Not now, not ever.

"What about us?" Beacon suddenly asked, a nervous gleam in his eyes. The Grims each looked at him, confused. "Won't we be recognized? Out there, I mean."

The gang appeared to consider this for a moment. He had a point. They were the three princes who had supposedly died over ten years ago as children. Out on the streets, they'd be worth a hefty price for ransom, and Enya had no doubt it would cause them plenty of trouble on the journey.

"We didn't recognize you," Finn admitted, scratching the stubble on his jaw. Maybe he didn't, but Enya had. She was sure anyone who'd known them as children would too.

Miriana pulled out a bag of dust from her skirts, one that

was tied with twine and what Enya guessed were fragile bird bones. "You can use this," she said, now whispering that secret language all magical creatures shared. Her eyes flashed black before going back to normal. "Close your eyes."

Rowan, Beacon, and Niall one by one obeyed, and she blew the dust onto their faces.

It shimmered before evaporating over their heads, and suddenly the crew was looking at three new teens. Rowan now had a smaller nose and black hair, which was almost the same inky darkness as Enya's own. Beacon had lost all his previous freckles and traded his own red hair for a deep brown. Niall now had more chiseled cheek bones and honey-blond hair.

Enya was in shock but a bit relieved. At least now they didn't remind her so much of her past at the palace. Maybe she could pretend they were different people and life could go on easier. But how long would it last?

"Will it wear off?" she blurted out, making them look at her with curious eyes. Miriana offered a weak smile in return, one that answered her question before she even managed to speak a word.

"It will eventually, but only when the goddess Eethra decides it should," she replied. Enya couldn't help but roll her eyes. *Who knows when that'll be?* She didn't like the idea of trusting some faerie goddess to take care of their business, but it seemed that was unavoidable right now.

The Banya's words appeared to placate the crew and the princes enough for now. At least for a little while they'd be drawing less attention than they would otherwise.

For a moment, Enya's thoughts drifted over to the palace and King Eamon. He'd locked them up, sure, but how long would it take for him to see that his precious sons had vanished? How much could they trust Farrell? She imagined the king strolling into their tower, finding it empty, and shivers ran down her spine. His rage would roar through the thunderous skies, and she was sure his wrath would not be gentle whenever it caught up with them.

"Does the king know you three have gone?" Enya asked.

The three princes all shook their heads.

"The queen took us in secret," Beacon explained. "Along with Captain Farrell. Our father didn't make visits often, in order to ensure no one discovered us alive. I guess that demon was the one who told the queen. For all these years we'd never heard of our secret being discovered. No one else knows." He scratched his head, grimacing. "For now, anyway."

Carson let loose an empty laugh. "Let's hope it stays that way. Otherwise, our lives might get much more interesting."

The moments after were calm, almost denying the impending danger that was headed their way. Some of the gang went down for drinks with the princes, but Enya lingered upstairs with Jackson, Maxon, and Carson.

So many thoughts still buzzed through her head, and it seemed some of the gang still had questions themselves.

"So, we're going to be helping royalty find a fancy sword," Maxon muttered, lighting a cigar and sucking in a deep breath.

He didn't seem at all concerned with letting his smoke out the nearby window. She wrinkled her nose when the stench found its way into her lungs, holding back a cough. Carson had turned the valves on the gas lamps sitting on the walls, sending brightness over the worn-out walls and interior. Those downstairs would have already done the same.

Enya sighed, locking eyes with Carson. He shrugged. Maxon wasn't the kind of guy to take this well after his kind of past. He wasn't going to let this go easy.

"They're willing to pay us eighty thousand pounds," Enya finally began. "Not to mention that we would have been hung by our necks if it weren't for them." She stood and paced to the open window. The city was still alive despite the night, with carriages and motor cars rolling along the road. But the streets were growing scarce; families were headed home for the evening.

It was in the night that monsters fetched their own suppers and humans did their worst deeds. The Raven knew this all too well.

"We owe them our lives." Carson nodded, making a face. A truth, while painful, true, nonetheless. They were in debt. "Which is unfortunate, given the circumstances."

Maxon blew out a few puffs of smoke, glancing at them with unsure eyes. "Their family killed my parents."

"Their family killed all of our parents—or stole them from us. We'll have our revenge soon enough." Jackson sighed, stretching his muscular arms and sitting back with his hands behind his head against the wall. "But will we kill them?"

"No, not now," Enya decided, pressing her fingers to her lips in thought.

She was certain that these boys hadn't had anything to do with what happened to this crew or the nation's people. But the question still stood: Why were they in hiding for over ten years, and why did the queen want them dead? Maybe they had more in common with their crew than it seemed.

Enya was dead set on finding out. She also didn't want

more of their family's blood on her hands than was necessary.

That wasn't who she was, or the Grims.

"I'm not sure yet," Enya finally said after a few moments. "We need to find out where their loyalties lie and whether that's with the people or with their crappy father."

Maxon angrily crushed his cigar in a nearby ashtray before pushing up from the table to stand. "Do what you want. I won't trust them until they've proven themselves." With that, he was stomping out the room, leaving them with a slammed door and a sea of uncertainty.

Jackson rolled his eyes. "I'd better go cheer him up. I'll leave you to it then." He gave a mock bow before leaving.

When the door closed for the second time, Enya and Carson were alone, and she didn't know if she liked the feelings this sort of situation created. The goosebumps all over her skin told one story, but the anxiety in her chest told another. Or was it all good?

Carson cleared his throat, sitting forward in his seat. "So, are you ready for an adventure, Miss Raven?" he teased with a grin, one that instantly melted her unease.

"I'm ready to get us out of this mess," she admitted, breathing out an uneasy sigh. "I'm tired of running."

"From your past, or the law?"

"Both, but the law is easier." Enya chuckled, looking down at her gloved hands that were clasped atop her lap. "The law doesn't haunt you at night." She wasn't even sure what was haunting her anymore, but the faces of the princes and wandering through the palace had given her a hint. Something happened there. Something that was fighting to be remembered.

He considered this for a moment. "I don't know. I see Chief Kelman in my sleep often." Carson laughed, the sound music to her ears. She loved it when he was in a good mood; it always put *her* in a good mood. "He tells me all about how I'm a lick away from landing in cuffs. While twirling his ungodly mustache, of course."

"I'm being serious."

"Okay. Seriously? My past haunts me too." Carson's smile faltered now, and his brows pushed together tight. "I think of my uncle every night. How he left … left me in that linen mill."

Enya frowned. She remembered rescuing him and how sad he had looked that day. It was as if all happiness in the world had been sucked out of his eyes. That look haunted her too—that of all the rebels when she found them. Varying levels of desperation and fear. Sorry souls that craved just a single shred of help to get them out of their predicaments. But they'd proven trustworthy, and that made them invaluable assets to her.

"But," Carson continued, now growing shy, "I also think about how you saved me. I was close to starving and you—you just swooped right in and took me under your crooked wings. You gave me a life again, Enya."

She blushed. "Yeah, I guess I did."

Throughout her time out in the city, she'd done her best to save everyone she could and take down anyone who dared take advantage of those in need. Considering Eamon and his heartless rule, that made plenty. Despite that, Enya wondered if it was ever enough. Sure, it gained her notoriety and praise, but she still felt empty. She still felt this strange void in her past, one that was beginning to claw its way out ever since they'd met the princes.

"But is it enough? I don't know." She squeezed her hands in her lap, her brows creasing. "Did I ever tell you how I came to know these princes?"

Carson shook his head. "No, you didn't."

She opened her mouth and then closed it.

Would he see her differently knowing that they had been friends? That she had done something horrible in that palace and to those boys that she couldn't remember? Enya didn't want to lose her closest confidant.

No. She couldn't risk his loyalty. Not when there was so much at stake now. She merely shook her head. "Never mind. I shouldn't have even mentioned it—"

"Enya," Carson interrupted, almost like a command in and of itself. It startled her so much she stared at him right in the eyes. "Do you trust me or not?"

Slowly, she nodded her head. "I do."

"Then know that I won't judge you for whatever happened in your past." He straightened up, grabbing her hand in his across the table. She flushed beet red in return. "Now, I don't know why you won't tell me what's going on or how you know these guys, but I know better than to ask when you get like this."

"Thank you," Enya whispered. "For trusting me too."

"I respect you and the rebel cause. Always have." He grinned, patting her hand. She was certain he was just being friendly. He had to be. Her heart fluttered and she yanked back her hand, regret filling her as his face fell.

"We should get some sleep. Big journey tomorrow."

Carson looked away, jaw set. She couldn't tell if it was embarrassment or anger or both. "Yeah. I guess we should."

She left him there at the table in the dark and cluttered meeting room, now going to her own worn-out mattress in the cramped bedroom they all shared, tossing a few tattered blankets over herself to fend off the cold that seeped in through the drafts in the windows.

Enya laid there, eyes on the ceiling, wondering what would happen next. Her hands drifted to the hidden paper and pen, her mind racing. She needed to write and get this all out—whatever it was. *Damn these thoughts*, she told herself, cursing.

This was a lot to take in. For anyone to take in, really. One thing was for certain, though. They had more to fear than just the royal family and their guards.

Arden, Skeyya

SOMETHING WAS pecking at Enya's legs above her wool blankets. Something with feathers and a really strange barn smell. With a start, she flew up in her bed.

A chicken clucked as it flew from her bed.

Chickens ... Why were there chickens in their bedroom?

The sun had only just begun to shine through the skyline attic-windows, indicating she'd slept well through the afternoon and night. Enya brushed a few feathers from her chest and took a look around the room. It was empty save for her, the pecking chickens, and an apologetic Jackson, who tried shooing the birds back out the door.

"Sorry!" He gave a nervous chuckle, fussing with his cravat. "I thought I had them locked up in the coop on Podge's balcony last night, but I guess not." Jackson picked up a hen as it tried to dart past him. "They looked lonely."

Enya sighed, fighting her own grin. She had to seem like she was in charge, after all. Another beak poked her side, and she flinched. "Put them back, please. You know Podge uses them for the eggs he serves downstairs. He'll have to scour the attic to find them all."

"I'll take care of it. I promise!" he exclaimed, rounding them up with a few waves of his hands, earning a flutter of wings that sent feathers flying up into the air as they were herded out the door, their clucking echoing down the hallway.

This boy was always a strange one to her. He had a not-so-subtle flirtation with the rebel witch and an uncanny knack for animals. And the very annoying habit of setting them loose at least once a week.

Enya took that as her cue to go downstairs and see where everyone had gone. Below their attic level, there was a floor for Podge's office, one that usually stayed empty except for the weekdays when he felt like being business minded. He'd drop off wares and grub to cook every day, but he'd quickly vanish with a tip of the hat and a curtsey from his woman of the week.

It was empty today, as well. The scents of porridge and steaming-hot bacon invited her to the bar and made Enya's stomach growl in anticipation. She hadn't even bothered to put on a change of clothes yet, but it wasn't like any of them had many clothes to begin with.

Aside from the voices of early patrons sipping on spiked coffee and talking about typical morning things like the frigid weather and how good King Eamon's head would look on a stake, there were the voices of her gang.

"You fed them *what?* That's horrible!" Prince Niall exclaimed, covering his mouth with his hands.

"It's just scrambled eggs. It's good for them!" Beacon laughed, toying with a pepper shaker on the bar. "Come on, man. Lighten up a bit. We've been holed up in that palace for long enough."

Finn chortled, giving him a high five. "That's unethical. I like your style! Maybe you'll fit in around here, after all."

"That's cannibalism." Niall began to tear up. "Those poor chickens," he cried, seemingly having lost his interest in breakfast. He grew quiet when Enya approached.

Beacon gave her a nod, still grinning. "Enya. How goes it?"

She raised a brow. "It goes. Ready for a big day?" she asked, stretching as she took a spot on the raised wooden seats. "It's go-time in an hour or two. There's no time to waste with jobs this big. That, and the whole demon thing."

They'd have to strap up and pack what was needed. They'd also likely need to bundle up to brave the winter weather properly, and especially in such a cold and watery place as Belsale. She hoped that didn't become their cold and watery grave as her stomach turned. Whether that was from hunger or fear, she didn't know.

Enya didn't like being afraid, but it seemed to happen much too often lately.

"We can leave as soon as we all finish eating," Rowan snapped, walking up to the gang. "I'm not going anywhere with you strange peasants on an empty stomach. I'd likely be sick." He cast her a wary sidelong glance.

Beacon's expression instantly soured. "Brother, is it really necessary to talk to her like that? Honestly, you keep—"

Enya interrupted, "I can arrange that. The being sick part, I mean." She offered Rowan a cruel smile, cracking her knuckles. "Though it would likely be from my fist."

His nostrils flared when he turned to face her head-on, seeming ready to fight right then and there.

"All right, all right. Settle down, you two." Maxon appeared from the kitchen, setting down a plate of food in front of Enya, who began shoveling it down immediately, ignoring the annoying prince at her side. "It's unhealthy for partners in crime to fight this much. We're all on the same side here."

That shut Rowan up. Or it did at least long enough for her to finish her food.

Enya couldn't shake the feeling of unease that gripped her when she realized she hadn't seen Carson yet. He was usually by her side as soon as she woke up.

Is that weird? Is it weird that I miss him? Enya ran a nervous hand over the back of her neck.

"I'm going to put on something not caked in gunpowder and the tears of my enemies," she said, getting up from the bar. "I'll be back in a bit, and we can get moving."

Back upstairs, in the tiny closet they all shared, she found a new black jacket and pants. Underneath she wore a blouse—the only clean one she had at the moment—and over that, she wore a black vest. Her boots were worn, but they'd have to do for now. There wasn't any money to replace them, but there was enough in her pockets to save them in a lick of trouble.

Her pistol and dagger hid beneath her clothes. One was strapped to her belt, the other in her pocket.

There would be no taking chances on this trip.

Her hair was a mess, but there also wasn't any time to really fix it. Not if they wanted to beat the morning rush at the train station. Her fingers, for once relaxed, undid most of the knots, and she was on her way back down the creaking steps of the pub.

She almost ran right into Carson at the bottom of the stairs. "Sorry," he mumbled, looking away and stepping aside so she could pass. Enya frowned, noticing his tired appearance. He looked like a sea of whiskey had swallowed him up and spit him back out.

"You ready to go?" she asked, brushing some lint off her jacket and trying to avoid his eyes.

Yesterday had been strange. She felt something then that she didn't know if she was comfortable with. But his face when she'd left him …

"Yeah, I have what I need," he replied curtly. He felt colder than usual, and she didn't know if she liked that. It wasn't like him to be this way, and she hoped they could mend whatever had broken between them soon.

For business purposes, at least, she thought, her mood darkening.

She passed him and went back up to the bar, now finding Miriana and Jackson there beside the princes.

They seemed much too preoccupied with each other to notice her walking up until she rapped the bottom of the bar with her boot a few times. When they turned, she raised an eyebrow, earning a blush from both of them.

Enya could have sworn she saw Beacon's eyes quickly dart away from Jackson and his own cheeks turn red, but she guessed it was nothing.

"Alright, boys. Grab whatever you deem necessary for a dangerous journey—though, I'd advise against all the trunks you felt the need to bring before. It'll only slow us down," Enya told the princes while they chugged down their glasses of goat's milk.

"I brought way too many fine things to leave them here with a bunch of thieving criminals," Rowan said with a biting glare.

Enya scoffed. "You're more likely to lose them on the trip than have them stolen by my Grims. Just lock them up in our closet. Anyone with a brain and two legs knows better than to go through our things." She gestured to the stairs.

It was true; no one would dare steal from the Grims unless they had a death wish, and no police bothered the Bowman's Pub unless they wanted to get shot by an unending number of bullets. That made this the safest place in the city for her gang and the rebels.

Rowan grumbled curses to himself as he disappeared.

Finn waited for him to leave before pulling out a rolled-up parchment. "This is a map of Belsale. Figured you might need one," he said, handing it to her.

Enya's eyes flickered over the worn-out map, which was dotted and drawn on with fading black ink. The paper was weak, even through her gloves, as if it could tear at any moment. Carefully, she put it within the pockets of her jacket.

It was then that Miriana strutted over and dropped three stones into Enya's hands. Each were etched with images Enya recognized to be of saints, like Saint Finthan, the sun saint, Saint Brigidda, the healing saint, and Saint Colline, the saint of storms.

She pursed her lips, waiting for an explanation from the Banya.

Miriana pointed to the golden stone. "This one will help if you run out of light." She pointed to the red one. "This will help if you are bleeding out. Only once, though. They all only work once." She pointed to the white one, grinning wide. "And this will help if you need smoke. I thought they might come in handy. Just say the words, 'help me in my final hour, the goddess has granted me the power,' and they'll activate."

Jackson was grinning from ear to ear behind her, likely impressed by both her charms and her pretty face. Most men were from what the Raven had seen during her time in the capital.

Enya nodded, placing them in her pocket. "Thank you." With that, she saw Rowan coming back down. She offered a half-smile to her Grims at the bar and left the gang, waving on the princes to the front door while she weaved around tables full of customers. Carson followed quickly on her heels, and they were out the door.

The cold wind of Skeyya's winter blasted their faces, almost burning them while ice sheets fell from the sky.

Bustling crowds rushed past to finish their daily errands, and a shiver ran down Enya's spine. It smelled of coal and horse slop, likely from the carriages riding up and down the road. She was sick of that smell, especially after all her years in the palace stables. Sleet and snow pranced around the sky above their heads and hit their shoulders, chilling them despite their coats. Enya sighed, crossing her arms to fight off the fierce weather.

"So, we need to go to the train station?" Carson asked, face stoic and unreadable.

She nodded, trying to avoid the ache in her chest while she walked with them down the street towards the station. It wasn't too far away, only several blocks, but it beat hailing down a carriage with this crowd.

"Yeah, but I don't have money for tickets. Do you?" she asked, earning a shake of his head. They turned their faces to the princes who paled. They didn't seem too keen to be spending their money. No one did, so Enya had a better idea. Though, this one was risky. "What if we steal the tickets?"

"Here we go again with the criminal activity," Rowan groaned, earning a swift hit from Beacon to his stomach. Niall snickered beside the two. Enya didn't think it was *too* illegal. It was just a few lousy train tickets. She didn't see how it was a big deal.

"Watch it, twinkle toes," she warned.

"Yeah, brother. Stop being such an ass for once," Beacon agreed, earning a roll of Rowan's eyes. "They're helping us."

When they arrived through the dusty glass doors of the station, the swarm of passengers was heavy. Strong cologne and scents of musky lavender perfume wafted in the air, making Enya cover her nose. Booming voices from porters loading luggage and that of those punching tickets rang through the air, almost drowning out the noise of the crowd.

They had two choices; they could either steal tickets, or they could sneak on the train.

Enya preferred the latter, as it avoided the annoying task of fishing through pockets and bags while avoiding prying eyes, of which there were many this morning. It would also likely avoid more incessant comments from Rowan about her "thieving personality," whatever that meant.

He was starting to really piss her off, but she didn't let it show. She wouldn't give him the satisfaction.

Enya's eyes scanned the train schedule posted on the brick walls near the east stairwell until she found one going to Belsale. It was leaving in only fifteen minutes. Now they just had to find it in the sea of steam locomotives.

Their steps rapped along the concrete floor while they neared their ride, and Enya and Carson exchanged a look when they noticed the police patrolling near the first few cars. That was typical of the station. There were always guards making sure no one was causing trouble, something that annoyed Enya to no end. Their idea of trouble and hers were very different, likely because they kissed the behinds of the palace, and she preferred to help the country's citizens. It wasn't unusual for them to target creatures of the woods or poor citizens for kicks.

"They'll know who we are the second they spot us," Carson muttered, easing back behind a group of traveling students and motioning for Enya and the princes to do the same. "We need a distraction. Something to keep them occupied long enough so we can sneak onto the last car."

Their eyes turned to see a mime performing just a few paces away, earning a hefty number of tips from those passing by.

"How much do you think causing a public disturbance is worth?" Enya gave the boys a wry smile. "In cash, I mean."

"Not enough. We shouldn't be wasting our money right now," Carson scolded. She sighed; he was right, as usual. But what else could they do? It's not like they could just ask someone to start trouble.

Beacon shifted back and forth on his feet. "Yeah, I'd rather not spend all our money if we can avoid it. We're not made of it, you know."

Enya let out a disgusted noise, earning a shrug from him when he looped an arm over his brothers. Niall looked disturbed by having this many people around him. Like a fish out of water, he seemed to be freaking the hell out underneath his seemingly calm demeanor. Rowan simply appeared to be revolted by seeing so many people who weren't rich in one place.

Typical royals. Don't want to spend a dime on anything beneath them.

"Okay, how about we create a diversion. I'll grab his tips, and while he's chasing me—and the cops, no doubt—you load the princes onto the train. Once I ditch them, I'll meet you on board," Enya said. It was a risky move, but they didn't really have another choice. She could try lifting the tickets off someone, but with this many people walking around, that was dangerous too.

Carson considered this for a moment, looking back up to the police beyond their makeshift hiding place. "And you're sure that you'll make it back?"

She cast him a sidelong glance. "Do I look like someone who gets caught?" This earned a raised brow, and she flushed. It was true they only just got out of the palace jail. "Would you just trust me? I know what I'm doing."

Finally, he gave in with a huff. "Fine. Just be quick, please." Carson paused, looking down at his black boots. "And don't forget to come back." Her stomach fluttered, and she had to remind herself that it was all just business again.

I thought he was mad at me. What's the deal with him today?

Enya nodded before walking over to the mime draped in black and painted in white. She'd have to be quick about this, for sure, or else maybe he'd be the one catching her, not the police. Either way would end poorly.

With a deep breath and wary eyes, she inched towards the performer's brown hat full of tips. Guilt almost stopped her—everyone had to make a living, after all—but her hand swooped down to grasp the hat tight, and she exploded into a run.

Curses flung over her head along with the shouts from police, but she didn't stop. She couldn't stop. Not when there was so much on the line.

Enya was sprinting through mildewed and damp hallways, nearly tripping over suitcases and trunks a few times as she did. Swerving around people and earning a few shocked gasps, she kept on, already feeling out of breath. She nearly felt dizzy and sweat had begun to drip down her neck, but she kept running. This place was massive, with two stories and countless trains boarding passengers and crew. Snow was also now seeping through cracked openings in the windows above the station's pathways, making the building cold despite all the warm bodies wandering about.

There was an entryway to her left that seemed to lead up metal stairs, so she bolted through, throwing down a pile of suitcases while she did. Grunts of pain echoed behind her, and a look over her shoulder said they had fallen back after running right into the luggage. Bystanders hollered for her to stop, but she ignored them.

This catwalk led not to the usual second story of the train station but to a more lonesome area littered with ropes, wires, and wooden planks jutting in from the rafters. She could see everything below with ease through tiny holes in the flooring of her narrow path with railings.

Air fought to reach her lungs, and it was becoming hard to keep up with her own feet.

She was tired of running—both now and in general. The hat fell from her hands, and whether that was on purpose or not, Enya didn't know. She only knew that the iron walkway she was on was leading right back to their train to Belsale. One whose steam and whistle indicated it was about to leave.

Enya could only hope that Carson and the princes had managed to sneak on board unnoticed. Otherwise, this would have all been for nothing, and she was going to be royally pissed off—no pun intended.

No one was behind her now, and her pursuers had likely grabbed the hat and forgotten all about her and her sticky hands. She was counting on that.

Enya slipped over the railing of her catwalk, being careful not to land too hard on the balls of her feet on the concrete ground below. Others passed by quickly, careful to avert their eyes and keep their voices down. If anyone noticed her dropping into a crowd out of nowhere, they knew better than to say anything.

This city's streets belonged to her. The only problem she ever had was with patrolling palace goons and their watchdog policemen.

Enya took a steadying breath, heart hammering in her chest from the exertion of the chase she'd only just escaped while she watched the train begin to roll by. A few steps later and she was hopping through the back door of the last car right before it rolled by and out of the station with the rest of the locomotive.

Enya was now on her way out of the capital of Skeyya and to a tiny fisherman's village up north. But she couldn't help but worry she had lost her companions in the process.

8

Belsale, Skeyya

THE TRAIN was much too full for Enya's liking, but that's usually how trains were.

The attendants meagerly sprayed lilac perfume up and down the corridors, making her cough. It was likely to mask the odor of so many humans and creatures of the woods being squashed together in one place. Various nymphs, goblins, and faerie creatures sat along the rows of seats, seeming to ignore the humans around them while they chatted. It was impossible for the humans to ignore them, though.

The sight nearly brought a smile to her lips.

Enya kept her eyes peeled for any sign of her companions, searching high and low, up and down each train car. Well, not too high. She doubted they were hiding in the overhead ropes above the seats.

Fear was tightening her chest now, but she tried to ignore it. Those kinds of feelings never did any good. She noticed a dark-haired man who could have been Carson from behind, but his face said he was well advanced into his older years. Her gaze fell to the carpeted floor in disappointment.

"Psst. Over here!" Enya heard a voice, one that sounded like Beacon, whisper from a row of seats to her left. It was there that she finally found Carson and the princes pretending to read the train safety pamphlets.

Beacon grinned. "Took you long enough! We're almost out of chocolate mints, but we saved you some." He tossed some over, and she deftly caught them in her hand, taking a seat next to Rowan near the aisle. He didn't look at all pleased that she'd made it.

Well, she wasn't at all pleased he'd made it, either. The cocky old lout was grinding her nerves. Just sitting next to him brought on a furious headache.

Sighing, Enya dropped the candies into her mouth, savoring the icy cool feel of mint and the delicate delight of milk chocolate. It was rare that she had time for sweets. Usually, the only food she ate was whatever they had lying around the Bowman's Pub and could put together quickly.

Like birds, they were constantly moving.

"There wasn't any trouble getting on board?" she asked, because of course she'd need to ask, being the leader of the Grims. This was a job, and they—she—needed to make sure it went off without a hitch. Or at least as small a number of hitches as possible. Payment depended on things like that.

Her sanity also did.

If something happened to these royals on her watch, she'd never forgive herself.

"Getting on board was easy. Carson saw to that after you distracted the guards. We're just starving." Beacon nibbled on an oatmeal bar he'd taken from the pub before they left.

Carson's eyes watched her every move carefully, as if checking a fallen bird for fractures or broken bones. It was as if he was scared she'd break. As if he knew her thoughts but wouldn't say. Enya wouldn't say, either. She averted her eyes, her heart racing at the intensity of the way he looked at her.

It seemed she wasn't the only one assessing for damage.

He cleared his throat and shifted his gaze out the window when he realized she'd caught him staring. A pink flush spread across his cheeks, but she told herself it was just the cold and nothing more.

"Do you think we'll get in trouble for sneaking on?" Niall spoke, and it had been the first time she'd heard his voice in a while. It almost startled her. A water faerie snuck a look over at them over a tattered newspaper, as if she too had heard the question. Upon meeting Enya's glare, she averted her eyes just as quick. Their group didn't need eavesdroppers getting them kicked off.

Enya shook her head, sympathy written across her face. He wasn't used to this life, and she didn't blame him for being scared. "No, not if we're careful."

That seemed to placate him enough for now.

"So, Belsale. What's it like?" Rowan asked, pretending to be interested as best as he could muster. It was likely for his younger brother's sake. Enya wasn't buying it.

"Smells like fish. And mud," Carson retorted with a matter of fact look. "Lots of it."

Enya held back a peal of laughter. His straight answer was as accurate as any she'd ever heard. This certainly wasn't going to be the most pleasant of trips. Maybe if they were lucky, they could grab some air fresheners once they arrived to wear as necklaces. That would be an entertaining sight, to say the least.

Rowan grimaced, obviously regretting having asked.

"It's a well-known fisherman village," Enya said. "But they keep to themselves. The caves aren't too far from the marsh. Lore says they're home to some pretty horrifying monsters." She cocked her pistol before laying it next to her on the cushion of the seat. "Let's hope the people are as quiet and out of the way as the rumors suggest."

And, she thought to herself, *Let's hope the rumors about the legendary creatures is overblown nonsense meant to keep outsiders away.* Otherwise, Enya was going to have her hands full trying to escort three snobby princes.

A silence settled over them then, and the hum of the train's engine slowed Enya's heartbeat, one she hadn't realized had still been racing. She settled back into her seat, finally managing to relax for once. Beacon and Carson agreed to grab a bite from the train's dining car, and they disappeared without much else to say on the matter.

That left her to watch Rowan and Niall, who sat across from her, without backup.

An attendant soon dropped off glasses of spiced wine and water, which they eagerly accepted. Enya inhaled the scent of cloves and cinnamon, licking her lips in anticipation. It went back smooth on her tongue, and the iced water was equally refreshing. The other two seated with her appeared to be just as satisfied.

When she caught Rowan smiling to himself, he turned his expression into a sneer. "The palace wine is better. It always will be," he snapped. Enya rolled her eyes and pushed away her drinks.

Leave it to him to ruin the moment. Niall didn't look too pleased with his older brother, either.

Her eyes caught onto a woman standing at the end of the car. She stared at her and the princes intently, as if she were a wolf watching sheep, while she casually leaned against a closet door.

Her curved figure didn't allow her long, embroidered coat to hide the dagger at her waist or the pistol in her right hand, the one hanging at her side. Her straight black hair was tied into a messy bun, and her red lips curved into a vicious smile.

Enya knew this woman, unfortunately. It was Jia, one of Sean's women of the night—though, she wasn't any older than Enya—and a notoriously deadly sharpshooter from the Tobuhan army across the Great Sea. Or she *was* from the army, until she started working for Sean's Wraiths after a supposedly hefty payout to her father.

It was rumored she could see the dead.

Enya sat there for a moment, trying to will her eyes to stop being so wide and her palms to stop sweating. If Jia was here, that meant Sean's gang had shown an interest in the Grims once again. Had shown an interest in those they were escorting.

Had shown interest in the princes.

"What are you looking at?" Rowan demanded, trying to turn his head to figure out what had unsettled her so much.

Niall copied his gesture, looking to be sick once more at the thought of something going wrong.

"It seems we have company. Be cool," Enya ordered, straightening up and grabbing her gun from beside her. The sharpshooter walked slowly towards them, as if savoring every moment before the kill. Hopefully, it wouldn't come to that.

"The Raven," Jia purred, placing one hand on the backs of their seats. "What's a rebel leader like you doing with … boys like these?"

Enya couldn't shake the feeling their new faces hadn't deterred them from this assassin. She knew the tricks of the trade, and she knew a glamour when she saw one. Enya had no doubt. She casually took another sip of her spiced wine, avoiding the woman's predatory gaze. "We're on a job. It's none of your concern," she replied.

Jia gave a dark chuckle, something that unnerved the two teens across from Enya.

"Funny. So am I." She leaned in, her breath now on Enya's cheek. "I've been sent to kill three 'dead' royals," Jia whispered in her ear, eyes never leaving the gun clutched in Enya's hand. She straightened. "They don't look very dead to me, and believe me, I would know. They also don't match the description I was given. Using magick to create a disguise, I presume?"

Enya's blood ran cold, and her cheeks flushed a bright crimson color. So, she'd ferreted out the truth already.

"How much money would it take to send you home empty-handed?" Rowan suddenly asked, eyes stern.

She gave a dark laugh, one that sent a chill down Enya's spine. "I would be killed if I came back empty-handed, but that was a good try," Jia said, eyes lingering a little too long on Niall, who flushed beet red. Enya didn't know if that was fear or flattery. "What a shame it is. I would say you're quite cute, too."

It was too bad he didn't look like himself. Otherwise, he could have taken that as a compliment. The boy grew flustered, nonetheless.

Enya cleared her throat. "Who sent you? Better yet, who told Sean about those I'm escorting?"

"The queen. She wants them dead," Jia said simply.

At least that didn't come as a surprise.

Enya couldn't help but feel like quite a few people were missing. Where was the rest of Sean's gang? He never sent one of his most valued shooters alone on a job.

"You're making the wrong choice here," Enya snapped, raising her gun to aim at the assassin's abdomen. She knew she needed to make this shot count.

And she would have, too, if someone hadn't tackled their adversary onto the floor.

Carson held Jia tightly to the ground, pinning her arms and legs with his own. Her gun fell to the floor, and Enya quickly kicked it away. She couldn't help the gasp of relief when she realized the danger had been stopped in time. They were fine, but the screams from the other passengers aboard didn't really second that.

A shot zipped above their heads, causing everyone in the train car to duck down, including Enya, Rowan, and Niall. Beacon was still nowhere to be found, likely hiding somewhere. One look up said that Sean's second in command, Lucian, had joined in on the melee.

Lucian was a tall and strong-built man covered in piercings. He, too, was a creature of the woods like Finn, having similarly pointed ears and faintly glowing eyes. His dirty blond hair was slicked back with an unholy amount of pomade as he watched her curiously, like an animal watching its lunch.

Enya didn't hesitate when she pulled the trigger.

Shards of glass rained down from the door she'd hit behind him when he dodged. She and the princes were trapped in their seats and needed to move before he closed in. Carson yanked Jia up to stand in front of him in a chokehold, likely to avoid being shot himself. Enya hoped he wouldn't be.

"Let her go," Lucian demanded from the other side of the train car. He knelt behind a few seats, now empty after their owners had run away during the commotion that had erupted. His pistol poked out from above the cushions.

Enya sneered. Coward.

"Neither of you will be getting off this train alive. Not after this stunt you've pulled," Carson hollered back, lifting his gun to Jia's head.

For once, the sharpshooter trembled. She was wrapped up in a game she couldn't escape.

Everyone knew Jia didn't have much of a say in working for Sean; they just didn't know why. This killer had never been known to falter, but here she was in the arms of one of the Grims about to finally meet her death all because of the Wraiths. Enya almost felt sorry for her, but not quite.

A slew of muttered curses rang out from Lucian's cover. With a hurried shuffle of feet, he began to retreat, hands up.

When he'd reached the cabin door, he barked, "She's an embarrassment to Sean and the Wraiths for getting caught.

Failures aren't worth my trouble, and I'll make sure the boss knows just how badly she's screwed up when I return to Arden. Light em up, boys!"

He disappeared out the cabin door, and passengers scrambled for the opposite exit, some opting to hide behind their seats when they no doubt realized time was of the essence. There was no way everyone could escape. Enya and Carson met each other's worried glances for a split second before she called out, "Get down!"

Carson threw Jia away, instead opting to duck behind the row of seats opposite Enya and the two princes. They each pressed against the floor, everyone on top of each other in most uncomfortable of ways, legs poking legs and elbows jabbing stomachs.

When Enya looked up from her tangle with royalty, Jia was gone.

"Are you sure he's not bluffing—" Rowan started before a cascade of shots blasted through the cabin.

An endless stream of bullets tore into walls, sending scraps of metal and wallpaper flying. Glass shattered, raining down on Enya and her companions and making other passengers scream. Shards tangled in her hair, and she removed them with hands trembling from adrenaline. One cut her index finger through her leather gloves, and her mouth twisted into a grimace as blood pooled at the seams and dripped onto her black pants.

The Wraiths must have gotten hold of an Incendia, a machine gun recently invented by the Brasovian army.

Enya didn't want to imagine the amount of Brasovian leus it would take to purchase something like that, but she was itching more and more to get one for her rebels with every fiery shot.

The seats around them shredded in a sea of hot lead and feathers, and she ducked down further. One stray bullet hit Carson in the shoulder. He grunted in pain, slumping further down to the floor. For a fleeting moment, fear stirred inside Enya's stomach. He'd never been hit by a bullet before. He'd never been hit by anything before.

"What's the plan?" Niall shouted nervously above the noise of gunfire. More screams erupted as other passengers started dropping.

Enya bit her lip, trying to recall what she'd learned of the weapon from the local papers—and eavesdropping on soldiers passing by in Arden's streets, of course.

She shook her head. "We have to wait until it runs out of ammo. After that, we get the hell out of here."

"And if they have more ammo?" Rowan pressed, scoffing.

"Then we get the hell out of here *faster*," Enya retorted, sputtering when a clump of feathers landed right in her face. She wiped them off, waiting for her cue.

Carson yelled out, "I'm not liking these odds, Enya."

She said nothing. It would have been impossible to count the number of bullets searing through the cabin, but she guessed it was in the hundreds. Brass casings fell to the floor, smoking hot.

"Come on," Enya hissed, readying herself. Adrenaline pumped through her veins, and her fingers practically shook with anticipation.

The firing stopped. She grinned.

"Move!"

They stumbled out from behind their seats, which looked nothing like seats now and more like a mess of ripped fabric and stray blood from other passengers. Corpses littered the cabin, but there was no time to dwell on death. Enya sprinted for the opposite door, hurried footsteps trailing behind her. She threw it open, guiding each of her companions to the next train car with her hands on their backs before hopping over to its ledge herself.

Winter winds whipped through her hair, sending the inky black waves flying. All around them, boggy wetlands stretched as far as the eye could see. The Raven's eyes landed on city lights and a tiny port off in the distance. Bingo.

Now the trouble was getting off.

"I'm here!" Beacon called out, appearing breathless in the next car's threshold with his hands full of baked treats. "They had free cookies and tea. What did I miss? I heard a lot of loud banging—" He was cut off by his brothers shoving him back into the cabin.

Enya glanced at her feet. Two massive pins linked the coupler between the cars. Just as she knelt down, the machine gun started up again. Cursing, she threw herself against the metal floor.

"Find cover! I'll take care of the rest," she hollered to Carson.

He cast her a forlorn look as he crouched beside her. "Just try not to die, alright?" With that, he was gone with the princes.

She scrambled to steady her hands as her body swayed against the freezing metal flooring beneath her. Below, tracks came and went, hinting at where she'd end up if she fell. Above, a hailstorm of bullets threatened to end her here and now.

Enya grabbed the first iron pin, heaving it up. Saints, was

this thing heavy. After it was out, the train shook violently, and she gasped, desperate to find a grip somewhere to avoid being bucked off.

Her gloved fingers removed the next pin, and the train car swerved slightly against the tracks. Then it began to slow, and so did her rapid heartbeat thrumming against her ribcage. The train in front of her kept going, but the Wraiths had lost their targets, stray shots hitting nearby trees instead.

They were safe.

Relief flooded her, and Enya fell back against the floor, staring up at the cloudy, gray sky as she tried to catch her breath. A few stray raindrops landed on her cheeks, and she blinked. The train car slowly came to a stop, jolting her. When she got up, she saw they were only about a yard or so from the ground atop the bridge.

Now they'd just have to hope nixies and other watery monsters didn't try dragging them to their graves once they disembarked.

9

Belsale, Skeyya

IN THE unmoving dining car, Carson sat beside her, gripping his shoulder in pain after having taken off his black jacket.

There had been a medic on board who'd managed to take the bullet out and stop most of the bleeding, but there was nothing they could do for the pain or damage inflicted. Meanwhile, glares followed their every move from other passengers.

Enya imagined it had something to do with disrupting their journey, making it impossible for them to reach their next destination anytime soon, and leading a rival gang here—even if none of the above was particularly intended.

It didn't seem like they'd be making any friends on this

ride. That wasn't an unusual occurrence in the slightest for the Grims.

Enya felt guilty now. She felt like if she hadn't accepted this job in the first place, maybe Carson wouldn't have been shot. Maybe these passengers wouldn't have been frozen in their seats with wide eyes and quick breaths. Maybe other innocents wouldn't have been butchered.

The blood that stained her right hand's white button-down shirt sent chills down her spine. *This is my fault.* She decided that was that, and nothing was going to change her mind. Enya would add it to her ever-growing list of things to think about at night.

"How do you feel?" she quietly asked, as if being too loud would scare him into hating her for what happened. Carson didn't meet her eyes.

"Like I just got shot in the shoulder," he retorted.

She assumed that she'd feel the same given the circumstances and nodded. The princes seated at the next table were quiet, so she decided a game plan was in order to get them back on track—no pun intended.

"I saw a city nearby. We're not far," she began, tapping her fingers against her leg, still rife with a need to keep moving. "I say we get off and check it out. We're in the right area, so I'm betting it's Belsale."

Carson hesitated before nodding. He exhaled, running a hand from his good arm down his face. "Yeah. It's worth a shot. If we stay here, we might get in trouble with the authorities when they show up." His eyes met hers, and she gave him a tight smile. "Just give me a minute to recoup. I need a drink to take the edge off."

Enya raised a brow. "Brandy?"

"Whiskey. On the rocks."

She stood. "Whiskey on the rocks it is."

Belsale did indeed smell like fish. An incredibly unbelievable amount of fish that bored into your nose and made itself at home. Oh, and manure. Or at least that's what Enya thought it was. She could only hazard a guess.

On the outskirts of the city, rain pelted hard, nearly soaking Enya, Carson, and the princes. They'd stolen a few dusty Macintosh ponchos from the train and wore them over themselves like children waddling through the mud, but that didn't spare their heads from the torrential downpour.

"Where to now?" Rowan shivered, blowing hot air onto his hands and rubbing them fervently together as he glowered at the weather. "Who has that map that thug at the pub gave us? Or did you somehow manage to lose it?"

Enya shot him a warning glare, yanking it out of her jacket. "Watch it, hotshot." With that, she whacked the old map out a few times to straighten it and they all peered close, huddled together. She saw rows of doodled cottages, fish markets, a bog, and even an old lighthouse at the very top of the steep cliffs that were so common in Skeyya's seaside, but no caves.

"Where is it? They said it would be there," Rowan demanded, eyes narrowing. "Typical magick creatures, always playing dirty tricks. Should have known."

Enya snapped, yanking him by the collar and pulling him close until they were nose to nose. "I'm about this close to continuing this journey with your brothers and ditching you in the dirty streets to fend for yourself." She'd already protected them against assassins and put her life on the line, and she'd risk a bog and whatever creatures lived there, but she wasn't going to put up with their childish antics. "Is that what you want? To come all this way just to end up dead because you couldn't keep your mouth shut?"

Rowan flinched but said nothing. He only shook his head slowly, as if scared she might strike him.

"Good." Enya let loose an angry breath and released his shirt. He stumbled back and turned his nose up at her but otherwise kept his mouth shut. The idea of leaving them behind and claiming the treasure for herself was ever the tempting option. "Now, let's figure out where those caves are shall we?"

In the street were several villagers trudging along with carts or short carriages transporting children to their daily lessons. Those around them held ragged faces, ones exhausted from hard labor and gaunt from lack of nutrients. There wasn't a friendly face to be seen in those kicking up muck with their beaten-up shoes as they walked. That is, until they saw a pale man passing out pickled herrings.

His blue eyes were kind, telling the story of someone who was tired of being hungry, but even more tired of watching others suffer the same fate.

She caught his gaze, and he offered a tired smile.

Without thinking, Enya walked over to him with the rest of the group in tow. His hand held out a fish for her, but she waved it away reluctantly. He deserved to keep what he earned, and she had no desire to take from him. So many others no doubt already had.

Her heart broke, but no one noticed.

"What can I do for you fine folks? You look like you're from the city," he observed, scratching at dirty, rain-soaked tresses.

"We are," Enya began without giving away much more. They needed to keep moving along, or else they might get distracted and do something heroic. She and Carson didn't need to be any closer to the noose. "We're looking for a cave. Know of any around here?"

"I do. There's one right in the middle of the bog," he said with a nod. If it was in the bog, that meant they might be running into Sean and Jia again. Enya remembered their splashes in the water, and her palms began to sweat. The man then added, "My name's Cormac, by the way."

"Cormac," she repeated. "Is it dangerous?"

"Please don't let it be dangerous," Niall muttered to himself while looking down at the dirt. She had to hide a smile. *Always a scaredy-cat.* Maybe he'd toughen up soon.

"Well," Cormac seemed to consider this. "Well … there are rumors that fear preachta inside guard some sort of amulet, but that's just rumors." He simply shrugged and took a bite of one of his herrings. He seemed to savor it when his stomach grumbled. Cormac didn't appear at all bothered by this, as if it was a usual occurrence.

Enya's heart sank even more.

Anger gripped her then, and she remembered once again why she started the Grims in the first place. To help people in need like this man and those around them.

She would make sure that rotten, obnoxiously arrogant king paid for his crimes against the people of Skeyya, and she'd take down whoever stood in her way.

"What kind of creatures are those? They don't sound too friendly." Beacon let loose a nervous chuckle, making Enya snap back to attention.

Fear preachta were said to be the undead remnants of those who died from frostbite, but she had never met one in person. Those were the kinds of stories old folks and faeries used to warn young children from the cold. They weren't supposed to be real, but maybe they were.

"Don't worry about that," Carson said, rubbing his hurt shoulder tenderly while gazing at the prince. "We're all armed, so it's not like we can't handle it."

"Ah." He cleared his throat and glanced warily between them. "So, you aren't just casual travelers, then."

Enya supposed they had looked as normal as a group of older teens could look. They always kept their guns and blades hidden; surprise was one of the best weapons, after all, aside from the ancient magick of the four faerie courts. She assumed there was much more magick she had yet to discover, as she'd never left Skeyya.

Maybe the sands of Cardek or the mountains of Tobuhan would hide something.

Enya hoped this job doesn't take them that far. Her near-empty pockets were almost screaming at the thought.

"Where in the bog did you say those caves were?" Enya asked, offering a sweet smile. They needed to play it cool so that they didn't attract any more unwanted attention. "We're just here studying, uh." She struggled to think of something. What did kids study these days? Enya hadn't taken lessons in ages.

"We're studying rock formations," Carson offered, batting his beady eyes in an attempt to look like a trusted pupil.

"Working on a big research project for the library in the capital." The princes nodded.

Cormac raised a brow. "Fancy." He gave a light cough, gesturing to nowhere in particular down the street. "It's on the west-most part of the bog. You really can't miss it even if you tried."

They bid him farewell and went on their way, trying to ignore the sad, wet faces around them as they did.

After a few minutes of trudging across the sloshy ground, Enya spotted a raven with a red tag on its leg perched on a wooden mailbox; a rebel symbol. The bird was busy cleaning its wings and fluffing its coat trying to sluice off all the rainwater.

She marched over to the raven, ignored its squawking hello, and found the paper and graphite that the guild kept inside the mailbox.

"What are you doing?" Beacon asked, watching her with curious eyes. His brothers did the same.

"Sending a message to the gang in Arden about our run in with Sean's gang," Enya replied. "Maybe they can deal with him while we're out on our little misadventure." She rolled up the paper and stuck it into a compartment on the bird's leg. With a few meager commands, it flew away into the clouds.

"Isn't that the bird you named yourself after?" Rowan asked with a condescending smile, his brows pulling up in mock surprise. She flushed red, her hands balling into fists at her sides.

"Ravens are beautiful creatures. They're more than just simple birds, you palace brat," Enya said stiffly. "Wipe that look off your face, or you'll get wrinkles." With that, Rowan rolled his eyes and finally managed to keep his mouth shut.

As they continued down the road, she could hear Beacon quietly chide Rowan from behind her, "Honestly, brother. Why are you so rude to them when they're trying to help us?"

Rowan scoffed. "Why do you care? They're just peasants."

"Seriously?" Beacon snapped, then he lowered his voice to a more controlled tone. "You sound just like Father."

"Don't you *dare* compare me to him," Rowan hissed.

Enya and Carson exchanged a brief glance but kept up their pace. It seemed the princes didn't believe they could hear them. Niall said nothing, his hands in his pockets and his eyes glued to the ground while they walked.

Beacon retorted to his elder brother, "Then don't act like him. These are our people, whether you like it or not. We both know what Father's been doing is wrong. How he treats people ... even us. It's wrong, Rowan. It's cruel and needs to stop."

The other prince let out an annoyed sigh. "You sound like a rebel."

There was a long silence before Beacon replied, "Maybe I do."

Enya paled, an unwelcome shiver running down her spine. Well, that was interesting. Surely, he couldn't have been serious. A prince supporting the rebellion? It was unheard of. Unthinkable.

She straightened, quickening her steps. No. She wouldn't let this distract her. Royals were nothing but trouble. One good apple didn't make a difference in a rotten bunch. They all came from the same tree.

The bog wasn't too far off. Really, it was just up the shoreline and past the docks. Colorful houses decorated the bleak and mossy hills of Belsale and brought brightness to an otherwise foggy village.

Enya couldn't help but wonder what kind of a person would choose to live here, but she didn't say anything. Her heart ached for the scene she'd only just witnessed, one that spanned almost the entire length of their walk to the outskirts of town.

The crooked docks they trudged past sat above murky water that held a few observant eyes of nixies and nymphs waiting for a bite. They peered up through the reeds and lilies above the dark blue haze of the sea, gazes watching their every step. Enya rolled her eyes, ignoring them. They couldn't reach them here, as far as she could tell. She did her best to put on a brave face while they passed.

A few fishermen's boats waded through the waves, and a child running near the water had caught the creatures' attention. They followed the boy, and Enya tried not to imagine what would come next.

Mud and muck coated their boots now, and water from puddles and rain soaked their shoes beneath their raincoats, making fairly dramatic squishing noises while they walked. Enya could hear Beacon and Niall stifling their laughs at how silly they must have looked. Five cold and hard souls braced for adventure with shoes that could barely keep out water.

It must have been a sight to see for the locals.

Upon further exploration with their map, their crew eventually found the entrance to the bog. Rickety wooden pathways crawled through a forest of dead, moss covered trees. The water beside the old boards was what really frightened Enya. Once inside the bog, it would be foggy, and sound would bounce around like a rubber ball on bare floors.

They'd have to stick close together or they'd quickly be

lost. All rumors aside, getting lost or eaten inside a bog was very easy to do if one wasn't careful.

A rotten sign at the entrance was perched on a tree.

Enter at your own risk. There's trouble afoot!

Enya didn't doubt it, and one look at her companions said the same. Now they just had to find the cave holding the Pentacle of Glac and face the terrifying fear preachta who guarded it.

She cleared her throat. "Okay, all fairytales aside, this isn't a playground; it's a bog. If you don't want to get lost or eaten, stay close and don't wander off. Keep the chatter down, too. Last thing I want is something in there being drawn to us," she ordered, stomping her way into the bog without a second glance at the terrified princes.

Moments later, she heard hurried footsteps fall in behind her.

10

Belsale, Skeyya

THE TREK deeper into the bog was less than ideal in terms of annoyance, but Enya had expected no less. That was simply how trips with royalty went. Well, this time with loads of muck and itchy grass.

Darkness and strange sounds enveloped them like a wicked blanket, sending shudders down Enya's spine. Their journey had yet to really test the willpower of their group, but she was afraid they'd soon be reaching that point.

The murky bog had quickly run out of helpful wooden walkways, and their path was practically non-existent as they moved through the sticky mud, having to yank their boots out of sinking holes with every step, earning nasty squelching noises. Rain pelted them from above, leaving them drenched from head to toe.

Enya was finally getting her bearings when mud suddenly turned into water. She slipped, nearly face-planting right into murky depths. Carson was instantly at her side, catching her and helping her regain her footing. She cast a glare towards the noxious waves licking at her legs, beckoning her further. Perhaps a hungry fae was waiting in deeper water, ready for a snack.

She mumbled a thanks, prying her hands off his jacket and stepping back onto more solid ground. Normally she would have given him a hard time about thinking he needed to protect her, but after everything they'd been through recently, what with the Wraiths and nearly being hanged at the palace, she figured he could use a break.

Carson rubbed his shoulder, wincing in pain from his still-fresh injury. Enya frowned, glancing first at him and then through the endless bog around them. That was just one more thing to worry about; was he going to need extra help getting through this mess?

Would he survive this trip? Would he be okay?

She mentally kicked herself for dwelling too much on the matter. No, they needed to keep going; to stay moving, no matter the cost. Sitting around worrying only got you killed.

They faced down the deeper waters together, their problems all but ending their young journey when it seemed there was nowhere else to go. The princes thankfully had missed the spectacle of her stumble, having fallen a few strides behind.

"What now?" Carson asked, sighing. It was growing darker, and the quickly disappearing sunset provided little in the way of relief from nightfall creeping through the bog reeds. There would soon be nothing but moonlight to guide them.

And nothing but trouble waiting in the shadows.

"I guess we can hope it doesn't go any deeper," she said, mustering more confidence than she felt.

Thankfully, the water didn't go past their knees. But the further they went into the bog, the more each groan and growl of the surrounding wildlife sounded like a beast hungry for human flesh. The dark water around their legs was full of mud, making it impossible to see what could have been swimming ravenous circles around them.

"How much farther do we have to go? My legs are tired of this nonsense," Rowan groaned, kicking a few twigs out of their path.

Enya rolled her eyes, tugging her coat tighter against her small frame, the tail of the fabric sending water droplets up into the air behind her. He'd been complaining for the past hour, and it didn't seem to be letting up anytime soon.

They were following Carson's compass now, one that said west was through thick brush and soggy grass.

Sickening noises erupted from the ground with each step they took, their boots sinking into deep sludge. The rain had dwindled down, too, but that didn't dry any of their hair. Enya was exhausted, and she could tell she wasn't the only one.

"Do you think there's anything out here that's … dangerous? Like, something that could eat us?" Niall asked so quietly that Enya could barely discern his words. He never spoke much, but ever since the incident on the train, he'd grumble here and there. Usually, it was something about monsters and how they were all going to die.

He wasn't the best mood lightener, but he kept them on their toes, to say the least.

"Probably," Carson shrugged, wincing at the pain in his shoulder. "But we're armed, so we should be fine."

Several sloshy steps later, they began to see a ground littered in shimmering specks of silver and white. Several steps after that, they saw ice seizing what appeared to be a dark entrance sunken into a hill. Frozen muck decorated its opening along with sharp, jagged ice shards.

Pentacle of Glac. Pentacle of Ice.

The group stood there seemingly frozen. No one wanted to be the first to go inside—which probably had something to do with the monsters they'd been warned about.

Enya swallowed hard, tightening her grip on the pistol in her pocket. They just had to stick together. There was no reason to be afraid, right? They were only rumors, after all.

"Well?" Rowan snapped. "Time to finish this, I suppose. Go on, then. Lead the way." Enya and Carson shot him dirty looks, but he was right; they did need to keep moving. If they had monsters to fear inside, she had no doubt there were also some lurking in the bog waiting to have them as their lunchtime snack.

Enya motioned for Carson to stay on her side as she took the lead. She needed to feel like she was in control. Not just of the group, but everything. The more she felt in control, the more confidence she had that she was one step ahead.

And the Raven was always one step ahead.

It sure as hell beat looking back on her past. Anything was better than that.

The inside of the cave was dreadfully dark, and Enya felt

anxiously in her pockets for a lighter. She wasn't scared, but she wasn't a big fan of all-consuming darkness either. With a small smile that she could barely see, Carson flicked his to life after lifting it out of his pocket with his good arm.

The inside was brighter than the bog, with glass-like walls reflecting back the flame in beams of blue-tinted embers. It was also deathly quiet, allowing the echoes of their footsteps to surround them while they trudged through.

Somehow, snow also covered the floor of the cave, causing their shoes to leave wet tracks as they trekked further. Deep inside revealed a worn, white door laced with etchings of snowflakes and skeletons. Enya's eyes went wide, and she glanced around nervously.

That … didn't belong there. If such an odd thing was hidden deep within the bogs of Belsale … were any of the stories true?

What was truly in this cave, waiting for them?

She could hear Niall fanning himself behind her, likely on the brink of another anxiety attack. She couldn't help but feel sorry for him. She knew all too well the coiling claws of fear; but he needed to toughen up. They all did. Giving into that sort of weakness only left openings for others to strike.

Enya steeled herself and reached out for the doorknob. It felt freezing in her grasp, nearly burning her skin through her black glove.

"You want to go in there?" Niall whispered. By the looks of it, he was close to passing out now. Beacon steadied the young prince's shoulders while Rowan scowled to himself in the dark.

"We have no other choice," Enya retorted, earning a curt nod from Carson.

"She's right," he admitted. "Come on."

With a slow turn, the door creaked open, revealing a steep drop that had to be at least several hundred feet. Faint sunlight shone onto a single pillar of ice in the center of the cavern holding what appeared to be a disk-shaped crystal.

The Pentacle of Glac.

The only way to reach the pentacle was a winding stone path around the cavern that began a few feet below the door. The path was almost too narrow for anyone to cross and seemed to go all over the place before coming anywhere near their prize. That didn't seem very promising to Enya or anyone else in the group, based on their expressions. She muttered a few curses to herself, earning an amused look from the princes and Carson.

Enya straightened up. "It's way too dangerous for all of us to go at once, but thankfully it doesn't take a team of five to grab a crystal." She and Carson exchanged a knowing look before they both gazed back at the three princes. It wouldn't be worth it to risk any of their lives, and they wouldn't get paid, either.

No, she and Carson should be enough to get the job done. It's not like they hadn't gone climbing before.

Granted, that was atop buildings with plenty of things to grab onto in order to keep from plummeting to their untimely deaths. Here, things looked a bit more slippery, but she was willing to give it a shot if he was too.

"We can handle it if you three can avoid being captured or killed." Carson didn't look too convinced that they could avoid either outcome.

"Why can't one of us do it? I'm sure I'd do a better job than either of you," Rowan huffed, angrily crossing his arms.

"I'm the heir to the throne, after all."

Beacon placed a steadying hand on his shoulder. "Relax, brother. We wouldn't want you bruising up that pretty face on the rocks, anyway. You love it way too much to lose it." Enya attempted to hide her grin behind her leather-clad hand.

"Besides, we're all terrible at climbing. Don't you remember that trip when we were kids?" Niall let out a nervous laugh. Rowan glared back. "You fell out that tree before anyone else."

Enya could faintly remember that herself, something that surprised her. They'd been competing to see who could reach the top first—when she wasn't working, of course, and the heir to the throne had fallen flat on his back. She remembered being one of the servants summoned to bring him to the former queen and getting him patched up from his bruises.

Meanwhile, Rowan had been a rude prick as usual. He couldn't dare believe that he had failed and blamed it on the creatures of the woods and their wicked magick.

Enya's heart clenched, and she made a face. Carson cast her a sidelong glance, but for once, she didn't like him looking at her. She wasn't feeling too great right now.

"I did not—" Rowan began before being cut off by Enya's raised hand. She'd had enough of the past and enough of everything. It was time to get this over with.

"Let's wrap this up," she said stiffly. "We can reminisce about this stuff when we aren't in an enchanted cave." With a scowl, the prince crossed his arms. The others offered apologetic looks while they nodded towards her and her right-hand man.

"What about the dark?" Niall asked, his eyes wide. The sun slipped through above their heads, but only enough to send shards of glimmering speckles across the cave.

They could see, but not very well.

Carson swiftly produced another metal lighter from his pocket and tossed it to the prince without a moment's hesitation. Enya and the three brothers looked at him with bewildered faces. "What? I always carry two."

With that, Enya and Carson carefully dropped down off the ledge and onto the path. It was dusty and falling apart, with rocks and sections vanishing before their very eyes into a bottomless, dark pit far below. When the rocks didn't immediately break at their weight, she gave a sigh of relief.

Bones and dust and blood were all interesting to Enya as long as she was none of all three put together.

"Try not to die, will you?" Rowan called out, his voice echoing throughout the cave. They couldn't see him or the other princes through the narrow sheets of ice growing haphazardly around every ledge. "Not that it would bother us." Enya heard a shove and Rowan grunted in pain. Niall then laughed outright.

What are they doing over there?

"Will you shut up already?" Beacon's voice rang out. Enya stifled a giggle, looking over to Carson. He was also fighting a smile, and she was happy to see him in a better mood. They needed to keep their spirits high.

The duo inched along rocky ledges, always careful to maintain their balance.

The path before them seemed never-ending with all its twists and turns covered in ice and snow, but she saw an opening not too far into the cavern walls on their left. Carson's eyes also seemed to notice it, and he signaled for them to make their way inside.

This narrow corridor was much darker than the faintly lit area they had been in before, as if all life had been sucked dry. An eerie wind swept through above their heads, leaving whistling noises to haunt their every step. If Enya focused hard enough, she could hear what almost sounded like singing. Horribly twisted singing.

A chill ran down her spine, and she wasn't sure if it was this creepy cave or the cold. Maybe it was a bit of both.

She caught Carson's gaze in hers and held a finger slowly to her lips. They needed to see what that was before going any further into this forsaken place.

Enya willed her feet to stop making crunching steps in the snow upon the ground. Carson's lighter flickered in earnest for a moment, wavering left to right as if screaming for help. Not a second later, it went out completely, and they were in darkness. The singing had stopped.

Their breaths caught in unison, and through the blackness of the cave, Enya could barely see that Carson looked as worried as she did. Then she remembered the gift Miriana had given them earlier. If those had somehow fallen out of her pockets, she was going to lose her cool—and fast.

Her hands fumbled through her pockets once more, this time pulling out three small stones. She struggled to remember which one was intended for light, but even still, it was hard to see in the blackness that swarmed them inside the cave.

She held the stones as close to her eyes as she could without poking herself blind and finally caught a glimmer of gold inside one of them. *Aha!* With furrowed brows, she tried to remember what to say.

Wasn't she supposed to say some spell?

Geez, let's hope I remember.

They'd be screwed otherwise. Enya remembered it being something about the moon.

With a small gasp of victory, she finally recalled the words. Enya took a deep breath, then spoke.

"Help me in my final hour, the goddess has granted me the power," she whispered to the stone. For a moment, nothing happened, and she sat there thinking what a cheesy and horrible prank that had been. Miriana would never hear the end of it—especially for making her say such a weird phrase in front of Carson.

She gritted her teeth, about ready to toss the stupid rocks right over her shoulder.

But then, something magical happened.

The stone in Enya's grasp shook violently in such a way that her entire arm hummed with magick.

A narrow white beam struck out. Then another, and another, until the entire stone was consumed with furious illumination. Her hand glowed beneath its warmth, and now so did the walls around them.

Enya couldn't hide the childlike smile on her face. She had to look away, and Carson too, as the light was creating impossibly red flashes in their vision nearly bleeding right through her glove.

Is this what magick felt like? Warm, powerful, and all-consuming? She wasn't sure, but she loved this sense of control she now had. They were going to be fine—hopefully.

"That's impressive," Carson said softly, watching her with admiring eyes. "I've never seen you do magick before."

Enya flushed. Of course, he'd find some way to catch her

off guard. "Miriana charmed these stones before we left. I didn't do anything." She gave a dismissive shrug, holding up the stone to get a better look down the seemingly never-ending corridor in which they'd found themselves.

There was another door at the end, one identical to the one they'd gone through upon entering the cave.

Was she seeing things?

She hadn't noticed that when they came in. Above the quiet sounded that strange singing once again.

"That ... wasn't there before," Enya said. She spoke her words carefully, as if some sinister creature was listening in. The hairs stood up on the back of her neck, so she didn't doubt the possibility of that one bit.

Fear preachta were known for playing horrible games to trick their prey into madness. Their ultimate goal was always to freeze their victims and feast on their souls. The mere thought of that now, while they were inside this quiet and dark space, made Enya's chest grow tight with fear.

This was so much more different than humans or faerie folk in the city streets. More different than unruly policemen and kings. This was wicked and vile and all kinds of wrong. It felt wrong just to be here in this cave, breathing this frigid air.

Enya braced herself for the worst.

We can take whatever comes our way.

She willed it to be true. Until the singing began again...

Belsale, Skeyya

THE DOOR stood there quietly in the light of the magick stone, as if it wasn't in any way out of place. Of course, doors didn't talk, but this one spoke a language of its own. One of despair and foreboding.

It called to Enya and Carson, and they followed suit.

With a careful turn of his hand and a bated breath from both of them, Carson opened the door.

It was like the cave had transformed. Inside this new corridor laid carefully polished marble floor and walls. Verdant plants and magick bubbles floated above their heads attached to the ceiling. It was enchanting and it was terrifying. But there had been nothing before … Where had all this come from?

Enya curled her once again aching fingers against her jacket, holding it tighter against her. How could any of this be real? It seemed impossible. But that's how fear preachta operated. They lured you in with impossible magick only to devour you whole, according to local legends and childhood stories told over lamplight. She couldn't help but wonder how many they were up against in here.

How would bullets fare against such creatures? Enya hoped they wouldn't run out of lead and iron anytime soon.

She walked further but was stopped short by Carson when he grabbed a hold of her elbow, sending shockwaves through her skin. Enya shot him a dubious look, and he pointed to three seemingly sleeping figures not far from where they stood around the corner on their right.

They were heavenly, gorgeous women, ones who appeared to sleep peacefully atop three featherbeds adorned with the finest gold and silver trim. One of them held a black key in her grasp, one with nails painted a deep red and rings on each finger. Their outfits spoke of a time long since passed, ones with layers of colorful skirts and tight bodices wrapped in lace.

It was a glamour. It had to be.

Enya groaned inside her head, her face twisting into a furious scowl. They'd probably need that key, no doubt. Of course they'd be put in such a situation.

Carson's eyes, however, were enamored. He watched them intently, but a bit of drool slipped from his lips, and she whacked him in the side. It was nothing but a trick. What was there to be googly-eyed about?

"Stop ogling. They're not real," Enya snapped, barely able to avoid the anger brewing under her hot cheeks. Something in her stomach coiled and made its way into her chest, but she didn't know what. She refused to examine that feeling too closely.

Carson shrugged, flicking out his pocket-knife. He gestured to them with it, and Enya nodded. They needed to handle this quietly, especially if they didn't know the creatures' true forms just yet. They could slit their throats, take the key, and be on their merry way.

It would be so easy. But that made it look that much more like a trap to the Raven's trained eyes. Enya and Carson inched closer to the women, blades at the ready to cut this short—no pun intended. With their weapons out, they looked to each other and nodded.

Enya breathed deeply, and then she struck … and nothing happened. The women didn't flinch as blood oozed down their porcelain necks and dresses. They didn't so much as move a muscle, and they didn't seem to breathe, either.

Nothing but eerie stillness … which meant nothing but trouble. Something was up.

Enya wasn't going to sit around and wait to see what trap was in store for them. She quickly snatched the key from the corpse and tucked it into her pocket beside the stones while Carson went to finish off the last of the three.

"Let's move," Enya ordered, kicking aside a few golden trinkets on the floor. She ran a frustrated hand through her waved hair. They were fine now, but escape wasn't guaranteed.

Carson nodded, eyeing the women carefully, as if at any moment they'd be ready to pounce—and not in the good way. "Indeed. I'd rather not be around when they decide to wake up.'"

They fled the scene down the slippery cavern passage, gazes drifting back over their shoulders at every suspicious noise and whistle of the wind against the ice surrounding them. Nothing was following them yet, but Enya guessed they still had a while before they were out of this creepy popsicle stand.

A wooden puzzle seemed to protrude from the floor and into a massive crystal wall at the end of the tunnel. Old and rotten oak engulfed several engraved pieces, ones that depicted a twisted and mixed-up creature needing to be put back together.

They'd hit a dead end.

"I guess we're solving puzzles now," she muttered aloud when they arrived in front of the contraption.

Carson shrugged. "Better than fighting water hags. Do you remember the last time we dealt with one? The wrinkly wench nearly sliced my head clean off with those nails of hers. And the smell was awful." Such creatures roamed the bogs of southern Skeyya. Luckily, they were straying north on their journey. Other creatures roamed in the shadows.

Ones they could meet anytime soon. Most fae could be reasoned with, but not all. And not ones hungry for flesh.

Enya exhaled, nodding. "You're right, but there's something I can't quite figure out. If the demon wants someone to set her free, putting so many obstacles in their way seems a bit counter-productive."

Carson considered this for a moment, scratching the stubble along his jaw. "I have a feeling it's the faerie folk who put these guardians here and these puzzles. They don't want anyone giving her what she wants." He pursed his lips in thought, staring at the contraption set up before them. "Any idea how to solve this puzzle?"

She pursed her lips, running a hand along the icy surface. The wood was freezing, and she pulled her hand back, feeling a slight burn through her black glove. Enya flinched. "Don't touch them for too long." The wooden pieces were painted to resemble a sort of figure with white ink. She stepped back, trying to get a better look.

"Here, let me try," Carson said, blowing hot air on his hands and fiddling with the tiles. It was starting to resemble *something* now at least. But what, Enya didn't know. With a few tries and a lot of cursing to himself, Carson finally managed to get them in order, and he gasped, stumbling back into her.

"What ... What is that?" Enya asked once he'd straightened himself, her eyes going wide. "It looks like a skeleton."

It was a corpse shrouded in ice, grotesque and ... terrifying.

Fear preachta. The creature's true form.

Their dance with danger wasn't over yet. Enya was certain there was some sort of trick to this.

The wooden slab violently shook within the ice, causing a few glistening shards to fall from the ceiling and narrowly miss the duo, earning a few more expletives from Enya.

It opened to reveal a silver key.

"What's with all these damn keys? We're in a cave." Enya groaned before Carson snatched it and tucked it into his coat pocket. "What would we need keys for?"

He was about to answer, but a sickening sound erupted from behind them. There was no singing now, but disgusting moans echoed through the cavern, earning a racing heart from Enya. Her hands shook for a moment in pain, worry forming a lump in her throat, and her wide eyes met his.

And then all went black.

"Carson!" Enya screamed, feeling her way around the cave, her boots crunching the snow under her feet with every hesitant step. Her leather-clad hands slipped against icy walls that seared through her gloves, nearly making her fingers numb altogether. Eerie blackness had swallowed them whole, and she couldn't detect any sign that Carson was even still there at all.

Faintly, she felt her right boot bump something small on the ground. She knelt down, feeling around with her hand.

Carson's lighter! Thank the saints.

She flicked it on, and a scream instantly tore out her throat.

Enya was surrounded by undead faces, each peering back from countless frosted mirrors. Torn skin hung in tatters from bony cheeks, and hollow black pits were void of any eyes. Nonetheless, that empty blackness bore into Enya from all sides. Without thinking, she yanked up her gun and fired, shattering the glass in front of her. Shot after shot rang out, sending jagged shards flying, and she scrambled to her feet, breaking out into a run.

Down the passage, she was met by a dead end. *Shit*. Enya glanced left and right, looking for a way out. Her eyes met with Carson's through a crack in the icy walls of the cave, one big enough to squeeze through. "Carson! Are you okay?"

He nodded, waving her forward. "Hurry! We've got to move!"

That she did. She slunk through the crevice, wincing at the way frigid stone poked her body as she did. Carson grabbed hold of her sleeve, pulling her all the way through and dusting her off.

There was another door down the passage on their left, and without a second to lose they were sprinting. Their feet pounded wildly against the slippery floor of the cave, breathing already ragged. This new door was identical to all the others. They just had to hope their keys would work if it was locked.

Something was following them. Something vile and wicked. Something that emitted screams and groans and all other sorts of horrible sounds.

Enya could hear the creature's feet trotting across the snow and slick ice after them. *Fear preachta.* Icy death, icy fear. Legend said they were corpses, and Enya had a feeling that if she looked back to find something like that bearing down on her, she might as well pass out. She didn't sign up for this; she signed up to find a stupid sword and save the world.

A harsh blast of air sent them flying into the door, earning pained grunts from both of them. She tried to use the knob, but it wouldn't budge. It was locked.

"Crap. My shoulder!" Carson groaned, gripping it in his hand. His lips curled back, and Enya had to steady him, something that made her heart ache. She hated to see him in pain, but they'd die if they didn't keep going.

"Carson, the key!" Enya cried, finally turning to look back at the monster. Her gun was up and firing, one shot after the other. But it wasn't doing any good.

It wasn't slowing down.

The creature was desiccated, with a ripped face and gnashing teeth. It stood frozen only a few meters away, watching them curiously before it began to slump towards them once more. It also wore one of the same dresses they'd seen on those three women before, black blood spewing from its neck from where they'd slit its throat.

"I'm getting it!" Carson exclaimed, struggling to force the black key they'd found earlier into the lock.

More bullets blasted into the fear preachta, and Enya bit her lip, hoping one would make a difference.

Another monster slammed into one of the cave walls, claws gripping the ice as it bared its teeth. Another century's old dress, another oozing neck. Shit. Enya swallowed her fear, aiming for their heads. If anything, lead shredded flesh, but the fear preachta crept closer, their movements unnatural and too fast yet too slow all at once.

"Saints, Carson," Enya said, laughing nervously and falling back a few steps. "Did you ever picture us going out like this?"

Carson threw the door open. "No, I didn't. Come on!" He urged her through with strong hands on her shoulders, kicking the creature back when it reared its ugly head through the threshold. Enya slammed the door shut behind them, falling back several steps.

All went quiet, and the door remained still.

"We made it," Enya gasped, grabbing his good arm.

Carson was still breathing hard as he nodded. "We did." He gestured down the cavern path, slicked with ice and more snow.

They soon arrived back in their original spot, with the unending abyss right below their feet slipping into black nothing. This time, they stood across from where the path had begun on the other side of the cave. But where were the princes?

"Beacon? Niall?" Enya called out, voice ringing against the crystalized ice that covered every inch of the cave. She hesitated before calling out the heir to the throne's name, worried he might think she actually cared about his well-being. With an exasperated sigh, she added, "Rowan?"

There were no sounds aside from the whistling of the wind and the dripping of water here and there around the cavern's interior. The sun was almost gone from the openings in the ceiling, and sunset had fallen upon the day. Enya *really* didn't want to be in here after nightfall had truly descended.

"We're here!" she heard Beacon call out, but she didn't see anyone. Could it be another trap?

"Define 'here' please," she shouted back. Everything about this place made her feel out of place. Out of her realm of expertise.

She was used to busy streets and musk and guns and running from police, not monsters in the mossy forests and bogs.

"If you climb up to the pentacle, you'll see us," Rowan's voice echoed. "Hurry the hell up. I'm cold."

Well, at least he sounded like his usual happy-go-lucky self. Enya held a rueful smile, sizing up their next challenge.

They moved carefully across the ledges before them. Any wrong step at this point could land either one of the duo in the dark, bottomless pit below them, and she wasn't a big fan of breaking all her bones. Well, most people wouldn't be either, she supposed.

She and Carson were so close to the pentacle now. There was only a steep climb and an old bridge between them and the object's resting place from what she could see through the crystallized ice walls in the cave.

"Do you think the princes are actually alright?" Carson finally said while they made their way up the cavern walls. He was careful not to drop his lighter showing the way, though it shook fervently in his hand. Carson's breathing was ragged, and sweat soaked his forehead. That bullet wound needed tending to—and fast. "You don't think they're dead or anything, do you? That maybe those are the fear preachta?" he added. Enya had to admit he had a point there.

It was possible that they'd used their glamour and enchantments to trick them once again. But then again, that did sound like something Rowan would have said. That voice had the same cocky attitude that so distinguished the eldest prince.

Enya had to think for a moment, grimacing as she almost slipped off the rocks. Her hands now stung with pain from holding up her weight. Saints, this was uncomfortable. With a grunt, she kicked herself up to the top ledge, hoisting herself over onto solid ground with Carson right behind her. She pulled him up as soon as she turned around, desperate to make sure her best friend didn't fall.

"Yeesh, I sure hope not. Think of all the money we'd be missing out on," she said in an attempt to make him laugh. He didn't, his lips forming a flat line.

Secretly she hoped she wouldn't be the one who'd led these three boys who trusted her into the unknown and right to their deaths. Her stomach turned with a sickness she couldn't escape, and her heart didn't feel much better at the thought. They trusted her, and she couldn't let them down. Enya might not have remembered exactly what happened in her past, but she knew she'd let them down before. She just didn't know how.

With a cold shrug, Carson was moving forward. Enya had no choice but to follow. Up on this ledge, they could see the pillar holding their prize wasn't too far off, and the exit to the cave was also in view. It was dark, but somewhat visible in the fading sunlight.

"Do you think they can last until we get over there?" Carson asked, holding a reluctantly steady hand on her waist as they neared the rope bridge.

"I'm sure they'll be fine," Enya replied, trying to avoid his gaze and keep her own on where her feet hit the now crumbling stone below. Not that they could get to the princes without grabbing the pentacle first. The bridge was rickety and dangerous, exactly how you'd expect a bridge in a forgotten cave to be. Snow still drifted in from the jagged holes in the cavern's ceiling, and their breaths only held a hint of frost while they walked.

Enya cautiously rapped a foot on the bridge, testing how much of her weight it could stand. It looked ancient, with rotting wood and tattered ropes. It was likely built by some of the first faeries of the region, or maybe it was even older than that. She couldn't really see the other side, only the reflections off the ice from the little light that shone in from holes in the ceiling of the cave.

"Please be careful." Carson gave an uneasy chuckle while he watched her. "Not sure how good of a leader I'd be for the gang if you fell and broke something important. Or, you know, died."

She knew that wasn't what he was really worried about— well, that's what she thought. Hoped? Her feelings had only gotten more confusing since they'd had so much alone time together. They made her feel confused and beautiful and scared all at the same time.

Enya merely nodded. The bridge *seemed* sturdy enough. It'd have to do. Now they just needed to grab the pentacle and escape with the princes before anything else devious and dastardly showed up trying to eat them.

Belsale, Skeyya

THE BRIDGE before them creaked with every step, and every step sent unwelcome shivers down Enya's spine and twists in her stomach.

Lucky for them, the journey across was surprisingly uneventful, and they both let out their breaths as soon as they hit the other side. They were fine. Everything was fine.

"That wasn't so bad," Carson admitted, eyeing the pillar up and down. It was then that he froze. "Oh my god." Enya followed his gaze before shock consumed her too.

Bones. There were bony corpses laced throughout the ice illuminated in stark detail by the flame of their lighter.

There had to be at least a few hundred bodies from the

top of the pillar all the way to the bottom of the cave, wherever that was in the never-ending shadows below them. Each of the figures had their mouths stretched in an ungodly fashion, teeth jagged and twisted.

Lucky for Enya and Carson, at least they couldn't smell what was inside. It would sure beat any stench Arden's slums had to offer.

They must have been victims of the fear preachta.

Or something worse. Enya didn't want to think it could have been the Crimson Witch. She much preferred to pretend that threat was far away. Something that couldn't touch them. It made this entire ordeal much more bearable.

"You were saying?" she asked. A shiver ran down Enya's spine before she collected herself.

The Pentacle of Glac was trapped inside this cursed ice pop. They'd either have to carve it out or see if there was some sort of mechanism that would make it release. To the left of their prize was a wheel with several different inscriptions, and it smelled rotten, to say the least, nearly making Enya gag.

"What do you think happened to them?" Carson whispered, his eyes wide in shock. She shrugged in an attempt to seem unbothered while secretly her stomach turned.

"I don't know, but let's try not to stick around and find out. Hopefully those three royals won't be meeting the same fate, either," Enya replied, taking a deep breath and leaning in to get a closer look.

Above the wheel held a sign that read:
At night they come without being fetched.
By day they are lost without being stolen.
"What the hell is that supposed to mean?" Enya muttered,

scratching her damp head and frowning at the knotted tresses that tangled around her fingers. "I thought this journey would only need manual labor, not pop quizzes."

Lost without being stolen?

She was never the best at solving riddles and today was no exception. Her specialty was more of a brute, in your face approach with a little pinch of conniving thievery in the city, not so much faerie messes like this place.

Carson furrowed his brows in thought. "What does the wheel say? I see some writing there." Enya squinted hard to read the words etched in wood. This was some crappy handwriting.

He brought the light closer and it all became clear.

"I think we're supposed to push this arrow to face one of them. There's the sun, the moon, the clouds, and the stars," Enya said, trying to avoid how close he stood.

Carson snapped his fingers. "Got it!" He slid his hand across her arm as he pushed past, creating butterflies in her stomach. "That makes sense. It's *stars*." Carefully, he pushed the arrow to face the words. With a click, the mechanism sunk into itself and turned. The ice pillar then opened the compartment holding the Pentacle of Glac, and a golden constellation shone onto the cavern ceiling.

Carson reached to pick it up, earning a quick swat of her hand. "What are you doing?" Enya demanded.

"Uh, grabbing it? We need it, if you hadn't noticed," he said with a frown.

Enya cocked her head. "And what if it's a trap?" she snapped, gesturing to the pentacle. There had been a lot of those lately and she was getting really tired of it.

"Then it's a trap. We have no choice," he retorted, offering her a sidelong glance when he snatched the pentacle out of the hole in the ice.

Nothing happened.

Enya let out a breath of relief. *Thank the saints.* Now they just needed to figure out the deal with the constellation.

"Enya, wait." Carson grabbed her arm, and her eyes went wide. "What if these people ... what if they were killed by the Crimson Witch? This is one of the keys to the sword and her army, after all."

"It's possible. But it could also be the guardians of this place having a field day with everyone who tries to get the pentacle. Remember how they like to eat souls and all."

He glanced at the pillar full of dead souls. "That's a lot of people trying." It was. If this many people had been after the pentacle, much less the sword, then maybe the Crimson Witch had a following. Who knew what other creepy corpses were stashed around this cave?

"Well, it has been thousands of years, I'm sure. Let's just get out of here before we get turned into ice cubes too, okay?" Enya tried to laugh it off, brushing his hand off her arm. He flushed and looked back up at the stars now littering the cavern's ceiling.

"What do you think all that means?" Carson asked in wonder. Some of the stars seemed to form a shimmering wand, while others made what looked to be coordinates over a map plane that stretched across the entire cave. It could have been a city if one tilted their head just right.

"It has to be the location of the wand in the picture. Or the next clue, at least." Enya squinted hard.

Carson, meanwhile, had yanked out a sketch pad from his

never-ending pockets and was furiously scribbling the coordinates and a rough sketch of the map down.

She wasn't really that familiar with coordinates herself, but her right-hand man never had a problem with maps or compasses. Enya couldn't help but feel envious of that talent. She'd have to work on that more when this mission was over so he couldn't one-up her.

Carson averted his gaze when he caught her staring holes at him. She quickly glanced away as well.

"The next clue, or the wand, should be in the city of Thomond near the mountains. Looks like it's in a church. The building has some kind of cross on it. We'll have to go all the way to the Brasovian border," he stated, stashing away his notebook.

Enya swore. That wasn't exactly close. It was at least a day's ride by train, and they were banned from that form of travel.

It was also at the forefront of a war between nations. Specifically, Skeyya and Brasova. Troops would litter the forest and city like rats in the capital sewers. And if there was anything Enya knew about soldiers, it was that they didn't mind roughing up a pretty face.

All it took was a general too familiar with the royal family, too familiar with the princes' faces, to blow their cover to smithereens. Those disguises had better be foolproof.

"Guess we'd better be on our way then. Time to catch up with those princes. If they haven't been eaten yet, anyway," she joked, trying to ease the tension that had smothered them both like summer heat, despite their frosty surroundings. That was usually how she dealt with situations like these; with humor and hoping that it went away. Secretly she *really* hoped they were still alive. Not just for the money, but because she'd hate herself if she did any more damage. It was strange feeling so empathetic towards the princes when she genuinely thought all this time that she hated every single royal.

Maybe they could be different.

"You think we can handle that many armed men, Enya?" Carson asked, giving her a wary look.

"Let's try not to piss them off then, shall we?"

Enya waved him on, and they began toward the path to the exit. It had a steep drop down to the doorway they'd come from, so they'd have to figure out how to get down without breaking their necks. Enya tried to convince herself it was just another job, and hopefully that was all this journey would ever be.

"Enya, wait."

She turned, meeting his hesitant gaze. "Yeah?"

"I'm happy you're okay, and that we made it out of that."

She swallowed. "Me too."

Across the icy ravine, Rowan, Beacon, and Niall stood waiting below while the heir to the throne held Carson's lighter high, sending flaming flickers across the cave walls. Meanwhile, the youngest prince held onto his pistol tightly, braced for action. Enya was surprised to see him this way. It looked like he was becoming braver by the day since they'd left the palace.

"Took you long enough!" Rowan muttered, kicking some rocks off the ledge. "We've been waiting for hours." This earned a quick eyeroll from Enya and an elbow from Beacon. Niall just looked ashamed to be related to this guy.

"Stop being a jerk!" Beacon snapped, but Rowan didn't seem like he'd be stopping anytime soon. They *seemed* to be normal princes after all. Otherwise, those creatures were better actors than Enya thought.

She turned to Carson. "You ready?" Enya asked.

He nodded, glancing from her to the darkness waiting should he fall. "I'll go first. At least I can catch you if things go wrong."

Carson prepared to jump, crouching down. With a strained noise that was likely from his injury, he was down through the door they had come through. He flashed a cocky grin to Enya while gripping his arm, and she chuckled.

"Try not to land on your head," Rowan mocked, earning yet another blow from both of his brothers this time. Carson just shook his head, holding out his arms for Enya.

She took a deep breath, and then she flew. In seconds, she was in his arms with a powerful thud, and something equally as powerful stirred in her stomach at the touch of his arms. Carson grunted in pain from the impact on his shoulder, and Enya bristled, regaining her footing and trying to put some distance between them. His skin had been warm. Much warmer than this cave.

"You good?" Carson asked softly, brushing some lint off her jacket. When the princes stared, he shoved his hands in his pockets. "Like, no trips to the hospital in Arden?" He attempted a smile this time, a genuine one. She returned it in earnest.

"Yeah, I'm fine. Let's go," Enya said, nodding to the exit and pushing along the three brothers.

As soon as she'd said the words, a sickening shriek echoed off the cavern walls. It was as if evil itself had blanketed the cave, its hems brushing along their bodies and sending shivers down their spines. All good feelings were ripped from the group, and a frigid cold settled over their skin, sending goosebumps up their arms.

It looked like the fear preachta wouldn't be giving up so easily.

Enya's gaze flew to the exit of the cave and back to the ebbs and flows of the ice they'd just escaped. She saw nothing until shadows began to slowly creep along the cave walls. The moonlight peeking through the ceiling slowly vanished into blackness.

Carson's lighters were more of a lifesaver than they'd initially thought. She'd have to remind herself to thank him later if they made it out alive.

One look over their shoulders showed hideous, bony figures stalking towards them and jumping across the various ledges, gnarly faces twisted into hideous grins as they neared.

She stepped back with one foot, then another, sweat dripping down her neck. Her heart pounded; she'd never seen monsters like these before.

"I think that's our cue! Run!" she shouted.

With barely any time to recover from their already exerting journey, they each sprinted towards the exit with the lighter shakily illuminating the way. Light glimmered off the cavern walls, which twinkled back and gave them some semblance of wonder rather than dread. But such was deceit.

"If we survive this, make that payment eighty-*five* thousand pounds!" Enya exclaimed. Rowan shot her a deadly glare, and she let out a breathless laugh.

When there were only a few feet between them and the bog, another door came crashing down. This one was just as locked as the last, nearly making their hearts stop altogether.

"What do we do?" Beacon yelled, trying to kick it, but it wouldn't budge. Niall looked ready to pass out.

"Royalty does not die in rotten caves and dirty bogs!" Rowan snarled, shoving past and joining him in his efforts.

The creatures were gaining on them, and it seemed like their trap had finally worked.

This was it. The Raven had finally met her match in the form of some ugly, skeletal creatures. She'd always thought it'd be at the hands of the king or a rival gang leader, but never this. Never losing her soul in the darkness.

Unless … she had the other key.

"I've got it!" Enya exclaimed, thrusting it into the lock and turning it all sorts of ways until she heard a lifesaving click. The door opened, and just like that, they were free. Once through, Carson slammed it shut right on a rotten face. *That was way too close*, Enya thought, glancing around the exhausted expressions of the group and grinning. *But at least we're alive.*

They were, and she'd never seen such relieved faces in her life. Her own heart still pounded in her ears, but they were fine.

They were alive and ready to face another day. Or night, considering the velvety darkness that swallowed the bog. Now they just needed to survive the trip to Thomond.

Belsale's colorful houses and shops seemed to be waiting for them once they returned, and the scent of torched seabass pulled them into a dingy inn called Clontart for an extremely late supper.

At first, they ate silently, flinching at every unnecessarily loud noise in their wake from the patrons around them in the Clontart Inn's restaurant. The taste of squid ink and radishes danced with that of the fish on their tongues. But then, something magical happened.

They started laughing. It could have been nerves, or maybe even relief, but they couldn't stop.

We're alive. We made it.

These words repeated themselves over and over in Enya's head. It had been such a rush to fight and escape. At least now they had a new crazy tale to bring back to the Grims if they made it all the way home. She hoped they would.

Enya looked at the princes differently now. Before, they'd been just another group of royals to take down, but now? Now, they seemed to be possible friends again. People she could depend on from her past in Renmare. Her mind told her they were just as bad as the rest of the palace lot, but her heart said otherwise.

She could only hope her heart was right. You'd never know how easily a heart could be tricked.

PART TWO

MONSTERS IN DISGUISE

13

Belsale, Skeyya

SUNSHINE SENT blazing light into their shared bedroom. The promise of a new day, and hopefully a less eventful day, loomed over Enya as she rose from her cot. This morning, she wasn't alone, and the thought comforted her. After what happened yesterday, she didn't really want to be alone.

She yawned, running a hand through her tangled black waves. Carson was across the room in his own bed, completely oblivious to her staring as he slept.

Someone else, however, was not.

"Good morning, wanted-criminal." Rowan rolled his eyes, throwing his blankets off his body and getting up to stretch. "Like what you see?" he asked, gesturing to her best friend.

Enya stayed silent and unmoving, quietly begging in her head for no one else to wake up. This wouldn't be a battle worth fighting. Not this early in the morning and certainly not with a jerk like him.

She and Carson were only friends. That was it.

Rowan shrugged, coming over to plop down at the edge of her own bed. "Listen," he said so low that only she could hear. "I may not know much about how friendship works in your little gang-run world, but I do know it's weird to stare at someone while they're sleeping. It usually means you feel very strongly about them. If you catch my drift." He raised a brow before getting up.

What the hell was that about? Was he trying to give her relationship advice? Unless this was an attempt to insult her. Rowan had barely spoken to her except to indulge in the latter.

"In case you four end up desperate for someone with a semblance of sense," he added with a splay of his hands as he inched his way towards the door, "I'll be getting breakfast." Rowan left, and Enya's cheeks turned beet red, and she quickly tossed off her covers, wincing at her throbbing hands.

There wasn't anything more than friendship to be spoken of here. It was strictly platonic. It was business. This wasn't … she wasn't …

Enya kept a brisk pace while she walked down the halls of Clontart Inn. Her stomach screamed with hunger, but she ignored it. Enya needed to rinse the grime off her face and figure out their next move. She needed to clear her head. Everyone else was asleep except for that haughty prince, so maybe she could catch a moment to herself.

Hopefully, he wouldn't stick his nose into her business

again. She almost felt like slapping him, but now wasn't the time for brawls. They had to figure out a way to Thomond without getting mowed down by enemy soldiers or Sean's gang.

Everyone was now awake and ready to go.

It wouldn't have been *too* far, but Thomond would have been far, nonetheless. Considering what happened on the train, it was unlikely they could sneak on at Belsale's station without being tossed right off as soon as the attendants recognized them. Horses would have to do this time. Besides, they would allow them to get closer to the border without the trouble of dodging military munitions on foot.

Enya stood by the front desk tallying who was present. "... three ... four ... Where is Beacon?" she asked, her brows pushing together. The prince had just been there a moment ago but had now gone missing. Fear clenched her throat, and she swallowed a lump as her eyes scanned the lobby.

"I think I spotted him going to the bar for a snack," Carson said, pointing over his shoulder with his thumb. "He wouldn't stop talking about saltwater taffy."

"I'm surprised you didn't join him," Enya replied with a smile, heart slowing down a little. "You love that stuff."

Carson shrugged, the corners of his mouth twitching with a shy grin of his own. "I'm trying to diet, remember. Can't be eating any junk when there's trouble lurking around any corner. Got to stay in shape." With that her smile turned wider. He was in a good mood today, and hopefully he hadn't noticed what happened this morning.

There would be no more weirdness between them. The thought eased her tangled mind.

"You look fine," Enya said, looking away. She was suddenly flustered. He seemed pleased at her comment, and she willed herself to believe it was only as a friend.

Rowan and Niall met each other's eyes and the heir to the throne had the audacity to smirk.

Enya gritted her teeth and stalked off to find Beacon. That bastard Rowan was always getting on her nerves. Lucky for her, the bar was just down the hall and soon they'd be on their way. She'd promised them protection on this trip, and unfortunately that meant babysitting a trio of practically grown men. How fun.

She found the missing prince at the sleek wooden bar inside the restaurant, and she couldn't hold back the shock from showing on her face at what she saw.

"But how could I ask for anything more," Beacon exclaimed over a mouthful of blue taffy while he leaned into another boy around his age sitting next to him, one with blond hair, blue eyes, and a devilish smile. "I'm huge on food, especially sweets."

"Perhaps I could be your next dessert." His companion laughed before whispering something in the prince's ear once he saw Enya barreling towards them.

She'd never seen this side of Beacon. Relationships with the same sex or gender were rare in Skeyya. She'd heard of these things in other lands and in small villages full of foreigners, but never from a royal prince who lived in the palace. It was unheard of. Not to mention she'd just seen him flirting with girls on their way to the capital before.

Enya tried to hide her surprise, but her face must have been doing a horrible job, as Beacon pushed the boy next to him away with a sheepish look. With a glare, the blue-eyed teen slunk off to find someone else to pounce on.

"Hey there," the prince said quietly with red cheeks. "How much of that did you see?"

Enya scratched her head. "Enough. I didn't know you rolled that way." She shrugged, trying to appear as nonchalant as possible. Anything else would likely embarrass him, with him being a prince, and all. She guessed that his brothers didn't know either. "Not that it's a big deal! It's fine—just ... It's not very common."

"No. No, it's not." Beacon sighed, fiddling with the buttons on his suit jacket. "I roll all kinds of ways. I'm not really stuck between boys or girls or anything else. He was just so cute, and he offered to buy me candy and—"

"I won't tell them," Enya said quickly before he asked. She knew he would, and she knew she could keep a secret. After all, Enya knew many secrets. What was one more locked away in her arsenal?

Her words seemed to settle the anxiety plastered on his face, and Beacon nodded. "It's easier to be myself here when I don't look like myself." He sighed, lifting off his seat and joining her to meander out of the restaurant and around countless patrons with hands full of breakfast and stout. "I can pretend I'm not a prince and let myself go."

Enya instantly felt a wave of pity. With Rowan being such a jerk, Niall being such a scaredy cat, and his father having locked them up for over a decade, he probably hadn't even had the chance to explore how he really felt.

She'd almost forgotten about the glamour from Miriana. Right now, it probably saved the prince from royal shame of serious proportions. That lifestyle wasn't so accepted around Skeyya, but things were changing. Maybe one day he could be honest and open and free. But today was not that day, and that really sucked.

"So, they don't know?" Enya asked. She paused their footsteps, needing confirmation before she promised to forget this royal secret of his. Beacon's eyes went wide before he gave a solemn nod.

His voice was low when he hesitantly replied, "No one does. Royals are judgmental enough as it is. I didn't need to hear more crap from them about … well, you know."

Indeed. That was that, and there would be no more talk of this.

If he was happy, she was happy too. That's simply how friendships worked. Could a wanted thief and a royal prince be friends?

With that, they were on their way back to the lobby. Rowan and Niall seemed relieved to have Beacon back, no doubt worried some bandit had made off with their brother.

"Okay, let's go find our ride." She motioned for them to follow her when she led out the door to the inn. Cold air stung her face and blew her hair off her shoulders, reminding her just how lucky they'd been to get a room for the night. Enya wasn't sure when their luck would run out, but her experiences so far had kept her eyes peeled for the worst.

Finding horses wouldn't have been hard. It was the purchasing of them that might. They needed to save their coin, and if she counted right, they'd need at least five beasts to bring them all the way to the city of Thomond.

The day wasn't gloomy for once, and despite the falling frost from the sky, the grassy land was bright and inviting.

Crowds, as usual, strung around the streets on their way to complete their daily dues, and children pushed past to beat their friends to the ration line not far from where Enya and the group stood. The locals still wore faces etched with exhaustion, but in light of the weather, they seemed to be at least more in the mood to trudge along.

In the distance, she could hear a group of local fishermen playing away at their instruments during a glimpse of free time from hauling in their daily catches, sending teetering notes from banjos, violins, and bag pipes through the freezing air.

"Over there," Carson said, gesturing to stables resting under a large oak tree.

Several horses of varying colors were tied to their stalls, eyes looking around absentmindedly while they munched on their breakfast. An old, overweight man with a diplomatic seal stood beside them smoking a cigar and messing with the mud on the ground with his boots. He clearly worked for one of the richer families of the region, likely supplying them with horses for long journeys. He wouldn't be able to chase them, and for that, he'd make an easy target to steal from.

Enya cast a wicked smile, reaching for the blade at her belt.

A bullet zipped by her then, narrowly missing her head. Pedestrians scattered, screaming and trying to escape the scene in a trod of horses and desperate feet.

The princes hid themselves behind carriage carts, and Enya and Carson flew behind barrels of fish. Right before they slipped through the mud behind cover, another shot rang out, hitting a child next to Enya. She gasped as blood misted her face, and the little girl fell.

More death, more senseless loss. Hollow eyes met hers from the ground, and hatred stirred in her heart.

Her hand instantly found her pistol while her other wiped the red from her cheeks.

A voice she recognized as belonging to Sean, the leader of the Wraiths, boomed over the surprised neighing of horses and civilian cries. "Give it up, Raven."

His boots crunched atop the soggy dirt and mulch road, and Enya saw that he paced with a rifle in his hands. Sean was an older gentleman, one that you'd never expect to be such a powerful gang leader. His salt and pepper hair framed a wrinkled face, and green eyes scanned the scene with contempt. Sean had never liked that such a young girl held so much power in the country, and he'd always done what he could to minimize that.

It seemed he'd finally found his opportunity.

Jia was nowhere to be found, likely hiding on the roof of a nearby shop waiting to strike—and likely also desperate to get back in his good graces after her recent failure.

Sean continued, "We're not in the mood to play these childish games. We want our money from the palace, and you know the Wraiths don't back down from a silly challenge." He fired a few warning shots in the air, making Enya flinch with each rumble through the streets. "You've made quite a bit of trouble for me recently. Almost cost me my best sharpshooter.

Do you have any idea how hard it is to find Tobuhanian soldiers these days?"

Carson already had his gun at the ready beside her. He only needed her signal, and they could take this guy down.

"You can thank Lucian for that!" Enya hollered before she could stop herself. Sean's head snapped in their direction, and she cursed, ducking further behind her cover. Carson gave her a dirty look, and she shrugged. Screw it. "He told your men to fire when she was still in the train car."

Sean tsked, slowly stalking closer. "I've taken care of him. Let's just say he's learned his lesson and won't make the same mistake again. Or any mistakes again." He cleared his throat. "Now, are you going to give me what I want, Raven, or will I have to take it myself?"

Enya's lips curled back into an unpleasant sneer. Even the Blood Spiders didn't give her Grims this much trouble. How much were these trigger-happy idiots being paid by the queen?

"You're outnumbered, Sean. It's not worth it," Enya yelled back. She lifted her head to peek at him and another bullet shot past her, this time grazing her jacket by only a few hairs. With her heart thumping, her head darted back down. "Let's talk about this."

Carson cast her a quick nod, running his hand quickly across her shoulders for comfort before moving to steady his gun over their cover. The action helped to settle her quickening pulse, but not the adrenaline rushing through her veins. Enya couldn't risk death. The Grims needed her intel to keep their upper hand in the rebellion and against Sean.

She lifted up a tiny mirror from her inner coat pocket,

using its reflection to search for Jia knowing full-well that if they could disarm her, they could get the hell out of here.

This member of the Wraiths was hiding almost too well, but not well enough.

Enya spotted Jia above a deli with her eyes glued to the Raven like a hawk as she aimed her weapon. It appeared she was using a scope to see better when she fired.

But how could she get up there and take her out?

Her eyes landed on a few wooden boards laying on a nearby cart, ones that seemed to form a ramp up to some signs and poles on the side of the building to her left.

Bingo. Enya grinned to herself, readying her feet to move.

"I'll take her out. Once I do, I need you to help the princes escape on those horses over there." She nodded over to the stables while speaking to Carson. This would work. It had to work. "I need you guys to meet me by the train tracks in the woods in the direction of Thomond—alive, preferably."

He frowned. "What about you?"

"There's enough for all of us. I just have to grab one on my way out," Enya said with a shrug, as if it would be so simple. Maybe it would be for once.

Carson gave a terse nod, and she was about to be on her way when he caught hold of her wrist. She turned to him in surprise, his grip warming her skin like a crackling woodland fire, raw with energy. "Be careful," he said gruffly before letting go.

With that, she was gone. She was lucky a rusty blue cart of coal kept her from being hit head on, but a few more of Jia's bullets sped by, ricocheting off the shop behind her and shattering glass windows. Enya flew behind the wall of the building, breathing hard. But she still couldn't shake the fear entrenching her body. Jia was much more skilled in military combat, and all Enya had to show for herself were some dirty tricks honed from her years on the streets. Even if they didn't use their weapons, there was still the matter of hand-to-hand combat, one that Enya wasn't sure she'd win against this Tobuhaian soldier.

With a grunt of effort, Enya was flying up the wooden planks, ones that threatened to break with every strangled creak. She caught hold of a fish-shaped sign and pulled herself up, holding back a cry from the pain in her hands.

Her weak fingers and feet felt for cracks and ridges in the building's brick wall, and soon Enya was up on the roof, laying low.

She crouched down, careful to stay behind the cover of chimneys and roof accents atop the gray tile at her feet. It only took one shot—one bullet to end this. But she wouldn't be going down without a fight, and she certainly wasn't going to let any of her crew get hurt.

So far, it didn't seem that Jia had noticed her escape onto the roof, and Enya let herself breathe a sigh of relief. She crawled across the rooftops. Soon, Enya reached a rope that would lead her to the top of the deli from the back and out of Jia's scope. With a grunt, she dropped down its tendrils, careful not to let go no matter how many obscenities her hands screamed at her. A few villagers caught sight of her, but she didn't falter. Not when there was so much to lose.

She carefully lifted onto Jia's hiding space, keeping low and out of sight. The sharpshooter was before her now but didn't seem to have heard her just yet while still aiming at

Enya's previous cover.

Without warning, Jia spun around with a snarl, knocking Enya to the ground just as she was about to take her down. Enya hissed in pain, cradling her now bruised knees which she'd used to land on the stone floor. She flew for cover behind an air vent, narrowly dodging a fire of lead that ripped through the metal by her left hand.

"This might sound trite, but any last words?" Jia purred. Her footsteps neared, one after the other.

Enya called out, "We can help you. We know Sean treats you like crap; he left you to die back on that train, for saints' sake. Help us. Do something right for a change." Not everyone was too far gone, and if rumors were true, Jia was not only Sean's best shot but also his best merchandise to sell around the slums.

As if realizing this, Jia hesitated, hand lowering slightly. But the moment was short-lived.

"He'd kill me if I left. I have to do this, Enya."

Without waiting to hear any more, Enya kicked out her foot, wincing at the bolt of pain that seared up her hip from the fall. Her leg looped around Jia's, and she came tumbling down on top of her. The rifle was skittering out of the woman's hands, and now Enya just had to hope she had no dagger. But that would have been a mistake to assume.

She deftly whipped out her blade, and they struggled on the ground. Jia took a hold of Enya's wrists and pinned her to the roof, her breathing slightly labored.

"Why are you helping these princes?" Jia asked between ragged breaths, sneering. "What's in it for you?" She smashed Enya's hand against the ground until she let the dagger go. It clattered harmlessly somewhere nearby.

Enya felt afraid. Afraid for her life, afraid it would all end like this … the princes left alone to care for themselves, her relationship with Carson teetering dangerously on the edge between friendship and something else. Panic seized her breath and nearly every ounce of courage she had left. "You think I'm doing this because I want to?" She wasn't sure why she was even saying this, but she was desperate. "No amount of money in the world would convince me to save a few royal bastards. Not after how they've treated this country."

In the gleam of faint sunlight through the clouds, she caught sight of a pendant hanging from Jia's neck. Saint Zopa, of patience.

How ironic.

Enya begged herself to believe they were worth all this trouble. That finding the sword and defeating the Crimson Witch just meant they'd have time afterwards to sort out the rebellion. Maybe they could find a new king. Maybe one of these princes would be worth defending as a king, too. Maybe the Grims could be a part of that—could be the *leaders* of that.

Maybe things would change.

She kneed her between her legs, and her adversary's breath caught. Jia groaned and fell back. Only a few inches, but it was enough.

Enya sprung onto her feet, catching the woman in a head-lock. Jia was fervently trying to buck her off, clawing at her arms, but it was no use. With serious effort, she managed to elbow Enya in the ribs. Air escaped Enya's lungs, and her arms slipped. Now this Wraith was running.

Enya reached for her pistol to fire, but the Tobuhanian

soldier had already disappeared over the edge of the roof. Her belt was also empty, which earned a hefty round of curses from Enya. That vile woman had stolen it during the struggle.

Enya sprinted to the edge of the roof, eyes searching for her crew. They were gone, and she could only hope that meant to safety and not captured. There was no sign of Jia or anyone else in the now deserted street. Curious locals and creatures of the woods were now hesitantly filling up the empty space.

Blood spotted the dirt behind the barrels of fish she'd hidden behind only minutes prior. Her breath caught. Carson was the only guy she knew she could rely on no matter what. He was her best friend, her closest confidant, and he already had an injured shoulder.

What if Sean had finished the job and taken the princes hostage? What if she'd failed them?

Enya's heart pounded in her chest, but it wasn't adrenaline now, though there was still plenty of that. It was fear, and she *was* afraid. Afraid all of this had been for nothing and she was responsible for the deaths of her friends.

She shook her head, begging those negative thoughts to stop. Now was time to grab the horse and hope they'd made it to the train tracks unscathed.

Icy air blew Enya's hair off her shoulders when she dropped down onto the sloshy earth below after grabbing her dagger. A few chickens scampered by, startling her, and she had to be wary there weren't any other surprise visitors waiting in the shadows. She didn't hesitate when she hopped onto the remaining horse in the stables, though he still seemed pretty spooked by what had just occurred. He was dark and beautiful, with black hair and an even darker mane.

He would do just fine. With her pained hands clutching his reins, she was off to find Carson and the princes.

Enya would thank the saints if she made it that far.

14

Thomond, Skeyya

SNOW WAS falling heavily now. It was damp and beautiful, stringing through Enya's hair and the horse's mane while they trotted along the train tracks north. The beast's hooves crunched atop the earth, cracking leaves and twigs that had managed to snag their way onto the wooden panels that lined her path.

Several horse tracks left indents in the earth and headed in the same direction, so she assumed that Carson and the princes couldn't have been far. She was right.

Their voices soon cut through the hollow quiet.

"…we can't just stay here! We'll be killed if we're caught—by humans or fae," Rowan exclaimed. "I don't know about you, pretty boy, but I'd rather not be turned into some troll's snack."

Enya flushed. He must have been talking to Carson and being a royal pain in the ass, as usual.

With a sigh of relief, she snapped her reins and swerved into their direction. The horse beneath her complied, huffing his displeasure at their change in pace. Enya ran a soothing hand over his mane, and he leaned into it eagerly, seemingly unused to such affections. Not everyone was kind to animals, especially those used for labor. It made her sick to think of how the king used to treat his own horses.

Enya eased through the mossy brush to find her crew all together in a clearing waiting for her. Each boy was seated atop his nickering creature, not seeming to have taken a break from riding. But considering the circumstances, none of them could really afford one.

They'd be reaching the war front soon. Bullets and bombs awaited them—and whatever new weaponry either Brasova or Skeyya had created for the deadly skirmish.

White, frosty plains would be covered in crimson speckles. Enya had no doubt.

"Took you long enough," Rowan muttered, taking a swig from a flask of water stashed inside his jacket. "We were just about to leave without you." Both Beacon and Niall's faces darkened. They too seemed to be growing exhausted of their brother's snarky behavior.

Carson didn't even try to hide his disdain, letting out a scoff. "No, we weren't. If anyone's getting left behind, it's you." His eyes shifted to Enya's as his hand ran slowly over his gunshot wound. A silent promise of protection even in the worst of times; of loyalty sworn even after everything they'd been through. Even after she'd rejected him. Warmth brewed under her skin at his comment, igniting summer inside her despite the wintry air, but she ignored it. Now wasn't the time.

Would there ever be a time?

"Good." Enya gave a light cough, gesturing to the endless trees with a nod of her head. "What do you boys say we hightail it out of here before Sean and his goons catch up?"

They turned their horses north. It seemed that surviving another day was something they could all agree on. Staying out here meant likely being eaten or shot at by elusive Brasovian scouts, and considering the looming threat of the Crimson Witch, Enya was all too eager to get out of Belsale.

With that, they followed Carson's compass north towards their destination. Their horses kept them awake, but exhaustion still clawed at their eyes, willing them to close and take them away with winter's never-ending wind. Sleep was so, so desirable in moments like these. Moments of focus and adventure out in the seemingly dark and foreboding woods were often plagued by such desires.

It wasn't nightfall yet, but it would be soon.

Signs of other villages and cities passed, but they didn't stop. They couldn't stop. The Grims and these princes had to get to Thomond before anything else got in their way. Before any more monsters—human or faerie—decided today would be a good day to cross Enya and her team.

Her fingers searched for a pistol that wasn't there, and her chest tightened with fear that wouldn't leave.

Their breaths were frosting now. Snow hadn't slacked off since Enya had entered the forest, and it didn't seem to be letting up anytime soon.

Winter flurries, reminding them of the desperate need for shelter, danced across the sunset sky, matching celestial orange and red with white. Wind swept the display down, earning a quick chatter of teeth and shudder from Enya. They found rest near a creek close to the train tracks with her and Carson taking turns keeping watch for creatures of the woods and all other kinds of monsters that could be lurking around.

And, thankfully, she'd actually been able to steal a moment to work on her next letter. Somehow the wrinkled and weak paper had made it this far. She could update the Grims on their journey and inform them of Sean's threat to the gang. More blood would be shed, but such was the way with scoundrels in the slums. Perhaps a few broken fingers. Or perhaps the loss of a few fingers.

Decisions, decisions.

But the cold wasn't letting up, and the princes huddled together for warmth. They'd need to find better coats—and fast. Their pitifully small fires did little to quell the ice stinging their faces and leeching the strength from their limbs.

Enya's bones screamed at her for sleep, and her eyes struggled to stay open.

She'd never taken on a job that lasted this long. Usually it would be work around the city. Maybe scouring factories or strongholds for supplies, but never so much walking, running, and riding. Of course, those jobs were usually dangerous, but never as much as the one they were currently on.

The Crimson Witch. A demon desperate to gain control

of the country and someday the world with the help of her army. One who could change faces and who knew what else. Just thinking about it sent further shivers down Enya's spine, earning a cock of the head from her right-hand man, his eyes lowering to take in her appearance. Flames made his soft irises nearly glow, and she had to look away, her heart picking up pace.

Enya could only hope that they'd survive and end this madness. If they could do that, she could go back to her gang and the rebels and maybe, just maybe, find some peace for herself once they overthrew the tyrannical king on the golden throne.

It was worth a shot.

Their journey to Thomond was a blur of trotting hooves and crunching leaves. Of snow and ice and cold whispering tales of frostbite and death in their ears, which stung from the increasing wind.

In a sort of guarding maneuver, Enya and Carson eventually decided to flank the three princes a few meters back with their animals. That way they could watch them from behind and make sure nothing grabbed them on their journey. It seemed a good enough idea. That is, until she realized she'd be more or less alone with him.

For some reason she couldn't name, that thought unnerved her like nothing else. Much more than the idea of guns or broken bones.

The trees were quiet on their journey and darkness settled over the lands like a wicked blanket, prompting Rowan to flicker his lighter to life. Enya thought it was too bad that the magick stone had lost its luster. It would have been way more useful now. According to Carson and his apparent knack for reading stars, they weren't too far from their destination. It would be only about an hour or so until they'd reach Thomond's gates.

"Did you ever think we'd get wrapped up in something like this?" Carson mused, finally breaking the silence which had so effortlessly wrapped around the trees that surrounded them. "Helping royalty. Saving the world. That kind of stuff."

Enya smiled slightly, turning to look at him beside her. In the dark, he was hard to see, but she could make out his features just enough to see that he was smiling too. "No, I didn't. I figured that any royalty crossing our path would earn us a good ransom, though," she said, shooting a glance back up to the princes. "But they seem different."

She hoped Rowan didn't catch wind of this conversation and mock her for it later, the royal prick that he was.

Carson nodded. "They do," he said, clearing his throat. His gaze cast upward for a moment, as if searching the stars for answers to questions he wouldn't ask. But Enya didn't press him. "Do you think we seem different?"

The question caught her off guard.

"Different how?" Enya let loose a nervous laugh, but her smile fell. What a strange thing to ask. Her horse neighed impatiently, as if also waiting for him to hurry up with his strange questions. She gave it a few soothing pats.

Carson shrugged. "I don't know. Ever since we left the city, things between us … they seem to have changed."

Her breath caught, and for a moment it felt like she could fly right off her horse. Did he notice her like she had been noticing him? Was it bad that she had? Was she going to lose her best friend? Enya gulped, unwilling to say anything and risk any of that happening.

He took her silence as a cue to continue.

"Not that I'm bothered by change!" Carson promised, scratching the back of his head. "Change can be good—better, even. I'm sorry. I'm rambling, aren't I?"

Enya nodded, her heart fluttering. "You are."

But she liked this kind of rambling. It made her feel good, but it also scared the crap out of her. They were best friends. He was her right hand in the Grims. This was a dangerous conversation to be having. Enemies could use this, whatever this was, against them. Her own stupid, annoyingly negative mind could use it against her, too.

But she didn't know if she wanted this sort of change.

What if she lost him? What if she lost herself?

"I realize this might not be the best time to say this, but Enya ..." Carson cleared his throat, wincing slightly as he held his wounded shoulder, his calloused fingers slicked faintly with dark red that gleamed in the moonlight. "You know I care about you. I always have ever since you rescued me. You're like this crazy force against nature. You're strong—so strong. You kick ass like it's nothing and fight to give this country what it deserves. Ever since we were kids, I've looked up to you, but now ..."

She stilled, holding her breath and trying to ignore the way her heart hammered against her ribcage.

"Enya, I think I want us to be more than friends."

With those few words, her entire world spun around her. This wasn't how she'd imagine their friendship going. Hell, this wasn't how she'd even imagine a relationship starting. Not while they were on the run in the woods with a bounty on her head from the king, tracking down an ancient demon, and escaping a rival gang.

It was unexpected, to say the least.

But did she feel the same? Did she want a relationship? Enya had never felt like that was something in the cards for her. It always felt out of reach. Something she'd *maybe* do once this whole rebellion thing was sorted out.

"Carson, I ... I really don't know what to say," Enya said quietly, and she meant it.

Silence was back, suffocating and cruel and filling Enya's mind with regret.

She snuck a look at him, and her chest grew tight when she saw how fast his face had fallen. As if sensing her gaze, Carson's features hardened. His stoic mask, one that was all too familiar when he was upset, was now back in place.

Carson had opened himself up to her. He was honest and he thought she was strong, a force against nature. *Her.* But instead of letting him in, she'd shut him out and practically crushed his feelings like acorns in the woods. Enya felt wrong and stupid and all sorts of messed up.

They were just supposed to be partners in crime, not ... lovers, or whatever else people who wanted to be more than friends did.

I'm just not ready. She really wasn't.

They had too much going on. *She* had too much going on. There was a rebellion to take care of and an evil witch to take out. Was it guilt that clawed up her throat and sealed her lips?

You lost him before he was even yours.

That thought sent a few tears running down her cheeks, and she gave a light kick to the horse's side. The creature sped up until she was beside the princes, and she breathed a sigh of relief to have some distance from the emotional carnage she'd wreaked only paces away.

With them, it was complicated, and it was messy, and Enya still didn't know why the hell her past scared her so much. But at least they didn't make her feel … like this.

When Enya and the others neared the crumbling outer walls of Thomond, she halted them with a quick, leather-clad hand.

The rumbles of war shook the earth, making trees sway and bricks threaten to give. In the distance, rifles popped off and bombs erupted, sending black into the faintly blue morning sky.

They had reached the border between Skeyya and Brasova, and spilled blood and shouts had come to greet them. Even from here, Enya could see the corpses of soldiers dotting the icy ground. This had once been a bustling city full of trade between two peaceful nations. But King Eamon's military seemed to have driven an iron wedge between such hopes and memories.

Slowly, Enya crept close to the ground, nearing a bombed-out hole in the outer wall. Peeking over, the coast looked clear.

Her breath frosted in the air as she whispered, "Come on." She locked eyes with the princes first, finally landing her gaze on Carson, who was almost as cold as the landscape around them.

Slowly, he sighed. "Keep it moving, you three. Up we go."

Enya, first up, climbed over the ashy stone, her booted feet crunching the snow on the other side. Carson helped Rowan, Beacon, and Niall over while groaning at his injury before leaping over to join them. His muffled cries of pain made Enya grimace, but they couldn't dawdle too long.

There were no soldiers in sight. Not yet.

Towering buildings sprung up out of the streets in the hazy winter sunlight. Gothic design and history were etched into every wooden and stone structure that had managed to withstand heavy bombings and hailstorms of bullets. Being on the border to Brasova, if any of these dilapidated shops were open, there would have been scents of cabbage rolls and strudels wafting through the air and making morning bellies grumble for breakfast.

Scarcely, Enya could see a few of the city's inhabitants scurry for cover from enemy fire in case the war spilled back into this street, ones dressed almost completely in black and adorned in fur. In the mix, Enya could spot faerie folk, like nymphs and shapeshifters, ones with pointed ears like all other creatures of the woods.

But they were here to find a church, of which there were likely countless scattered around the city. Based off what Enya knew about the Brasovians, most of them more or less followed the fae religion centered around the goddess Eethra. Being that Enya had to make deals in the capital with visitors from all over the world, it was only practical that she learned the names and meanings of their saints.

Her mother had believed in them. But that hadn't saved her from an untimely death.

Enya refused to believe in anything but herself. Faeric magick was just that: magick. You didn't need to believe in some deity to believe in spirits or powers. There were some questions that she was content not knowing the answers to.

"You've been rather quiet," Rowan observed while they tied their horses' reins inside a set of stables on the outskirts of the city, away from sight. Enya had been, but she didn't think anyone would notice. "Something wrong?"

"Oh, no. I'm great." She forced a smile, but he didn't seem too convinced. With great restraint, she tugged her black gloves tighter against her hands, trying to ignore his gaze. She quickly added, "Leading three princes through demonic caves and war-torn countries has always been a dream of mine."

Why was this jerk even bothered?

"You don't seem fine," he pressed, eyeing her carefully. "Did something happen on the way here?"

Niall and Beacon were watching them now, but Carson had disappeared, likely to get a break from their group and smoke. Probably a break from Enya too. How funny this must have been to him. Royals caring about petty thieves and gang leaders? If she looked hard enough, she could see concern in his eyes.

It made her gulp. But she was also angry.

How dare he care for her? How dare any of them care for her?

She felt like a mess, and he must have noticed. Rowan looked over to where Carson had vanished before meeting her eyes. Whatever he saw shut him up.

"We need to get going," she said curtly, flipping her long waves over her shoulder. With one last pat on her horse, Enya led the princes through the crumbling city. Whether Carson followed or not was his own problem.

Never-ending shops and homes strung along the cobble-stone streets while fallen carriages and even a few run-down motor cars sat empty and abandoned in the street. If they want-ed to find this church, they needed to get in touch with some-one who knew the lay of the land. Maybe even someone who knew all about this Crimson Witch.

"Have any ideas of where to go, or are you just sight-see-ing for fun?" Rowan muttered, fixing his hair in the reflection of a nearby window. It seemed his arrogant attitude was back in full force. Enya thought he was honestly much more pref-erable that way.

"We need to find someone who knows where this church is, *Your Majesty*. Someone who knows about this whole … demon thing," Enya retorted.

Her eyes fell when she saw Carson catching up. If she tried hard enough to act like he didn't bother her, maybe she could even pretend things were still normal between them. When Carson arrived, his arms were crossed as best as some-one with a bullet wound in their shoulder could cross them, and he refused to look at her. *Or maybe not.*

They peered around the square, searching for anyone who looked like they might fit the description—and for any signs of the battle. Blasts still echoed through the city, but they sounded like they were getting farther away. Enya couldn't help the relief that spiraled through her chest, but her heart sank when the consequences of war really set in. When the sorrow and loss of the bodies littering the ground sang out to her and made her stomach turn.

This had once been a gorgeous city full of people. Full of mothers, fathers, children. Eamon's greed had led to a pointless war that had taken who knew how many lives? That would take how many more? She had no clue, but his reign of tyranny had to end.

A young man raised his head from behind a broken sign, eyeing Enya and the others warily.

He seemed innocent enough, with short honey hair and a pinch of stubble atop a young face. His hazel eyes were friendly, and despite his tall, built figure looming over them in the sunlight, he didn't look to be an army man. A long black suit jacket was draped over his shoulders and he had a fur hat, one that sparkled in the sun.

"Do you all need help?" he asked, now moving over to stand before them. His voice held the typical sharp, melodic accent of a native Brasovian. "My name's Andrei. You don't look like you belong out here." His eyes raked over their ensembles, likely noting their lack of uniforms, and the princes shifted on their feet, straightening their coats and avoiding his prying gaze.

Enya hesitated. He seemed too eager, like he'd expected to find them here. "I'm Enya," she said carefully. "We actually do need help. We're looking for a church." Carson handed over his sketch of the map from the cave. Andrei pursed his lips, looking the wrinkled paper up and down before handing it back.

Andrei nodded, clicking his tongue. "Yeah, I've seen that place before. Do you need some help finding it? It ain't far."

Enya glanced up at their crew before speaking, trying to gauge whether there was mutual agreement on the matter. No one seemed to object to his suggestion. "That would be great."

With a gesture of his hands down the street, they began walking. Andrei kept rambling on about how it wasn't far and pestering them with way too many questions about where they were from and what they were doing so close to the border. But replies were kept to a minimum, considering the battle raging what had to be mere miles away and the fact that they hardly knew the man. Maybe it was just cultural differences that made him so friendly.

He had a friendly face, but in her experience, most monsters did. Enya held onto the dagger in her pocket the entire way to the church.

15

Thomond, Skeyya

THE CHURCH was beyond beautiful, but most Brasovian architecture was.

Stained glass windows, ones of every color, lit up the dusty white pews that filled up the space. Vessels of holy water made of faerie statues were strung along the ornately decorated walls, and a vast ceiling covered in art smiled down at Enya. She paced hesitantly along the aisle towards the alter. It was striking and sweet, something she'd never seen before.

Her heart felt full, and her mind was at peace, but that could have easily been from the colorful faerie charms hanging from the lights above them or the smells of sage and earth. This building was a striking contrast to the devastation waiting just outside the front door.

How had this church gone untouched? Unnoticed?

Enya stuffed her hands into her pockets and tried to act nonchalant while churchgoers regarded her and the gang curiously, as if they were specimens they'd like to observe. Or eat. Some of them watched them with dangerous eyes, as if they knew something they didn't. Winter Court fae were nearly always suspicious, and they preferred to kill first and ask questions later, making them brutal when it came to fighting.

Miriana was the only exception to that, but Enya liked to think of her as not being defined by normal standards when it came to, well, anything. Trauma had changed her for the better.

"Here we are," Andrei announced, plopping down casually on a scratchy white bench near the alter. "The Church of Astru. Finest Unseelie church in all the lands."

Enya couldn't help the odd feeling that clawed its way into her gut at the thought of Andrei accompanying them any further.

"I guess we'll be seeing you around then," she said with a dismissive wave, motioning to the exit with a nod of her head. Something didn't feel right, and she wanted to be rid of the rat before he bit anyone.

This didn't seem to faze him. "No, I'd like to tag along. You all seem like you're going on an adventure, and that's my specialty."

Carson and the princes exchanged uneasy glances, and Enya's hand on her dagger tightened.

One of the nearby faerie priestesses hissed through her pointed teeth once she'd spotted Andrei. Her long tendrils of silver hair whipped behind her as she crept up to him. At her pale throat were several bones woven into a necklace, and she wore a billowing black dress that brushed along the stone floor. Without hesitation Enya flung out her blade and Carson his pistol.

"*Orias,*" she spat. Enya knew enough of the language of Brasova to translate that as *monster.* "You have no place within these sacred walls. Leave now."

The creatures of the woods and Banya who had cultivated in the church turned to look at him with hatred in their eyes. Sparks of power brewed at their fingertips, dark as night in their smoke.

"What are you guys talking about?" she demanded, unsure whether to turn her weapon on the faerie folk or the stranger sitting before them. The gut feeling was only getting stronger, making her nearly bend over and gag. Saints, she felt sick.

Carson didn't hesitate. He sprung onto Andrei and caught him in a headlock, pointing the gun directly to his temple.

"Now, now, no need to get hot and bothered," Andrei said flippantly with a roll of his eyes. There was no hint of emotion in his voice. It was as if his veins had filled with ice. Enya swallowed hard.

What the hell had they gotten themselves into?

"Who are you?" Carson barked, pressing his pistol harder against the man's temple. This only earned a sinister laugh, one that chilled Enya to her core. It sounded vile and wrong, like fingernails on chalkboard.

The priestess whispered a few words in that magical foreign language so many faerie creatures shared, one accented by her Brasovian heritage, and manifested a sword made of ice before their eyes, one bedazzled with onyx and jade crystals. Gasps and murmurs filled the church as patrons huddled together, eyes on the newfound visitors and their companion.

Enya refused to be afraid. Not in front of all these people. She shoved past the building crowd, lifting her dagger up to Andrei's face.

"Tell us what you know, or we'll gut you like a trout," she snapped, running the blade down along his cheek until reaching his neck, where she pressed against his jugular. She would show no mercy here, and especially not to a demon's pet. "The Grims don't like playing games, and you're beginning to take up way too much space in this church."

"Find the sword and then we'll talk," Andrei said with a smile. In a sudden flash of mist, he was gone.

Carson nearly fell over when the man vanished, and Enya had to steady him, much to his dismay. He shrugged her off and she flushed. Maybe this was their new normal: avoiding each other.

The priestess spoke, drawing their attention back towards the sea of deadly fae. "I'm Galina, the leader of this sacred place and devoted follower of Eethra." She watched Enya and her crew with distrustful eyes, and Enya didn't blame her considering they'd shown up in company with a sworn enemy of theirs. The priestess continued, "Why have you come to this place?"

Lying risked the penalty of death. Enya weighed her options carefully. If they told them the truth, they might earn another ally here. Since the fae courts trapped the Crimson Witch, perhaps they'd like to ensure she didn't escape. Or end the world and kill everyone.

She sighed. *Very well.*

"We come seeking a wand, and eventually the Sword of Bas. We just got back from finding the Pentacle of Glac," Enya finally replied, lowering her dagger back into her belt.

"So, you seek to set the Crimson Witch free." Galina let loose a deadly chuckle. "For that you will die." She raised the shimmering sword above her head, poised to strike, and Enya heard an intake of breath from the faerie folk who had gathered around them.

"Wait!" Beacon exclaimed, shoving Niall and Rowan behind him with hands on their chests. "We're trying to kill her."

Galina paused the weapon in mid-air. "You are?"

Carson exhaled in relief at her hesitation and added, "She's got a hold on the palace right now through the queen. We think she's trying to take over the world."

"So, you seek the Sword of Bas to *kill* the Crimson Witch. How noble of you," Galina scoffed, making her sword disappear just as fast as it came to be with a quick flourish of her hands. "No human has ever made it this far. We faerie folk put many pieces in place to make it impossible, and yet here you stand."

Another priestess and Banya, this one draped in a deep, maroon dress against dark brown skin lifted her head to regard the bunch. She came to stand beside Galina, placing her hand on her shoulder. Golden bands wrapped around her neck and wrists, ones that shone in the faint lantern light from above their heads.

"Perhaps they have proven their spirit then," she remarked in a silvery voice. "Or perhaps they have proven their stupidity. It's a fool's errand to try and kill this demon, especially for mere humans."

Enya rolled her eyes at her backhanded compliment.

"We didn't come here to be talked down to. We need that wand if we stand any chance against the Crimson Witch," Rowan retorted, clenching his jaw to hold back what Enya had no doubt would have been a biting remark.

"The Wand of Tine," Galina said flatly, her expression growing dark and haunted. *The Wand of Fire.* How inviting. "With every object you find, the Crimson Witch's power only grows."

Enya gaped at her for a split second before quickly shutting her mouth, trying to piece together this new information as the gears turned in her head.

That changed everything. This entire time, they thought they were getting one step closer to taking away her power and taking her down. But to know they were only giving her more leverage to use against them and the country? An unwelcome shiver ran down her spine, igniting a fierce wave of nausea in her stomach. Carson met her gaze, and a million thoughts passed between them. Above all emotions in his expression, guilt was the most noticeable. Even the princes appeared displeased, what with their frowns and scowls.

This wasn't what they'd planned. Not at all.

What kind of darkness were they allowing to spread across the country? Across the world?

Her hands balled into painful fists at her sides. *Murderer. Traitor. Deceiver.* Those thoughts were back, and her past was upon her once again, clawing at her like a wounded animal in a trap begging to be noticed. Begging to be seen. It almost knocked the breath out of her to acknowledge. She had to get those memories to shut up.

"What kind of power has been growing?" Niall asked quietly, breaking the deafening silence. "What have we done?"

Galina said nothing for a moment, instead walking over to the center alter of the chapel, her back to them as she rested her hands on the pages of a massive tome. She flipped through the pages with her slim, ringed fingers, and Enya neared to get a better look.

It was in Brasovian, but on the gold-edged paper were illustrations. Ones of a black female figure guiding an army of denizens in swirls of foreboding smoke. Of faeries both fleeing and fighting. Of fire and monsters that endlessly captured the homes of innocents.

Enya cut her gaze to Galina, who briefly closed her eyes in thought.

Her dry tone rang out, "This is the history of our people. The chronicles containing information on the four fae courts. We've faced many foes, but this one ... has given us significant trouble. It's not every day all courts must work together against a common adversary, and you should know some of us are practically at war with others in the fae realm. Do not step into this task blindly.

"I believe you're aware the Crimson Witch can change the faces of herself and her followers. That's common knowledge to all creatures of the woods and Banya alike. But with each magick item set free from where we've hidden it, she gains back one of her old powers. Before, she was trapped in the Black Lake with all her remaining creatures. Since you've discovered the pentacle, now some of them will be able to roam free and wreak havoc."

Out of the corner of Enya's eye, she could see the other priestess give a solemn nod, bowing her head. "If you find the Wand of Tine, she will be able to invade the dreams of those in the world who have connection to these magick items, and she will be able to possess them," the woman added.

Galina raised her head to look at her companion, obviously pleased with her recollection. "Yes, she's right. You're lucky that you haven't experienced any visions yet. The closer you get to the haunted woods that hold the wand, the more you'll experience hell on earth."

Enya swallowed the lump in her throat, straightening her back and trying to quell the sea of nerves in her belly. Hushed murmurs waded through the crowd of fae dotting the pews of the chapel.

This all sounded like some odd folk tale gone wrong. Like some sort of dark and twisted story an old woman might tell her grandchildren to keep them from straying too far in the woods, lest they be consumed by monsters.

"But," Galina continued, her index finger running down another illustration of demon-induced torment before she stepped away and turned back towards Carson and the princes. "I'm sure you're aware that the only way to stop the Crimson Witch and her army is to find these magick objects and use them against her. Aside from the obvious risks, we would be grateful to be rid of her. If she already has a hand in the palace, something must be done to stop her."

Enya kept her expression emotionless and cool as steel as she moved to stand by her companions. "Where is this haunted forest?" she asked. Now wasn't the time to show fear. They were promised payment, and now the world was depending on them to see this job through. "We came here to finish this, to destroy that demon and her army, and we aren't leaving this city without the wand. You can either help us, or we'll find it on our own."

Galina flashed an approving smile, one filled with sharp teeth, as she laced her hands behind her back. "What strong words coming from a wanted criminal. You shouldn't be surprised that a priestess of the goddess is well informed of the Raven and her deeds," she commented.

In some ways, Enya would be flattered that they were keeping tabs on her, but it was more than likely they only noticed her past when they walked into the church. High fae and their priestesses were always capable of more skilled abilities than their counterparts.

But Enya wasn't that important to the rebellion. Not yet.

"We can help you find the forest, but we would not dare enter," Galina continued. "It is overrun by our guardians, but they've been possessed by the Crimson Witch. Unfortunately, we underestimated her power in that regard. Doina here can assist you." She motioned to a creature of the woods standing up against the far wall.

The woman had pointed ears that held several metallic earrings. Her pale arms were laced with bands covered in runes and foreign markings, and she wore an embroidered blue coat lined with black fur. Her dirty white hair was twisted into a long, tight braid across her shoulders. Doina flashed them a sarcastic smile, one that showed full lips painted in red. She was beautiful, just like all the rest of the women in the church.

"I'll help you humans, but only because my priestess wills it." She shrugged, kicking off the wall and stalking towards them. In the light of the lanterns above them, Enya could make out a jagged sword at her belt. "Let's just hope you can keep up with a Winter Court fae."

Enya rolled her eyes. She wasn't going to be outdone by some strange Brasovian creature of the woods, wicked or otherwise. But that didn't keep her from flinching when she realized how Carson wouldn't stop staring at Doina. He looked her up and down, mouth agape. He might as well have been drooling.

Something powerful made Enya's blood boil and her fists clench tightly at her sides, but she refused to believe it was jealousy. She'd just told him she didn't know what she felt, and she meant it. But she couldn't help the tightness in her chest when she looked at the ground feeling … whatever it was she was feeling.

A rumble outside made the building shake, those inside letting out cries of surprise at the intensity. That blast was close. Too close. The battle had returned in full force, and shouts and shots howled outside. Galina's expression turned sour, like spoiled milk, and her lips curled back in disgust.

"That settles it then." She flattened her palms against her dress, trying to regain her stoic demeanor. She turned to a few nearby followers. "Grab these visitors some weapons and garments more suited to the conditions surrounding our harsh mountains. We'll all go into our shelter below and remain until the streets have cleared. We can worship in the dining hall, if need be."

Enya hadn't realized how gross they must have looked. Clothes soaked in bog water and ripe with gunpowder. They hadn't bathed in days and probably smelled awful. Galina shot her a cold, knowing look, as if reading her thoughts.

"And get them a bath. I don't want them stinking up my church or our living spaces below-ground," she ordered, waving everyone towards a nearby wooden door.

203

"Wait," Enya said, startling the priestess as she had just begun to leave. "My friend here, Carson, his shoulder is hurt from a gunshot wound. Can you fix it?"

Galina considered this for a moment, looking Carson up and down while he stood beside Enya, gripping a wooden pew for support. "Very well. I'll have a healer see him before you rest for the night."

It looked like they were in good hands. But after what happened with Andrei, Enya couldn't help but keep her guard up. Who knew what other followers of the Crimson Witch hid among them?

16

Thomond, Skeyya

BENEATH THE Church of Astru, dimly lit corridors held various rooms for guests, baths, and storage holds for a plethora of packaged goods and sweet-smelling spices.

At the end of one such hall, in their bathhouse, row after row of lanterns hung from the ceiling, giving the room a vivacious, golden glow. Steam wafted up and swirled in the humid air as Enya lounged, eyes closed. She sighed happily as she relaxed further against the stone backing of her pool, which smelled faintly of jasmine and sandalwood. The water did well to alleviate the stress and sore muscles resulting from the arduous journey to Thomond.

Enya opened her eyes.

Moonlight seeped in from an opening in the ceiling, and she could faintly make out a few stars in the sky. The priestesses had installed some sort of cover in the exterior of the building, keeping any black smoke from the explosive commotion outside from flowing in.

Beautiful was a word Enya liked to save for special occasions, and it seemed to fit well in describing the scene before her.

Galina had mentioned on their way underground that the only sort of plumbing in this section of the city was all linked up to a hot spring nearby, so the water was thick with minerals and fresh against Enya's skin as she sunk deeper into her stone tub.

She breathed in deeply and tried to forget the day. But unfortunately, the day would not soon be forgotten.

They were being watched.

She didn't know exactly by whom, but she knew the feeling of curious and malicious eyes when they bore into the back of her neck. Ever since they'd arrived in the city, something had felt off. After the incident with Andrei, Enya was certain that they'd need to be more on guard if they wanted to finish this mission.

The Crimson Witch could change the appearance of any of her followers to make them do her bidding.

Anyone around them could be a traitor.

Enya sighed and rose out of the water, flinching at the frigid air that quickly caught her in its embrace.

Her hands felt for a towel, and soon she was on her way back to her room to get dressed, passing woven tapestries depicting Saint Dumitru and Saint Dina, those of sacrifice and spirits. She may not have been religious by any means, but knowledge was power, and power allowed her to succeed over her enemies. And avoid zealous mobs, if need be. On more than one occasion the Grims had desecrated a religious monument in their scuffles and, well, Enya would prefer to avoid such fallouts again.

Thankfully those in the Church of Astru seemed to be more or less tame. She grimaced to herself in thought.

Enya hoped it stayed that way.

Her feet left small puddles with every step on the cold, uneven stone floor. No one else seemed to mind her bare flesh; they were fae, after all. Carson and the princes were likely already in the main room having supper.

Inside her room was nothing particularly remarkable. Sheep skins and pelts adorned a feather mattress on the stone floor. Brasovian artwork covered much of the walls, and a simple Banya charm kept three glowing orbs circling each other on the ceiling to chase darkness away. Enya noticed most lanterns were simply magical orbs, but the thought brought her peace.

Magick could keep one safe if done by the right faerie.

"Do you require anything, human?" a female voice sounded behind her, making her heart pound and her feet nearly slip before she spun around. Where the devil was her dagger when she needed it? She hated being caught off guard. Before her was the priestess who had spoken with Galina in the chapel. "You may call me Sorcha, as well."

Enya felt a flush of embarrassment heat her cheeks, and she clenched the towel around her chest tighter, earning a throb of pain from her joints. "Yeah, some privacy would be nice. And to not be snuck up on in my own room," she replied curtly, furrowing her brows.

Sorcha nodded, her face emotionless and still.

"Very well. Supper will be down the hall. It's going to be meatball soup with sour cream. One of our followers also thought to roast some local vegetables if you're not the meat-eating type. Though, we source from our own pigs the soldiers haven't found yet." She said the words carefully, as if a human would not understand as easily as a Banya or faerie could.

Meanwhile, Enya, still dripping wet and practically naked, waited impatiently for her to leave. She did not. Enya held back the urge to toss her out, instead rolling her eyes practically all the way back into her raven-haired head.

"Thank you. I'll be down shortly," she said with a tight smile. With that, Sorcha left in silence, closing the bedroom door behind her. Enya sighed, her shoulders falling in relief.

She couldn't remember Miriana acting so ... odd, a thought that made her smile become more real. At least these folks were taking care of them. It would serve her well to remember that when their attitudes occasionally made her want to throw them from a balcony. She would not soon forget their acts of kindness; without them, they would likely be shivering out in an abandoned building somewhere, out of food and reeking of bog swamp. Maybe once this was all over, her gang could help them out in some way or another. Perhaps return the favor.

The clothes Galina had set out on the bed were not much different than the ones Enya had arrived in.

A black, wool trench coat buttoned above the waist and lined in black fur met her gaze. Equally dark slacks and a cotton shirt were placed beside the ensemble, and boots were stacked on the stone floor at her feet. They'd even had the courtesy to leave black gloves for her.

Her gloves made it easier to forget the pain that constantly plagued her fingers and joints. The burning that would come back every so often beneath her skin. But why? She didn't know. Recollection prickled her mind, reminding her she had done something horrible with those hands, but she could never remember what.

After putting on her new Brasovian getup, Enya headed to the main room where her companions were waiting with Galina and her followers. Beyond those with pointed ears were a few families seeking shelter from the war. They looked up from their cots, ranging from wee babes to old women. But the turmoil and loss outside made their faces haggard, with bags under their eyes and gaunt cheeks. Hope was minimal, but it shined in the eyes of a small child who stared at the Raven with her mouth agape.

Inside this expansive space laid several rows of wooden tables coupled with a small crowd feasting on the mentioned grub, whether on wooden benches or on the stone floor in their makeshift cotton beds. More Brasovian artwork hung neatly from the walls, and candlelight hanging from the ceiling sent small shadows flickering through the room. The food smelled inviting, and Enya's stomach growled. They hadn't eaten for a while, and it seemed that her body was finally noticing.

Standing to her left near the banquet table full to the brim with steaming delicacies, Enya saw Carson with Doina. He was chatting her up with charming small talk and laughs that had been so normal for Enya not too long ago. He moved his shoulder with ease while he caressed the girl's hair with his fingers. The healer must have already seen him.

Enya bit back a terrible scowl, something rude and wicked

rising in her chest. He'd moved on. Or perhaps this was pay-back for her rejection.

Doina was busy toying with his new acquired outfit after they sat together on the far side of the room. Her painted nails scraped playfully along the fur trim at his neck, and they laughed at some joke Enya couldn't hear. Without warning, their lips met.

Enya's stomach fell, and suddenly she wasn't very hungry at all. She might as well have been sick. He seemed to have moved on in no time at all. Like she was nothing. Like they were nothing.

If this was to make her jealous, he'd never hear the end of it from her or the other Grims. She'd make sure of that much. It was stupid, and it was cruel. A firm hand on her shoulder brought her away from her thoughts, and her eyes met Rowan's.

His stormy expression met hers, and he sighed.

"I know what you're thinking," he said, his brows knit-ting together. That only made her angrier. She was about to say something very nasty before the next few words left his mouth, stopping her dead in her tracks. "You deserve better than that, Enya."

She stared at him in shock. "What?"

He frowned, shrugging. What an odd thing for a prince to say. What an odd thing for a prince to … care in general.

Shaking her head, Enya looked away. "Never mind. Let's go eat."

He nodded, leading her to the banquet table first to load up on food, then to his brothers who were seated with Gali-na. The priestess gave her an indifferent nod, her eyes flitting briefly to Carson and Doina's display, then back to her. She knew, and perhaps she felt pity—if a Winter Court priestess was capable of such emotions.

The thought didn't comfort Enya while she spooned several hot bites of soup into her mouth. Its spiciness did well to distract her for the time being, though. With several gulps of plum brandy, she felt light enough to fly.

"This is the best food I've ever had," Beacon said with a grin, slurping a giant spoonful. He picked up his bowl and gulped it down, then turned to Niall. "Ah, man. Remind me to tell our chef back at the palace to serve more of this stuff."

Niall's lips twitched with a small smile. "There's the issue of war, brother. Do you think those back at Whitstone would enjoy eating their enemy's delicacies?"

"You and I both know this war is utter nonsense," Beacon retorted, pointing his spoon at him and dripping red sauce into his bowl. "Father is being a greedy buffoon."

Niall shrugged, staring down at his meatballs as he absently poked them with his fork. "What's new?"

Rowan straightened. "When I am king, we will no longer have these pointless wars. They're a waste of money and resources. Look around you," he said, gesturing to the crowded dining hall. "Do they look like monsters to you? Like our father tells us?"

"Like he tells the world," Beacon echoed, shaking his head. "You know he only does that to justify expansion."

Rowan let out an exasperated noise, earning a curious look from Enya as she dolloped some sour cream at the table onto her meal. Never in her life had she imagined royals talking like this.

Galina's voice made them all look up. "We can speak to

Eethra if you'd like. For guidance on the issues that brought you to our city." Her voice startled Enya and nearly made her knock over her glass of brandy. She'd been so quiet that the Raven had almost forgotten she was there at all.

Enya considered this. She'd always had her doubts about Finn and Miriana's religious beliefs and charms, but help was help. Anything they'd like to try she was willing to try too. Or at least watch *them* try.

The princes nodded in encouragement.

"That might be useful," Enya allowed, watching her carefully. "But I'm a little unsure how that would work. Doesn't the goddess have, uh, magick business to attend to?"

Galina laughed outright, the sound chilling and lacking any warmth, as expected from an Unseelie faerie. "Yes, she does. But with the right offering we can handle it. Just leave it to us."

She lifted out of her seat to meet with other church members conversing with a few of Thomond's refugees, ones who were organizing their meager belongings in tiny piles. Not long after, she circled the main room holding a wooden bowl stuffed with chicken and cow bones and herbs, murmuring in that unintelligible language once more.

The eyes of the priestess went black, and mist fell from the bowl and floated in the air around her curvy figure. It swallowed her like a gentle caress from the goddess, and those around her looked on in awe at the sight.

Enya was thankful for the help, but the scene erupting before her was starting to make her nervous.

She'd never been very religious, and most of the Grims could second that notion, but she couldn't deny the power rippling through the air from Galina's hands.

Other women of the congregation, this time Banya, gathered to dance in a circle around the priestess. Their dark linen dresses whipped around them just as much as their long hair, and suddenly screams erupted from their mouths. They froze, and Enya held her breath. Their arms came down to their sides, and Galina shot her savage black eyes to where Enya stood. Her mouth was agape, as if words would spill out at any second.

"The queen will turn into an abomination, a servant to evil and evil alone," Galina began, hands frozen in the air still holding the bowl of bones. They shimmered in the lantern light above. "The Crimson Witch will turn her smooth, pale skin into matted fur. Her pristine teeth will become jagged, ones that are capable of tearing flesh. Her eyes will be as red as the crimson blood flowing from the wrath of the demon herself.

"The Crimson Witch will test you. She will show no mercy in her viciousness. Be wary, visitors, for there is more to come. Do not believe everything you see," she said, voice echoing off the walls of the room. Her eyes turned back to normal, and the bowl of bones came to rest at her waist.

The queen will become a monster like no other.

Would she kill any of the royal family when that happened? Enya sighed, pinching the bridge of her nose. If the queen managed that, there was no telling what chaos would ensue.

"We still need to find the Wand of Tine, and we don't give up too easily," Enya finally said, looking at Carson. He was still wrapped around Doina, much to her dismay. At least the princes had the decency to keep to themselves.

Beacon nodded. "We have no choice. When can we leave?"

he asked, gazing over to Galina.

Niall grimaced, as if the thought of leaving would make him lose his dinner. Enya didn't blame him. It was going to be one hell of a ride.

"No, you must leave tomorrow when day has broken. These woods are not safe. When you reach the haunted forest, there are a few marked trees that will guide you," she explained, placing her bones on a nearby table and crossing the distance between them. Sorcha came to meet her, her hand now resting at Galina's waist.

If Enya didn't know any better, she'd say that they were lovers. Unless the Brasovians in Thomond had suddenly found a knack for invading personal boundaries, that is. That idea wasn't too far-fetched given the incident in her bedroom earlier.

Rowan gave her a bewildered look, but kept his mouth shut. Niall did the same.

Beacon just looked happy to see someone like-minded, based off his impossibly wide grin. Enya remembered his secret then and couldn't help but wonder if he'd reveal it soon. Hopefully, he would be accepted as they were here. He deserved not to live in the darkness with no one knowing who he really was. He deserved to be free.

What a strange thing to think about a prince.

"Tomorrow, then," Enya agreed, standing up to shake Galina's hand. She would make sure to give the Grims a good reputation in this city and the neighboring country. Maybe they'd get more help taking down Eamon in the future if they could manage to keep up their kindness. "We appreciate all your help, Galina."

The priestess smiled. "Good. You stand for the rebellion

and against that nasty king of yours who is to blaze his way into our country. You will return the favor down the line. I'm certain of this."

Enya almost sensed ... approval from the woman.

A tiny voice in the back of her head wondered at what secrets this priestess knew of her past.

Enya had offered many secrets to the capital city in return for favors during her time on the streets. She didn't like the idea of someone else holding all the cards, especially being the leader of the Grims. She was supposed to have a hand above everyone else, but lately she felt small. She felt like she was coming apart at the seams.

Galina spoke again, distracting her from her incessant thoughts. "Doina can cast a charm that will keep those on the war front from seeing you, should they cross your path. That and any spies lurking within the trees. But be warned, it's not an easy path to tread upon. You must be careful," she urged before returning to the festivities of the dining hall with Sorcha.

The rest of the night was a blur of blades and gunpowder. Of magick and dust. The members of the Church of Astru did their best to ensure Enya and her gang had more than enough in the way of weapons, and surely all the fur and wool in their outfits would protect against the frigid winter temperatures outside.

When Enya reached her bedroom after the flurry of small talk and being hurried around underground tunnels, stars of the northern sky danced across the walls in another sort of Banya charm. Sleep couldn't come soon enough to her. And sleep she did.

Her dreams did well to distract from the journey that

waited for them the next day, but the unease she felt never left. It sat beside her as she tossed and turned in her sheets.

Enya woke with a gasp, flying up in her bed. Her heart pounded wildly against her ribcage.

She had begun to remember glimpses of her past. Something about darkness coating the palace stables. Something happened there that had scorched her mind so horribly that she'd blocked it out. There was so much guilt teeming inside her as a result. So much shame.

The charm above her head, swirling with Banya magic, lit the room like a horrifying fire, like the waking nightmare she couldn't be rid of. She closed her eyes tight, and when she opened them, the room was normal once more. Thank the saints.

Her hands stung atop the sheepskin blankets, and she shook them, willing them to stop hurting and willing her memories to go away. She wasn't supposed to be like this. The Grims were strong, ruthless, and determined. They weren't scared. They weren't ashamed.

She hated this side of herself.

Ever since Enya had met those three dead princes again, all these strange feelings kept popping up. Flashes of memories she'd thought gone forever.

She had to be strong. She couldn't forget who she was.

Enya threw the covers away in a whirl and jumped to the stone floor. Her soiled clothes were in a wrinkled pile on a table against the far wall. She missed the normalcy of those clothes, but she clenched her jaw and left to meet with her companions.

If her past was shrouded in darkness, the least she could do was walk boldly into the bright new day. Any fearful thing those forests could muster would not be ready for her.

17

Thomond, Skeyya

THE ROAD to the mountain forest was bleak and empty, as if others knew better than to travel this path—including Brasovian and Skeyyan soldiers. Maybe her group didn't know better at all, but Enya held her head high, nonetheless, swaying inside her saddle.

"It's not that far now," Doina called over her shoulder to no one in particular. She seemed bored with this entire situation and much more interested in flirting with Carson. The two had been riding side by side, inseparable since they'd left the inner city of Thomond.

Enya didn't bother hiding her disgust. But she refused to believe it was jealousy. She chalked it up to Carson and

Doina's obvious ploy to piss her off. Perhaps it was working. Perhaps she'd hit him over the head later when she'd reached her limit.

She sighed, focusing on the path ahead.

Far in the distance, the booms of battle raged on, but they seemed to be in the clear as they maneuvered their beasts along the rocky and uneven dirt. Sunlight peeked through gray, foggy clouds. Snow would return soon, but for now they were only dealing with winter's stormy aftereffects. The trees around the stone path whistled and swayed in the freezing wind, and the slightest glimmer of ice pelted the ground below their horses' trotting feet.

Enya couldn't help but imagine life back in Arden and what was waiting for her after this mess of a job.

Miriana, Jackson, Finn, and Maxon were all waiting for them and watching the rebel bases in the capital—as responsibly as that bunch could, anyway. She'd probably have to sort out the finances of the Bowman's Pub and bolster up their warehouses when she got back. But what of the princes?

Enya glanced up at Rowan who was only a few paces in front of her. But what of the heir to the throne?

Would she have to kill him and his brothers or strike some sort of bargain with the palace? It seemed much more proactive to get Rowan on the rebel side. Though, she deemed that unlikely from the moment she met him. Beacon and Niall might have stood a better chance of that. The rebel cause needed them, even if they weren't the first in line for the throne. They could help overthrow the king and bring about a real change to the country.

But she knew now that she might hesitate to kill them or

harm them. Things were different. They'd seemed … changed. Maybe they could be the leaders this country needed after all.

"This has been a pretty peaceful ride, wouldn't you say, brother?" Beacon tossed a coin playfully at Niall who rode beside him, breaking the eerie silence. "It's too bad there isn't much to do out here. I'd give anything to be riding with a beautiful woman—present company excluded, of course."

Niall grinned slightly at his brother's attempt to lighten the mood. "When this is over, I'd prefer to hide back in my bed in the palace, thank you. I've had enough 'fun' for four months." He shuddered, clearly back to being nervous. "I want to go home."

"Yeah. I do too." Beacon sighed. Rowan looked over his shoulder at them with a frown.

Enya hoped he wouldn't notice her staring. Why was she staring, anyway? She darted her gaze to her hands clutching the reins of her horse, feeling heat rise on her cheeks.

"You boys are so dramatic. I'll bet you've never gone a day without some guard right on your heels and saving your asses," Doina groaned in exasperation, messing with the piercings on her right ear. "What kind of a man hides in his bed from the world? You should be living your lives free to roam, free to see life as it really is. You should be seeing how the majority of Skeyya lives."

Rowan scoffed. "Don't pretend to know us."

Doina spun her horse to face them, halting their group dead in their tracks. "You're the three dead princes. No one in our church needs magick to see that. You're spineless, empty, and think nothing of others, like all royals do. Don't pretend you couldn't use this advice. You know nothing except what the king has shown you."

There was once a time when Enya and Carson would have agreed with her on all accounts.

She met his eyes and for once after their talk the other day, didn't flinch. These were pretty aggressive words for an escort, and they didn't come all this way to have the princes attacked. They both held the guns at their waists, ready to step in if needed.

So much for romance with the faerie girl. At least that would give them something to finally talk about.

"If you are to rule this country, you should know how *real* people live, not just those who kiss your asses in the palace. You're pathetic, spineless royal fools. That's all you'll ever be," Doina finished, spitting on the ground before the princes. Hatred was too kind a word to describe their expressions.

"Hey," Enya raised a hand, approaching with her horse. Rage spiked through her, warming her cheeks. "They might be royal, but they've changed a lot since we left Renmare. Your job is to take us to this haunted forest and go. I didn't realize mouthing off about utter nonsense was part of the package deal."

Doina's lips curled back, and Carson sighed. "Doina … don't be like this. We were having a pleasant journey."

She threw up her hands, clucking her tongue. "I will lead you to the haunted forest, pretty boy. But after that, we are done. I've kept my mouth shut long enough for your soft kisses," she retorted, turning to face Enya with a scowl. "You have turned your back on the rebellion to become a royal pet."

Her words stung, but Enya knew the truth. She was doing the right thing. Well, she hoped she was.

Carson fell back from riding next to Doina after that,

which only seemed to piss the creature of the woods off more. He rode beside Enya on her right with the princes wedged between them and their escort, just like their trip to Thomond.

The princes were quiet, and she could faintly sense guilt brewing on their stiff backs. She felt guilty too, but only for allowing herself to keep getting caught up in her emotions. She'd let prospective friendships and romances distract her.

After a while, the forest around them grew dark, and their horses began to grow restless and weary of the path ahead. It was at this point that Doina stopped.

"This is it. I refuse to go any further, otherwise my mind will get as messed up as yours are about to be," she said with a dismissive wave. "I still think this is a ridiculously stupid idea, but I've never been one to stand in the way of those. I prefer to watch and laugh, personally."

Enya smiled, then reached for her pistol when the woman's back was turned.

"Enya," Carson warned, shaking his head in exasperation.

"Joking … sheesh." She just wanted to imagine what it would feel like. Besides, Doina was still technically helping them, even if she was ordered to do so and even if she was being a bitch about it. "Thanks for the help," Enya said finally when the Unseelie fae glanced at them again, trying to control the annoyance rippling through her. "Guess we'll see you later." She hoped not. Saints, she was sick of her.

The creature of the woods smirked, then vanished with her galloping horse, and their crew had never seemed so relieved.

Enya would prove her wrong. She wasn't just doing this for the money. One day, she wanted to rule the rebel cause entirely and save these people from the spineless shrimp on the golden throne. This was all part of that long and arduous plan.

They stayed their course, but the horses beneath them shook their heads in anguish, silently begging them to stop. Enya offered a few gentle pats to the one she rode, stroking his mane, but it did little to soothe him. They were almost there. She was sure of it. They'd already passed two marked trees.

"I'm not too thrilled over what she said about our minds getting messed up," Niall said, voice warbling in the now darkening forest. Snow laced through their hair, and shadows seemed to dart through the brush.

"It's going to be fine," Carson called back. "Think of how nice it'll be to get this over with and go back to that fancy palace of yours."

She smiled, momentarily forgetting his fling with Doina and her anger about it. "With all its fancy paintings, food, and music around every corner," she added. Their joking did little to ease the tension, as the woods had grown ever darker and more foreboding around them, with briars and shadowy mist. And ... Enya could feel it.

They weren't alone.

A black figure darted across the road and into the trees, prompting their horses to pull back, shrieking. Another ran behind the group, and Enya's head spun, wondering where to look next. Her weapon was out, and she wasn't about to be caught off guard. They each held out their pistols, ones with iron bullets, courtesy of the Church of Astru.

Screams, ones of terror and agony, echoed through the woods, warning them to go back from where they came.

Instead of doing that—and Enya's instincts were begging her to—she smacked the reins of her horse, prompting the creature to sprint forward. The sound of her companions following helped ease her racing heartbeat, but adrenaline still pulsed in her veins, keeping her going.

The woods were a blur of ghouls and hags, their hideous and gnarled faces coming and going beneath a black fog that had settled over the trees.

If at all possible, the woods around them grew ... darker. Ominously so, considering the trees were all almost entirely dead. Above them should have been a gray sky, but there was a haze there that hung in the boughs, cutting off the sunlight above and allowing only the smallest patches of glimmering light to slip through.

Enya sucked in a breath, her eyes searching aimlessly for any sort of assurance that they weren't just wandering around with no sense of direction. When she saw no more markers, she felt defeated. This couldn't have been for nothing. They'd come so far to get here.

A fork in the path had all of their group coming to a sudden halt. Enya turned in her saddle, trying to figure out which way their group should take. Neither road stuck out, and both were equally lost in the darkness of the forest. Just a few strides down either and you'd barely be able to see the tall, twisting tree that sat between them.

Enya narrowed her eyes. "The priestess didn't say anything about a forking path," she said flatly.

Carson's mouth formed a tight line. "That she didn't."

"Then maybe we should split up," Beacon whispered, earning several dark looks from the others in the group. He flinched. "I'm just saying we could cover more ground."

Carson seemed to weigh this for a moment. "That might

not be a bad idea. We'd cover double, maybe even triple the area if we split up," he admitted, scratching the back of his head.

"And we'd have double or triple the chances of being caught or killed," Enya retorted with a deep frown.

Rowan bit his lip, turning to look around them with furrowed brows. "Would we, though? I'd say we're doing just fine. Besides, we have the weapons to handle it—unless you're scared." He raised a brow, and she rolled her eyes.

"I'm not scared. I'm just not stupid."

He let loose an annoyed sigh, now facing the others they rode with. "Everyone for splitting up, raise your hand."

Everyone but Niall and Enya complied, meaning they were outnumbered. This earned a cocky grin from the heir to the throne and a sickening feeling in Enya's stomach.

"It seems our little gang takes my side today, little thief. Don't forget that," he said with a chuckle. With his hands tight on the reins of his horse, Rowan continued, "Carson and Beacon, you two should come with me. I'm sure the big, bad Raven can handle my little brother by herself."

"So, you think you're the one calling the shots?" Enya demanded. How dare he assume that he was in control.

"No," he said simply, meeting her eyes. "We had a mutual agreement here. Unless you're more into a dictatorship sort of thing. I'm sure my father would like that."

His words cut into her, making her flinch.

As if knowing how much he'd hurt her, Rowan paused, regret flashing over his features. What a rare sight for this prince, indeed.

"Just keep moving. Me and Niall will do our search," she said, her voice cold. He nodded, now leading his brother and

Carson away towards the left path. They vanished with the noises of crunching leaves and chirping forest creatures waiting in the branches above.

There was no telling how deadly those creatures were.

Niall and Enya meandered slowly down the right path, stopping every so often when deadly noises echoed over their heads from beyond the trees. In moments like these, she missed her spot at the Bowman's Pub even more, and she couldn't wait to get back. One look at the prince's face said he had a similar idea.

"So, what's up with you and my brother?" Niall asked, breaking the silence that had engulfed them in the ever-growing darkness.

Enya's breath caught. "I'm not sure what you mean. He's the heir to the throne, and a rude one, at that. What more is there to say?"

"He's being nice to you."

She had to hold back a chortle of laughter. If that was considered being nice to royals, perhaps there really was no hope.

"And?" Enya prodded.

"He's not normally like this."

"Not normally an arrogant ass? I find that hard to believe."

Niall sighed, casting a cautious look around them as if something were waiting to pounce. Enya didn't doubt it. "Did something happen?" he asked hesitantly.

Well, something did happen. Carson happened, and apparently Rowan had noticed. But she figured almost anyone could have noticed considering her sulking lately.

"Nothing important," she said with a shrug, avoiding his gaze. He didn't look convinced but didn't press further.

It was quiet for a little longer before he spoke again.

"Do you think we'll survive this?" he asked.

Enya paled, pained hands tightening on the reins of her horse. She sucked in her cheek, willing her face to stay stoic and strong. "We can handle whatever this crazy witch throws at us."

"You mean *demon*," Niall corrected, earning a weak chuckle from her. "I think it's pretty likely that we're screwed. More or less, anyway."

"Gee, thanks." Enya rolled her eyes. "That's so comforting," she said, her voice dripping with sarcasm.

The prince shrugged. "You're welcome."

He sure was talking a lot, which was rare for him. Maybe he felt more comfortable away from his brothers. She definitely did, anyway, especially from Rowan. Then again, he also seemed scared from head to toe.

She tried her best not to be scared too.

After a while, they stumbled across stone ruins, ones gleaming in the bare sun still left from the day with magick and power in the color of black gemstones. If Enya had to guess, she'd say that was a sign, but she wanted to investigate to make sure.

Hopping off her horse and walking over, feet crunching in the snow, she was met with the etchings of a woman, one draped in mist and death. The ruins pictured her using the wand to rule over dozens of monsters.

Looked to be a sign if she ever saw one.

Enya ran her fingers across the ruins, flinching at the cold and jagged stone. The wand was pointed north. "I think we're supposed to go in that direction," she exclaimed, gesturing with her hand. Niall followed her motion with his eyes, cringing at the look of an even more foreboding scene of darkness and cold waiting within the forest. The sun touched the earth, but just barely, leaving shadows to dance within the trees before them in a strange, unnatural way.

"That looks safe," he sighed, nodding over to her horse. She mounted, not being much concerned with safety or otherwise. "There's no chance we could turn back?"

"Absolutely not. Let's just keep moving, alright? If we sit here, we're good as gobbled up by night creatures."

That seemed to shut him up. With that, they trudged north, much to the growing dismay of their horses who whined and pinned their ears back. The frigid blast of the winter breeze was growing, and an ominous feeling spread over their backs and up their necks, giving them goosebumps. Her uneasiness only grew the further they slipped away from civilization, and it didn't seem to be letting up anytime soon.

Follow me. Enya started at the feminine voice seeping through the frost flying through the air.

Her gut told her it was leading them through the trees to the left. It also told her that it was likely an awfully bad idea to do as the voice said. Well, Enya decided that wasn't of concern right now. Based on what Galina and her followers said, it was more likely that the witch would lead them to the wand and eventually the sword, since she wanted to be freed so badly.

She glanced over to Niall, who looked as white as the snow around them. He'd heard it too.

Follow me. I will show you the way. It echoed again above them, serene and terrible all at the same time. It sounded smooth as velvet and as sinister as any banshee or hag of the bog.

But it beckoned them, and they followed.

Shivers ran down Enya's spine, and she wasn't sure if it was from the cold surrounding them or the way this … creature unsettled her. Their horses had given up their calm demeanors, refusing to budge and kicking at the dirt in protest. With a sickening feeling, she lifted a leg over and jumped to the ground, earning a confused look from Niall.

"We're going to have to leave them," she said, the thought striking pain through her chest. After growing up with horses, she'd grown fond of them and hated the idea of leaving them to the monsters of this forest.

"They'll get eaten or worse," Niall shot back, eyes wide. "You can't mean—"

"I do. We can't keep going if they're going to be like this. We have no choice," Enya said stiffly. It was a horrible thing. It was. But they'd get no further otherwise.

Niall was quiet for a moment, unmoving. Finally, and with obvious effort, he slumped off his horse. Hesitating, he brushed a hand over the animal's mane, his lip trembling.

Enya felt for the young prince. But he would have to grow up. They all would if they wanted to survive in this world.

Showing mercy was a good way to get oneself killed out in territory like this. She'd seen enough of what that mindset did on the streets in Arden. Of how people ended up when they let their feelings catch a hold of them.

Life was unforgiving in that way, and she wouldn't allow herself to be the next dead soul in mercy's wake.

Her eyes stung, but she started walking. After a moment, she could hear Niall's footsteps crunching the dead leaves behind her.

Follow me. Let me help you to see the truth.

Enya grimaced, but she forced herself to keep going.

When they eventually reached a magical haze of red caked in ash seeping up from the ground and humming along to the tune of the winter wind, she could hardly believe her eyes Had they not already found the Pentacle of Glac, she would have thought her mind was playing tricks on her. It was massive, nearly reaching the clouds above their heads. The portal was like a wall of glistening light, impenetrable and foreboding all the same.

That voice whispered again through the air of the forest, beckoning them onwards.

"I'm not so sure this is a good idea," Niall gulped, hands shaking at his sides. Enya felt pity for the scared look on his face, but they couldn't stop now. Not when they'd come this far.

"We have no choice," she said simply, echoing her words from earlier. That seemed to be a common theme on this trip.

With caution, they inched closer to the portal that was only mere yards away. It called to them, begging them to enter. Begging them to get this over with and cross the distance.

As they stood in front of it, Enya gulped, taking Niall's hand in hers. She knew that when they crossed over into that portal, everything would change. Something would break in them, that much was certain.

Would the others face the same fate?

They stepped over the threshold of the magick haze, and an evil feeling, one like death itself, spread over Enya's skin. She wasn't in the forest anymore, and Niall was gone from her grasp.

What stood before her shook her to her core.

18

Renmare, Skeyya

BUSY SERVANTS belonging to Whitstone Palace bustled around with their carts and their platters, completely oblivious to Enya's presence and nearly running into her in the process.

The scent of lavender and jasmine wafted by, along with that of the palace garden outside the large open windows to her left. A few soldiers laughed to themselves while they went to the armory not far ahead. Nighttime was falling upon the palace, urging all who dwelt within its halls to finish their daily chores and go to their rooms.

Enya was back in Renmare. In that place she'd tried so hard to forget from her childhood. And before her stood a young girl, one no more than nine or ten years of age, by the looks of it.

The child had black hair tied into a dainty bun, and her rosy cheeks looked beautiful atop her fair skin. She wore a small, black pair of trousers and a white blouse above dark boots caked in mud and hay. This girl worked in the stables, and suddenly Enya couldn't breathe.

"Enya!" a voice called, making both their heads turn.

Her blood ran cold, and the little girl bit her lip, now moving swiftly down the hallway to follow the voice.

It's me. I'm the girl. Her hands shook and throbbed while she followed meekly behind the child, unseen and unheard by those around her. They arrived through a set of white double doors, ones that revealed a foyer constructed of marble and polished stone.

"Where have you been, child?" an older woman cooed, one dressed similar to her younger self except for the satchel of horse treats hanging at her side. She kept her frizzy, dark hair tied at her neck, and her wrinkled eyes met the young Enya's with warmth.

This had been her mother, Orla, the keeper of the stables so many years ago. It was too bad illness had taken her so young; Enya had only found out herself from local newspapers after leaving the palace. But no one ever really lived long as a servant.

"I was trying to find the princes," the young Enya admitted, rocking back and forth on her feet with pursed lips. "They said we could go play by the kitchen, but I couldn't find them," she sighed dramatically, crossing her arms.

"Now, you know there can be none of that until we finish our work, young lady," her mother scolded.

"But I already finished shining the horseshoes and feeding them," the young girl whined, earning a stern look ... and then a small smile from Orla.

Enya shook her head. The sight of her mother alive was almost too much to bear. What was horribly depressing about the entire ordeal was that she'd forgotten all of this. She'd remembered small fragments of her past but nothing more. Nothing tangible.

She was living this moment with her younger self, and it felt like it was the first time.

"Ah," her mother tsked, folding her arms. "But you didn't clean the stalls or water the troughs."

Enya's younger self sighed dramatically, trudging off no doubt to finish the job. The Raven was inclined to follow.

They crept along the now-silent halls of Whitstone Palace, being careful to not bump into the last of the servants lighting the gas lamps on the walls. Her younger self huffed, no doubt annoyed to have missed out on the chance to fool around with her royal friends, Rowan, Beacon, and Niall.

The three dead princes. Enya hated the sinister feeling snaking up her spine.

At last, they reached the stables outside, now illuminated by moonlight. A few ravens fluttered about its roof, curiously watching those on the ground below. One seemed to catch Enya's eye, but there was no way it could see her if no one else could, right?

Her younger self whistled a few times, and one of the birds came down to rest upon her waiting arm. It pecked her lovingly, as if greeting an old friend, before flying back up into the trees.

The child slipped inside the stables, now picking up a

rusty wash bucket to rinse the stalls. It smelled of hay and animals. It smelled like home.

"Marlow, you sly dog," her younger self said with a giggle. "You think you can just steal all the apples now?" The little girl picked up an empty satchel in front of a black horse's pen.

Marlow had been her favorite. That much she remembered. It was so strange the things one's mind would latch onto and what things it would forget.

Little Enya began mucking the stables, toiling hard with a scrub brush. After that, she brought water to each of the creatures, making sure they each had their fill. Finally, she plopped down in a stack of hay with a paper and pen, determined to write about the day.

The sight made present-day Enya smile to herself, taking a silent seat on a nearby wooden barrel to watch in amusement, noting the little tricks she'd learned over the years. It almost made her forget about her worries or even where she was. She could forget about the gang, the king, the rebellion.

She could breathe for once, and it didn't seem anyone was inclined to stop her from this relief.

This wasn't so bad. This didn't seem scary at all.

That is, it didn't until a sinister noise sounded outside the barn. It reminded Enya so much of the sickening feeling that had loomed over her ever since they'd arrived in the haunted forest.

They weren't alone.

The horses around them shrieked, backing up into the wooden walls of their confined spaces, ears turned back in earnest. Little Enya set her pen down with a sudden, paralyzing fear before rushing to comfort them, cooing to no avail. It was then that the lanterns of the stables went out, one by one, leaving them in total black.

Her younger self froze. At the sound of creaking wood, she slowly turned her head towards the stable doors. Present day Enya rose from her barrel, now wielding her pistol with iron bullets. She wasn't going to take this, whatever it was, sitting down by any means.

Darkness pooled together in front of the entrance, fizzling in and out in sparkles and mist until it created a figure of a woman. She stood there, draped in a vermillion cloak, a hood over her head. Only her wicked red smile could be seen in the shadows of the night.

Enya's stomach turned and suddenly she felt ill. Was this encounter what she'd blocked out for so many years?

"What a fine child you are," the woman purred, lifting the hood to watch her with stunning, gold eyes. Her ears were just barely pointed beneath long tendrils of white hair. Her pale skin was obvious, even in the darkness. "I wonder why they have you working so late."

The younger Enya yanked out a small knife, her hands shaking. "Who are you?" she demanded, though her words were just as uneven.

The woman in red seemed to consider the question for a moment, pacing around the child.

"I go by many names. Some call me the bringer of life, others call me the bringer of death. But some simply call me Ballora," the pale visitor replied with a shrug, now toying with a glass eye she'd produced from thin air.

She turned to the girl, lips pursed before forming a wicked smile.

"Would you like to look into my little eye here?" she asked, watching the younger Enya carefully. "It's got quite the charm to it, I must say. You can see all kinds of magical things, like your future, your past, or maybe what will become of those pretty little palace boys you frolic with all day."

"Leave her alone," present-day Enya ordered, earning nothing but a slight twitch of a smirk from Ballora, as if she'd heard her but refused to acknowledge her presence. The thought of that made Enya feel almost as small as the child no doubt did in this situation.

Her younger self bit her lip and shook her head.

Yes. Please don't listen to her.

Ballora cocked her head curiously, as if a vicious snake toying with her food.

"Oh, trust me dear girl, there's no reason to be afraid. Hm, well at least there's no reason to deny me." She laughed, the sound like nails on a chalkboard. "Why, I'm in death and life. I'm everywhere giving life to those I choose and darkness to the rest. You cannot escape me; I am inevitable." The demon woman paused, then put an arm around the trembling girl. "I need you to do me two favors, child." She raised two long, bony fingers.

"What kind of favors?" the young girl asked, standing straighter. Favors for demons? For faerie folk? That was asking for trouble. Present-day Enya silently begged the child to know this, to understand.

She didn't.

"It's a simple matter, really, one that you mustn't know the details of just yet. When the time comes, I will call you to do the deeds I require," Ballora said with a dismissive wave of her hand.

"What will I get in return?"

The demon's eyes sparkled. "Clever one, aren't you? Very well. You'll have power. You'll even rival these princes of yours with your wit and strength. Truly, you'll hold the fate of many in your hands. I'd imagine that's quite better than mucking yourself up in the stables for that nasty king. How does he treat you, girl?"

Ballora's eyes flickered to the fresh bruises on Little Enya's arms, ones she hurried to cover with her sleeve. Such was the punishment for daring to befriend King Eamon's sons.

The younger Enya watched her with furrowed brows, earning an innocent splay of the Crimson Witch's hands.

Finally, she said, "Fine. I'll do these favors for you. Only if you hold up your end of the bargain too, Ballora."

"I knew you'd see it my way. I'll be seeing you very soon, little one." The Crimson Witch laughed, clapping her hands together. She took hold of the girl's hands then, and a crescent shape appeared on the younger Enya's palms. "Consider this a mark, sealing the deal."

The demon said nothing else when she vanished into a pool of mist. Present-day Enya didn't even remember exactly what she'd done yet, but she already felt disgusting. Her skin prickled with that now familiar feeling of the Crimson Witch's presence, and her salted tears burned while they streamed down her face.

The younger Enya stared down at her hands in wonder.

Time was a blur. She saw the child's face flush with excitement as she rushed to finish her chores, and then she saw nothing at all.

Night had passed and gone a few more times. The sun came and went in flashes, and moonlight was upon Enya once again. It was a new day, maybe even one a week later. It had only felt like a few minutes.

Enya was waiting now, alone in the rose and lavender scented courtyard outside of the stables in Whitstone Palace. Waiting for that horrible thing she'd been brought to her past to see.

Three young princes came into view with her younger self in tow.

"You can't tell me what to do. I'm going to be king one day," a child with a familiar arrogance sneered, kicking aside a few stones on the ground.

That must be Rowan. It has to be. I know that face.

A shorter boy beside him coupled with one around the same height nodded, casting looks over at the younger Enya who stood with her arms crossed.

"He's right, you know," the youngest looking, presumably Niall, said, earning a pout from little Enya.

"For as long as I've got two feet and two arms, I'll be bossing you all the way to the mountains, royal or not," she retorted, earning oohs and aahs from Rowan's brothers. He flushed red and tagged her before running away.

With a flourish of finely made jackets and servants' clothes, they chased each other around the flowers strung around the courtyard. Trying not to hit anything too expensive as they did, of course.

The present-day Enya shook her head ruefully, a smile now on her lips. This wasn't so terrifying. Maybe she'd been brought here by mistake. Maybe this was all some weird dream.

"Fine, you win," Rowan groaned while the younger Enya stood over him on the ground in triumph. She'd pushed him onto a flowerbed, and his servants would no doubt begrudge having to clean up the mess. But that didn't stop her in the slightest.

"I'm sorry. What was that? I can't hear you," she taunted, holding a hand close to her ear and leaning in with pursed lips. Beacon and Niall snickered beside them. "I feel like you said something, but I'm just not sure. Say it again."

Forever the troublemaker. Enya grinned to herself.

Rowan glared back while he climbed to his feet. "I said you win. Now, if you'll excuse us." With his nose turned up and his hands now stuffed into his pockets, the heir to the throne was on his way back to his quarters with his brothers in tow. Niall turned his head to look at the girl before shooting two thumbs up.

Little Enya beamed with pride, and so did her older self.

When they were gone, the child skipped along to her room, ready to catch some rest after a long day in the stables and chasing the princes. Enya quietly followed, careful to avoid bumping into any more furniture from the past. She felt tired too and began to wonder when this haze of a dream would be over.

Once the younger Enya had settled into her cot and put out the gas lamp beside her bed, her eyes closed, and the world of royalty and games were gone. A few feet away, her mother snored in her bed.

Without warning, darkness began to climb up her covers, much to the horror of her present-day counterpart.

The girl's blade was instantly out, but it was no use. It wouldn't work against something this powerful, this ancient. Mist near the child's face formed into the head and hands of Ballora, and suddenly her grasp was over the younger Enya's mouth, halting her scream.

"Today's the day you will complete this first task for me, little one."

19

Brasovian Territory

THE WORLD was spinning, and nausea had wedged itself inside Enya's stomach as she hit the snowy ground. Her skin prickled with both fear and disgust at Ballora's words, at the realization that struck her harder than any physical blow could.

She'd assisted the Crimson Witch. She'd struck a deal with her.

No. No, this had to be a mistake—an illusion, maybe. It couldn't be true. She would never have agreed to help her. Her younger self surely would have fought her at every turn. Her stubborn nature would have won out.

And yet …

Enya tore the gloves off her hands and looked down at

her scars. They were there, same as they had always been. They carried with them a true, weighty guilt of her past.

She's made a deal with a demon, something straight out of stories of old. And for what? For the promise of future rewards? For strength that rivaled even that of the princes? Her best friends? Enya looked up dizzily at the pitch-black sky above.

But what could Ballora have wanted a little girl to do?

Then a sinking feeling returned to her gut and she knew … something horrible. Something worth forgetting forever. And she didn't want to face it. She had pulled herself free of the portal. It stood before her, tall and glimmering, red and foreboding.

"Niall!" Enya screamed brazenly at the dark woods surrounding her on all sides. Two tracks still led into the portal, hers and Niall's. But he was nowhere to be seen. She stepped cautiously around, just to be sure. There were no tracks on the other side and none when she'd come tumbling back out.

Which could only mean one thing. She stared into that glowing red, horrifying light … Niall was still in there. Maybe he was still dreaming, still suffering through an eternal nightmare, or maybe—

He had done it. He had suffered through and made it to wherever that portal led.

Damn it, Enya, she thought to herself, *Are you really going to let the youngest, most scared prince of that bunch get the better of you?*

Was she really going to let him do it alone?

"Saints, I know I'm going to regret this …"

Enya gritted her teeth and ran headlong at the portal.

Enya appeared back in the palace, stumbling right into a barrel of coffee. She winced and steadied herself, taking in her surroundings.

Before the younger Enya and Ballora in the empty kitchens was a tea set perched on the counter with a spoon. It smelled of sage and lemon, making the child lick her lips.

"There now. It's simple, really. Take the tea to the queen." Ballora clapped her hands in delight.

Enya's heart stopped, and for a moment she couldn't breathe.

"That's it?" her younger self asked, tilting her head in confusion.

"Indeed." The demon woman nodded, waving towards the tea, her long fingernails gleaming in faint candlelight that scarcely illuminated the room. "Come on, now. Hurry up."

There was silence as the younger Enya stilled, weighing her words. Then she said, "Won't the king see me bring the tea?"

Ballora laughed her signature, sinister laugh. "He's with one of his weekly whores. No one will even know you were there." She gave the younger Enya a sidelong look. "My dear child, it's only tea."

Present-day Enya balked at this, falling back one step, then another, until she hit a wooden kitchen cart full of sugar and honey.

Had she been the one to … No. This was surely a nightmare.

Ballora turned her head slightly, amusement splaying over her features, but she remained quiet. Her eyes met the present-day Enya's, and a wolfish grin set in her lips. It was almost like she was challenging her to even dare to stop this. But nothing could be done.

The child lifted the tea platter with trembling hands, earning a hissed scolding from the demon.

"Be careful. It was extremely annoying to procure that tea."

Present-day Enya's heart panged with every step towards the queen's chambers, and there were plenty of steps considering that Her Majesty was practically on the other side of Whitstone Palace.

Ballora hummed to herself the entire way, dancing within the shadows of the corridors of the palace, fading in and out of the darkness. Nothing seemed to top the obvious glee on her face at this predicament.

It was wicked, oh so wicked, and Enya hated it. For a moment, she couldn't breathe. *This can't be real. This can't be real.*

When they reached the queen's chambers, the demon held up a hand to stop the child from going any further, and for a moment, hope sparked in both her and Enya's eyes. It didn't last long.

"I can't enter. The king put some sort of faerie protection spell over the room, locking me and my kind out," Ballora whined sarcastically, crossing her arms and toying with the glass eye she'd once again produced from her billowing black cloak.

The child gasped, eyes frantic. "I'm doing this alone? I've never even been in her rooms before," she exclaimed.

"It's easy as pie. You give her the tea, and you go. Now, about your appearance," the demon woman muttered, giving a dismissive wave. Ballora then strung up her hands in a circular motion, and a sparkling mist fell over the child, disguising her as a handmaid. "Go on and get this done. I have other things on my schedule for tonight."

The present and past Enya both grimaced.

With a deep breath, the child rapped her knuckles on the door once, twice, then three times. The knocking echoed through the palace hallways, sending shivers down Enya's spine. They were so utterly alone here, which was uncharacteristic for these chambers.

After several long moments, it almost seemed that Her Majesty wasn't coming to answer, and hope blossomed within the present Enya. But it was too good to be true.

Queen Layla emerged in a long cotton nightgown, with tired eyes and lips set into an annoyed frown. Her long, light brown hair sat in a loose braid over her shoulder, exposing her cream-colored skin that somehow managed to stay young despite so many years of life.

Before she could say a word, the younger Enya spoke.

"Tea, Your Highness," she said quietly, almost shoving the tray into the woman through the door. Present-day Enya silently pleaded with the queen to walk away, to forget this.

"This late? I don't recall requesting any tea." The queen sighed, looking around the corridor outside her door.

Relief flooded Enya. Maybe she would turn her away and this night could be forgotten. Maybe this horrible, horrible thing didn't have to happen. She could stay innocent, live a long, happy life, and this could all fade away with time.

The princes could grow up with a mother, and she could grow up without the clawing of unwanted memories at her chest.

A frigid breeze ruffled the queen's gown and raised goosebumps on Enya's arms, a breeze no doubt sent by Ballora. She could almost hear her cackles again. The queen shivered, adding, "Well, it would be welcome in light of the night's chill. Come in, child."

The younger Enya complied with the present-day one not too far behind, slipping in carefully across the threshold. The door shut with a slight creak, and guilt flooded the Raven's veins, shaking her bones to their very marrow.

The room dripped in wealth, with decorated white walls covered in golden designs and trim.

Beige velvet furniture littered the interior with sculptures of every sort standing atop a sparkling marble flooring which rivaled that of the throne room. A canopy bed sat at the center of the far wall, one whose white blankets were mussed from recent use.

It was enough to make any servant stare in awe, much less a wanted criminal who had lived for so long on the streets of the capital.

She gestured to a wooden accent piece on the far wall. "Set it on that table over there," the queen ordered, walking over to a plush lounge chair facing a large window and plopping down. Moonlight spilled in through the glass panes, casting faint blue light over her elegant features. "After that, you may take your leave."

The child nodded, placing the tea set where she had been instructed, her hands quivering nervously all the while. She walked back towards the door, opening it briefly—just enough to hint that she had gone—then closing it and hiding behind one of the stone pillars lining the wall to her left.

Enya could hear the child's breath catching while she tried to stifle it and keep quiet, adrenaline no doubt flooding her limbs. Perhaps she was waiting to see what was so important about this tea.

What made a demon fetch her in the night for such deeds.

The queen's footsteps could be heard tapping lightly on the floor. Her serene and elegant figure approached the table with a slight exhaustion, as if she were ready for a long day of royal duties to be over with. Her Majesty then added a few sugar cubes which she had stashed inside the cabinet beneath the tray, her tiny spoon clanking against the porcelain of her cup. Finally, she lifted the glass to her lips and took a long, deep swig of the tea.

More footsteps came, and the queen had now gone to lay down in her bed for a peaceful night's sleep.

The silence was deafening, unnerving the Raven and making her legs tremble in anticipation. Saints, this was madness.

Minutes later, Queen Layla gasped, struggling to throw the covers off herself. She thrashed, legs and arms shaking violently and a weak cry building in her throat when she landed hard onto the floor.

"What have you done?" she exclaimed, though her voice was small and breathless. As if desperate, the queen pulled herself as best she could to the alarm bell next to her bedside table.

If she rang that bell, Enya had no doubt her younger self would be killed—or worse.

The younger Enya flung herself onto the queen, trying to move her away with as much strength as her tiny body could muster. Little Enya had to do it. If she didn't, the entire palace would know what she had done. The princes would have known.

She did this. *She* killed the queen.

"I'm sorry. I'm sorry. I'm sorry. I'm so, so sorry," the child wailed, crying into her hands and slumping against the bed as she sat on the floor. "I didn't want to do this. I promise."

It didn't take much longer until the queen went limp, eyes glossed over and lifeless. One final gasp let loose, and both Enya and the child knew she was dead.

She had killed the queen of Skeyya. She killed her best friends' mother. She was a murderer.

The girl lifted slowly off the queen, hands trembling. She cried out in pain, and red burned into the crescents on her palms, an eternal reminder of what she'd done to the queen. Of what she had done to herself. Of what she had done to the princes.

Her younger self fled, not even turning back to shut the door to the queen's chambers. Enya could see the Crimson Witch's wicked grin in the shadows while the child only pressed on faster.

She sprinted down the hallways, down the stairs, and down the cobblestone leading to the stables. She had to get out. She had to get away from all of this. How could she face the princes after this? How could she face her mother?

Seeing her reflection in a wooden trough of water inside, the younger Enya could see the demon's disguise had begun to fade away, her dark hair shining through locks of blonde and her servant's clothes revealing themselves under the maid's outfit.

In disgust she tore them off. She threw on one of the stable boys' ensembles of black and brown, one coated in dried muck and scented like the worst kind of horse slop, but she didn't care. Anything was better than what she'd worn to murder the queen.

After fretting about and throwing what little supplies were in the nearby closet into a woven bag, the child paused.

"Mother, I didn't even get to say goodbye. I'm sorry."

With one final look at the stalls full of her beloved horses and the small, printed photograph of her and her mother taped to the wall by the door, she fled into the night on Marlow, the black stallion.

It was then that Enya's heart stopped, and the evil of it all consumed her. She screamed until she couldn't see or hear the world around her anymore, until it all went black.

20

Brasovian Territory

THE WOODS howled with something sinister, the leaves on the trees above rustling in the winter breeze.

The world was pitch-black for several painfully long seconds, nearly sending Enya's mind into a tailspin until specks of the stars and moon finally began to illuminate the forest floor, the only semblance to anything normal this awful forest had to offer.

She was out of the portal. She'd made it to the other side.

Enya fell to her knees and heaved, throwing up onto the damp earth beneath her. She was a killer. She had killed the queen. She had killed their mother. It was *her*. But what happened after that? Where had she gone, and how had she survived?

What else had she forgotten all this time?

So many questions, so many unavailable answers.

"Are you okay?" Niall's voice cut through the darkness, startling her. He must have escaped the portal too. A hand on her shoulder, however, made her recoil as if she'd been burned. "What's wrong?"

"Don't ... Don't touch me." Enya said, voice as unsteady as she felt. She climbed shakily to her feet. When she met his gaze, it looked as haunted as her own. He'd seen something too. Something horrible. His disguise from Miriana was also gone, likely having been erased by the portal's magick. Niall was back to his inherited red hair and hazel eyes, looks that were common for the royal family.

"What did you see?" he asked, his voice tinged with worry.

"I don't want to talk about it," she snarled, pulling her coat tighter against her now shivering frame. It was snowing again, the white flakes only making her colder as they landed on her skin. Or maybe it was fear that caused her to shiver. Either way, Enya was ready to get the hell out of this place. "Let's just go."

Niall looked taken aback and hurt flashed over his features, prompting regret to grab hold of her.

Damn the saints. Now she'd made this worse.

"Look, I didn't mean to be a jerk. I just ... I just saw some shit I didn't need to see," Enya muttered, looking down at her boots.

"That makes two of us," Niall sighed. She hoped it wasn't anything *close* to what she had seen. But wouldn't he be trying to kill her if that were the case? She definitely would if she were him. "Come on. We need to find the wand and the others." She cast a wary look to the foreboding jet-black trees before them. There was barely any light.

Niall followed her gaze and pursed his lips before snapping his fingers and producing a lighter from his pocket. Enya raised a brow. "Carson lent me one before we split up. Figured we'd need it."

"Well, for once he's right." No, he was usually right. She sighed deeply, gesturing for him to flick it on.

The lighter sprung to life, sending brightness to dance along the shadows of the forest surrounding them. He let out a nervous chuckle, no doubt unnerved at the sheer amount of emptiness around them. There was barely even the chirping of crickets to fill the silence of the night in the Crimson Witch's woods.

"Guess we better start walking, then," Enya huffed, stomping through the trees and getting wet mud all over her shoes, the prince in tow. She tried to appear confident, but she was shaking both inside and out. How could she lead Niall and the others knowing that *she* had killed his mother, an innocent?

Enya was a murderer. A real, nightmarish, actual murderer. She did this to him and his family. She was responsible.

A part of her wanted to deny it. To accept that it was her deal with Ballora that had led to this, but the rest of her wouldn't accept that. No, she had poisoned the queen. She had strangled the life out of her. She had watched her writhe in agony and her eyes go blank.

For once, the leader of the Grims didn't feel like a Raven at all. She felt like a fraud. A killer.

On the streets … she faintly remembered someone taking her in. That she'd started stealing to fill her stomach. That eventually led to sneaking innocent children out from factory labor and unsavory conditions. Eventually, she'd even used the king's secrets overheard in the quiet palace halls against him, earning notoriety across the country.

Memories she'd forgotten, happy and sad ones, faintly shone through the wall she'd had up for so many years. It had all been too much, what she'd done to the queen and to her best friends. It was all too much, even now.

Enya was the leader of the Grims, but at the cost of Queen Layla's untimely death. Her murder. Maybe that's why she subconsciously hated them so much, apart from their usual horrible demeanors.

Maybe it was because she hated herself for what she'd done.

"Enya?" Niall asked, startling her out of her thoughts.

"Yeah?" she replied, clearing her throat and trying to ignore the sinking pit in her stomach.

"I think I can hear them over there," he said, pointing west, beyond several sickly thorn bushes full of dead roses. Most everything in this forest was either dark or dead, with no exceptions.

Enya felt pretty lifeless too.

After several moments of shimmying through and getting cut up with jagged pricks, they emerged to find the rest of their group huddled around a small fire. They looked as though they felt as crappy as she did and considering the circumstances, she couldn't blame them. Rowan and Beacon's appearances were also back to their former states, both with crimson hair and eyes matching Niall's.

"You're alive!" Carson gasped, running over to sweep her into his arms in a not-so-friendly embrace. She wasn't sure whether she enjoyed it or felt disgusted by it. She really just felt disgusted by herself. "You both were gone for so long we thought you'd been caught."

Enya smiled back slightly. She didn't want to seem too eager, though she pulled away to put some distance between them. Behind them she could almost swear she saw Rowan scowl to himself.

"Have some faith. Grims don't go down that easy," she retorted, looking to see the distraught faces of Beacon and Rowan. "Did you guys go through the portal too?"

Of course they did. Everyone who went through the forest did, and now she had just reminded them of that horrible experience.

"Yeah, we did," Carson said, his expression darkening. "It was pretty rough, Enya. We all saw some bad shit out there."

She stayed silent, observing the others. Could they tell what she had done? Had they seen it too? No one spoke up, so she hoped not.

"I saw my brothers die," Rowan admitted. "My worst fear above anything else. It was horrible." Enya tried not to be relieved at that.

Beacon stoked the flames of their makeshift fire pit with a stick, gaze stuck on the ground. "I saw myself alone. There was no one. It felt like hours of just empty nothingness."

It went quiet for a few moments before the next person spoke.

"I was trapped underwater, and I could see nothing but dead bodies everywhere. It looked like it was near the palace. Like I had been killed. There was a stone tied to my foot, and I couldn't breathe no matter how hard I tried," Niall explained, straightening up his jacket and letting loose a nervous laugh. "It wasn't real."

He seemed to say this as much to comfort himself as to remind the rest of those around him.

"I was back in the linen mill. What I saw was definitely real. It was my uncle leaving me there to die," Carson muttered with a scowl.

They each turned to Enya, who had yet to reveal her vision from the portal. She swallowed the lump in her throat, avoiding their eyes. "I saw something horrible from my childhood. I'd rather not talk about what it was," she snapped, her face falling back into a stone-cold mask.

If she pretended that she was fine, that she was hard and emotionless, maybe they'd believe it. Maybe she would believe it too.

Carson cleared his throat, putting on a reassuring smile. "Alright then. Let's go find this wand."

"Did you guys find anything that could lead us to where it is?" Niall asked, rocking back and forth on his feet with his arms crossed. The snow fluttering above their heads now felt wet against Enya's jacket, making her shiver. If anyone else was cold, they didn't make any mention of it. The wind of the Crimson Witch's forest that spun around them was as frigid and foreboding as the demon herself.

"We did, actually." Rowan lifted a hand with a smirk before tossing over a sheet of paper likely torn from Carson's journal to his younger brother. Niall looked it over for a moment before nodding and passing it to Enya.

In black ink were a few *very* poorly drawn sketches of the Wand of Tine floating above a mountain pass covered in flames. Inside the drawing of the mountain were strange symbols. They looked to be part of the Brasovian Zodiac, the signs representing constellations during various parts of the world's spin around the sun.

Enya knew enough about Brasovian superstitions after so many trade deals in the capital, coupled with chats with Miriana, to know that the two in the picture were *Berbec* and *Leu*. The ram and the lion, the second also being the name of Brasova's primary currency. Both represented fire to the Banya witches.

"Where did you guys see this?" she asked, pushing her brows together. "And when?" She handed the paper back to Rowan.

Carson shrugged. "On our way to the portal we saw this scratched onto some old, dead trees. Mister Heir to the Throne here thought it'd be a good idea to sketch it out," he said, pointing over to Rowan with a thumb over his shoulder.

"So, there's a mountain in these woods? You'd have thought we would have noticed that on our way in ..."

Murderer. Murderer. Murderer.

"We did spot some high ground above the cliffs we were on after we split up. Almost fell and broke my neck again." He laughed uneasily. "Looked like it was northwest."

Enya met the eyes of the princes, none of which seemed too happy to be here. She wasn't either. Especially not to pretend she was some innocent girl who didn't kill their mother when they were kids.

"Let's get moving, then."

Their feet crumpled a wake of leaves and mulch while they followed Carson's compass through the darkness—with the exception of the faint glow of their lighters, of course. It was eerie and uncomfortable, almost like someone was watching them. There wasn't a doubt in Enya's mind who that might be.

"Wouldn't there be a huge lake of fire or something leading the way? This is kind of underwhelming," Rowan yawned, stretching his arms above his head while they walked across a rickety, old wooden bridge in the center of the trees. "I was expecting a lot more doom and gloom, to be honest."

Carson quickly spoke up, ignoring him, "Check that out." He pointed to a stray cabin nearby within the trees.

Screams echoed through the forest, and shadowy figures began flitting through the woods, filling the space with an awful chill that made Enya's teeth chatter. She said, "Guess that's our cue. Get inside!"

They hurled themselves inside and slammed the door with a loud thud, nearly shaking the entire cabin with its force. Whistling and moaning sounded just outside the entrance, and cackling figures taunted them from the frail glass windows that littered the wooden building. Enya and her companions ducked down, flattening themselves against dusty wooden walls. A large figure crept past, one made of pure darkness. Out of the corner of her eye, Enya could see a large eye look through the windows, and then it was gone.

Silence fell, and she let out a gasp of relief. Whatever had been out there was gone, and they were alone once more.

That is, until Enya saw a flash of crackling lightning that showed the Crimson Witch's face against the glass pane beside her for a split second. She held an evil smile before disappearing with her ghouls, and a shiver ran down Enya's spine.

Murderer. Murderer. Murderer.

It was like the demon and that word wouldn't let go of

their hold on her. That was what she was after all, a murderer. Enya did this to herself and to the princes. She swallowed hard, backing up with one foot, then another, until falling right into Rowan.

"Sorry," she stammered, straightening herself and dusting off stray specks of old soot that floated in the air. The prince smirked but kept quiet; he'd save any witty comebacks for later when their lives weren't on the line, most likely.

Finally, Enya turned to survey the scene before her. The smell of rotten wood permeated the air, almost making her gag. It was near black inside, save for a worn-out fireplace.

A fireplace that was lit and crackling.

"Why have you come to this place?" a haunting feminine voice echoed throughout the cabin.

An old woman wearing peasant's clothes slinked towards them from inside the shadows, her skin almost transparent in its fragility and her hair so wispy it was as if she could fade into nothing at any moment. Two pointed ears poked out, signaling that she was—or had been—a creature of the woods.

"Have you heard of the Wand of Tine?" Carson questioned, hand never leaving the pistol at his belt while his eyes watched her warily. The others followed his move, grasping their weapons.

The old hag cackled, the sound shrill and unnerving. "Have I heard of it? I'm here because of it. Do you really think you're the first to come to this forsaken place?"

Enya stepped forward, her own gun out and ready. "No, but we were told that whoever resides here is a soul taken by the Crimson Witch. Ring any bells?" she challenged. The woman narrowed her eyes.

"Yes, this is unfortunately true," the faerie admitted, her skin now turning pale blue. "I am cursed to live here for as long as Ballora sees fit. You could say we made a bargain, her and I." She took a few steps closer, eyes raking up and down the lot of them with a condescending smile. "I suppose you think that you can find the wand and save the day? How noble of you all."

"What kind of bargain did you make?" Beacon asked, eyes wide as he shielded his two brothers with an arm.

She sighed. "I must kill anyone who enters these woods, just like everyone else who is stuck out here. Only, if I keep this up until she reigns, I get to be freed from my servitude. It's rather boring, really."

Enya's blood ran cold, and her grip on her weapon tightened almost painfully.

"Are there any rules that say you can't give us some friendly advice first? Like, say ... on where to find the wand?" Niall piped in while loosening the collar of his shirt. "It wouldn't hurt your deal, and at least we'd know before we, uh, kicked the bucket." Enya shot him a warning glare, but he waved her off, eyes pleading. Fine. She'd let him try what he wanted. They'd kill this woman either way.

The hag flashed a wicked grin, showing pointed teeth. "That's a cute try. Very well, I suppose it wouldn't hurt. Once you reach the mountain's northernmost face, you will find a pass of fire. The wand sits on the other side, guarded by the flames of the damned."

She cocked her head, waiting for any protest. When none came, she simply shrugged.

"That's not intimidating for you? Oh well. Let's get this

over with. Try not to make too much noise. It's really annoy-ing—"

The creature of the woods was cut off by several shots from Enya's gun. Her eyes went wide, and she fell into a heap on the wooden floor. Not a few moments later did her body crumple into ash and mist, floating out through the cracks in the cabin.

Carson and the princes turned to her in surprise.

"What? We have places to be. Let's get moving," Enya ordered, motioning for them to follow when she kicked open the front door and stomped out. They didn't have time for this, and she certainly wasn't going to let that creature get any more time to prepare her attack on them. After what she had done, the least she could do was protect them and finish this whole "find the sword" thing.

I'll be better. I'll do better. I won't let my past define me.

To be ruthless and cunning came easy, but ultimately, she had the Grims and now the princes to protect. They had to keep going. To stay moving, no matter the cost.

And now they had all kinds of hell to face.

21

Brasovian Territory

THE TRAIL leading toward the cliffs was sharp and dangerous, and the crunching of twigs and leaves signaled there was more than one unfriendly foe on their tails. Something was watching, always watching their every move.

Enya sucked in a deep breath and let her eyes focus on the path before them. Jutting rocks covered in black dust and greenery threatened to cut into her legs, and the others did well to avoid them while they followed. If they managed to keep their wits about them, they'd be just fine.

Murderer. Murderer. Murderer.

The words threatened to undo her with every step forward, and she bit the inside of her cheek to try and distract herself from the never-ending slew of negative thoughts.

"Looks like we're almost there," Carson called out, prompting her attention back to the now and away from the evil twisting and turning her mind. He was right. There wasn't much left between them and the intimidating, rocky edges casting over the Great Sea.

"Ugh, more cliffs," Rowan muttered to himself. "Did I ever mention I'm not the biggest fan of heights?"

Beacon nudged Niall in front of Enya as they walked. "It's probably because of that time you fell out that tree." He laughed, earning a smile from their younger brother.

The heir to the throne rolled his eyes, stuffing his hands into his pockets. "So you keep reminding me," Rowan replied. "But at least I had the balls to climb it." He smirked.

If Beacon noticed the jab, he didn't remark on it. "Saints, I'm so hungry. Did anyone bring snacks?"

"You're always hungry. No, we don't have snacks," Niall retorted, lacing his fingers behind his head while he walked with his brothers ahead. "You'll just have to wait until we finish saving the world."

"I thought this was just one stop!" Beacon cried.

With a few more laughs, they went silent.

Their feet echoed across the cold stone of the cliffs, with each footstep uneasy, as if the rock could give way at any moment. Winter winds ruffled Enya's coat, sending chills down her spine, and the darkness of the sea almost warning them of what waited if they slipped.

There were no doubt plenty of faerie folk beneath the waves, eager for a bite.

But right now, it was possessed souls and deadly spirits

they had to worry about. Iron bullets usually did the trick, and she gripped her pistol so hard it was painful. A nervous sweat lingered on her neck beneath her thick black hair, and her heart pounded in anticipation. Anything could happen at any moment. They had to be ready.

The rustling of their followers stopped, and all went quiet. Enya could almost cut the tension in the air with a knife.

"What is that thing?" Niall shrieked, making them all whip around. A tall beast sitting higher than a woodland bear covered in red fur was slowly approaching. Its features resembled that of a wolf, and vicious teeth snapped while its black eyes watched their every move.

A morrigan.

A morrigan was a wicked creature of the woods, one who predicted death and battle for the evilest of beings and rulers. It was commonly used on faerie warfronts to sniff out enemies. What a coincidence.

"I'm going to take a wild guess and say that thing works for the Crimson Witch," Carson remarked, aiming his weapon at the beast. Enya did the same, her hand just barely trembling with uncertainty.

The monster inched closer, its giant set of teeth gnashing in anticipation of a sizable dinner. Two shots rang out from their guns, zipping right into its head. It froze, only for a moment, before toppling to the earth at its feet. Black blood oozed from its wounds and a faint sigh let loose.

"That's not going to hold for long, guys. Come on," Enya urged, pushing the princes further into the rocky terrain awaiting them. "Unless you'd like to start counting worms with the nixies."

"Yeah, no, I'd rather live. Thank you," Rowan snapped back, fixing his hair. The beast stirred, its eyes opening. The prince paled. "Crap."

"Move it!" Enya yelled, and they broke out into a run.

Massive paws thudded behind them, stalking them along the rocks and listless grass. Enya sped up, her eyes taking in the landscape and searching for a way they could be rid of this thing. At least temporarily. She stumbled along the rocks, tripping over jagged edges.

Claws tangled in her hair, dragging her back. A massive jaw lunged for her throat, and she rolled, crying out from the pain in her scalp. Enya's stomach lurched when she realized she was mere inches from the cliff's edge. Watery depths called to her from below, a dark abyss of nothing but salty waves.

Her eyes darted up to the giant wolf above her, whose drool dripped onto her cheeks, then briefly to the princes and Carson who stood behind the beast, trying to distract it.

It was worth a shot.

Enya rolled completely over the edge, grabbing a stray branch sticking out the cliff's side. She gasped for air when the ground fell out from under her. The creature's dagger-like canines narrowly missed her throat before it flew past into the waves below. The splash sent icy water droplets into her clothes, and wind rustled her hair. Saints.

But now she was dangling with no way up. The branch was too far from the ground above, and her gloved hands were slipping.

"Enya!" Carson called out, skidding to a halt on his knees at the edge of the cliff. "Shit. Guys, get over here."

Rowan, Beacon, and Niall appeared, and she started feeling dizzy. If they knew the truth, would they save her?

"We've got you," Carson added. He glanced around, then pointed to something she couldn't see. "There!" He disappeared for a moment, reappearing with another large branch.

"What the hell is this supposed to do?" Rowan demanded.

"What do you think? You three, hold this." Carson shoved it into their hands, guiding the thickest side down towards Enya. Her eyes widened, and he called down, "Think you can grab it, Enya?"

She nodded, scrambling with her feet against the dusty cliff edge. Her boots struggled to find purchase, but she found a sturdy spot and propelled herself upwards. For a moment, she was flying, and she was sure death would capture her in the Great Sea. Then her hands grabbed hold of the new branch. Her palms burned beneath her black gloves, and she gasped.

"Pull!" Carson ordered. "We've got you."

Solid ground grew ever closer, and they all grabbed hold of her jacket, heaving her onto the rocks.

"*Saints.* That was too close," Enya managed, trying to catch her breath as she crawled further from the edge. Her hands grabbed fistfuls of grass, and she almost felt like kissing the earth in relief.

She spared a glance back over to the water endlessly spanning across the horizon. The morrigan had fallen, but she was sure they weren't out of the woods yet. The princes beside her helped her up, and Carson immediately took her into his arms.

"Please don't do that again," he pleaded into her tangled hair before pulling back. "You almost gave me a goddamned heart attack."

Enya flushed, removing his hands from her arms. She composed herself, standing up straighter with a cool expression. "I'm fine. Let's keep going, you four. We have a wand to find."

Carson nodded, furrowing his brows. He gestured back towards the forest. "Lead the way."

They must have walked for miles. It had to have been, based off the incessant aching in Enya's knees and feet, but no matter how much time it took, the moon never went down, and the sun never came up. It was as if they were trapped in a perpetual state of night.

Soon, their steps began to crunch material at their feet, and there was plenty of it littered across the dirt and moss of the cliffs. It was hard to see in the dark, so Enya simply guessed that it was twigs or more dead leaves.

"That sounds kind of weird," Beacon admitted. "Hold on." He took a lighter from Rowan and peered close to the ground before stumbling back in shock and dropping the device. He grabbed onto his brother, his chest rapidly rising and falling.

"What's wrong?" Niall asked, his voice wavering slightly. Enya came closer and gasped.

Bones. They were walking on bones.

"Do you think those are real?" Niall moaned, gagging into his hands. Enya could feel her own stomach grow queasy. These must have been more victims of the demon. The remnants of those who had failed to pass through.

Carson quickly snatched back up the lighter, face brave despite the horrific scene spread out before them. "They look real enough."

Eventually they made it across and back into the undergrowth of trees and briars, relief plastered on each of their faces. The morrigan had yet to follow them after it fell. It was both relieving and unnerving. Something was waiting for them; the Raven was sure of it.

"That wasn't so bad, right?" Beacon offered with a hesitant smile once they'd stopped to take a breather. "We made it, you guys."

It was then that they heard voices in a clearing up ahead. Enya motioned for everyone to get down. Crouching, she shifted closer, peering through a rotten smelling bush.

Visible behind the foliage were dark tents inside a chest-high, pointed fence. Oil lamps hung around the clearing, ones which illuminated various ghastly faces and near-translucent figures. Sharp teeth and black eyes caught in the moonlight. Some possessed wolfish figures, others that of banshees, or even goblins, and each looked more sinister than the one before. These were the worst of Seelie and Unseelie faeries, the most vile and evil of them all.

But why were they here in this wicked place?

Enya felt for her gun but thought better of it and grabbed her blade. There would be less noise and less attention that way.

They'd have to be silent as hares out here in order to avoid detection. Quiet feet led her slowly, ever so slowly, through the brush to her left, careful to watch both the forest floor and her adversaries at once while the rest of the gang followed close behind.

"Hey! I spot some live ones!" a burly voice shouted.

Enya bolted, the balls of her feet pounding into the earth the faster she ran. It was hard to see without their lighters, and it took plenty of effort to avoid tripping.

Cries of protest sounding from behind said otherwise. She looked over her shoulder to find Beacon and Niall captured and thrown to the ground. Two furry ghouls hissed, claws drawing blood as they tied up the princes. Carson struggled with another lizard-like foe, slashing with his knife. When he tried to reach for his gun, a paw across his face sent him flying into a nearby tree. He laid still, unconscious.

"Foolish mortals," the scaled creature muttered, shaking his head. He grabbed Carson by his leg and flipped him over. His hands were next bound with rope, and soon he and the two princes were smacked into a tree trunk. Enya's heart sunk.

And then she held back a scream when claws snaked around her from behind. She was spun to face hollow eyes and a skeleton-like face that managed to twist into a jagged smile. The bony creature sliced into her chest with its long nails, taking advantage of her surprise and creating deep red gashes in her pale skin.

Biting back curses, she stumbled back right into a tree, and the scent of burnt cedarwood filled her nose. Rowan was at her defense in seconds, striking the creature down with a charred log. It batted at him, sending claws deep into his leg and earning a pained hiss from the prince. Enya quickly snaked out with her blade, severing its head as she tried to catch her breath.

It fell into a heap of ash, and Rowan staggered into her, holding onto her for support. "Come on," she urged, pulling him further through the woods so they could hide behind a nearby tree before they were spotted again.

Hearing more agonized cries from the other princes made Enya's blood ran cold. She'd tried so hard until now to protect them, all of them, and now it might have been for nothing. Any ounce of making it up to them for what she'd done, whether they knew that was what she was doing or not, would all have been for nothing.

There would be no redeeming herself if she failed.

When she peered through the brush back towards the clearing, she saw that Carson was still slumped against the tree with his eyes closed, but she saw his chest rise and fall. He was still breathing.

The other two princes were now bruised and bloodied, but alive.

In her focus on their captured friends, Enya had failed to realize how close she was to that royal pain in the ass. And they were pretty darn close. When she turned back to the tree, Rowan was nearly right on top of her. His chest rested not even an inch away, and his breath brushed against her cheeks. If it weren't so perpetually dark out, she would have sworn that he was staring at her.

No, scratch that. He *was* staring at her. What the hell was this guy thinking? Now wasn't the time for this. Any of this. Enya wasn't even sure how she felt about Carson, and that was a serious mess in and of itself. No, she and Rowan were just friends, if she'd even call it that. Most of the time he was just a royal prick, and she was just a gang leader, and that was that. Right? Right.

With cheeks blazing, she pushed back, eyes on the ground. "Don't do that again," she said gruffly.

Rowan rolled his eyes, his jaw now set as he leaned against the trunk with his injured leg. "You put me in that spot. It's not like I chose to be there."

"Just—can you just shut up for a moment? We need to rescue everyone before they become undead ghouls."

"No, really? Here I thought we were just having a late-night picnic in this innocent forest. We're rescuing people too? Anything else you'd like to do while we're here? Sight-see, maybe?"

"Saints, you are such a pain. Out of all the people to be stuck with, it just had to be you," Enya snapped, careful to stay quiet so those in the clearing couldn't hear. "We have to be smart about this. You have weapons from the Church of Ast-ru, right?" she asked, earning an annoyed nod from the prince. "Good. They didn't happen to give you any *magick* weapons, did they?"

The prince gave her a pointed look. *I'll take that as a no.* Great. That wasn't going to be super helpful.

Options, options. What were their options?

"Stealth, then. We'll have to sneak over there and hope we don't get caught trying to cut them free. You do know how to work that thing, right?" Enya asked, gesturing to his pistol. This time she earned an exasperated sigh.

Rowan crossed his arms, glowering down at her from his tall height. "If we make it out of this, you're looking at ten thousand pounds less for the sheer amount of annoyance you manage to contribute to my day. *All* of my days."

"Wasn't in the deal, hot shot," she retorted, tightening her black leather gloves and blowing dirt off her gun. It barely shone in the moonlight. That's about all the light they had, one that sent a silvery glow over the snow on the ground and the forest around them.

"So, you think I'm hot?" he asked with a smug grin.

"Saints, are you always this—ugh. No," Enya stammered, now pinching her nose in frustration. The nerve of this guy.

They were quite literally in the middle of a life or death situation and like usual, all he could think about was himself. Specifically, his looks. "Just be ready, alright? We have to be careful."

Rowan smiled further, clearly pleased with himself.

If they did manage to make it out alive, she'd have to find some creative way to wipe that smirk off his face.

But her chest began to pulse with pain, and Enya clutched it with her gloved hands, wincing. Even Rowan looked off-beat with his leg, jaw rippling with vulnerability he dared not show her.

"We can't go out there like this," Enya finally said.

He scoffed. "No. Really? I thought we stood a good chance."

Saints. "If you're going to keep talking to me like that, I could just ditch you, you know. I'd fare better than some royal fool with a bad leg out in these woods," she retorted hotly.

Rowan closed his eyes, sighing deeply. "We should find cover. Assess the damage." He opened them and met hers. Something warm flashed between them, and she held out her hand. Unsure, he took hold, and she slung his arm over her shoulder.

Enya cleared her throat. "You're no good to this country dead, Rowan. Being the heir to the throne and all."

He shook his head, letting her guide him along the forest floor with a rueful smile. "And here I thought you were starting to like me."

"You know, I've never had a rebel leader bandage me up before. A bit ironic, don't you think?" Rowan asked with a smirk as

Enya tied a piece of fabric she'd ripped off his shirt around his thigh.

She narrowed her eyes and tightened her grip, making him wince. "Very ironic, Your Highness."

All around them, the forest was eerily silent. Black mist swirled at their feet as they sat within their makeshift shelter of bundled twigs and leaves stashed between two trees. It wasn't much, but it would do.

"Alright," Rowan said, nodding towards her. "Now you."

Enya shook her head, trying to ignore the blood still oozing from the gashes in her chest. "I'm fine. There's really no need."

The prince gave her an exasperated look. "Seriously, Enya? Stop being so proud and let someone help you for a change. Just look at yourself. Does that look *fine* to you?" He waved at her chest, and she flinched. The cuts still stung, but what was there to do about it?

"We have nothing for this. No healing balms, no bandages—"

His face darkened, and she shut up. Reluctantly, she fanned out her jacket and spread the collar of her shirt wider, which was caked with dark red. Rowan scooted closer and raised his hand, pausing, waiting for her to give the okay. Enya nodded, and he brushed the collar even wider, his thumb smoothing slowly over her exposed skin.

She'd never felt more on fire in her life.

"T-That's enough, Rowan," she stammered, pulling back from the prince and flashing a nervous smile. "It's bloody. It's gross. I think we've established that."

His face was unreadable, a stoic mask. But she could have sworn she saw something else when his skin touched hers.

Finally, he sighed. "We should at least clean that up, Enya. Do we have any water? Anything?"

She frowned. "No. Just the clothes on our backs ..."

Without hesitating, Rowan tore off another piece of his shirt, and she flushed after seeing a glimpse of the toned muscle underneath. He held it out to her, and she took it with a trembling hand. Out of the corner of her eye, she noticed the corner of his lips turn up into a small smile. *Damn him.* Enya dabbed at her wounds, hissing in pain when the fabric touched the exposed flesh.

It was quiet for a while as they pondered their next move.

"How's your leg?" Enya asked finally, breaking the silence and glancing down at his thigh. The fabric was soaked with blood.

The prince stretched it, grimacing. She helped him stand, and he walked a few steps, testing it out. "The cuts were deep, but I'll manage. How's your ..." He trailed off, nodding towards her chest.

"Good enough. Ready to save Carson and your brothers?"

He flashed a haughty smile. "Ready for anything, Raven thief."

PART THREE

DEALS WITH DARKNESS

Brasovian Territory

IT WASN'T exactly the easiest thing to sneak around a bunch of ghostly foes, but Enya and Rowan weren't going to let that stop them in the slightest.

The muffled chatter of the demon's henchmen could be heard in the darkness, nearly covering up the crunching of dead leaves and twigs under Enya and the prince's footsteps through the brush and beside the spiked, wooden fence against their backs.

Her eyes were locked onto their friends held captive while her head just barely poked out from above the fence line. Her hand tightened around her iron knife from the Church of Astru.

Adrenaline kept her heart pounding in her chest, or was it in her ears? Either way, she was ready.

Rowan crept down beside her on the forest floor, only mere feet away from Carson and his brothers once they'd crawled through an opening in the wood, now stalking through briars that cut into their skin. Pain wracked through her, but she pushed on.

With the dim light of the lanterns, Enya could see the rope binding their hands. If she were fast enough, she could slice it without anyone noticing.

Or she could always slide them the knife and let them do it. It would be way more subtle that way. But doing that meant catching their attention in a way that they knew what she was planning.

"Why don't we just kill them now?" a gruff voice demanded, one coming from a figure with pointed ears and sharp teeth who stood a few yards away from the oak tree holding their friends. His skin was as pale as the fading snow on the ground. "I want to taste their flesh and feel their souls slip into the Black Lake."

Enya backed away, closer to their escape route in the fence. Rowan mimicked her silently, eyes wide and ready.

A fist slammed on a wooden table covered in dried blood next to him, this one coming from a hairy figure resembling a faoladh, a wolfish creature said to be the protector of innocent souls. Such a shame he'd been stolen into the Crimson Witch's grasp. But based on how many monsters there were in the clearing, and there had to be dozens, he definitely wasn't the only one captured.

The monster's eyes sparked with fury, his lips curling back

from canine teeth. "Ballora said these humans were to be kept alive until we captured the Raven and the heir to the throne. She has plans for those little rats." He pulled back, staring down the others in the clearing. "They're going to help her find the Sword of Bas so she can be freed."

Next, a sinister laugh from a feminine voice. This one resembled a siren, her near-translucent blue skin now covered in rotten kelp and fish bones. "So we can all be free to reign over the world once again, my brothers and sisters."

Enya's blood chilled and a queasy feeling found its way into her stomach. Catching Rowan's gaze, she could see he felt the same.

After a few more moments of talking about doom and gloom and their plans for world-domination, the ghouls walked away beyond a few tents and bushes, leaving just the one lizard-like faerie to guard Carson, Beacon, and Niall. Now was their chance to strike.

Enya scanned the clearing once more, making sure that no one would notice if one of their little demon buddies went missing.

When she was certain he was all alone and facing away from the tree, she pounced forward, leaves scraping along her exposed hands.

She pushed up on her toes to catch his scaly head in a headlock. Not a moment later, Enya's blade was against his throat, pressing against green and yellow-tinted flesh, now faded with death. He felt surprisingly solid for a lost soul. There was no pulse in his neck, no indication that his heart was keeping him alive. It must have been the Crimson Witch's magick that made him—them—so real, so deadly.

But hot rage boiled inside Enya when she recalled what this one had done to Carson. She pressed harder, drawing black blood.

"I'm going to take a guess and say that you're the Raven," he said slowly, his voice shrill. But his face was stoic and if anything, a tad bit amused.

"You have a knife, right, Rowan?" Enya asked quietly, almost dangerously. When the prince nodded, she continued, "Cut them loose and be quick about it."

For once, he did as he was told without some snarky comment. He crouched down by their friends, setting them free one by one.

"We thought you guys were dead!" Niall cried, catching Rowan's hand in his for a quick pat on the shoulder. Beacon did the same, and they both got up from the ground. They nudged Carson, and he stirred, mumbling to himself.

Enya's eyes narrowed, and her lips curled back. He'd better be okay enough to walk or there would be hell to pay.

"We're fine, but we need to get out of here," Rowan reassured him. His eyes scanned Carson and his brothers. Finally, Enya's right-hand man opened his eyes, and they widened when his gaze landed on her predicament with the creature.

"I'm going to kill you," she murmured in the lizard-man's ear, sneering. "You and all your little friends."

Her threat was met with an emotionless scoff.

"Do you think I'm scared of you, little girl? You and your bunch of royal misfits," he scoffed, careful not to push closer into the knife at his throat. "No. No, I'm more scared of Ballora than I'd ever be of you. She has true power."

Enya didn't wait to hear more.

She plunged the iron knife into his throat, wincing at the black liquid that spewed out. He fell out of her arms, stumbling forward while his hands clutched his neck desperately. After a few moments of choking on his own blood, he crumpled into a pile of ash on the ground. Enya covered the mess by kicking and stomping it into the dirt.

There would be no evidence of foul play, save for his absence and that of the Crimson Witch's missing captives. Well, on second thought, maybe that was enough.

"We have to move. Now," Enya ordered, motioning for everyone to stay down. She hurried over to help Carson up, relieved to find he wasn't disoriented but rather calculating with every step and glance around their surroundings. Pride swelled inside her chest.

Enya led them through a tear in one of the surroundings tents. Inside was nothing more than an empty mess of fur blankets. She crept to its front, checking to see if the coast was clear. Winter seeped into her clothes, her breath now frosting before her in the darkness as she waved Carson and the princes towards the fence line to her left. They knelt down, hidden by stray bushes.

Her hand never left her iron knife as she took in the nearby firepit. The scent of burned flesh caught itself in Enya's nose, and she had to stifle a cough. What in saints name would they be burning out here?

"These wrenches wouldn't give in to Ballora. What a shame, too. That one looks pretty bulky. Got nice muscles on him," a feminine voice nearby said. "It's too bad she won't let us eat them, either."

Sickness churned Enya's stomach and she grimaced.

Footsteps atop the crunching dirt sounded above their heads, fading as whoever, or whatever, it was walked away. She let out a sigh of relief, looking back to Carson and the princes who looked equally disgusted. She motioned with two fingers to go behind another tent on her left, one not too far from where they were posted.

In the shadows of the lamps, the coast looked clear, so Carson nodded in understanding.

They each hurried toward the designated area. That is, until they saw shadows approaching in the lamp light.

Crap. Crap. Crap. Crap.

Enya froze, Rowan running right into her side and shooting her a deadly glare. She motioned wildly with her hands for everyone to duck behind a stack of wooden crates full of more bones and ash. It was no doubt other poor, unfortunate souls who had fallen at the hands of these demons.

Her and the rest of the group flew behind the crates. Whether anyone else was holding their breath, Enya didn't know, but she certainly was. More footsteps approached, lingering for several moments before walking away. Their owner muttered something about forest foxes and pixies.

Saints, Enya thought, furrowing her brows. *That was way too close.*

With so many people to hide, this would be difficult. She wished that they still had those invisibility charms from Miriana. Moments like these made them pretty damn handy.

There looked to be tables covered in torn, white cloth up ahead near the outskirts of the clearing. When the coast was clear again, Enya skid across the dirt behind it, leaving fresh tracks atop the mossy earth. The others followed quickly, with

Beacon sliding his feet under cover right before another lost soul passed by. This creature looked to be human above the waist with its dark fur coat, but below their body was that of a black horse, one decayed and twisted by the demon's magick.

It trotted west, away from them, and Enya breathed another sigh of relief. Ice filled her veins just as quick when several shadows approached on the other side of the table they hid behind, stopping only a few feet away to chat.

"Do you ever get tired of being undead?" a shrill male voice asked, earning snorts of laughter from those with him.

One male voice scoffed. "How could I possibly get tired? I'm dead. I don't need sleep," another male voice retorted. The first let out an annoyed sigh. "No. With all the power Ballora has promised us, I could never get tired of this."

"What if it doesn't happen? What if she fails?"

The screeching of metal against metal sounded through the night air, making any chatter of monsters or shaking of tree leaves from the wind go silent.

"How dare you even speak those words?" the second demanded with a growl. Another clash of metal, likely swords drawn in anger. "Once she has captured them and retrieved the other items with their help, we will all be free to roam the world as we did before, brother. Well, a little rotten, but still."

"Not if they kill her first," the shrill one muttered. Not a second later, a guttural cry let loose, and a body slumped to the ground. Enya's eyes went wide, her entire frame going stiff. These guys were ruthless. They'd be a serious pain in the ass to try and take out, too.

"No one speaks of the Crimson Witch that way. She is practically our queen," the second voice growled again.

"Relax, Brendan," chided another voice, this one feminine. After a moment, she added, "Someone take care of that. Burn it with the others."

Footsteps came and went until all was quiet once more. Shivers ran down Enya's spine, and she snuck a glance over at her grimacing companions. She sucked in a deep breath, her eyes scanning for their next hiding place. After a moment, she realized they were more than halfway through the clearing.

But could they make it through without being caught?

The howl of the morrigan echoed through the night, making all the hairs on the back of Enya's neck stand up.

"Our captives are missing! Tell Ballora!" a female voice shouted.

The clamor of metal and wood pounded around the clearing, battle cries not far behind. They knew they were there. The morrigan had announced it. He had just given away any sense of stealth they'd been hoping for. They had no choice but to run now.

This was it. They had to move or risk a horrible fate. She could only hope that these monsters were confined to the space around the camp. Hope was all they had at this point.

"I see them over there!" someone cried.

Crap. Crap. Crap.

Enya pushed Carson and the princes around a nearby cart of supplies. Her gun full of iron bullets was out and ready, and she fired shot after shot. One bullet zipped into the head of a fire nymph, another into the chest of a dark-furred beast. Her shot was joined by several more as Carson joined her side. His bravado and smugness truly never felt so deserved than when he was shooting.

His shots were just as accurate as Enya's, every single bullet. One sliced through the head of a lizard fae, next through the heart of a ghoul. They dissipated in spews of black blood and ash.

In their desperation, the princes finally found their courage and had begun popping off rounds. Rowan took three shots to finally turn a wicked fae to ash. Beacon fired wildly into the crowd of demons, howling in both excitement and fear.

But Niall struggled against a ghoul. The smaller demon had the prince's gun, he was unable to reclaim his weapon. Enya spun from her last kill to help Niall, her finger ready on the trigger before she was blind-sided. Whatever creature hit her caused her to miss wide, thankfully not taking out Beacon in the process.

She found her knife just as a serpent-like creature grabbed her by the hair and flung her to the ground. The impact sent pain up her side and through her legs.

"Shit!" she exclaimed, grabbing a hold of its claws atop her scalp. Enya's pistol came up in a quick flick, her bullet blowing out the creature's abdomen in a gruesome black mess. The sound of her defense made her ears ring, and she winced. The creature staggered to the ground before crumpling into a heap of ash.

Enya had no time to turn back to her friends. Another was on her in an instant, this one more of an undead wolf, one who was half human. The monster lunged for her throat with long canines, and for a moment she was afraid. She shoved her gun inside its mouth and pulled the trigger, the bullet and brains blowing out the back of its skull. But not before her arm was torn by jagged teeth.

She sucked in a breath, biting her lip to try and ignore the pain. Red blood ran down her arm, and the world began to spin. But she wouldn't go down that easily.

Battle cries rang out from the Crimson Witch's followers, piercing through the air and making all the hairs on Enya's neck stand up. She and the group took down another wave of undead foes sprinting from all sides, more blood coating the ground along with their bullets.

Bodies covered the clearing, all of them turning into ash and disappearing from her view just as fast as they had come. But there was no safety here.

They ran. They ran, ignoring all the shouts and screams and growls behind them, threatening to catch hold and drag them back into the Crimson Witch's grasp. They ran beyond the exit, beyond the beaten path leading out of it, and beyond more jagged cliffs begging for them to slip and fall.

Finally, they stopped when they were certain that they'd ditched those undead soldiers.

Enya's breathing came in ragged gasps and her limbs felt sore from the constant walking and running for the past several days. Her stomach rumbled with a weak reminder that she hadn't eaten in a while too. She desperately needed to rest, and her torn up arm needed bandaging. But would they find respite in these haunted woods?

Brasovian Territory

THERE WAS nothing but silence when Enya opened her eyes, taking in the stars in the perpetually blackened sky. Cold was what she noticed next, raising goosebumps on her arms and making her shudder.

It smelled of burnt lavender and weeds, making her crinkle her nose. She sat up, taking in her surroundings.

It was still dark, but of course it was, considering where they were. She was surprised nothing had killed them while they slept. Bushes and trees surrounded them on all sides, but otherwise the space was clear.

Enya faintly remembered that their group had somehow managed to wrap her arm up in a torn-up scarf, courtesy of

Niall, before dozing off. She raised her arm, cringing at the bloodstains spotted over the cotton material.

Carson laid a few feet away, still dozing. Rowan was closer … just slightly, his leg pressed against hers. Her eyes widened and she scooted back an inch. His brothers were also still asleep, but they'd have to get up soon.

They needed to finish this once and for all.

Enya lifted onto her feet, dusting off her clothes and tightening her weapons to her belt.

The sound of the crunching leaves below woke Rowan, whose eyes flashed open to meet hers. He glared, getting up slowly to join her so they didn't wake up the others. She motioned through the bushes with a hand, and he followed, flicking out a lighter to illuminate their way. Dust floated around in the shadows exposed by the flame in the prince's grasp, and they stopped by a pair of trees.

"Got a plan, wanted criminal?" he asked casually, leaning up against a trunk with his hands behind his head. As if they were on some sort of field trip from the palace.

"We just keep moving. We reach the mountain pass, find the wand, and then go home." She sucked in her cheek, avoiding his eyes. Thoughts of him so close to her in the forest came to mind, and her cheeks flushed beet red.

Rowan sighed. "I hate when you do that."

She pushed her brows together confused. "What are you talking about?"

"When you make that face," he replied simply, as if it were obvious. His lips curled down into a frown. "You do that when you're thinking about Carson all the time."

What gave him the right to assume that?

Enya didn't have the guts to say that she was thinking about him this time. Instead, she plastered on an emotionless expression, one that she hoped was unreadable.

"I'm not thinking about anyone," she said stiffly.

He scoffed. "Sure you're not."

"I'm not! What gives you the right—"

Rowan interrupted her, "You're thinking about *something* then. Something that makes your face look ... strange." He swallowed, his gaze now glued to the ground. He must not have been used to girls having feelings. That must have been it. Surely, he didn't feel something like Carson did. That would be one hell of a mess.

Footsteps drew near, crackling stray woodland debris, and Enya turned her head to find Carson, Beacon, and Niall had joined them. When Carson noticed her alone with Rowan, his jaw set.

"Alright, so, uh," she scrambled to find the words. "Is everyone well-rested enough?" She had the feeling no one would ever be prepared enough for what they were about to face, but she wasn't going to say that out loud.

Niall paled, earning a comforting pat on the back from Beacon. Rowan just looked bored, silently glowering at Carson. Was the heir to the throne *jealous*? Of a gang member? It seemed crazy but plausible if the murderous expression on his face was any indication.

Carson nodded. "Let's get going, Enya."

"Maybe I don't feel like going anywhere," Rowan muttered, stomping away into the woods and disappearing into the night.

Carson shot Enya a hesitant look, pausing for a moment

while he looked after where the prince had disappeared to. Finally, he said, "I'll go check on him and make sure he's good for the trip." He lumbered off in the direction Rowan had gone, his footsteps soon fading.

Beacon yawned, rubbing his bloodshot eyes. "As much as I'd love to get this party started, I'm guessing we're waiting for them."

Enya smiled slightly. "Yeah. Let's take this time to rest a bit more."

For several long moments, they sat in awkward silence on the ground. Enya stared at her boots, ones now caked in bone dust and stray flesh, making her nose wrinkle in disgust. She sure had a lot of explaining to do when they returned to the Bowman's Pub for this mess and her new Brasovian get up. The thought brought a little bit of levity to this dark situation.

"So, where to after they come back?" Niall asked, breaking the silence as he stretched his arms.

Enya shrugged, feeling a headache brewing inside her skull. Saints, she just wished she could sleep. Actually sleep without the threat of devilish foes waiting to pounce. "We head north, like that ghoul said."

"You trust her?" Beacon asked, grimacing.

"No, but we have no other leads," she retorted flatly. "I'd rather not be wandering these woods aimlessly forever, if you don't mind."

Her mind drifted back to Rowan and Carson, and she frowned. They still hadn't come back yet, and it had been a good while by now.

"Should we check on them?" Niall asked, his voice wavering slightly with worry. "To make sure they're still alive?" He loosened the collar of his shirt.

Beacon nodded. "Yeah, we need to make sure they're okay. Come on," he said, waving for Enya to follow while they walked through the forest, following where their companions had vanished. Cold air stung their faces as they trudged on. All was quiet and unmoving. Not even woodland animals stirred.

"Where are those two?" Beacon muttered. "It's not like Rowan to want to stay out here. He'd start complaining about everything,"

Enya smiled. "He already complains about everything without being in a haunted forest." She raised a brow. The two princes laughed, but there was a nervous undercurrent to it.

She heard footsteps to her right, and immediately her pistol was up and ready to shoot.

It was Rowan and Carson, both looking wide-eyed, but safe. They weren't harmed, at least, not that she could see. Enya lowered her weapon, awash with relief. Her pulse gradually slowed back to normal.

"We thought something happened. Where the hell were you guys?" Enya demanded, giving Carson a light shove.

He watched her, his face empty and hollow. After a moment, he replied, "We were talking, but we're back," he said, but his voice felt off. It didn't sound like his usual warmness at all. Rowan looked equally distant, not even bothering to approach his brothers before he began walking through the forest. Carson wasn't far behind.

They continued in silence, their path once again lit by lighters. Moonlight danced through the trees, and the scent of pine and wilted flowers filled their noses with every step. Soon, the ground became more rocky and jagged. Hills grew higher, trees grew taller, and their path sunk within the earth. They had reached the Galtymore Mountains that spread throughout the borders of Brasova and Skeyya.

But the night sky before them was full of flames. Fire filled the valley that cut through the mountain, sending hues of red, orange, and yellow in a constant stream through the valley.

Lighters were off, and finally part of their journey was bright enough to see without assistance.

Smoke and ash filled the air yet somehow it didn't choke their group, though it did burn their eyes. The smell of burnt wood filled Enya's nose and she gagged, covering it and her mouth with a leather-clad hand.

At the center of the valley was an array of pillars, all flanking each other and perfectly equal in size. They were much lower than the cliffs they were on now but would require they climb once they'd reach the bottom of the valley.

A single bauble of magick, full of blue and white lights, floated at the center of those pillars, one holding a glowing wand. *The Wand of Tine.* They'd finally found it. Only, how were they supposed to get there? Those pillars and foreboding flames beneath didn't make for an easy smash and grab.

"I'm going to take a wild guess," Beacon began as he took a steadying breath. "We're going to have to climb up those pillars in order to reach that thing."

Enya sighed, flipping her hair out of her face. "We are." Tightening her boots and gloves, she looked up at Carson. "Are you ready?" she asked him. His expression was as it had been for miles, blank ... empty.

After a brief pause, he spoke. "I am."

"Uh, good," she said carefully, turning to face the princes.

Rowan was equally expressionless, and her pulse quickened. Something was very wrong. "Beacon, Niall, and ... Rowan, do you think you can handle climbing with us? It might be the only way through to the other side of this valley."

"Are you kidding? Y-You think it's safe out here?" Niall cried, shivering in disgust. "I'd follow you any day."

"What he said," Beacon agreed. "Besides, I don't think Rowan would let anyone venture on without him. He has a brave reputation to protect, right brother?" he asked with a smile, now facing the heir to the throne who stood still as stone.

Enya quickly pulled Beacon and Niall to the side, casting a weary look over to Carson and the oldest prince. "We'll just be gone a minute. Don't go anywhere, okay?" She kept marching them another few feet and through a few bushes. Leaves and thorns scratched at her skin, making her wince. Finally, she whispered, "There's something going on with those two."

"Seriously. I've never seen him shut up for more than ten minutes before," Beacon huffed. "It's a new record."

Niall shook slightly, swallowing the lump in his throat. "Do you think they'll be okay?"

Enya shrugged. "It might be shock or something. But ... I've never seen Carson act like that. Just be on your guard, okay? Don't trust them." Her eyes filled with pity at the princes' expressions. She understood. But she also felt sick to her stomach that they still trusted her, not knowing that she had killed their mother. They'd hate her if they knew the truth, and she deserved that hate.

Beacon and Niall gave solemn nods, and the trio headed back with spirits just a little lower than before.

Carson and Rowan stared at them expectantly, as if they

knew what had been discussed in the bushes. Enya's cheeks flushed, and she motioned for them to keep walking toward the valley.

They couldn't afford to stop now and have some big, group heart-to-heart. Not when they were so close to finding the wand and getting out of this mess.

Hopefully, the wand would give them a clue on the Sword of Bas. That was the key to ending all of this business with the Crimson Witch and her army. Well, that or it would be how she gained control over their country and the world as they knew it if for some reason the Grims and the princes happened to mess up.

The entire valley was deserted, save for the burning chasms below the stone pillars. Enya hoisted herself up onto the nearest one, hands screaming obscenities at her for the strain of pulling her weight. She grimaced. The pain of remembering what those hands did to Queen Layla's neck was almost just as painful.

Murderer. Murderer. Murderer.

She swallowed hard. Up here, Enya could see the wand better, but there were still several rows between them and their prize.

Carson was right behind her before slipping past her with ease. Enya watched him a cautious moment before grabbing hold of Beacon's hand and pulling him up. Niall came after, pushed up by Rowan. The last prince followed, stoic and unreadable.

Up ahead was some sort of star-shaped disk made of stone etched into a rock wall.

Enya sighed, trudging up to peer closer. Inside the star

were two faded keyholes, one shaped like a ram and one like a lion, each having Brasovian Zodiac symbols. She had to squint a bit to make them out, but they definitely looked familiar.

"Hey, hand me that paper from earlier. The one you guys sketched from that tree thing, or whatever it was," she asked, holding out her hand to Rowan. He watched her without saying a word. "Uh, pretty boy, the paper please?" Almost mechanically, he reached into his coat pocket and produced the crumpled-up drawing from before, handing it to her slowly.

Her brows pushed together, but she didn't comment on his weird behavior again. She swallowed hard, turning her gaze down to the paper in her hand. She rolled it out and tried to straighten it a bit in her palm until she could make out the signs below the fiery mountain it contained. *Berbec* and *Leu*. The ram and the lion. That seemed to match what was in the star.

"What are we supposed to do now?" Beacon asked, uncertainty coloring his features. "Go on some kind of scavenger hunt for keys?"

Enya nodded. "Seems like it. Let's start looking around and see what we dig up." She held up the paper so they could get a better look.

With determined nods, they set off.

Enya went with Carson to the left and the princes went to the right. The looming rock had more than enough room for them all, spanning several yards before running into ones taller and shorter in size. Small stones shaped like different animals littered the dusty ground, ones with various symbols.

Looking closer, Enya realized this was exactly what they'd been looking for. "Beacon, Niall," she called out. "Come check this out." They hurried over, a few stones in their hands similar to the ones she was gazing at.

She raised a brow. They'd found the keys already? Rowan and Carson didn't show any inclination that they'd seen anything.

"Check this out," Beacon huffed, tossing over one shaped like a lion. "Isn't this what we needed?" It had the right shape, but the sign etched into it was wrong. Enya shook her head.

"No, we need these symbols here, Berbec and Leu, remember?" she said, once again displaying the paper. The thought of dropping it in the flames below sent a shiver down her spine.

Niall scratched his head. "There was another star thing in a wall on our side. Same shapes different symbols."

Enya cocked her head curiously. That was odd. "Show me what you mean."

The duo complied, marching over to a new stone slab depicted just like they had said. She bit her lip. No, what they found in the woods clearly depicted these specific zodiac signs. Something was off here.

"This could be a trap," Enya admitted. Beacon and Niall's faces fell, and so did her hopes for keeping their spirits high. "Let's go find the ones for the first star and go from there, alright?" The two boys shrugged, and they all resumed their search for the right keys.

Enya lowered to a crouch, her hands brushing the black dust at her feet aside and feeling for anything unusual. Finally, her hands struck something pointed and round. When she held it up in the light of the flames, she saw the symbol for Berbec.

She dusted it off and stuffed it into her coat pocket, taking a steadying breath as relief washed over her. "We just need Leu now, guys. I found the other one," Enya called out.

"I think we just found Leu," Niall hollered back. Thank the saints.

"Meet us by the first star," she replied. Hesitantly, she glanced over at Carson to find him equally as expressionless as before. Her face paled and she looked away.

Once they'd approached the star in the stone once more, Enya and Niall placed the keys in simultaneously.

For a moment, nothing happened, and she braced herself for another sarcastic remark from the heir to the throne. But then, the rock before them rumbled, causing the ground below their feet to tremble, nearly putting them off balance. It quivered and slid down, revealing a clear pathway through the pillars and fires around them. At the end was the Wand of Tine, waiting in its magical vortex.

Galtymore Mountains, Brasova

ENYA COULDN'T help but feel that their sweet victory had come far too easily. She proceeded with caution, one foot after the other, until they reached the massive stone formation that stood below the Wand of Tine.

"Are we sure this isn't a trap?" Enya asked skeptically.

Beacon and Niall shrugged, with no response coming from Carson or Rowan. That made their behavior seem even more suspicious.

"Maybe we just got lucky we found that thing in the forest," Beacon suggested, stuffing his hands into his pockets and sizing the wand up. "What do you think about lifting me up so I can grab it? It doesn't look that high." He began raising the sleeves of his jacket and cracking his hands.

"N-No! That's a horrible idea," Niall cried, partially covering his face in horror. "Who knows what that thing will do to you?"

Enya nodded. "Yeah, he's right. Maybe there's some sort of lever to turn off the magick stuff around it or some kind of spell we should say," she sighed, crossing her arms and peering around the rocky platform they stood on. The flames surrounding them licked at their feet, and the night sky was full of smoke that somehow didn't affect their breathing.

If I were some wicked demon-witch thing, where would I hide a magical lever? This situation was becoming more frustrating the longer she saw nothing but bare and empty stone. Were they going to have to plunge their hands into the fire below to find it?

"Hey, I think I see something," Niall exclaimed, stumbling right into her while looking over her shoulders in excitement. "But it's all the way on that wall over there."

Enya turned her head to see what he meant and did indeed find a lever. The only problem was that it was several dangerous jumps across the rocky pillars. Whoever dared to try that had to be crazy. But there was no turning back now. She stretched a bit, wincing at the pain in her hands and legs. And ignoring the protests of her growling stomach.

Once they got out of this fiery valley, she was excited to grab another crab sandwich at the Bowman's Pub and catch up with the Grims and the rebels.

For a moment, her mind wandered back to that time in the palace with Queen Layla ... No. No, she wouldn't think about that. Not right now. Not when they needed her.

"Alright," Enya said, clearing her throat. "I'll do it."

The princes balked at her. "By yourself?" Beacon demanded. "You'll be killed. Do you seriously think we could make it if something happened to you?"

Probably not. Her chest grew tight with worry, but she shoved those feelings aside. Who else would be able to do this? Carson? She glanced over to him and instantly regretted it when she saw the emptiness on his face.

Finally, he met her eyes and flashed a wicked grin.

"I'll do it," Carson said, his voice a hollow shell of what it once was. Now it was Enya's turn to grow wide-eyed.

"Are you sure you'll be able to handle it?" she asked, words wavering slightly. She couldn't lose him on top of everything else that was happening. It would be too much to bear.

He nodded. "Just leave it to me."

In a flash, Carson was off. He landed on pillar after pillar, leaving Enya gaping at the impossible distances he'd managed to cross in mere seconds. Once or twice, he almost lost his balance, but he was undeterred and smooth in regaining his composure. Finally, he reached the lever. Carson flipped it, and the wand glowed above their heads.

The magick soon vanished, and the wand fell neatly into Enya's waiting hands.

It was magnificent, dazzling, and all-around beautiful. It also scared the hell out of her. Though they needed this to take down the demon, it also made her stronger along the way.

But now she would be able to invade their dreams. The Crimson Witch would be able to possess anyone who touched the magick artifacts, according to Galina. She'd be able to possess Enya. The Raven gulped, slowly shoving the wand into her belt and turning to face the princes.

"Okay, we have it. Now let's get the heck out of here please!" Niall offered a nervous laugh. "This place doesn't feel right at all." Beacon nodded solemnly beside him.

Shrill squawking startled them, and they looked up to find inky black birds, ones whose feathers were tipped in flames. *Huma.* These were monsters that had somehow immigrated from the sandy dunes of Cardek, no doubt summoned by the demon's magick. The creatures swooped down repeatedly, attempting to jab their group with sharp beaks or burn them with their fiery wings.

"Run for it!" Enya exclaimed, pushing the princes down the rocky pillar and hoping Carson followed behind. They scampered across, ducking low to avoid their newfound attackers. Enya fearfully tried to cover her head with her hands before grabbing her gun. She fired several rounds to no avail, eventually giving up and running faster. There were way too many for shooting to make a difference.

The pounding of their feet sent echoes across the mountain pass, and the darkness of the night sky did little to hide the flock of flames above.

The air reeked of death, and Enya was afraid hers was drawing near. Her heart pounded when she leaped onto another pillar, then another, slowly making her way to the other side of the mountain with Carson and the princes in tow. For a moment, her life flashed before her, and with every swoop of the huma, she gasped harder and harder for air in her screaming lungs.

Smooth, grassy land didn't look too far off, so she pressed the balls of her feet firmer against the stone beneath her, begging them to hurry up while her muscles screamed obscenities at her.

One of the huma dove down, nicking and slightly burning her face in its aim for her neck. Fresh blood leaked out, the skin burned like hellfire, and the bird squawked in delight as she swatted it away. *Saints.*

Enya blew shot after shot with her pistol once more, aiming blindly at the night sky, which was scorched with feathery flames above their heads. In this trek to the haunted forest alone, she'd managed to spill plenty of her own blood and now endured stinging burns. Those at the Bowman's Pub would surely have legendary tales to tell the Grims gang's enemies upon her return to her flock.

"We're almost there!" Beacon shouted, just as out of breath as she was. "Please don't die, you guys. I'd miss you."

Enya scoffed, smiling briefly before flinching at another swooping bird, cawing in her ear.

Saints, please let us make it. I can't make any promises, but I might consider being sort of religious for a few days.

They flung across the rocks and above the fiery pits below, landing hard on the grass outside the mountain pass. Enya stumbled, rolling over and back onto her feet. The princes tried but were a lot less graceful in their attempts.

Just like that, the huma vanished against the edge of the valley, and all was quiet.

She looked over her shoulder to find the flaming valley and rocky terrain had gone, as well, leaving a simple mountain covered in dust and dirt. It was as if it had all been some sort of twisted dream.

"That was close," Enya said after several moments of

standing with her hands on her hips trying to calm the adrenaline in her veins. "Is everyone in one piece?"

"Feels like it," Niall huffed, eyes wide. "B-But I'm ready to go back home and away from all these monsters."

Enya sighed, sympathy written across her features. But then she turned to Carson and Rowan who still wore cold, stoic expressions.

She glanced around, taking in the dense trees surrounding them from all sides and the incline of the mountain that would send them down a grassy hill. The foliage looked much more alive here, absent of the eternal darkness that had blanketed the haunted woods in a sinister shroud. Night was turning into day, and for once since they'd entered the forest, the sun shone onto their faces. Enya savored the warmth of it flooding her skin.

If they were north of the mountains, that put them further into Brasovian territory. Maybe they could find somewhere to hole up while they figured out what to do next.

"Carson," Enya asked, turning to face her right-hand man. "Which way do you think we should go? You have the compass still, right?" Several awkwardly silent moments later he produced it from his pockets and handed it over, his eyes never leaving hers.

Okay … that was odd. Enya swallowed, flipping it open in her palm. Carson was usually the directions guy, not her.

"Northwest sounds good," she offered with a hesitant shrug. "Maybe set up camp a little ways away from all this demon stuff." Yeah, that sounded reasonable enough.

Beacon exchanged glances with Niall. "Do you know where you're going?" he asked.

"Not really," Enya let loose a nervous laugh. It would have been nice if she did. She'd never crossed into Brasova before. "Do either of you know your way around this side of the border?" They both shook their heads.

"It can't hurt to try northwest," Niall admitted.

With no objection from either Carson or Rowan, they were off.

The sun was shining in full force now, sending rays of light to fill the forest floor. Leaves fluttered around their feet, and the noise of woodland animals filled their ears. It smelled of sage and roses, something that helped ease Enya's racing heart. They were safe for the time being.

Several minutes later, she finally slumped against a large tree trunk laced with vines, her hands taking in the wound on her chest and the burning gash on her cheek. She must have been a sore sight to see, and her exhaustion was beginning to get the better of her.

"I think we need to rest." Her feet ached and her hand stung with memories of the past. Her mouth was dry from lack of water. Her stomach was rumbling in protest from lack of food. Even the forest floor was starting to look like the most comfortable bed on earth.

"That's the best idea we've had today," Beacon sighed, He turned to face Niall, who was already dozing while standing up.

Enya pursed her lips, looking around them for any signs of trouble. After seeing none, she said, "Yeah. Let's camp out here. Carson, can you start a fire?"

Silence. Then finally he replied, "I can manage it."

Enya's heart ached and an uneasy feeling slithered its way down her spine. He was being so different. Something was wrong and … and she realized how much she missed her best friend. Her closest confidant. His stupid jokes and his stupid way of knowing exactly how she was feeling all the time.

The group gathered to create a makeshift shelter against a large oak tree out of twigs, foliage, and several lavender stems they'd found nearby. Carson, as promised, started a fire to keep them warm if need be, and the sun began to set.

Aside from the buzzing of bees and the chirping of birds, it was empty. Enya wasn't sure if that was a good thing or not.

The crackling of the wood and kindling filled the silence surrounding them, burrowing deep into Enya's coat and warming her legs against the chill. Rowan was seated with his brothers while acting just as strange as usual, and Carson stood against a tree with his arms crossed. He stared blankly at the ground at his feet.

Enya sighed, looking between him and the princes. Finally, she gave in and marched over to him. Screw just being friends. She needed to get a few—no, make that *several* things off her chest. Business be damned.

"Follow me. I need to say something," Enya said gruffly before stalking past a few briars and bushes.

The breaking of leaves signaled he had done as requested, and when she turned, she found him less than a foot away. His eyes met hers, but there was no warmth to be found. Enya swallowed hard, stuffing her hands into her pockets.

"Carson, we've been through a lot on this trip, right?"

He nodded.

"And … a while ago you told me something. Something about wanting to be more than friends. Is that still, um, true?" she asked. Carson shrugged, his mouth set in a tight line.

Enya gripped the insides of her pockets hard, dreading the next few words coming out of her mouth but knowing they had to be said. He needed to know.

"Listen, I don't—I'm not really good at the whole relationships thing. I've never done that and never thought I really *would* do that. You're my right-hand man. My partner in crime. I didn't want to see you as more than that and potentially ruin our friendship." She was babbling now. Enya knew it, but she continued anyway. "I didn't want to feel anything … I still don't. In general. There's so much about me you don't know—still don't know."

She stopped for a moment, watching his expression. It didn't change and her heart fell to her stomach.

"Carson, when I saw you with Doina, it really messed with my head, okay? And apparently the princes noticed it too—er, noticed our connection. If you want to call it that."

Enya sucked in a breath, hating every single moment of this. Why did she have to feel like this?

"My point is that I have … feelings for you too."

He said nothing and she said nothing for a while after that, both unmoving. Her heart hammered in her chest and her stomach dropped in anticipation. It felt like forever had passed when Enya finally looked up from her dirty boots and back up to his face. It held nothing. It was as cold as the winter air around them.

"Damn the saints, Carson," Enya snapped, turning around to grab her long hair into fistfuls in her hands. "Do you have any idea how hard that was to say? To get that off my chest?" She spun back to face him. "Say something!" she demanded, shoving him.

He didn't, and her frustration only grew.

She stood there and huffed, eyeing him up and down. This wasn't like him at all. Carson didn't act like this. He was kind and nurturing and witty and all sorts of things she liked and hated that she liked.

"Screw it," she muttered. There was only one option left now, one that truly pained her to do. She hadn't wanted it to come to this. Enya flew forward and crashed her lips into his.

And her blade into his heart.

It was then that tendrils of black and gray smoke surrounded them. A wicked laugh, one that Enya had grown to recognize all too well these past few days, echoed through the woods. The Crimson Witch. Enya pulled back, but not before seeing an evil, twisted look on Carson's face.

"Your friend is gone," he whispered, his eyes wild and fanatic when they found hers. "Find the sword." Not a moment later, he was a heap of ash on the forest floor.

Enya sneered. She knew it.

Hurried footsteps came from her right. Enya's head whipped up to see Beacon and Niall with torn expressions. There could only be one reason they came here without the heir to the throne.

"Rowan's gone. He practically disappeared right in front of us! What the hell was that?" Beacon burst out.

Murderer. Murderer. Murderer. You failed them again.

This time, though, she wouldn't let the demon get away with what she'd done.

25

Brasovian Territory

A COLD sweat broke out on Enya's neck when she realized the severity of their situation.

Just moments before, they were victorious. They'd found the Wand of Tine, they'd escaped the Crimson Witch's grasp, for now, and she'd kissed Carson. Well, a fake version of Carson, which definitely didn't count but still left Enya with a mix of confusing emotions.

But now, Carson and Rowan were gone, and she was left to stare into the worried eyes of the other two princes. Her right-hand man and the heir to the throne were gone. They'd been captured by the demon.

"What do we do?" Beacon demanded, his eyes frantic and

heartbroken. "We can't just let her have them. We have to do something."

Enya's eyes were focused on nothing when she rose to her feet, her expression solemn and empty. This was her fault. She brought them here. She let them go out alone. For a moment, Enya said nothing. How could she? She'd murdered the princes' mother, led them here to the demon's haunted woods, and now let their brother get kidnapped by the very same creature who tricked her into killing the former queen in the first place.

Think, Enya. Think.

She cautiously pulled out the Wand of Tine, keeping her eyes peeled for any sign of trouble all the while. It shimmered a deep orange, the light sending glistening rays to dance across her skin. Enya felt in her pockets for the Pentacle of Glac. It wasn't there.

"Shit. Carson has the pentacle," she said, cursing under her breath. "That means the Crimson Witch has it."

"You don't mean …" Niall trailed off, horror written plainly across his face. He lifted a hand to cover his mouth.

Enya nodded. "She's only three objects away from gaining back all of her powers, escaping the Black Lake, and unleashing her army. That is, unless we figure out how to take her down and get back the pentacle."

"And get back Rowan and Carson," Beacon added. He regarded her with a challenging look, jaw set with determination.

She swallowed hard, a lump now in her throat. "And get back Rowan and Carson," Enya agreed, her heart heavy with guilt. She paused before cursing again.

"What's wrong?" Niall asked, voice wavering slightly.

"Usually, we find some sort of clue for the next object. We forgot to look this time because of the firebirds," Enya sighed, kicking a few twigs at her feet into the tree beside her. She really wanted to smash someone's head in. "*Saints*, could this day get any worse?"

"So, we have to go back in there?" Niall asked, now pacing around Enya and Beacon with his hands shoved tightly into his pockets. "Back to face those *things?*"

Enya crossed her arms before looking at the mossy ground at her feet. "I'm not exactly thrilled about it either, but what choice do we have? Honestly," She took a deep breath and met his gaze. "Do you want to save your brother or not? This is the only way to do it."

He stopped short, glancing back and forth between Beacon and her. Finally, "A-Alright. Let's go."

Once their feet crossed back into the valley of flames, night descended upon them once more. Though, there were no flames to be seen and no rotting ash stench making them wrinkle their noses.

The valley was barren, save for trees and greenery. It looked about as normal as any old mountain would, and it smelled of pine and honeysuckle.

But Enya and the princes knew the truth.

Hidden among the normalcy was that dreaded feeling of being watched. Of being cornered by some unseen and sinister force lurking in the shadows. The Crimson Witch was watching them, no doubt, and waiting to strike.

It was quiet. Much too quiet.

A fluttering of bats set them all on edge, almost making her heart stop completely. Enya was just about to breathe a sigh of relief when she realized that nothing past the valley looked even remotely like it had before.

"Uh, Raven—er, gang leader person," Beacon cleared his throat. "This doesn't look familiar."

"No, it doesn't," Niall seconded, gripping his brother's arm so hard his knuckles turned white, earning a dirty look from Beacon. "Oh. Sorry." He let go, moving his arms to hold himself against the cold air.

Enya's hand stayed locked onto her weapon while she crept further into the brush and briars laced throughout the forest. They needed to find a clue. Something that would point them to the next object. But they didn't even have a clue of what it looked like.

Murky, gray fog was seeping up their knees now, and the silence around them only seemed to be growing.

"Why, hello there," a familiar male voice said from behind them.

They each spun around, weapons up and glinting in the sunlight, daring their newfound foe to come closer.

Andrei.

He raised his hands innocently, grinning from ear to ear. "I come in peace."

Enya scoffed, cocking her pistol. "State your business before we spill those cocky guts of yours."

He slowly paced around them, their muzzles following his every step. "I want what you want."

"And what's that?" Enya challenged. "Last thing you said to us was to find the sword. Now, boys, who does that sound like?" She tilted her head towards the princes, who both nodded.

Andrei tsked. "I want it for the same reasons you do. To take this Crimson Witch down."

This had Enya taken aback and for the briefest of moments, her gun-wielding hand wavered. "Why would you want that?"

He shrugged, still circling with his hands up. He even had the nerve to raise a brow. "Why wouldn't I want that? Haven't you met her?" He paused, his mouth twitching with amusement. "Besides, don't you want those pretty boys of yours back, safe and sound?"

Enya swallowed, weighing their options. They could wander these forests aimlessly, searching for a sign of either the next clue or their captured companions. Or they could make a new deal with the devil.

"Perhaps. What's in it for you?"

Andrei lowered his hands from above his head, moving to cross his arms, his expression darkening. "I want revenge for what she did to my family. To me. Killing her with the power of four fae courts combined sounds like a good place to start. How do you think she created this little army of hers? Surely, you didn't think we all held hands and frolicked into these woods by choice."

Niall's breath caught. "So ... the creatures ..."

"Men, women, children. All twisted by her dark magick."

Did this demon's torment know no bounds? Enya's stomach turned violently, and nausea inched up her throat.

"How do we know you won't turn on us?" she said next, forcing herself to be emotionless. Feelings made you weak and left you exposed to your enemies. After what happened with Carson, she refused to be controlled by them any longer.

Andrei shrugged. "You don't, but it looks like you're running out of options, little Raven." He tilted his head curiously, his lips curving into a smirk. "Do you even have any idea how to get to the Black Lake, where she's stashed your friends?"

No, Enya did not. Damn him.

She gritted her teeth, slowly nodding. "Fine. But first, show us to the next clue—and don't forget we're armed. I won't hesitate to take you down, *Andrei*, if that's even your real name."

He had the nerve to laugh. "Call me Anders. I have many names, but that one is reserved for those I know personally. I'm sure we'll be friends, little Raven. Good friends."

Smug bastard. She gestured with her gun towards the forest, and he began walking past them, further through the valley. Beacon and Niall's footsteps followed close behind.

When it felt like they'd trudged for eons based off the incessant aching in Enya's feet and the exhaustion clawing at her eyes, though it could have only been a mere half an hour, her eyes widened at the scene before them. Illuminated speckles of green slime, ones varying in size, knotted themselves across the grass at their feet. The speckles glowed brightly, even in the sunshine, almost like magick. No, scratch that. It had to be magick. There was no other explanation.

It seemed like the speckles had formed a sort of path through the darkness. "This way," Anders said, waving them on. Enya and the two princes exchanged unsure glances, but this looked promising.

They followed the glowing lights, their shoes kicking aside leaves, pine needles, and dust. There was no wildlife to be seen when they neared a giant tree, one whose trunk was three sizes too big. The green speckles vanished inside a hollow in the center, far up into the air.

"Ta-da!" Anders did a flourish with his hands. "Here's your clue."

"A tree," Enya sighed. "I'm guessing we need to climb that thing?"

He nodded. "You guessed correctly."

She yanked her gloves tighter, flinching at the pain in her hands and the memories that pain brought forth. Once they were tight enough to her liking, she pulled on her boots for good measure.

Niall frowned. "That doesn't seem very safe."

Enya shot him a dubious look. "If I remember correctly, I could climb both you and your brothers out of a tree any day." She flexed her fingers, willing the burning in them to go away. Enya cleared her throat. "I think I can handle it."

If Carson were here, he'd be lifting her up himself. If Rowan were here, he'd be complaining about why the tree had to be so big and the weather so annoyingly cold. And also bragging about how climbing was much too easy for him.

"Just be careful, okay?" Beacon chimed in, his hands laced behind his head while he watched with weary eyes.

Enya nodded back, meeting his and Niall's gazes with a reassuring smile. She had to be strong. She had to keep them safe and fix this. All of this. As the Raven and leader of the Grims, it was the least she could do. And as a decent human being.

Murderer. Murderer. Murderer.

"Break a leg!" Anders called. "Or don't!"

Gritting her teeth, Enya approached the trunk. Her feet searched for an opening to latch onto, and once they'd found their mark, her hands grasped sturdy branches. Hand by hand and foot by foot, she climbed up the seemingly endless tree. Her fingers stung with the weight of her body and the scratching of the bark against her already dry skin. Once or twice, she had to blow her black hair out of her face to see where she would go next.

After a long while of climbing, Enya reached the hollow in the tree, pulling herself inside and then taking in the mix of wonder and magick.

The glowing green slime was splashed throughout the hole, and from it grew flowers and leaves. Despite the forest having been so empty and void of life, a tiny family of squirrels had made the hollow their home. It smelled of the sweetest wild cherry flowers and roses.

In the middle of the hollow was an etching of circus tents and stars, ones covered in black smudges.

There was only one place Enya knew of anywhere near Skeyya that held circus performances: Dredias in Brasova, near the capital city. It was full of Unseelie faerie folk, those from the Autumn and Winter courts. They were a cold and conniving bunch, but they put on a good show—at least according to those she traded with in Arden.

"Hey, I think this is the clue—" Enya began before losing her footing. She was falling, and then she wasn't. Something had caught a hold of her from the air.

She looked up and gasped. A massive beast with raven-like

wings held her in a vice-grip, baring its sharp teeth. Feathers ran along the length of its body, leading to what resembled a human head. A very twisted and grotesque human head.

"Beacon, Niall, get out of here!" Enya screamed before being knocked out the monster's grasp and thrown to the forest floor. She landed with a hard thud, the wind knocked right out of her. When she looked up, she saw Anders battling with the creature, ripping it in half with his hands, ones that now held long claws.

Blood spewed across the dirt before her, and soon she was being helped up by the princes.

Anders appeared seconds later. "See? Aren't you happy I'm here?"

They were surrounded, with Ballora's goons closing in from all sides. There was no time to wait for her next move. Enya's pistol came up to shoot three adversaries in the head, each going down in a heap of blood and ashes. The others slowly stalked closer, claws and teeth ready to taste human flesh and bone.

Anders snarled, baring his teeth. "Come and get me, boys!"

More appeared, some flying and some on four legs. There were at least dozens. Anders took out another five, ripping them apart, but others managed to land a few bloody blows, sending him flying back, growling obscenities.

But his attack had earned them an opening to their right.

Enya grabbed him by the collar and hauled him back through the trees, hastily waving for the princes to follow with her gun. "We're outnumbered. Move it!" she shouted, out of breath.

Howls of anguish and fury followed their hurried footsteps, with the Crimson Witch's ghastly ghouls gaining on them. There had to be some use to the Wand of Tine. It couldn't just be some faerie prop. Enya pulled it out, shaking it a few times for good measure and wincing at the scarred skin on her good arm from the earlier attack. Did this need some sort of spell to work?

She didn't have time to think more on it. A massive black bear, one disfigured with dark magick, grabbed hold of Niall. Its jaws clamored for his neck, seeking blood and bone.

He screamed, and then went limp in its giant paws.

"Niall!" Enya and Beacon yelled in unison. She shot at the bear several times, but the monster showed no signs of stopping. It bared its teeth before fleeing, leaving a broken and bloodied prince on the forest floor before them. "Stay and keep watch. Shoot anything that moves," Enya snapped at Beacon, her pulse quickening like mad.

He nodded, firing off several rounds into more tyrannical creatures rushing toward them. Anders followed suit, rushing out to tear more beasts apart with his claws.

This couldn't have been happening. None of this felt real anymore. Like it was all just some horrible dream.

"*Saints*," Enya muttered to herself, her eyes raking over his body for the wound. A growing pool of red blood stained the side of his shirt, right above his stomach. This was bad. This was really bad. Her vision blurred.

"Can you fix this? Will he make it?" Beacon demanded from behind her. Several more shots rang out from his weapon, ones met by cries of anguish and death.

For a moment, she doubted it. She doubted herself. Niall was lifeless before her, save for barely open eyes and a chest rising and falling, but even she knew it wasn't going to last. He had lost too much blood, and there was no way they'd be able to get him to a medic in time.

"Will he make it, Enya?" Beacon urged.

Wait. The stones! Enya gasped in relief. She pulled out the red stone Miriana had given her to help stop a situation exactly like this. That Banya must have known bleeding out was a risk when facing the Crimson Witch. It was lucky she did. Enya scrambled to remember the saying Miriana had told her. Something about the goddess … *Got it.*

"Help me in my final hour, the goddess has granted me the power!" Enya cried, her voice shrill and desperate when she placed the stone on him. This had to work. She couldn't lose him along with everything else.

At first, nothing happened, and she was about to lose all hope that Niall could get better. But then a bright, hazy light erupted out from the stone. It entered Niall with a force that made the ground shake below them. In seconds, the blood drained from his shirt, leaving its usual pristine white appearance. Niall heaved a breath before his eyes flew wide open. The stone slid to the ground, now gray and useless.

"He's okay!" Enya called over to Beacon. She almost laughed in disbelief herself. "He's alive!"

Their celebration was interrupted when a wicked laugh drifted through the trees, one that Enya had grown to know so well since they'd come to this horrible place. She froze, unmoving. Not that she had a choice; she couldn't feel her limbs anymore.

When she looked up from the prince, she saw the Crimson Witch standing there, her hands resting on the beast that had attacked Niall. The demon's white hair flowed past a black gown, one rife with smoke and lace.

"Hello, Enya." Her eyes narrowed, flitting to their new-found companion. "Anders. I'm so glad you could make it to our little home we have here," the demon purred, stroking the bear beside her. "Queen Ciara here is glad too, I'm sure. Not that she could talk, of course." Ballora laughed, the sound sinister and mocking.

They now faced the demon herself, accompanied by the queen of Skeyya as her prisoner.

26

Skeyya/Brasovian Border

TERROR COULDN'T adequately describe the intensity of emotion Enya was feeling, but the word did well enough.

Ballora crept closer, hands gripping the chains around the royal queen's now-furry neck. This was it. She'd found them, and now she was finally coming to claim that final favor. Enya swallowed hard, eyes frantically searching for a way out and finding none.

Anders remained quiet, still as stone beside her. She almost wished he could somehow magick a way out of here for them.

Anything to avoid what came next.

"You look well, Raven thief," the demon mused. Her

mouth was twisted into a cruel smile. "It's been some time since I last saw your face, hasn't it?"

"You know her? Is that the Crimson Witch?" Beacon demanded. Several of the wicked faerie's henchmen tried apprehending him and Niall, but not without a fight. "What have you done, Enya?" He struggled against the ghouls grabbing at him. One finally yanked his arms behind him, pushing him against a tree.

Niall didn't try as hard to escape, however. His mouth hung agape in unadulterated shock.

"Are you working with them?" Beacon shouted, his words slightly muffled by the bark pressing against his face.

Ballora pursed her lips in thought. "Well, I suppose she is now. Aren't you, little Enya? Remember, you owe me one more favor. That was in our deal from so many years ago."

Niall's face turned as white as a banshee. "What's she talking about? Enya, I thought you were our friend."

Murderer. Murderer. Murderer. You let them down again.

She tried to open her mouth, but no sound came out. The Crimson Witch snapped her fingers. "Oh dear. My mistake," she remarked, disinterested. She ruffled her hair with her black-stained nails. Whether that was blood or nail polish, Enya wasn't entirely sure. "You may talk to your princes now."

Enya rotated her jaw, startled by the sudden looseness. But even then, what could she say?

"I—I'm your friend. I've been trying to help you all this time to take the Crimson Witch down. We came all this way. When have I shown you otherwise?" she pleaded.

"What deal is she talking about?" Niall pressed.

"I—"

"Oh, *saints*, this is so dreadfully boring. Since you won't just get on with it, allow me." Ballora sighed, flipping her white waves over her shoulder. She turned to the princes. "Your friend here made a deal with me as a child. In return for a few measly human gifts, she had to kill the queen."

In mere seconds, the world stopped moving.

"You did *what*?" exclaimed Beacon.

"We trusted you!" shouted Niall.

In mere seconds, every ounce of trust she'd gained, every bit of friendship she'd worked for, was gone. They knew about her darkest secret. She killed Queen Layla. The princes fought against their captors, kicking and screaming.

"Oh, *dear*, this is rather sad," Ballora said, now facing Enya. "You're lucky I don't need those two. I only need you. You must help me find the Sword of Bas."

"And if I don't?" Enya challenged, her jaw going taut.

"Then I will kill your two friends I stole. Rowan and Carson, isn't it? Or maybe I'll have my fun with them. They'd look so nice all bloody and delicious." The Crimson Witch cackled, nearly giddy at the thought. "Or maybe I'll turn them into monsters, like Queen Ciara here."

Enya shot a worried look over at the princes, ones gazing back with faces full of hatred. She did this to them. She allowed their brother to be taken. The least she could do was save his life.

"Andrei," Ballora said, almost sweetly, and his head snapped in her direction. "Is there a reason you've been smiting your brothers and sisters? Explain yourself."

"Only to lead the Raven and her companions to you, my queen. I live to serve only you."

Anders finally budged, this time to kneel in reverence, but that only brought him closer to Enya. She spun to face him, to understand. Surely, she hadn't allowed herself to be duped.

He whispered, "Do as she says, Enya." Anders lifted his head slightly, his eyes meeting hers. He mouthed, "Trust me."

She narrowed her eyes, turning back to face the Crimson Witch. "What about these two? Will you let them go?"

Ballora let loose a frustrated breath. "Details, details, details. How annoying. Very well. Boys, bring those two royals to the edge of the forest and let them loose. Try to keep our other more vicious friends from eating them, will you? It's the least we could do. We aren't animals, after all." She paused. "Maybe that's a bit of a stretch. Is that enough for you to shut up and do as we agreed? You owe me two favors and two favors are what you will do."

The consequences for breaking a deal with a demon or faerie were worse than death, that much Enya could remember. At least if she complied, there was a chance of saving her best friend and the heir to the throne. When the demon's henchmen marched off with Beacon and Niall, she nodded.

The Crimson Witch scoffed. "See, now wasn't that easy?"

"Just get this over with," Enya snapped back. "I'm tired of your stupid games."

Ballora shot her a deathly glare before straightening her dress and fixing back up her pale tresses. "You humans really take the fun out of things sometimes. Alright then." She peered around, eyes setting on the ash littering the forest floor around them. "Fionn, Hughes, come grab the Raven. We have a little field trip to make."

She stepped towards Enya, staring her down mercilessly.

Two creatures, both tall, sinister, and covered in fur, grabbed Enya by her arms and lifted her to her feet. Seconds later, the Wand of Tine was out of her pocket and in the Crimson Witch's hand. Her other one held the Pentacle of Glac, no doubt stolen from Carson.

Now she was only two away from taking over the world.

At this point, all hope seemed lost. Enya had failed Carson, she'd failed Rowan, Beacon, Niall, and the entire Grims gang. She'd failed the world, too, if she really thought about it.

Her chest tightened and her eyes burned with unshed tears. Nothing could possibly make this worse. Everything she'd worked for, the trust she'd fought so hard to earn, was gone. Forget being a leader of the rebellion. At this point, she just wanted to fix all of this and make things right.

The world around them shimmered with black and gray smoke. Trees faded into stone walls, and the mossy ground into dark, marble floors. Stained glass windows, ones of purple, blue, and red, illuminated the large room Enya now found herself in while the smell of wilted roses filled her nose. She'd almost say it was like a church, but this was much more twisted and lacked any pews. At the end of the room was a single black throne covered in blood and bones. Outside the window was murky and bubbly, like water.

They were within the depths of the Black Lake, the Crimson Witch's prison, courtesy of the four faerie courts.

"Welcome to my little corner of the world. I'd say home, but my true home resides in the plains of the hidden realm. Ah, well. This will do for now." Ballora chuckled darkly, with Anders moving to stand beside her with his head downcast towards the stone floor. "Men, take the prisoner to dungeon."

"So that's it? You're just going to lock me up?" Enya spat. She wasn't too keen on being treated like some palace dog. "Aren't we supposed to go find this sword?" She didn't want to be stuck here; it was suffocating. At least on land she had hopes of escaping.

The Crimson Witch gave her a funny look, as if hearing those thoughts. "You so easily forget that because you found the wand, I have access to your mind, human. I may be a demon, but I realize humans need rest, food, and water, things you seem to be lacking. How are you meant to be useful to me if you collapse and die during our journey?"

Enya had nothing to say, knowing that her words were true.

She kept quiet when the monsters dragged her away, flinching when the souls of the damned stared at her from the colorful windows littering the corridor.

They, like her, were trapped with little hope of freedom.

Inside the dungeon was a space littered with dust, cobwebs, and more bloodstains, as if someone had been tortured down here. Knowing the nature of the Crimson Witch, Enya didn't doubt it in the slightest.

It also housed Carson and Rowan.

"Enya," Carson said in disbelief. He stood to greet her, and she met him with a hesitant hug back. She felt disgusting and untouchable, like she wasn't worthy of love or comfort from anyone. Not after what she'd done.

Rowan rose to his feet and watched her, almost as if unsure of what to say. She turned to him and gripped his hand tightly, meeting his eyes and being surprised by the warmth she found there. "I'm glad you're alive," he said gruffly, pulling away to stuff his hands into the pockets of his coat. A red tinge spread over his cheeks. "I'm guessing she caught you too. Where are my brothers?"

"They're … She let them go."

"Why?" Rowan asked, lines creasing his forehead. "Why would she take you and let them go? They're royalty."

Enya rose a brow. "I'll try not to be offended by that. She wants me to help her find the sword." She thought for a moment. What could she say without telling him the truth? She didn't want him to hate her too. Not yet, anyway. "Ander— Andrei showed up, that guy from Thomond. He's apparently on our side."

"Well, at least that's something." He sighed, crossing his arms and looking at the iron-bar coated door that held them in this disgusting room. "It would be good to have some eyes and ears down here."

"She has the pentacle and the wand," Enya added, her stomach turning with something vile. If it was fear or shame, she didn't know. "She forced me into helping her find the Sword of Bas, but she wasn't careful with her words. She said she wanted me to 'help her find the sword,' but that doesn't mean I *have* to find it, just that I have to help her. Maybe my help doesn't have to be so helpful."

She tried to appear confident, but inside she was screaming for this to be over. She was so tired.

"Okay, that's another positive," Carson said after a moment with a slight nod. "Right then, we have to think. What can we do to get out of here?"

326

Enya stared at the ground, her eyes unfocused and blurry with tears she refused to let fall. They were trapped. Beacon and Niall hated her guts. Pretty soon, the Grims would know what she'd done. Rowan and Carson would find out too, soon enough. This was a mess.

But the Raven would fight. She wouldn't let the Crimson Witch get away with destroying her life or the world. In this darkness, she remembered the motto of the Grims, and her hand tightened on the silver feather in her pocket.

To stay moving, no matter the cost.

Niall was still in shock when he and Beacon arrived in Arden, being greeted by the smell of ships and factory soot. They'd lost Rowan and found out their childhood best friend killed their mother. There was nothing easy about coming to terms with any of this, but Niall was determined to stop being so damn afraid of everything.

He'd start by confronting the Grims.

The gang needed to help them save Rowan. It was the least they could do when their leader was a murderer. After she'd led them on for so long … Niall sighed, his hands starting to tremble for the fifth time since they'd set off back to the city. His chest was too tight and his breathing too shallow, but he'd make it.

"Do you really think they'll help us?" he asked Beacon. He cleared his throat, hugging himself tighter against the frigid wind around them.

They were on horseback, having sold the last of their

already meager belongings to a dodgy old man in Calway near Thomond. The ride was brutal, scary, and lonely without Rowan to protect them. Maybe Beacon wasn't scared, but Niall was.

Rowan had always been there to keep them safe. This didn't feel right at all. For a time, Enya kept them safe too, but that fact only made Niall feel worse.

Snow pelted above their heads, turning their already grungy clothes soggy and freezing. Just their luck, it seemed.

"I think so. If not, we can have them arrested and hanged," Beacon suggested, his voice void of any sympathy.

But they had to show no mercy. These people were monsters. Or at least, they were harboring a monster.

"But what if they didn't know? We didn't."

"Then we'll figure it out. Point is, we need our brother back and to stop the Crimson Witch. Everything else doesn't matter," Beacon shot back. Niall could see that his brother's jaw was set. It was strange seeing him so angry. Out of the three of them, he was usually the most easygoing. "I think I see the Bowman's Pub from here."

The bustling street full of carriages and wandering pedestrians barely made way for them to cross, but they managed to hastily slip through between a motor car and merchant's cart. Upon reaching the other side, they hopped off their horses and tied them to a street post. A man waiting out front eyed them up and down, his arms crossed over his chest. Wind whipped up his coat, and a leather-clad hand snaked up to stroke his long black beard.

"I recognize you," he said, narrowing his eyes. "You left with the Raven and Carson a while back. We've been waiting for your return." He waved them back towards the door. "Follow me."

The pub looked emptier than usual, but maybe that was normal for this early in the morning. Niall didn't really like being around too many people, either. It set him on edge more often than not. Several rows of wooden chairs and tables sat vacant, and Maxon and Finn stood cleaning up the bar on the far side of the room. Their brows raised in unison when they noticed the doorman with the princes in tow.

"Hey, you two. Where's our famous Raven and her trusty sidekick?" Finn asked carefully as the doorman returned to his post by the entrance. His eyes seemed to search for any possible weapons while Maxon already had a knife in his hand. "And didn't you have another brother or something?"

"They were captured by the Crimson Witch," Beacon said flatly. "We need your gang to help us get our brother back and take down that crazy demon."

"Enya gave us all very strict orders to watch this place while she was gone. How do we know what you say is true?" Maxon retorted.

Beacon looked around the pub carefully to make sure no one was listening when he spoke his next words, "Do you really think members of the royal family would be waltzing around without an escort or disguise with nothing but the clothes on their backs? Come on, man. We'll pay you exactly what we promised before."

Finn and Maxon exchanged a wary glance.

"You know there's a bounty on you two, right? If you're playing any tricks with us, if you're spies for the king—" Finn began before being cut off.

"We're not!" Niall cried. "Please. Our brother is in trouble. Besides, you already know who the Crimson Witch is and what she's capable of. Are you really willing to risk losing everything you know just to blow us off for being royals?"

It was quiet for several long moments.

"We want at least double what you were going to pay before, and we want half up front. Consider it an insurance policy so you don't betray the Grims," Maxon finally said, crossing his arms and leaning against the floor-to-ceiling shelves behind him covered in glass bottles.

Finn nodded in agreement. "That works for me. We'll need a lot of our gang to get the job done anyway, which means more guns and more transportation fees."

"And more likelihood of getting stopped by police," Maxon chimed in with a smirk. "That's my kind of adventure."

"So, you'll do it? You'll help us?" Niall asked eagerly.

Finn shrugged. "Yeah, we'll do it. Just don't stiff us on payment. I'll go grab Miriana and Jackson and we'll figure out a game plan," he said before leaving to trudge up the stairs to the attic.

Maxon returned his blade to his belt and went back to scrubbing wine glasses, but his gaze traveled back up to watch them. Niall and his brother took a seat at the bar, keeping quiet.

"So, you guys don't drink tea, if my memory isn't as crappy as they tell me. Want some grub and mead? Podge dropped off some clams today, and I'm cooking up a mean chowder for lunch."

Niall's stomach growled with a fury, and he nodded sheepishly. Beacon did the same. They hadn't eaten since they'd arrived at the haunted forest. If it weren't for how starving he was, he probably wouldn't have eaten at all. This was all too much to take in.

He shuddered, gulping down the drink Maxon slid over.

But it was going to be okay. They'd regroup and get Rowan back. Maybe they'd even get revenge for their mother's death along the way.

The Crimson Witch would pay for what she'd done, one way or another.

ACKNOWLEDGMENTS

Congratulations! You made it all the way to the end. Thank you so much for picking up this book to learn all about the harrowing tale following Enya, the Grims, and the three princes. I'd also like to thank you for flipping through a bit further to discover a bit about my own story.

Growing up, I never imagined I'd be a writer. Sure, I combed through library after library as a teenager, eagerly devouring up to 30 books each trip. I'd also read all of those books in class, much to the dismay of pretty much all of my teachers. I always knew that I was an avid reader, but I never thought I'd end up writing a book until I became a professional editor.

Seeing all those people write such amazing stories and bringing life to so many different worlds made me think that maybe I could do it too, and I did. Ta-da! *Jazz hands*

So, here's the part of the book where I thank every awesome person who helped make this happen.

First, I'd like to thank my mother for supporting me all the way. She's always been there encouraging me to pursue my dreams, and for that I'll always be thankful. She also took me to the library and bookstore and didn't complain when I grabbed tons of books each trip, thus helping me delve further into the magic of fantasy novels. For each special occasion, she'd get me a new YA novel, and here we are now. Thanks, Mom. You're awesome.

Next, I'd like to thank Naseem, my partner in crime. He's

always been my rock, keeping me calm and present every day. I've never known true love before him. Hopefully, that'll last forever (as it does in most romance novels). He's strong, caring, and devilishly handsome, which makes for a good male protagonist, if I do say so myself.

I'd also like to thank the rest of my family for their support. They've always been impressed with how far I've come for my age, being in college and all, and hopefully I'll keep impressing them for many years to come.

I'd also like to thank my cats. Specifically, Watson, Rose, and our newest addition, Kaz. It may seem strange to mention them in this section, but I have to be honest, they've gotten me through a lot. Heck, my former editing page was literally called "The Crazy Cat Editor." During the writing of this book, my first cat Watson unfortunately died from Hemangiosarcoma cancer, FIV, and anemia. It was a brutal condition, and he had to be put down within eleven days of finding the tumor. This experience taught me a lot about handling death, as it had been my first experience with it. I hope this section, and his inclusion in my logo, are good tributes to his life. My furry friends will always be the best writing assistants anyone could have, but unfortunately for everyone else, their services are exclusively mine.

It wouldn't be an acknowledgments page without thanking my friends too. I've had so many wonderful readers and authors supporting me from the indie community, and each one was more lovely than the last. They provided me with a lot of wisdom and guidance, and I couldn't possibly thank them enough.

Thank you to my talented cover designer, Bianca Bordianu of Bianca Bordianu Design. She made my cover an absolute masterpiece. You can find more info on her by searching her company on Facebook or Instagram.

Thank you to my developmental and line editor, Nick Beard. Without your help in fleshing out my story, this book wouldn't be as awesome as it is. With countless months of developmental work and brainstorming, we were able to make The Raven Thief a reality. Again, no amount of thanks would be enough.

I'd also like to thank my proofreader, Carolyn McSharry. After no less than three other proofreaders looked through the manuscript during the time it took to finish this book in its entirety, you found over 200 additional errors they missed. You did exactly what I was looking for and needed, and I'm very happy we got to work together on this book. Thank you!

Thank you to my formatters and designers at Qamber Designs Media, run by Nada and Najla Qamber. Your creativity truly helped bring my novel to life, not only through the interior design, but also with the magical map, chapter headings, and scene breaks that artist Melissa Wright created. Out of all the companies I checked out, yours really went the extra mile. Their Instagram is @QamberDesignsMedia.

Thank you to my amazing character artist, Corinne Taylor, otherwise known as @Sncinderart on Instagram. She has the ultimate touch when it comes to creating the most realistic and human character art I've ever seen—and I've searched plenty.

There's no way I could forget to say thank you to Skye Phimpha, owner of the FahSkyeCreations store on Etsy, for making my quote bookmark for The Raven Thief. I'll admit, it took me a super long time to come up with something worth quoting, but she was able to turn my words into a work of art, and for that I'll always say thank you. Her Instagram is @ FahskyeBookmarks.

Thank you to Nicole McDonagh, the creator of my watercolor Raven Thief bookmark and the owner of BTBookmarks on Etsy. Her Instagram is @Bt.bookmarks.

Thank you to Catarina Book Designs for making the designs for my merchandise! Her art is absolutely gorgeous, and I'm very thankful to have worked with her. Her Instagram is @CatarinaBookDesigns.

Thank you to Jane Conklin, owner of Wick and Jane Candles. Her Instagram is @Book_and_Jane. I'm still amazed at the scents she came up with! It was as if the characters were really captured inside her metal tins. There's the Raven herself, scented as warm earth, jasmine, and sarcasm. Rowan, who is scented as pine needles, mint leaves, and brooding. Beacon, who is scented as berries, sandalwood, and free spirit. And finally, Niall, who is scented as fresh flowers, black tea, and anxiety. You can request any of these wonderful candles over at the Wick and Jane Candle shop on Instagram.

Next, I'd like to say thank you to my beta readers, all 120+ of them, for rolling up their sleeves to rake through my unedited work and figure out exactly how many diamonds were hidden inside that mess. I couldn't have come this far without you guys.

Of course, I'd also like to thank my ARC readers for taking the time to check out my novel and give their honest opinions on it. I'm always welcome to feedback, and theirs were really helpful and uplifting. Without the initial feedback on the first

ARC, the book wouldn't be as awesome as it is. I really needed the criticism, and I'm so thankful I got it.

Finally, I'd like to say a big thank you to my readers, every last one of you. You find wonder in the stories and the little fantasy worlds we authors create, and you continue to inspire me with your dreams and words of encouragement. You believe in the faerie magick, the haunted woods, the royal palaces, and the mystical lands, and for that I thank you. There really wouldn't be a story without you.

ABOUT THE AUTHOR

Ashley Olivier is an aspiring writer based in the busy capital city of Baton Rouge, Louisiana. When she's not writing, she's working as a full-time editor with a specialty in fiction and fantasy. You can usually find her spending an unusual amount of time in coffee shops taking advantage of free Wi-Fi and refills.

She prefers matcha green tea almond milk lattes over coffee, sushi over pretty much anything, and cats over humans.

When she's not working, she's getting her zen on with yoga, reading young adult fantasy—usually on the adventurous side, running her bookstagram, creating messy masterpieces in the kitchen, petting her cats, and going on midnight adventures.

Instagram: @AshleyOlivierAuthor
Facebook: @AshleyOlivierAuthor
Email: ashleyolivierauthor@gmail.com

Printed in Great Britain
by Amazon

Penny Holmes
Susan Mallet

simply british

Photographs by Akiko Ida
Styling by John Bentham

contents

Puddings

Tea time

introduction

A change in
British cooking

Over the last decade, the quality of food available for those wanting to eat out or cook at home in Britain has improved enormously.

Public demand, driven by the increasing number of television cookery programmes and wider travel, has forced a revolution in the quality and presentation of food available in restaurants, pubs and cafés.

A wide range of international cuisine is now available all over Britain.

A traditional cuisine
brought up to date

Until recently, the strength of British cooking was in home-cooked food – Sunday roasts, teatime cakes and scones as well as puddings. Now, thanks to up to date equipment and an emphasis on fresh, seasonal local produce, the great traditional recipes are now re-emerging in a lighter, healthier and more interesting way in restaurants and 'gastro-pubs'.

The recipes in this book are based largely on this inheritance of home-cooking and aim to demonstrate the diversity and quality of delicious dishes now available in Britain.

Culinary heritage and
regional produce

The demand for fresh, good quality, seasonal ingredients has resulted in a wide range of excellent products being available almost everywhere in Britain – from supermarkets to farmers' markets.

British chefs are experimenting with their culinary heritage using local produce - organic meat and fish and excellent fresh vegetables and fruit which have always been very important in everyday cooking in Britain.

Dairy produce of course also has an important role in British cuisine – Welsh salted butter, Jersey double cream and the surprising variety of regional cheeses.

Afternoon tea

The ritual of teatime is a moment to share with friends, whether it be using a teapot, a porcelain cup and a tea strainer or a tea bag in a mug.

The way to make a good cup of tea is firstly to boil the water and pour a little into the teapot. This warms the pot and enhances the flavour of the tea leaves. Then empty it. Immediately measure the tea leaves into the pot – one heaped tea spoonful for each person and one for the pot! Meanwhile, bring the kettle back to the boil and immediately pour the water onto the tea leaves. Leave to infuse for 3 – 6 minutes. Then stir the tea and pour it into the cups through the strainer.

Either drink the tea with a drop of fresh milk or with a slice of lemon, according to taste and the type of tea.

Tea time

The cup of tea can be accompanied by a cucumber sandwich, a biscuit such as shortbread, a piece of cake or, of course, a scone with jam and cream.

Pea and mint soup

Pea soup comes in many variations in England. There is even one called 'The London peculiar' which was as 'thick as London Fog' in days gone by (hence the term 'a pea-souper'). This recipe is a light subtle version and can be served hot as a delicious winter warmer, or a chilled on a summer's day.

Serves 6

700g (1 ½ lbs) (or 1 medium sized bag) frozen petit pois

2 onions chopped

1 apple, peeled and quartered

50g (2 oz) butter

bunch mint, roughly chopped

750ml (1 ¼ pints) chicken stock

250ml (10 fl oz) single cream (or full fat milk)

salt, pepper

In a large saucepan, gently fry the onion and apple in the butter until soft. Add mint, salt, pepper. Add the chicken stock and bring to boil.

Add the peas and gently simmer 3 minutes until the peas are tender, do not overcook or the peas will lose their colour. Add cream (or milk) and process in a blender until smooth.

Serve in warm bowls garnished with either croutons or small strips of crisply cooked bacon.

Variation:

As an alternative, you can pass the soup through a sieve and serve chilled, garnished with a little fresh cream and a sprig of mint.

Smoked salmon tartare

Nothing beats Scottish salmon at its best. This recipe combines the distinct flavours of smoked salmon with the delicacy of good, fresh salmon.

Serves 6

300g (10oz) fresh Scottish salmon fillet, skinned

150g (5 oz) smoked Scottish salmon

1 shallot, very finely chopped

juice of 1 lemon

the finely grated zest of ½ lemon

pinch of cayenne pepper

a few drops of Worcestershire sauce

salt and freshly ground black pepper

To serve

some salad leaves or 12 cocktail size blinis

125g (4oz) crème fraiche

50g (2 oz) lumpfish roes

Cut the salmon fillet and smoked salmon into very small dice with a sharp knife. Place in a bowl, add the remaining ingredients and mix well, chill for 2-3 hours (no longer).

Either serve by placing a little green salad on individual plates, drizzled with a little oil and balsamic vinegar, and a tablespoon of the tartare on top. Or as a delicious canapc, serve the tartare on cocktail blinis spread with a little Crème fraiche. Garnish with lumpfish roe.

Pear and stilton salad

An unusual light salad using a traditional combination of Stilton cheese and pears. Stilton, a creamy, blue cheese was first introduced 200 years ago at the Bell Inn in the village of Stilton in Leicestershire.

Serves 6

2 pears

225g (8 oz) Stilton, coarsely chopped

2 celery stalks, chopped

12 walnut halves, coarsely chopped

mixed green salad leaves

Vinaigrette

1 Tbs white wine vinegar

3 Tbs virgin olive oil

½ tsp sugar

2 Tbs chopped chives

salt and pepper

Prepare the vinaigrette in a bowl.

Assemble celery, Stilton and nuts on top of the salad leaves on individual plates and peel, core the pears and cut into 8 pieces. Arrange on top of the salad.

Drizzle the vinaigrette over the salad and serve immediately so that the pears do not discolour.

Fish pie

An assortment of fish in a delicate white sauce topped with mashed potatoes - a comforting pie.

Serves 6

800g (1 lb 12 oz) fresh fish (salmon, cod and smoked haddock)

250ml (9 fl oz) fresh, full fat milk

25g (1oz) flour

25g (1oz) butter

125ml (¼ pint) crème fraîche or single cream

50ml (2 fl oz) white wine

2 Tbs chopped fresh parsley

Mashed potatoes and leeks

mashed potatoes (see recipe on page 36)

2 medium leeks, trimmed and cleaned, chopped finely

25g (1oz) butter

salt and pepper

Skin and remove bones from all the fish and cut into about 2cm (1 inch) cubes.

Preheat the oven to 180 °C (gas 6).

To make the sauce, put the milk, flour and butter in a saucepan and heat gently, stirring constantly until sauce thickens and begins to boil. Take off the heat and add the cream and white wine. Season well and allow to cool.

Add the raw fish chunks and parsley to the cooled sauce and place in a pie dish.

Prepare the mashed potato (see recipe on page 36). Melt the butter in a frying pan and add the chopped leeks. Gently sweat until soft for about 10-15 minutes. Mix the leeks into the mashed potato.

Pile the mash on top of the fish mixture and roughly level out the top. Dot with a little butter.

Cook the pie for about 40 minutes until the top is golden and the fish mixture is bubbling hot.

Serve with a bowl of petits pois.

Cod Welsh rabbit

Welsh Rabbit (or 'rarebit') was traditionally served on a slice of toast at the end of a meal, in gentlemen's clubs! Try this fish 'rabbit' as a supper dish. Delicious on a bed of spinach or with roasted cherry tomatoes.

Serves 6

6 x 150g (5 oz) fillets of cod, each cut into 2

225g (8 oz) grated cheddar cheese

2 eggs lightly beaten

½ tsp mustard

A few drops of Worcestershire sauce

Salt and pepper

Put the cheese, eggs, mustard, Worcestershire sauce and seasoning in a food processor (or use a wooden spoon) and mix well. Put the mixture in a plastic bag and leave in the fridge for 2 hours.

Preheat grill.

Season the fish with salt and pepper and arrange on a greased baking sheet.

Divide the cheese mixture into 12 portions, and pat out on your hands to about 2-3mm thick, lay these on top of the fish.

Place under the grill until golden and puffy. The fish should be just firm.

Kedgeree

Kedgeree began life as a spicy Hindu dish, 'discovered' by the British during the years of the Raj and served for breakfast. If fish and rice aren't your 'cup of tea' for breakfast, serve this as a starter or as a light lunch or supper.

Serves 6

450g (1lb) smoked haddock (preferably tail and undyed)

6 quail's eggs (or 3 hen's eggs)

4 Tbs chopped, fresh parsley

350g (12 oz) basmati rice

75cl (1 ¼ pint) chicken stock

1 onion, chopped

2 tsp curry powder

1 bay leaf

1 Tbs olive oil

1 tsp salt

black pepper

Place the fish in a pan and cover with fresh water, a bay leaf and some freshly ground pepper (no salt). Gently increase the heat until nearly boiling and simmer for about 10 minutes until the smoked haddock is firm and cooked. Remove from the pan with a slotted spoon onto a clean plate.

Meanwhile, fry the onion in the oil for a minute, add the curry powder, rice and salt, stir and ensure the rice is well coated with the curry. Add the stock, bring to the boil, cover with a lid, reduce heat and simmer for approx 10 minutes until the rice is tender and the liquid has evaporated.

In a separate pan, boil the quail's eggs for 3-4 minutes (or 8-10 mins for hen's eggs), plunge into cold water and peel the shells.

To assemble the kedgeree, flake the smoked haddock into chunks and fold into the rice, with half of the parsley then turn onto a serving dish. Halve the quail's eggs and arrange on top of the rice. Scatter the rest of the parsley.

Variation:

Hardboiled eggs are traditionally used as a garnish but try a warm, soft-poached egg on top of the kedgeree for a more substantial meal.

Fish and chips

The British are well known for their fish and chips! An early take away food, traditionally wrapped in newspaper, fish and chips originated from the North of England in the 19th Century and later became popular in the rest of Britain.

Serves 6

6 x 150g (5oz) thick cod or haddock tail fillets (or use hake, plaice or sole)

I kg (2 ¼ lhs) potatoes

vegetable oil

150g (5 oz) plain flour for the batter plus 75g (3 oz) to flour the fish

3 egg whites

300ml (½ pint) pale ale or lager

pinch of salt

Peel the potatoes and cut into 1cm thick chips. Rinse in water and drain well on kitchen paper. Heat vegetable oil in a deep fat fryer or heavy based saucepan until very hot. Carefully cook the chips in the oil in batches until soft but not coloured. Remove, place on kitchen paper and set aside.

To make the batter, gradually whisk the ale into the flour until smooth. In a separate bowl whisk the egg whites with a couple of pinches of salt until it forms peaks. Carefully fold the whites into the batter.

Check the fillets for bones, then lightly flour the fish. Heat 10cm depth of vegetable oil in a deep fat fryer or heavy based saucepan until a little batter dropped in will brown in 5 seconds.

Carefully dip each of the floured fillets into the batter, in batches and fry for about 4-5 minutes in the oil until golden. Drain on kitchen paper, and keep warm in a low oven.

When ready to serve, heat the oil again and cook the chips, for a second time in batches, until golden and crisp. Drain well on kitchen paper.

Cottage pie

A traditional recipe, a nice and easy meal in one which appeals to all ages, and is ideal for family and friends.

Serves 6

1kg (2 ¼ lbs) minced beef

2 carrots, diced into 1cm cubes

2 onions, chopped

2 Tbs vegetable oil

25g (1 oz) flour

450ml (¾ pint) beef stock

1 Tbs tomato puree

1 Tbs Worcestershire sauce

1 tsp dried thyme

mashed potatoes (see recipe on page 36)

10g (½ oz) butter

salt and pepper

Preheat the oven to 200 °C (400F or gas 6/7).

Heat 1 Tbs of the oil in a heavy bottomed saucepan, add onion and fry gently until soft. Add the carrots, stir well and cook for 2-3 minutes. Remove from the pan with slotted spoon and put to one side.

Heat the rest of the oil in the casserole dish, fry the meat, breaking up with a fork until browned. Return the vegetables to the pan, sprinkle the flour into the meat and vegetables, mix well and add stock, tomato puree, Worcestershire sauce, thyme and seasoning, and stir well. Bring to the boil, then reduce the heat and gently simmer for about 45 minutes until tender (stir occasionally to stop the meat sticking to the bottom of the pan).

Spoon into an ovenproof pie dish and leave to cool.

Meanwhile make the mashed potatoes (see recipe on page 36). Spoon the potatoes on top of the meat, trace lines on the mash with a fork, dot with butter and bake in the oven for 35-40 minutes until the top is golden.

Variation:

Use minced lamb instead of beef to make a 'Shepherd's Pie'.

Irish stew

There are many versions of this celebrated dish. It was originally an economical way to using cheap cuts of mutton by slow cooking over an open fire. Now it is best to use shoulder of lamb for its flavour and tender meat. If you can't find pearl barley, use a tin of flageolet beans.

Serves 6

1.5 - 2 kg (3 ½ - 4 lbs) shoulder of lamb, cut into large cubes

50g (2 oz) flour

3 leeks, trimmed and sliced

2 carrots, peeled and sliced

1 onion, chopped

1 clove garlic, crushed

2 Tbs vegetable oil

1 litre (1¾ pints) stock

2 Tbs tomato puree

2 Tbs chopped fresh rosemary

125g (4 oz) pearl barley (or a tin of flageolet beans)

salt and pepper

Preheat the oven to 150 °C (gas 5).

Season the flour in a bowl with salt and pepper, and coat the lamb cubes lightly.

Heat half the oil in a heavy bottomed casserole, gently try the onion, leeks, carrots, garlic, salt and pepper for a few minutes. Remove from pan and put to one side.

Heat the rest of the oil, and fry the lamb until just browned. Add the vegetables and stock. Bring to the boil, cover with a tight lid and place in the oven for about ¾ - 1 hour.

Check the stew, skim off any fat. Add the pearl barley and herbs, and return to the oven for another hour. If you are using flageolet beans, rinse in water, drain and add to the meat about 15 minutes before the end of the cooking time. Check the seasoning and serve with mashed potato or bubble and squeak. (See page 36).

Variation:

This recipe can be made using a whole shoulder or leg of lamb. Increase the cooking time to 2 - 2 ½ hours before adding the pearl barley.

Roast beef and roast potatoes

The British have been known as expert cooks of roast beef and its partner Yorkshire pudding since the 18th century. Just as important is the rich gravy made from the pan juices and the golden, crisp roast potatoes.

Serves 6

1 ½ kg (3-3 ½ lbs) cut of beef, either on the bone or top side

25g (1 oz) beef dripping or use vegetable oil

1 kg (2 ¼ lbs) potatoes (King Edwards, or other floury potatoes)

50g (2 oz) olive oil or goose fat

Gravy

1 Tbs plain flour

250ml (½ pint) vegetable stock

salt and pepper

Preheat the oven 220 °C (gas 7/8). Put a little beef dripping (or vegetable oil) in a large roasting tin, and heat in the oven for 10 minutes until extremely hot. Season the beef with ground pepper, place in the tin and roast for 15 minutes turning midway, to ensure the meat is 'sealed'.

Reduce the heat to 180 °C (gas 6) and continue roasting. Allow 25 mins per kg (12 minutes per pound), and baste regularly.

Peel and cut the potatoes into even sized quarters, and parboil in plenty of salted water for about 5 minutes until just soft around the edges. Drain well and shake gently to slightly rough the edges. Put the goose fat in another large roasting tin, heat in the oven for 5 minutes until hot. Transfer the potatoes to the pan and ensure they are well coated with the hot fat. Roast in the oven for 1- 1 ½ hours until golden crispy.

Remove the beef to a warmed serving dish and allow to rest for 10 minutes while you make the gravy. Pour off any excess fat. Sprinkle the flour over remaining juices and use a slotted spatula (or fish slice) to mix well. Make sure you scrape all the bits from the pan. Return to the heat and brown the flour for a minute or two, stirring.

Deglaze pan with the vegetable stock, a little at a time, stirring constantly with a balloon whisk until you have a thin, rich gravy. Slice the beef thinly, serve with roast potatoes, Yorkshire pudding, gravy and some green vegetables and horseradish sauce for a traditional Sunday lunch.

Yorkshire pudding

Britain is known for its traditional Sunday lunch of Roast Beef and Yorkshire pudding.

Serves 6

2 large eggs

150 g (5 oz) flour

250ml (8 fl oz) fresh, full fat milk

pinch of salt

Heat the oven to 220 °C (gas 7/8).

Mix all the ingredients together with an electric beater (or balloon whisk) until you have a smooth batter.

Place a small 'nut' of goose fat or beef dripping in 12 individual bun tins (or use a 15-20cm square baking tin for one big Yorkshire pudding). Place the tin in the oven for 5 minutes until the fat is extremely hot. Divide the batter into the bun tins and cook for 15-20 minutes until well risen and golden.

Serve immediately with roast beef.

Fruit stuffed loin of pork

This recipe involves a wonderful combination of dried fruit and meat. The pork is cooked in cider to make a slightly sweet gravy.

Serves 6

1 ½ kg (2 ½ lbs) boneless pork loin (tied with twine)

150g (5 oz) dried apricots

100g (4 oz) dried, pitted prunes

1 clove garlic

salt and pepper

100g (4oz) butter (softened)

1 tsp dried thyme

300ml (½ pint) cider

Preheat oven to 180 °C (gas 6).

Using the handle of a wooden spoon, make a hole through the length of the centre of the loin. Push the dried fruit into the the hole (alternating prunes and apricots).

Cut the garlic into thin slivers and make deep slits in the meat with a sharp knife and push the garlic into the slits, without cutting the twine. Rub the surface with salt, pepper and thyme, and smear with butter. Place the pork in a shallow roasting pan. Pour the cider around the meat.

Roast in the oven for 1¾ hours (approx 1 hour per kg/30mins per lb plus 35 minutes), basting frequently. When done, remove the meat from the oven and let it stand (cover loosely with foil) for about 10 minutes. Cut into thin slices and serve with the pan juices and Bubble and Squeak (see page 36).

Steak and kidney pie

Steak and kidney have been cooked together for at least 150 years. Traditionally made as a steamed savoury pudding, this recipe has a puff pastry crust, which is a lot easier to prepare! This is a popular national dish, and, if well cooked using fresh ingredients, there is nothing better on a cold winter's evening. Good quality kidneys in particular are key to the richness of the gravy.

Serves 6

750g (1 ½ lbs) braising steak, chopped into 2cm cubes

250g (8 oz) lamb kidney chopped into 2 cm cubes (fatty parts removed)

2 Tbs flour

2 onions, chopped

1 ½ litres (2 ½ pints) beef stock

salt and pepper

2 Tbs beef dripping if possible (otherwise sunflower oil)

puff pastry (about 350g/12 oz)

1 egg

Preheat the oven to 150 °C (gas 5).

Soften the chopped onion in 1 Tbs of the beef dripping in a good size casserole, removing when done.

Season the flour, and place in a bowl. Toss the beef and kidney until well coated.

Meanwhile melt 1 Tbs of the beef dripping until spitting hot in the casserole then fry the meat in batches until a good colour. Return the onion with the meat to the casserole, add enough stock until just covered, season with salt and pepper.

Bring to the boil, cover the casserole with a tight lid, put in a low oven and simmer for about 2 hours until very tender (check every so often and add more stock if it looks dry). The kidney will make the most wonderful, rich gravy.

Pour into a 1.5 litre (2 ½ pint) pie dish. Allow the steak and kidney to cool until just warm (or you can make it the day before).

Preheat the oven to 200 °C (gas 7).

Roll out the pastry to 5mm thick. Cut a strip to sit around the rim of the dish (this will guarantee the top stays in place), then place the rest of the pastry on top and trim. Crimp the edges for a neat finish, and decorate the top if desired. Brush with a little beaten egg, and bake in the oven for about 30 minutes. Serve with green vegetables.

Coronation chicken

This recipe was devised for the coronation of Queen Elizabeth II in 1953. It is a very popular summer lunch dish.

Serves 6

6 breasts of chicken, skinned and boned

120mls (4 fl oz) chicken stock

2 Tbs clear honey

3 tsp mild curry powder

4 Tbs mango chutney

4 Tbs mayonnaise

6 Tbs crème fraîche

2 Tbs toasted flaked almonds

300g (10 oz) green grapes, deseeded and cut into halves.

Gently poach the chicken in the stock for 10-15 minutes until cooked.

Melt the honey in a pan, stir in the curry powder and chutney. Cook on a low heat for 5 minutes. Take from the heat and then cool.

Stir the mayonnaise and crème fraîche together and then add to the cooled curry mixture.

Cut the chicken into strips. Fold into the curry mixture with the grapes (keep some for the garnish).

Put onto a serving platter and sprinkle with the nuts and the remaining grapes. Serve with green salad and bread.

Chicken tikka masala

Now one of Britain's favourite dishes, Chicken tikka masala is of Indian origin. The traditional tandoori chicken tikka (a dry curry) has been adapted by the British with the addition of a tomato curry sauce. Don't be put off by the long list of spices – all of them are worth having in the larder, and the success of the recipe depends on them.

Serves 6

6 boneless chicken breasts, skinned and cut into 2cm chunks

6 Tbs tandoori paste (ready made in a jar)

3 Tbs natural yoghurt

3 Tbs vegetable oil

1 cinnamon stick

8 cardamon pods

1 large onion, finely chopped

1 Tbs grated fresh ginger

2 cloves garlic, crushed

2 tsp ground cumin

2 tsp ground coriander (seeds)

1 tsp turmeric

1/2 tsp cayenne pepper

200g (7 oz) tinned chopped tomatoes

200ml (7fl oz) chicken stock

2 tsp garam masala

juice of ½ lemon

½ tsp salt

Marinate the chicken in the tandoori paste and yoghurt for 2 hours (or even better overnight) stirring occasionally.

Heat the oil in a casserole, and when hot add the cinnamon, cardamon pods and onion. Fry for about 5 minutes until soft, then add the ginger, garlic, cumin, coriander, turmeric and cayenne pepper. Allow the spices to cook for a minute, then add the chicken with the marinade.

Fry for a few minutes and add the tomatoes, stock, garam masala, lemon juice. Bring the curry to a gentle simmer, stir well and cook very gently for 15 minutes.

Take out the cinnamon stick and serve with basmati rice or naan bread, and a green salad.

Bubble and squeak

This recipe is a traditional way of using left over green vegetables, but of course it is delicious made fresh. The name comes from the sound the vegetables make when cooking in the pan! It is an ideal accompaniment to meat, or served as a light lunch with a fried egg on top.

Serves 6

mashed potato (see recipe below)

2 onions chopped

200g (7 oz) green cabbage, shredded

50g (2 oz) butter

1 Tbs olive oil

2 Tbs flour

salt and pepper

Make the mashed potato (see recipe below). Meanwhile heat the oil in a pan and fry the onions gently for 5 minutes until soft.

Steam or boil the cabbage in a small amount of salted water until just done (about 2-3 minutes). Drain well.

Mix the cabbage and onions into the mashed potato. Make 12 little rounds of the mixture, flatten and flour lightly each side. Heat the butter in a non stick frying pan, gently cook the rounds on each side, until golden and crispy.

Serve with fruit stuffed loin of pork (see recipe on page 28), or with cold meat and chutney.

Mashed potato

Serves 6

1 kg (2 ¼ lbs) floury potatoes

150ml (¼ pint) fresh milk

50g (2 oz) butter

salt and pepper

Peel and cut the potatoes into quarters, boil in plenty of salted water for about 20 minutes until tender. Drain well.

Put the potatoes back in the pan, add the milk and butter and mash well until very smooth (for an even texture use a hand mixer to 'mash' the potatoes perfectly).

Summer pudding

A favourite English summer pudding using the fruits of the season. Use a variety of different berries to give a good mix of colour and texture. This version uses less bread and the fruit is uncooked which results in a lighter, fresher taste.

Serves 6

400g (1lb) brioche loaf (or white bread)

½ litre (1pint) blackcurrant coulis

250g (9 oz) strawberries, hulled

75g (3 oz) blackberries

75g (3 oz) blueberries

1 Tbs caster sugar

125g (4 oz) raspberries for decoration

crème fraîche or vanilla ice cream to serve

Prepare the fruit: Slice the strawberries into rounds, halve the blackberries and blueberries. Sprinkle with sugar.

Remove the crusts from the brioche and cut the loaf into ½cm slices. Cut 24 rounds from the brioche slices with a 5-6cm cutter.

Lay a small square of baking parchment on a board and place 8 circular metal rings on top.

Arrange a layer of overlapping fruit slices in the mould and cover with the next slice of brioche, dipped in coulis. Repeat until there are 3 layers of brioche and 2 layers of fruit. Press down lightly. Refrigerate until ready to serve.

To serve, slide each of the puddings off the paper and on to the serving plate and carefully remove the mould.

Decorate with raspberries and a trickle of coulis over the top. Garnish with a mint leaf and serve with crème fraîche or a scoop of vanilla ice cream.

Eton mess

A very easy and comforting dessert which was invented at the renowned British public school, Eton College.

Serves 6

750ml (1 ¼ pints) double cream

300g (10 oz) ripe strawberries, hulled

2 Tbs caster sugar

225g (8 oz) good quality meringue

Sprigs of mint for garnish

Put half the strawberries and half the sugar into a blender and process until a smooth coulis.

Whisk the cream with the rest of the sugar until just stiff.

Slice the remaining strawberries. Put a few to one side for decoration.

When near to serving time, break the meringue into small pieces and fold into the cream with most of the coulis and the sliced strawberries. Do not mix thoroughly – it should be marbled.

Pile the cream mixture into a glass bowl and spinkle the remaining strawberries on top. Drizzle with the rest of the strawberry coulis and decorate with a mint sprig.

Little glasses of trifle

There are always arguments about whose grandmother made the best and most authentic trifle. Each is different and each delicious.

Serves 6

200g (7 oz) fresh raspberries

4 sponge fingers (or 4 slices of Victoria sponge)

50 ml (2 fl oz) sherry

4 Tbs good quality raspberry jam

200ml (7 fl oz) double cream, whipped

30g (1oz) toasted almond flakes

Egg custard

200ml (7 fl oz) single cream (or full fat milk)

3 egg yolks

25g (1 oz) icing sugar

2 tsp cornflour

2 drops vanilla essence

First make the egg custard. Heat the cream (or milk) until very hot in a little saucepan.

In a bowl mix the eggs yolks with the cornflour, sugar and vanilla with an electric beater until thick and very pale in colour.

Add the hot cream little by little, beating with a wooden spoon continuously.

Strain the mixture back into the pan. Over a low heat, stir continuously until the custard thickens and coats the back of a spoon. Do not allow the custard to boil or it will curdle. Take off the heat immediately. Pour into a cold bowl, add the vanilla and leave to cool.

To assemble the trifles, take 8 little glasses and put 3 or 4 raspberries in each. Spread the biscuits (or cake) with raspberry jam. Cut into small pieces and put a layer into each glass, then pour 1 Tbs of sherry on top.

Then pour the egg custard equally into each glass.

Finish with a spoonful of whipped cream and decorate with grilled almonds. Refrigerate until ready to serve.

Chocolate bread and butter pudding

Bread and butter pudding has recently enjoyed a renaissance in Britain. This is an extremely rich version that is utterly delicious.

Serves 6

About 6 slices of thick white bread (or brioche)

400ml (14 fl oz) single cream (or full fat, fresh milk)

100g (4 oz) castor sugar

75g (3 oz) butter

3 eggs

150g (6 oz) best quality dark chocolate

Remove the crusts from the bread and cut the slices diagonally into triangles.

Place the chocolate, cream, sugar, butter in a bowl set over a saucepan of gently simmering water, (or melt in a microwave on a low heat). Stir until the chocolate and butter are completely melted and all the ingredients are well mixed. Remove from the heat and allow to cool slightly.

Butter a gratin dish, then spoon a layer (about 1cm) of chocolate mixture into the dish. Arrange a layer of bread triangles (overlapping) on top, then another layer of chocolate mixture, then bread, finish with a layer of chocolate. Press down the bread carefully to ensure it is well covered. Allow to cool completely.

Cover the dish with clingfilm, and refrigerate for 24 hours.

To cook, preheat the oven to 200 °C. Remove the clingfilm and bake for about 20 minutes until the top is crunchy and the inside soft. Leave to stand for 10 minutes before serving with vanilla ice cream.

Apple and blackberry crumble

The most popular of British nursery puddings, which never fails!

Serves 6
900g (2 lb) tart apples

125g (4 ½ oz) blackberries

10g (½ oz) butter

2 Tbs caster sugar

Crumble
150g (5 oz) flour

100g (4 oz) butter

50g (2 oz) soft brown sugar

Preheat the oven to 200 °C (gas 6/7).

Peel and cut the apples into chunky slices. Melt the butter and sugar in a frying pan and add the apple. Toss until lightly caramelised.

Put the apple in a pie dish (or individual ramekins) and add the blackberries.

To make the crumble, rub the butter into the flour with fingertips until it resembles breadcrumbs. Add the sugar and mix lightly.

Sprinkle the crumble mixture in a thick layer on top of the fruit, and put in the oven for 20-30 minutes until golden (15 minutes if using ramekins). Serve with whipped cream or vanilla ice cream.

Christmas Pudding

A classic Christmas pudding should be prepared a good couple of months in advance so that the flavours can combine properly. The pudding can be kept for several months, and some people keep theirs from one year to the next!

Serves 6

250g (10 oz) currants

200g (8 oz) sultanas

75g (3 oz) candied orange peel,softened by boiling for 10 minutes, then drained

75g (3 oz) candied lemon peel, softened as above

40g (1½ oz) chopped walnuts

50g (2 oz) coarsely grated apple

50g (2 oz) grated carrot

250g (10 oz) fresh breadcrumbs

100g (4 oz) softened butter

1 Tbs mixed spice

juice of 1 orange

juice of 1 lemon

250ml (9 fl oz) brandy

3 eggs

Brandy Butter

200g (7 oz) creamed butter

100g (4 oz) icing sugar

7 Tbs brandy

Mix the sultanas, currants, peel, nuts, apple, carrot and breadcrumbs in a bowl. Then add the lemon and orange juices, and the mixed spice. Cover and keep cool for 24 hours, stirring from time to time. Add the butter, the brandy and lastly the eggs lightly beaten.

Pile the mixture into a deep, 6 inch diameter pudding bowl. Cover with a round piece of greaseproof paper and then a piece of muslin measuring about 22 inches square. Wrap a length of butcher's twine round the edge of the bowl to secure the muslin, tie very firmly. Take two opposite points of the muslin and bring together on the top of the bowl, knotting firmly. Do the same with the other points.

Put the pudding into a bain-marie and cook for 6 hours. The pudding can then be stored in a dry, cool place for several weeks.

When you are ready to serve the pudding, reheat it in a bain-marie for about 3 hours. Turn it out onto a plate, warm 10ml (3 fl oz) of brandy in a small pan, pour over the pudding. Light the brandy and bring to the table aflame.

To make the brandy butter, beat together the butter and the sugar until the mixture is very creamy, add the brandy and mix well. Keep in the fridge until needed.

Sticky toffee pudding

A wicked, indulgent pudding!

Serves 6

175g (6 oz) stoned dates, chopped

175ml (6 fl oz) boiling water

½ tsp vanilla essence

2 tsp strong black coffee

¾ tsp bicarbonate of soda

75g (3 oz) butter, softened

75g (5oz) caster sugar

2 eggs, lightly beaten

175g (6 oz) self rasing flour

Sauce

175g (6 oz) brown sugar

100g (4 oz) butter

6 Tbs cream

Preheat oven to 180 °C (gas. 6).

Lightly grease 8 little metal moulds and place a disc of parchment paper in each base.

Place the chopped dates in a bowl and pour boiling water on them. Add the vanilla, coffee and bicarbonate of soda and leave to one side.

In another large mixing bowl, beat the butter and sugar until a pale colour and fluffy. Gradually add the beaten eggs, a little at a time.

Carefully fold in the sifted flour with a metal spoon, and then fold in the date mixture with the liquid – the mixture will look very sloppy!

Divide the mixture between the tins and bake for 25 minutes. When cooked, allow them to cool for 5 minutes then loosen the sides with a palette knife carefully turn them out, and place in an ovenproof dish (this can be done ahead, and frozen).

To make the sauce, combine all the ingredients in a saucepan and heat gently, stirring until it forms a smooth, toffee sauce.

When ready to serve, preheat the oven to 200 °C (gas 6/7). Pour the sauce over the puddings and place in the oven for about 8 minutes. Serve with crème fraîche or whipped cream.

Banoffi pie

Invented at the Hungry Monk Restaurant in East Sussex in 1972, this has become a popular dessert worldwide. There have been many imitations from Russia to USA and it is rumoured to be Mrs Thatcher's favourite pudding!

Serves 6

300g (11 oz) shortcrust pastry

a tin (440g) of condensed milk

4 firm bananas

250ml (9 fl oz) double cream

1 Tbs sugar

6 squares of dark chocolate

Immerse the unopened can of condensed milk (note: remove the label first) in a deep pan of boiling water. Cover and boil for 5 hours. It is essential that the pan does not boil dry, as it can cause the can to explode so check regularly and top up the water as necessary. Allow to cool completely before opening the can, which will be filled with a soft toffee filling. However it is sometimes possible to buy ready made banoffi toffee.

Preheat the oven to 200 °C (gas 6).

Lightly grease a loose bottom 25cm tart tin (or individual ones), roll out the pastry and line the tin. Prick the pastry all over with a fork and bake blind until crisp. Allow to cool.

Whip the cream, with the sugar until thick and smooth.

Spread the toffee over the base of the pastry case. Peel and slice the bananas, arrange them on top of the toffee. Finally spoon the cream over the top and coarsely grate a little chocolate to decorate.

Variation:

Instead of using pastry, try a biscuit base. Combine 100g (4 oz) crushed digestive biscuits, 50g (2 oz) melted butter and 40g (1 ½ oz) sugar and spread over the base of the tin, press down firmly with the back of a metal spoon and allow to cool.

Dundee cake

This is a rich fruit cake which was created in the city of Dundee during the 19th century. It is good with a cup of tea particularly after a long walk or at a picnic!

Serves 6

175g (7 oz) softened butter

175g (7 oz) sugar

3 large eggs

225g (9 oz) flour

1 tsp baking powder

1 tsp mixed spice

2 Tbs ground almond

175g (7 oz) currants

175g (7 oz) sultanas

50g (2 oz) glace cherries, chopped

50g (2 oz) mixed candied peel, chopped

Finely grated zest and juice of 1 orange and 1 lemon

4 Tbs whisky

50g (2 oz) whole, shelled almonds (for decoration)

Preheat the oven to 170 °C (gas 5/6).

Grease a deep, 20cm cake tin with a little butter and sprinkle with a teaspoon of flour. Line the cake tin with greaseproof paper.

Beat the butter and sugar with an electric mixer until light and creamy. In a separate bowl beat the eggs well and then combine with the butter and sugar mixture. Make sure the mixture is well incorporated.

Sift the flour with the baking powder and the mixed spice, then fold into the mixture. Then gently fold in the ground almonds, the fruit, orange, lemon juice and the whisky. Do not over stir but make sure that everything is thoroughly mixed - it should be a soft, dropping consistency if not, add a little milk.

Pour the mixture into the cake tin. Level the top and decorate with the whole almonds.

Place in the oven and bake for 2 hours. If the top of the cake becomes too brown after an hour, cover with two sheets of greaseproof paper and continue to bake. Check to see whether the cake is cooked by inserting a skewer into the centre - if is cooked it will come out clean. Take the cake out of the oven and let it cool for 5 - 10 minutes before turning it out of its tin.

Suggestion

This cake keeps well wrapped in greaseproof paper in an airtight container for several weeks - it will even improve with time!

Scottish shortbread

Shortbread is a delicious, buttery biscuit from a rich Scottish baking tradition, perfect for afternoon tea or accompanying a sorbet or mousse.

Makes 18 biscuits

175g (6 oz) plain flour

100g (4 oz) butter, softened

50g (2 oz) caster sugar

Mix the ingredients together in a large bowl, using a wooden spoon until a smooth paste. Turn onto a floured surface, and form into a long 'sausage', wrap in clingfilm and chill for about 30 minutes (the dough can be frozen).

Preheat the oven to 160 °C (gas 5/6).

Cut the dough into discs about 5mm thick. Arrange well apart on a baking sheet, prick the surface a couple of times with a fork and bake for about 30 minutes. The biscuits should be a pale, straw colour, not golden brown.

Sprinkle with sugar and allow to cool.

Victoria sponge cake

Named after Queen Victoria, a simple tea time cake.

Serves 6

175g (6 oz) flour

2 tsp baking powder

3 large eggs, at room temperature

175g (6 oz) butter, softened

175g (6 oz) caster sugar

½ tsp vanilla extract

raspberry jam for the filling

a little sifted icing sugar for dusting

Preheat oven to 170 °C (gas 5/6).

Lightly butter two 18cm loose bottom baking tins then line the bottom with a circle of greaseproof paper.

Into a large mixing bowl, sift the flour and baking powder together. Add the butter, sugar, eggs and vanilla to the bowl and mix well with an electric hand whisk until the mixture is smooth.

Divide the mixture between the two tins, and bake in the centre of the oven for about 25 - 30 minutes. Do not be tempted to open the door of the oven before or the cake will sink!

Check the cakes are cooked by pressing gently with your finger and if the top springs back and leaves no impression then they are cooked.

Remove from the oven. Allow to cool for 5 minutes and then turn out onto a wire cooling rack, peel off the paper and allow to cool completely.

Sandwich the cakes together with plenty of raspberry jam, and whipped cream if you like. Dust the top with icing sugar and place carefully on a serving plate.

Scones

Afternoon tea in a fine hotel or a little village tea shop is a unique British tradition. The West Country created the ultimate indulgence, the cream tea; a good pot of tea, warm scones topped with a generous spoonful of clotted cream and homemade strawberry jam.

Makes 18 pieces

450g (1lb) flour

4 tsp baking powder

good pinch of salt

50g (2 oz) butter

50g (2 oz) caster sugar

2 eggs

about 200ml (7 fl oz) fresh, full fat milk

Preheat the oven to 220 °C (gas 7/8).

Sift the flour and baking powder together into a large mixing bowl. Rub in the butter, until the mixture resembles breadcrumbs. Stir in the salt and sugar.

Beat the eggs lightly with the milk. Using a table knife, mix the liquid into the dry ingredients by making cutting movements until a soft dough is formed.

Gently roll out the dough on a floured surface until about 3 - 4cms thick. Cut out rounds using a 6cm cutter. Arrange well apart on a baking sheet, dust with a little flour and bake for 10-15 minutes until well risen and golden.

Cool the scones on a wire rack. Serve them warm with clotted cream (or crème fraîche) and strawberry jam.

Orange marmalade

**For 5 kg
of marmalade**

**1.5 kg (3 ¼ lbs) bitter,
Seville oranges**

2 kg (4 ½ lbs) sugar

3.5 litres (6 pints) water

juice of two lemons

Wash and dry the oranges well. Cut them in half and using a lemon squeezer, squeeze the juice. Pull the pith from the orange halves and put in a muslin bag with the pips. In a large jam pan place the orange peel, the water, the lemon and orange juice, and pips wrapped tightly in a muslin bag.

Bring to the boil and simmer for about 1½ - 2 hours until the orange rind is very soft and the contents has reduced by half. Allow to cool (you can do this a day ahead). Remove the muslin bag, and squeeze until all the 'pectin' (white, syrupy liquid) is extracted. Cut the orange peel by hand into thin strips, or put the orange peel with the cooking water in a food processor, pulse until the peel is roughly chopped into approximately 2-3mm pieces. Do this in batches. Put the orange peel and the cooking liquid back into the cleaned pan. Add the sugar and slowly bring to boil. Increase the heat and boil for 15-20 minutes, until the jam reaches setting point (to test, drop a little of the marmalade onto a cold saucer, place in the fridge for a few minutes and check it has set). Carefully skim off the white scum and discard. Remove from the heat, cool for half an hour before ladling into cleaned, warmed jars, then allow to cool completely before sealing.

Suggestion

In the last minute of cooking, add a glass of whisky.

Lemon curd

Makes about 1 kg

**100g (4 oz) butter, cut in
dice**

300g (9 oz) sugar

**grated zest and juice of
3 large lemons**

4 large eggs, lightly beaten

Melt the butter in a bowl over gently simmering water. Add the sugar, lemon juice and zest, and stir until the sugar is completely dissolved. Add the eggs, heat gently, stirring all the time until the mixture is thick. While still hot, pour into thoroughly clean, dry and warm jars and seal. Store in the fridge and eat within 2 weeks.

For Heather and Camilla

Part of the profit from this book will be donated to Breakthrough Breast Cancer of Great Britain.

The authors would like to thank Brigitte Husson, James Viaene, Gwen Hamilton,
Jane Hodges and Isobel Abulhoul.
John, Sarah, Lucy and Emilie
Stephen, George, Mim and Elizabeth

Published in 2006 by JERBOA BOOKS
PO BOX 333838 Dubai UAE
www.jerboabooks.com
ISBN 9948-431-18-9
رقم إذن الطباعة: 1249
التاريخ: 30 October 2006

Copyright © Marabout 2004 for the French Edition
Published in France

Photography Akiko Ida
Styling John Bentham

English Edition © JERBOA BOOKS

Printed in the UAE